I0766155

STORM PRINCESS

3

USA TODAY BESTSELLING AUTHORS
AYMIN EVE & EVERLY FROST

For all our readers.

We honor you.

PROLOGUE

BAELEN RATH

My shoulders are sunk low, my chest bleeding openly. The rain falls in all directions now. I've lost track of what is up or down. Water streams down my chest, blood-tainted liquid trickling along the sword's blade onto the patch of dirt where I stand. Waiting.

I search for Marbella in the images beyond the field, praying for a glimpse of her auburn hair, her determined eyes, praying that she's safe, unharmed, waiting for her to tell me it's time to stop waiting.

I saw her forced to eat beside our enemies, to swallow their food and their twisted conversation, to stand in the face of their threats.

I saw her hunched beside my cage.

Still she doesn't call me.

Still I wait in this scorched field, dripping blood onto my sword, the weight of the rain driving my chin toward my chest.

I want to act, but I have to trust her.

I have to wait for her voice.

Baelen, I love you. I always will.

My head shoots up. I search the images beyond me but I don't see her. I see only an empty room. "Marbella!"

A new image forms in front of me, but it's not inside the room. It's here with me in this field: a woman with pure white hair and eyes like blue crystals, glittering wings and a dress made of diamonds dragging through the mud. She stops one step away from me.

"Baelen Rath, you called me."

She speaks with Marbella's voice, her gorgeous, strong, sweet voice, but she's not my love.

I demand, "Who are you?"

"I am Incorruptible."

My eyes narrow, assessing her for possible threats. "Where is Marbella?"

Incorruptible turns her head slightly as if she's checking something behind her. There's a hiss. A hum. A distant clatter and a far-off scream. "She is avenging the life of someone who loved her."

My jaw clenches. Someone has lost their life and it's caused Marbella pain. Too much pain. Cold fingers wrap around my heart. Fear shoots through me. My fingers twitch around my weapon. For the first time in all my waiting, the tip of the sword begins to form, taking the shape of solid steel.

Marbella, what have you done?

"Don't worry. She didn't love him like she loves you."

That's not what I'm concerned about. I trust Marbella with my heart, without question. She's free to make her own choices. My fear is because I can't sense her. My fear is because there's a female gargoyle standing here in Marbella's place. "Why do you speak with her voice?"

"Because I don't have a voice of my own anymore."

"If you've hurt her, I will destroy you."

Her chin shoots up, outraged, as if I've insulted her. Her mouth purses with a retort, but at the last moment, it softens. "You love her."

"More than anything. More than life."

"Ah… Just like Rath loved Mercy. I knew him, you know—your ancestor. He was just as strong-willed, the protector of his people, but his love always came first." She widens her eyes at me with a self-assured smile. "He was never afraid to show it either. I envied that. Much like I envy you."

Another raindrop slides down the back of my neck, following the angry chill racing down my spine. "Then you know I mean it when I say that if you've hurt her, I will hunt you to the ends of our world and beyond."

"Don't worry, Wrathful One. Marbella is unharmed." She leans forward into my anger, daring me to step toward her. "But when you wake, you need to be prepared."

"Prepared for what?"

"For what she has become."

I won't wait any longer. I force my legs to move, my muscles screaming against the force that opposes me. With a roar, I wrench the sword from the ground and this time, I do not allow it to return to the earth.

Incorruptible considers me with alarm. "If you leave this place, you will die, Baelen Rath."

My angry eyes meet hers. My arm muscles bunch with the strength it takes to hold the sword aloft.

Her lips set in a resolute line. "Very well. I can show you how to survive, but you won't have long. In return, you will do something for me."

I grit my teeth, sweat dripping down my chest, mingling with my blood as I fight the downward force of the sword with all my remaining strength. "Whatever it takes."

She leans forward. "You will stop Marbella from destroying our world."

I grit my teeth, rage spiraling through me. I have to go to her. I will go to Marbella.

I say, "Show me how."

1

MARBELLA

Death was never part of the plan. When I crossed the border into gargoyle territory, my goal was simple: heal Baelen and get the hell out of there. But the gargoyle king had different plans for me. Forced to work in his mine, I joined the enslaved gargoyles digging for heartstones to increase King Howl's power. Finally finding a heartstone—the Prime Heartstone—we saw our chance to rise up against him.

I fought side by side with the miners against Howl's army, fighting a battle for our lives. My friend, Llion, was badly injured, and Cassian was killed, but not before he brought the Queen's deadly heartstone to the battle: a weapon that only a gargoyle with royal blood can safely touch. In an act of desperation, I forced Howl to hold it. As Howl flew me high above the battle, I pressed the Queen's heart into the harness around his neck where he kept the other stones that gave him the power to enslave his people.

Howl was anything but royal. The stone's power shredded him before my eyes.

But I touched it, too.

Now, I am about to die.

Released from his arms, I tip backward. The Queen's heart floats up and away from me, defying the press of gravity. The tip of my finger taps the stone, a glow rippling out from it as if it was dropped into water, and we're both sinking under the surface.

A thick cloud of debris fills the air above me where Howl used to be. The Queen's heart burned him to ashes. Gusts of wind sweep his remains through the open sides of Crimson Court, past the pillars and flags bearing the shadow panther crest, out over the cliff's edge, blowing the dust away in a single, sharp burst. Howl is gone.

Darkness presses in on me from all sides, and I'm falling. Falling to the floor of Crimson Court where I will break on the hard stone. The final light of the day shoots across the Court, warming me for the last time. A long time ago, the Elven Queen gave her life to become the sun that lights our world. As her light bathes my body, I sense the rising of the distant moon. After the Elven Queen became the sun, the Gargoyle Queen became the moon. Her name was Incorruptible and it's her heart that killed me.

The sunlight winks out.

I take one last breath and inhale the scent of battle, of blood and death. The fighting continues around me. Only the nearest soldiers saw Howl die, his death cry swallowed by the sounds of clashing swords and roaring gargoyles. Llion has collapsed to the ground, badly injured, one of his wings almost torn off. Liliana runs to him, crying his name.

Jasper fights his way to me, his clothing and weapon both bloody, his face cut and bruised. Welsian races toward me too, the bulky gargoyle moving faster than I've ever seen as he leaps over bodies trying to get to me. The leader of our mining team, Roar, took flight the moment I started falling, his blue-veined wings glowing in the new dark as he zooms toward me, desperately reaching out.

They think I'm falling because Howl dropped me. They think they can catch me. They don't know the stone has already killed me. I close my eyes. My friends are free now. They will rebuild their lives and bring peace to their country. I know they will.

"*Baelen...*" I whisper his name one last time, exhaling my final breath.

I brace for the final impact.

Out of nowhere, a gust of wind rushes under me, bursting upward and taking me with it, spinning me around, elevating me above the fight. I'm too stunned to fight its force, letting it take me and carry me high to the ceiling, pushing me upright so my feet point downward, and I stand on nothing but air.

Roar flies to my side, his wings beating hard, surprise shooting from every angle of his body. "Lady Storm!"

Welsian shouts from the floor, his face upturned to mine. He tries to approach me, clearly alarmed by this new force, but a tornado springs up between us. It buffets Roar backward too, pushing his wings around as if he's a moth and not a massive warrior. He fights it, angling his wing daggers forward in an attempt to cut through the shield, but the gusty barrier forces him back again.

The tornado widens, extending all the way around me. It's transparent so I can see through it, but the way Roar rolls backward every time he tries to get to me tells me that the barrier around me is impassable. I'm completely separated from the rest of the battle.

I'm worried it will rip Roar's wings off if he tries again. I push my hand out to tell him to stop, not daring to extend my arm into the whirlwind. "Stay back! It's okay. I'm okay."

I think.

I do a mental check of all my limbs. I'm still in one piece. I'd expected to be nothing more than dust by now. I'd expected to die a painful death like Cassian. To be torn apart like Howl. But for some reason, the Queen's heart hadn't shredded me into fragments.

What's more, all four heartstones have gathered inside the eye of the tornado with me. The Queen's diamond heart floats in front of my chest while the emerald Virtuous heart and sapphire Lightsworn heart drift on my left. On my right side, the golden Prime Heartstone gravitates toward the Queen's heart, but that is not a surprise to me. When I read the Queen's journal, I found out that Queen Incorruptible had been in love with Prime. She never acted on her love or betrayed her husband, King Supreme, but when she gave her life to become the moon, her heart fell from the sky to Prime's resting place so their hearts could be together forever. We'd unearthed both of them.

A commotion draws my attention to the far end of the Court where Howl's soldiers have herded all of the clan leaders and the old Priestess into a group. The soldiers hurry out of the way, shouting and trying to rally as another gust of air forces the group to part, creating a clear pathway from the Court entrance all the way to me.

A figure appears in the gap: a male silhouette, his armor catching the light of the moon and glinting across the space between us. From head to toe, he's covered in finely sculpted metal plates, linked to protect his body and decorated in crimson and ochre markings. At his side, he carries a sword, its sharp blade pointed outward, handle gripped hard.

He towers over the nearest warriors while the air around him glows red like a bloody sunset. As he enters Crimson Court, the ground lights up beneath his boots and the stone floor blazes, leaving a scorched trail behind him. The scent of rain hits me. Acid rain.

My breath catches in my throat. My heart stops.

He is the most dangerous man I've ever seen.

He is the only man who's ever held my heart in his hands.

"Baelen!"

But this can't be true. He can't be awake. He won't last more than a few minutes before his wounds kill him. The Elven Commanders stabbed him with swords strengthened with sorcery. Baelen took four deadly wounds through his chest. He used his storm power to suspend the damage before he died, to pause himself in time, but now he's awake, the wounds will continue their course and he will die.

I hold up both of my hands, palms out, even though I'm in danger of pushing them through the barrier that could strip the skin off them. *Stop. Please. You can't be awake. You can't... die. I won't let you! I will rip the world apart before I let that happen!*

As soon as these desperate thoughts form inside my mind, a light flares in front of me. I wrench my focus from Baelen to stare sharply at the Queen's heart, not sure what I just saw. Did it just spark? Did it just react to my thoughts?

Inside the Court, Howl's soldiers have used Baelen's arrival to rally and regroup. They abandon the task of imprisoning the clan leaders and race to form a cluster at the far side of the wind tunnel Baelen has created.

Jasper responds by shouting at the miners to rally to him,

gathering on the opposite side closest to Llion. Jasper appears both relieved and concerned to see Baelen. Jasper is one of Baelen's best friends. They attended military training together, and Jasper knows that Baelen is unrivaled on the battlefield. Having Baelen in this fight will tip the scales in our favor. But Jasper knows as well as I do how close Baelen is to death.

The miners form a protective barrier in front of Llion and Liliana. I'm worried about them, but glad to see Jasper and Welsian take up defensive stances in the front row, weapons held aloft and ready. They're joined by Badenoch, Erit, Iago, and Arlo, and within moments, the clan leaders also race to join them, moving as quickly as they can with the old Priestess at their head.

The battleground inside the Court is now divided into two: Howl's army on my right and the miners on my left, each on one side of the path Baelen has created. The division has made clear just how many soldiers there are—and just how few miners are left. Even the addition of the clan leaders has done little to boost their numbers. On top of that, most of the clan leaders are old men, the ones Howl knew couldn't challenge him.

How many miners have died? Sadness overwhelms me as I scan the bodies lying on the floor, afraid of what I'll find.

Roar zooms up in front of me, his face pale and drawn, wings spread, trying to block my view. "Lady Storm," he says. "Don't look."

But it's too late. I've already seen them. Half the miners lie dead where the central battle was fought. I knew all of them, had heard all of their stories, and knew the names of their wives and children, their mothers and fathers.

"They fought with valor," Roar says, his eyes burning bright. "You've already avenged their deaths by killing Howl."

Rage burns inside me. The Queen's heart flares again, but I'm too angry to care. "That doesn't bring them back, Roar."

"Then we will mourn when this battle is over."

The fallen miners were Roar's friends for longer than they were mine. He hides his pain well, but it shows in the clench of his jaw and the slow beat of his wings, the slump of his shoulders. Pain flares through every nerve ending at the loss of these honorable men. I want to scream it out. More than anything, I want to fight. I want to kill every soldier in this place.

A sharper flare of light makes me gasp. This time I'm sure the Queen's heart responded to my anger.

As if he senses my fury across the distance, Baelen tightens the whirlwind around me so I can't act on my instincts; his focus zeroed in on me. I can't read his expression from this distance, can't see his eyes, but there's definitely something different about his face, something that I can't make out…

I want to hear his thoughts like I could when we used the storm's connection to communicate with each other. I need to know that he's okay—need to tell him to let me down because I want to fight—but he's closed off from me.

I am his focus as he strides along the pathway between combatants, heading straight for me with stunning purpose. Now that his path is clear, the wind tunnel dies down around him, but the tornado around me remains strong. I may not be able to read Baelen's thoughts, but I can sense his intentions.

He's coming for me.

He's more than halfway to me when he pulls up sharp. I'm not sure why until a soldier steps forward, blocking his path. Baelen shoots me a last determined look before turning his attention to the new man.

This man has a sharp nose and dark-gray wings slightly spread, wing daggers pointed forward in an aggressive gesture. For a long time, I suspected that many of Howl's guards were forced into serving him—I still think that's true—but many more of them followed him willingly. They saw an advantage for themselves in their positions of power over others.

It looks like they have a new leader.

I recognize this gargoyle. He was one of the men who blocked Jasper from helping Cassian. This man knew what he was doing. He thought Howl would win, so he gave no thought to Cassian's suffering.

Nearby, Roar leans toward me, speaking through the whirlwind. He snarls as he inclines his head at the gargoyle standing in Baelen's path. "That is Gerst from the Grievous Clan.

He was the one Howl sent to take our wives and children away from us."

Roar's wife is imprisoned in Harem Hall, like many wives of the miners. Roar once told me that Howl took away the wives and children of all the men he believed could challenge him, using their loved ones as leverage to ensure the gargoyles did not rise up against him. I'd met Roar's wife, Gilda, a beautiful ebony-haired woman and vowed I would reunite them.

Roar continues. "Gerst was next in line to be General if something happened to Cassian. As long as Gerst thinks he has a chance to get his hands on the heartstones, he won't surrender. He's the highest ranking soldier now. He wants to be the new king."

That would explain why he was so happy to let Cassian die. But he has no idea what he's facing now that Baelen is here. Even Howl was smart enough to fear what would happen if Baelen woke up.

"I won't let that happen, Roar."

He nods. He trusts me, but his next glance has a question in it. He was a leader among the miners for many years and needs to get back to the others. Jasper can lead them temporarily, but they won't follow an elf for long—even if there's a possibility that Jasper is part-gargoyle.

"Go," I say. "They need you."

As Roar flies back to the main group, Gerst calls out to Baelen, loud and harsh, a snarl in the tense silence. "You will lay down your weapons, elf. You have no place in this fight."

Baelen responds by narrowing his eyes. His whole body thrums with anger. He pauses before he speaks, commanding the attention of everyone in the Court. "Only the Gargoyle Queen can command me. I will lay down my weapons when she tells me."

It's been so long since I've heard Baelen speak. The connection we used to talk with each other while he slept is no comparison to hearing his voice now. A shiver races down my spine. I don't care that the Queen's heart glows. I close my eyes and let the sound of his voice wash over me like cool water.

But my eyes fly open as I consider what he just said. *Gargoyle Queen?* Is he talking about the Queen's heart?

His response causes a stir. The soldiers turn to each other. Even the miners are confused. One question is repeated over and over: "What Queen?"

Baelen half-turns to me, shooting me a sudden smile across the distance. It's a smile just for me, making his face light up. It takes my breath away, burning the air between us. His smile should be reassuring, but it only serves to make me more confused. And afraid. It's only been moments, but he's still alive. Like me, it seems impossible. How have we both defied death today?

Baelen's smile fades as his focus returns to Gerst. "I recognize you, Grievous Gerst. I was not sightless while I slept. I know what you have done, and I will not let your actions go unanswered."

A shiver shoots down my spine at the violent intent behind Baelen's speech. I was never sure how much Baelen actually saw or heard while he slept. He spent the last month living as a statue in Howl's Royal Residence. Howl, who maimed, tortured, and killed his people at will. I don't want to imagine what Baelen might have seen.

Gerst responds to Baelen's declaration with a surprised step backward. Fear shoots across his features, quickly hidden. Baelen often has that effect on people. All men and women in the House of Rath were formidable warriors—the biggest and strongest, sworn to protect others. He trained his whole life to be the warrior that he is today.

A thunderous scowl quickly turns Gerst's expression to anger. He won't like that everyone saw his fear of Baelen. He screams a command, and two of the biggest soldiers leap out from the group behind Baelen, a surprise attack.

Baelen is unfazed, his sword swinging out in a fluid movement to impale the first man through the chest. At the same time, he evades the other man's weapon and grabs his sword arm before the gargoyle can complete a downward stroke. Baelen wrenches the man's arm outward, and the gargoyle screams. I have no love for these soldiers, but the way the attacker's arm dangles makes me wince. Baelen moves swiftly, twisting left, his sword whispering through the air. The second gargoyle's head rolls across the floor and hits Gerst's boot at the same time the first man's body thuds to the floor.

Gerst screams a battle cry and all of the soldiers race at Baelen and the miners at once. They don't make it twenty paces before the side of the wind tunnel springs up again, creating an impassable barrier from floor to ceiling between the guards and miners. The attackers can't even fly over it.

On the miner's side of the barrier, Roar had already taken flight, and Jasper had urged the miners forward, but they pull up short, unable to get through, protected on all sides.

Baelen has chosen to take on all of the soldiers by himself.

An ear-popping shriek is the only warning the nearest soldiers have as Baelen's sword crackles with lightning. A single swing drops ten soldiers to the ground before he clashes with ten more coming at him from every side. He plows through them while blocking any attempts to attack him from behind. One after the other they fall in rapid succession, a trail of bodies lying in Baelen's wake.

Gerst's wing daggers slice through the air a moment before he roars a challenge and launches at Baelen. Fear shoots down my spine. A gargoyle's wing daggers can tear through rock. Baelen ducks, feints left, and comes up on the right, his sword tearing through Gerst in a single, deadly swipe.

My fear evaporates.

Gerst wobbles on the spot, eyes wide, before he topples to the floor. He is dead within seconds.

Baelen spins to the remaining soldiers as they swerve away from him, scrambling out of his path. Their leader is gone. Nobody is making them fight now.

"Who else?" Baelen roars from deep within his chest, an echoing shout. "Who else wants to die today?"

The nearest soldier drops his sword, throwing his hands into the air, starting a chain reaction among the others.

Baelen waits a mere beat before he turns his back on them and strides toward me. Swords and daggers clatter to the floor behind him as the soldiers lay down their weapons. The lightning fades from Baelen's body as he approaches me. My heart enters my throat as he stops three paces outside the shield he has placed around me. He eases the tornado and allows me to descend from up high, but not by much. I'm still elevated too high to come close to placing my feet on the ground.

This close I can see what's different about his face.

His eyes are full of fire. Literally. Normally green, his eyes now glow like hot coals, resembling the scorched stone he burns beneath his feet.

"Marbella." He growls my name, drawing it out like he doesn't want to stop saying it. The corner of his mouth lifts into a smile, the intensity of his gaze burning through to my heart. His voice washes over me like a lifeline, breaking through the tension in my entire body.

"Baelen… how are you here?"

"You were falling," he says as though that explains everything. At my questioning look, he adds, "I'll never let you fall."

He's so calm, so controlled that it sends me into a spin. I can't begin to understand why he isn't worried about his own life right now. I burst out, "But how are you still alive?"

I'm so worried about him that I'm going to leap out of my skin. Fear consumes me as completely as the flames filling his eyes. After everything that's happened, after everything we've been through, I can't lose him now. My own eyes burn with tears I can't seem to shed.

Baelen's smile fades, concern flashes across his face. He half reaches for me before he reconsiders that action. "I'm alive because I'm not all here. My heart is still suspended." He shrugs his broad shoulders. "I am a shell made up of storm power while my core remains safe." He closes the gap between us, one pace away from the shield. His nearness is like balm on my fear, his expression telling me not to worry. "I'm okay. I promise."

"What about Elyria? Where is she?" The Storm is nowhere to be seen. The last time I saw her, she was unable to move from Baelen's side, tethered to him because I gave him all of my storm power when I cut the connection between him and me. It meant she couldn't move more than a hundred paces from wherever he was.

Baelen's expression falls. "She's as far away from here as I could get her, further away while I'm in this state, but it's not far enough."

"Where?"

"Outside the deep springs."

The deep springs are located in the heart of Mount Erador, across a ravine only a thousand feet west of Crimson Court.

Nobody goes there for healing anymore because Howl blocked the entrance. The way he blocked it was horrifying, he'd put up a barrier made of living gargoyle wings.

"She's struggling, Marbella. She's caught in the nightmares of her past as well as the nightmares of her present. She needs your help. But first, you have to help yourself."

He withdraws a little, a cautious crease appearing on his forehead. "I need you to trust me right now. Can you do that?"

I whisper, "Always."

He takes a deep breath as if he's bracing for my response. "I need you to take hold of the Queen's heart."

"What?" I glance in disbelief at the stone floating within arm's length in the air between Baelen and me. It rotates slowly, a glittering, powerful force. Is he really telling me to touch the diamond heart again?

"Take her heart, Marbella. It belongs to you."

How can it belong to me? I'm not a gargoyle, let alone one with royal blood. A thousand denials rush through my mind, but Baelen persists.

"It didn't kill you. You're more powerful now than you ever were."

"But… it *did* hurt me. I hurt everywhere. My head, my arms, my skin, my heart…" I press my hand to my chest where pain burns like a fire inside my chest. "It *hurts*."

"That's because you're grieving. You're in pain because you lost someone important to you."

He inclines his head toward the floor, and I follow his gaze, looking down at Cassian for the first time since he whisked me above the battle.

He lies directly beneath my feet, one wing covering his chest, the other spread out beside him where he fell, its massive length stretching out across the floor. Baelen seems to sense what I need him to do, gently using his power to lift Cassian's outstretched wing and cross it over his chest, cocooning him. Cassian saved my life in the mines. He warmed me when I was cold. He believed in something that can't be true: that I carry royal gargoyle blood.

Now he's gone.

I shiver, suddenly cold. "Cassian brought me the stone. It's my fault he died."

Baelen meets my eyes. The shake of his head is slow and deliberate, giving me time to think while the fire in his eyes dims, stern but strong. "He died believing in the truth. He made a choice. Now you have to make a choice, too."

Choose.

That single word echoes around in my mind. It was the last thing I heard before I began falling: a command to choose between life or death.

My response to Baelen now is small, a reluctant admission. "I don't think I can do this alone."

"I'm here, Marbella. I'm not going anywhere. And when you heal me, all of me will come back to you. But right now, you need to know that you've changed. You've changed inside and out."

His mouth transforms into a gentle smile. "I wish I could touch you, show you how beautiful you are right now, but you have to heal me before it's safe to make contact again. In the meantime, the best way to accept who you are is to take hold of the heartstone that belongs to you."

I trust him. With all my heart. He would never hurt me. He has only ever protected me. I don't understand what's going on right now or why, but I believe him.

My fingers flex, reaching out through the air. My hand closes around the Queen's heart.

An electric shock shoots through me, and a surge of power follows it. The power stabs through my arms, legs, and torso, making my spine arch. The Queen's heart blazes into life inside my closed fist, casting sharp pinpoints of light across the floor and watching gargoyles. I gasp as webs appear above me, forming out of nothing, and glowing brightly across the entire ceiling, a glittering, tangled mass. At the same time, external light fills the space within the Court as the moon outside reaches its brightest point, dominating the sky with its large, round face as if Incorruptible herself is watching.

The other three heartstones gravitate toward my left hand, hanging in the space above it. I feel them as if they're alive. Just like

I feel the Queen's thoughts. All four stones are a hammer in my mind, beating hard like drums in unison.

Baelen smiles again, the curve of his lips making my heart race. "Take a seat, Marbella."

The air around me shifts, slowly transferring my body weight behind my thighs, supporting me as I lower to a sitting position. Baelen has given me a seat of air. I hold the Queen's heart in my right hand, elevated at my side, while the other heartstones hover over my left palm.

Baelen assesses the stunned gargoyles. He takes up position beside me like a sentinel, guarding more than my body but also my heart. He finally allows the wind barrier to die down around the miners and clan leaders, releasing them from the protective shield.

The floor lights up beneath him. Fire bursts around his feet as he says, "I give you your Queen."

2

———

MARBELLA

I'm certain my eyes are as wide as everyone else's. They stare at me while I stare back at them. *Queen?* I don't think so. I loosen my grip on the heartstone, preparing to release it as I whisper to Baelen, "You should let me down now please."

He gives me a firm shake of his head—*no*—causing my forehead to crease. He's not going to let me down?

The old High Priestess races toward us, covering ground faster than I expected the ancient woman to move. She runs so fast that her wings catch the air, fluttering and elevating her in large leaps.

She shout-whispers, "Lady Storm, do not move! Do not let go of that stone!"

"What—?"

Jasper strides toward us too, not far behind the old Priestess. But we aren't his only focus. He turns his head, searching the space around us. "Where's Elyria?"

He doesn't even get close to us.

The Priestess whirls, her bony hands pushing against Jasper's stomach so hard he doubles over. *Oomph*, the air leaves his lungs as she propels him bodily backward.

His startled eyes shoot up to hers. "What—?"

"Get back Jasper, son of Grace! Stay away from Lady Storm unless you want to die."

"But I need to—"

18

"You need to live. Which you won't if you step into her space."

"What are you talking about?" Jasper glares at the Priestess, his eyebrows drawn down, challenging her. "Baelen's standing right beside Marbella."

"Baelen Rath is the only living creature who can share her space right now and survive. Even he is in danger if we don't act soon. Now get back and let me do what I must."

Jasper backpedals as she shoves and flaps at him, blocking his every attempt to get to me. She waves her hands at all of the gargoyles who have taken steps toward me. "All of you. Get back. Now!"

If my eyes were wide before, they've turned into lakes now. She's always been a bit odd, but this takes the cake. As she forces everyone backward, even the soldiers, ordering them to form a very wide circle at the edges of the Court, I sense genuine fear in her voice, desperation in her body movements.

She definitely knows something I don't. I murmur, "Baelen, what's going on?"

He answers me with a firm, but gentle command. "Hold onto the Queen's heart, Marbella. Don't let it go."

In the distance, Jasper paces, resembling a caged beast. He formed a bond with Elyria before he was forced into the mines with me. Now that he knows Baelen is safe, he needs to know where Elyria is. I understand his frustration. It's the same desperation I felt at being separated from Baelen.

The old Priestess flutters back to us, bowing low to Baelen, her chest heaving. She's visibly trying to calm herself down. "Thank you, Wrathful One," she says, still bent low to Baelen. "Without your power containing the heartstone's force, none of us would be alive right now."

She rises and peers cautiously at me. I notice that she has chosen to stand further away from me than she ever did before. "Lady Storm, you control the destructive power of the Queen's heart now. But it is a fragile control. The heart responds to your thoughts and emotions. A single thought from you can have a thousand consequences. You are either our salvation or... our greatest enemy."

I can't get rid of the crease in my forehead. "I should have died when I touched it."

"But you didn't."

"Cassian said… impossible things." I shake my head. He said I smelled like the Queen, but I have no gargoyle heritage and I know my mother never had eyes for anyone other than my father. No matter what they say about children always looking like their mother, I'm as certain as I can be that she never had an affair with a gargoyle. Let alone with the former King.

The Priestess's fingers flex as if she wants to leap across the distance, grab me, and shake sense into me, but I guess the whole single-thought-can-destroy-her thing stops her.

"Only someone with Supreme Incorruptible blood running through their veins can hold the Queen's heartstone like you are now," she says. "How this happened is not important right now. We will figure it out soon enough. For now, you need to establish control over the stone, or we are all in terrible danger."

In the distance, Jasper paces halfway around the watching gargoyles. He stops in front of Llion who is very pale. Even from this distance I can tell that Llion doesn't look good. Roar supports him on one side and Welsian on the other, while Liliana presses close to him. I have to get to them and figure out how to help.

I have to get to Elyria and help her too.

I say to the Priestess, "You're telling me that I'm dangerous right now. Well, I refuse to stay in this cage forever. Tell me what to do and I'll do it."

She seems relieved, rather than annoyed. She points at the Queen's heart, her finger forming a delicate line to the most powerful heartstone unearthed. "You must tether the Queen's heart to your own. Then the other heartstones will follow. That is the only way we will have peace in Erador."

I scan the distant faces. The clan leaders wait and watch me too. Now that Howl and Gerst are gone, and with all of the royal family deceased, the danger is that the clans will go to war to determine their new leader.

The Priestess gestures from the stone to my heart. I know what I have to do. I watched Baelen do this very same thing during the Heartstone Ceremony when he bound himself to me.

I draw the Queen's heart to *my* heart and press it against my armor. It feels right that the inner suit of my armor is made out of Elyria thread, the light and life of a gargoyle's nest. As the stone presses up against it, warmth spreads through me. Light flickers around my torso and it feels like the storm. It is lightning and thunder, a tornado of tears like rain, a torrent of emotion. It's so much. And it's... *mine.*

Still pressing the Queen's heart to my own, I focus on the three other hearts as they continue to spin in a slow, lazy circle in front of me. They revolve slowly enough that I could reach out and grab them, but I decide that isn't what I should do. The sense I get from each of them is so different: Virtuous responds to my sadness, Lightsworn responds to my determination, and Prime, well, Prime responds to the Queen's heart with the same bond I've seen in Baelen's eyes when he looks at me.

I don't want to force a connection with the other heartstones like Howl did. Instead, I extend my free hand, palm open beneath them. Inside my mind, I ask: *May I have your permission?*

All three hearts drop into my palm. They're too big to fit all at once but each one balances on the tips of my outspread fingers, weightless, not heavy. A glow spreads up my arm and I can't help but smile at the happiness I sense from them.

As I open my fingers, preparing to release the Queen's heart —*my* heart—the Priestess visibly braces. Baelen plants his feet. He thickens the tornado around me just in case.

I release all four heartstones into the air and a thread of light forms between the Queen's heart and my chest. As soon as the diamond floats into sync with the others, the thread extends between them all, connecting them in a circle that is connected to me.

It looks just like the thread of storm power that used to link Baelen and me: a thread of deep magic.

The Priestess sags with relief. "Thank the ancients. Now that they're all tethered, the Queen's heart is not volatile anymore. It will only react to your conscious and deliberate thoughts. And what's more..." Her gaze flicks back to the watching clan leaders and remaining soldiers. "Nobody else can claim them. Remember this, Lady Storm: the stones are yours and yours alone. Even Howl was not tethered to them."

I have a feeling I should be afraid, but I'm not. For the first time, I understand why Cassian believed so strongly in this, why he gave his life for this. My purpose now is to keep the stones safe. To never allow them to be used like Howl used them. Never again.

The Priestess rocks back on her heels while Baelen eases the windstorm around me, lowering me to the ground, shifting me away from Cassian. The gusty wind dies down, but Baelen retains his position as my quiet sentry, staying out of the Priestess's way while remaining close at my side.

I meet his fiery gaze. While he's in this state, I can't read anything in his eyes, but the quiet curve of his lips and the angle of his shoulders tell me he will help me, no matter what I have to do.

Everyone has moved closer to me now that the threat is over. I expected to see Jasper at the front, given that he was determined to get to me before, but instead, he pushes his way back through the crowd. I follow his line of sight with a gasp.

Llion has collapsed to the floor. Liliana crouches next to him, crying.

That's it. I'm not staying put any longer. "Llion needs my help."

The Priestess blocks me. "You need to convince the clan leaders to accept you."

I glare across the room at the older men standing apart from the others. "Their acceptance is not more important than my friend's life. They can wait."

Her lips compress but understanding warms her eyes. "Very well, I will do what I can to hold them off."

That's good enough for me. My heart hammers inside my chest and the heartstones flare. I take off toward Llion with Baelen close behind. Baelen uses a firm but gentle breeze to lift onlookers out of the way, setting them down at the side, creating an opening for me straight to Llion. It's just as well because the gargoyles nearest to me scatter as soon as I approach. They obviously don't want to touch the stones that fly after me wherever I go. I growl inside. If being Queen means I'm going to end up isolated like I was when I was the Storm Princess, then I'm going to abdicate very quickly.

I've tasted a life where I was part of a larger community and I don't want to go back.

When I reach Llion, it's my worst nightmare. His breathing is labored, and his skin is pale and tinged with a shade that reminds me of death. Liliana clutches a cloth soaked in blood. Jasper holds his head and both Roar and Welsian support his wings on either side. One of his wings is a gruesome mess from shoulder to tip. A gargoyle's wings are indestructible but Howl used the heartstone's power to tear Llion's wing apart.

Jasper's solemn expression breaks my heart. "He's dying, Marbella. He doesn't have long."

My jaw clenches. "Llion is not dying today, Jasper. It's not happening."

I'm not letting him go. I've lost one friend today. I'm not losing another. Tears fill my eyes as I meet Llion's.

He sighs, trying to smile. "Lady Storm, you are Supreme Incorruptible now…"

My shout echoes through the suddenly quiet Court. The heartstones crackle around me. "You're not dying today!"

I seize the Queen's heart in my fist and drop to my knees beside him, drawing on its power. I will heal Llion. I will save his life—

"Stop!" The Priestess's shout breaks through my concentration as she races back to my side. Once again, she moves faster than expected. "You can't use the stone to heal him."

Incredulous, I raze her with a fiery glare. "Why not?"

"Because the Queen's heart can't heal. It is a destructive force. Only Virtuous's heart can heal, but it will only heal you, not anyone else. The heartstones belong to you now. They will only destroy others. That is the balance in Erador. All the good went into our beautiful moon, our majestic mountains. All the bad remained in the hearts. It is why our ancestors buried the hearts beneath the mountains."

"Are you seriously telling me that all of this power is useless to me right now?"

"I'm sorry, Lady Storm. Deeply sorry. Only the deep springs can heal Llion, and they are closed off—"

"Not for me." I jump to my feet. "Liliana, I will not let your husband die. Do you believe me?"

Her response is immediate, her trust complete. "Yes."

I spin to Baelen. "Can you help me move Llion without hurting him?"

Baelen responds with action. He barely moves when he uses the storm power, but Llion rises from the ground his legs gently tucking under him, and his good wing curled around his torso and knees. His damaged wing remains at the exact angle and position it currently is, protected while he floats.

While Baelen moves Llion, I grab Roar and Welsian's attention, speaking quickly. "Roar, please, will you go and free the women in Harem Hall and the gargoyle in Slave Station? Make sure they find their families." My expression softens. "Your wife will be so happy to see you."

Roar's expression is a mixture of hope and sadness as he immediately calls a group of miners including Iago and Arlo to follow him. Roar's wife Gilda was forced into Harem Hall while Iago and Arlo's wives were enslaved to work in the palace. They have waited years to see their wives again.

To Welsian I say, "Would you please tend to the fallen in this Court? I want each fallen gargoyle treated with the same respect, whether they were miners or soldiers."

Welsian bows low to me, before he calls the remaining miners to him. To my knowledge, he isn't married and has no children, so I hope he won't mind staying behind. "Lady Storm, I will wrap them in their wings as is the gargoyle way."

"Thank you, Welsian."

Finally, I snag Jasper's arm. "I'm taking Llion to the deep springs. You must come with me. Elyria is there and she will need your help."

He gives me a quick nod. I follow Baelen as quickly as I can. The remaining guards and clan leaders part for me, but this time—maybe for the first time—they watch me with respect as I lead the procession to save Llion's life. The Priestess, Jasper, and Liliana stay close behind. Outside, I judge the distance across the ravine to the deep springs. I remember standing at this exact spot when I realized how close the springs are located to the Court. At the time, that was a bad thing, but now I'm grateful.

"Baelen, can you fly Jasper and me over to the springs?"

"Of course." He is already floating across the space with Llion held securely in front of him, and within minutes, we alight onto the cliff in front of the springs. Jasper wobbles as he finds his feet, but his focus is the woman huddled against the side of the cave.

Elyria sits with her knees drawn to her chest, her hair hanging down over her face, and her shoulders slumped. She's listless and absent and doesn't even seem to notice our arrival. I can't imagine the cruelty she's witnessed. She has shut herself off, stopped looking, creating a mental barrier to protect herself.

Jasper runs straight to her, refraining from touching her at the last moment, but his hands hover around her face and shoulders. "Elyria?"

"Jasper?" Her tiny voice is frail and lost, gaining a little bit of strength when she sees him through the curtain of her hair. Her eyes widen. "Jasper!"

"I'm here."

She starts to sob, her chest heaving. Jasper gathers her into his arms, pulling her against his chest, wrapping her up as much as he can.

My heart wrenches. I want to go to her, but I'm very afraid for Llion now. He has lost all his color and his head sags without any strength left in his body. Elyria is safe with Jasper for now, so I return my focus to the task in front of me, narrowing my eyes at the monstrosity blocking the entrance to the deep springs.

Shivering gargoyle wings stretch from one side to the other, glued together by Howl. In the moonlight, they appear to breathe in and out, struggling to be released. When I first arrived here, I discovered that the wings were still alive. My stomach turns and my anger boils at Howl's cruelty. Approaching the wings, I run my hand across them. I will not destroy them. My target is the magic that holds them together.

Running my finger along the seams between the wings, I draw on the stone's destructive power. All at once, the wings slide apart, lifting out from the jigsaw puzzle they formed. I was prepared for them to collapse, but they don't. Instead, they pair up, folding neatly into each other. Pair by pair, they float down to ground level, lining up against the cliff face next to the opening. There are at least ten sets of them: ten gargoyles who lost their wings. One of those gargoyles was Rhain, a man who used to be a miner. The one who found the Virtuous Heartstone. He tried to use it to free his wife, Carmen, from Harem Hall. Howl punished Rhain by cutting off his wings.

Within moments, the entrance is clear. It's sickening how long the springs were blocked, but I'm relieved at how quickly I undid it. I inhale the surprisingly fresh air wafting out from the cave inside.

Liliana whispers at my elbow, "If you would do me the great help of asking the Wrathful One to keep Llion afloat, I would like to take it from here."

Elyria once told me that the deep springs is a place where the women can harness deep magic. It makes sense that Llion's wife should be the one to heal him.

"Of course." The truth is that I'm glad. I came here to heal Baelen. Now I've come full circle, and my journey has given me friends and knowledge about myself that I never expected to find. But something tells me I can't go inside unless it's with him. Nearby, he gives me an affirming nod: he will make sure Llion doesn't fall.

I say, "Go safely."

I return to Baelen's side. I want to reach for his hand, for the comfort of sharing this moment of anxiety as Llion and Liliana disappear into the darkness. I need this to work more than anything, because if the springs heal Llion, then they will heal Baelen too.

"Marbella." Jasper calls me from the side of the cave, and I hurry to him. He crouches with his back to the cliff face, Elyria wrapped up in his arms, her face hidden against his chest. "You need to untether Elyria from Baelen. It's killing her to be like this."

I agree, but I'm not sure how. The Priestess said the power I hold now is only destructive. Is it dangerous to Elyria? Could I hurt her?

"Marbella." Jasper is growling now. There's definitely gargoyle in his voice. I glance between them, from the way she clings to him, begging him to help her, to the way he pulls her closer trying to draw the agony out of her body into his own.

"She's in pain," he says. "It's destroying her. You have to free her. *Now.*"

He's never give me an order before. He's always nudged me in the direction he thinks I should go, but there's no give in his expression now.

I have to trust his instincts.

"Okay." I draw my focus to the force that exists between Baelen and Elyria. Several paces away, Baelen senses my intentions, and he braces but doesn't try to stop me. The force between them is not a thread like the connection Baelen and I had. It's more of a wide pull, like a magnet. I gather the destructive force inside the stone and push against the connection, physically leaning into the space between them as I try to claw it apart.

I shoot Baelen a worried glance. I don't want to hurt him either. But he nods: *keep going.*

The connection rakes through my bones, thick and heavy, pushing back at me. I extend my fingers and exert all my strength, the heartstones flaring and gleaming at my side. There's a final burst of power from the stones and the connection breaks. I stumble forward, losing my balance without the opposing force against me.

Two things happen at once. The first is that Elyria slumps in Jasper's arms, but her deep, indrawn gasp tells me that she's more alive now than she was before. In fact, it sounds like her first real breath since we arrived in Erador.

The second is that there are multiple gasps behind me where a crowd of gargoyles has gathered. Some of them point, others whisper. My eyes widen for the thousandth time today. They're pointing at Elyria. I'm guessing this means she isn't invisible anymore.

I really hope you know what you're doing, Jasper.

Elyria raises her face to his. "Jasper, please, take me away from here."

He scoops her up into his arms. He's still wearing his mining clothes. He's still splattered with blood. But none of that matters. He looks to the sky as a brilliant blaze grows in the east.

Phoenix!

The firebird responds to my mental cry. *I am here, Princess. In the sky above you.*

You're free! The last time I saw the phoenix, it was imprisoned in a dungeon beneath Howl's palace.

I broke free when Howl died.

A streak of burning light precedes the phoenix onto the cliff's edge. Proud and beautiful, it glides above our heads, dropping into the widest space it can find. It folds its wings to the side as I run to it while Baelen watches on. The stones follow me, slipping neatly behind me. For a long time, the phoenix was the only creature I could touch when my storm power was dangerous. I throw my arms around its large neck, barely able to reach around it, and bury myself in its fiery feathers.

Phoenix, it's so good to see you.

You too, Princess. It lowers its solemn face to me, nuzzling my cheek. *I'm glad to see you looking so... luminous.*

My eyes and skin changed after I came into contact with the Queen's heart in the mines, becoming pale and silvery; even my hair became a lighter shade of auburn.

The phoenix smiles, not with its mouth, but with its voice. *You have a long path ahead of you, Princess.* Its tone becomes solemn. *But it seems Elyria needs my help now.*

I make way for Jasper as he carries Elyria to the phoenix, tucking her wings into her side, gentle with her broken one. His hands are full, but he takes a moment to speak with me.

"Thank you, Marbella."

"Where will you go?"

"Wherever makes Elyria feel safe. I'll contact you as soon as I can."

The phoenix extends its strong wing so Jasper can walk up it with Elyria in his arms and settle behind its neck. Then they disappear into the night sky, the phoenix's fire forming a graceful arc beneath the moon's white glow. I check the sky for evidence of Elyria's storm power, but the sky is clear. She used to rage every day, and every day I had to calm her, but now... She isn't raging at all.

I don't know where Jasper will take her. I just know it's going to be far away from here. I have to trust him to know what he's doing, and I know the phoenix will take care of them both.

A gargoyle drops to one knee in front of me, drawing me from my thoughts. I'm surprised to see Rhain, the gargoyle who lost his wings.

He begins to speak. "Supreme Incorruptible…"

Okay, that seems to be my name now.

"Will you grant me my wings?"

I blink at him in surprise. He doesn't need my permission. A quick glance at the line of wings tells me there's a pair straining forward as if they know who their owner is.

"Your wings are your own, Rhain. Take them and heal."

I look for Carmen, Rhain's wife, but it doesn't look like any of the women from Harem Hall are among the gargoyles gathering at the edge of the cliff. Rhain collects his wings and waits at the entrance to the springs for his turn to heal.

When I turn back to the crowd, I find countless gargoyles waiting in the air at the edge of the cliff, remaining in a holding pattern that takes my breath away. There are at least a hundred. Some of them carry wingless ones. Others are injured themselves. I gesture them forward while Baelen helps those who can't fly for themselves.

"Anyone with injuries or who has lost their wings, come forward to heal." My voice lowers. "Um… Priestess?" I spin, finding her at my elbow.

How does this woman manage to stalk my heels so closely?

"Can you please make sure they access the springs in the order of greatest need? Anyone who is badly injured needs to go in first."

"Of course, Supreme Incorruptible. Your ruling on this is wise."

My ruling?

She relays my instructions to the waiting gargoyles and sets to work assessing their needs as they come forward. There are so many. Half of their wounds aren't fresh, but days old. Not from the battle but from mistreatment over time. The female slave whose neck Howl nearly broke on the night he made me prove I didn't have my storm power, bears deep bruises around her neck and is unable to speak. She tries, but I stop her.

"I'm sorry I couldn't stop him," I say to her.

She shakes her head, swallowing, still trying to speak. Finally she taps her chest and places her hand over my heart, nodding at me before the Priestess leads her to the growing line.

My eyes well up. I freed her. But it wasn't soon enough.

A cheer breaks out and I turn to find Llion and Liliana beaming at the entrance. They cross the distance to me, and their happiness is like a warm hug. It sings through me, soothing the worry I feel for Elyria.

I say, "You made it."

Liliana's tears have dried, and her hands are entwined with Llion's. "Thank you, Supre—"

"Marbella," I say firmly.

"Thank you, *Lady Storm*," Llion rumbles, a smile lighting up his golden eyes.

"I guess I can live with that." I bite my lip before tears fill my eyes. "I'm glad you're okay."

He presses his big palm against my cheek, a gesture of appreciation, but his expression swiftly becomes solemn. "My children."

I nod. "They're in danger. The Elven Command has increased its efforts to kill gargoyles who cross the border."

"I trust High Priestess Talia to look after them, but the Elven Command is corrupted by sorcery. There's no saying what could happen."

I shudder. "Could their sorcery defeat Talia's deep magic?"

"I don't want to find out. I need to go to them and bring them home." He looks at his wife as she squeezes his arm. "*We* need to go to them."

Llion had escaped across the border with his newborn children after he believed Liliana was killed. He hid them for a year, escaping detection, but the Elven Command made a deal with Howl to kill any gargoyles who tried to escape Howl's rule.

"Take whatever you need from the palace and bring your children back safely. Bring the High Priestess home too. Your people…" I clear my throat. "*My* people need her here."

When they fly away, the old Priestess appears at my elbow again. "Do you wish to heal Baelen Rath now?"

I glance at the line of injured gargoyles, surprised to see that they're waiting for me. Baelen himself gives me a confirming shake of his head.

"Not until the others are healed. Baelen is safe. I will wait my turn."

"Your ruling on this is also wise." She bustles away again, and I have a feeling this old lady is going to become my advisor. I'm not sure how I'll feel when she tells me my decision is *un*wise. That day is bound to come. It's impossible to get everything right.

I wait as the line of injured gargoyles grows shorter. Rhain emerges whole and bows low to me before he flies away. The woman with the injured throat returns with tears in her eyes to tell me that her husband was killed in a mine two years ago, but she's going to the orphanage to find her children now. I wait for all of them to heal until the moonlight changes color around me, deeper, darker, and only Baelen and I remain on the cliff.

The Priestess is the last to leave. "Come to the palace when you're ready. There's a lot of work to be done. Not least, you will need to deal with the clan leaders."

"I will." It's a simple promise but carries so much weight. There are mines to be closed, families to be reunited, homes to be rebuilt, and so much damage to be undone.

She places her hand on my arm before she takes flight, a gentle gesture, the first she's shown me. I'm certain I won't see this soft side of her again. "It's time to heal Baelen Rath."

3

———

MARBELLA

I stand on the cliff with all my emotions raging through me and they scare me like hell. Finally, I can heal Baelen and I'm suddenly afraid of so many things. Right now, he's a shell of storm power. His heart still sleeps. He looks and acts like my Baelen, but what will happen when he wakes up? Will he remember any of this? Will the Storm's power return to me or stay with him? There's also a lot he doesn't know because he was trapped in the Royal Residence all this time. How will I tell him everything that happened in the mines while he slept?

Mostly I'm afraid because we might finally have the chance to be together, and I'm terrified something will rip it away. What if he's wrong and his heart is gone?

"Marbella, I'm here."

With those simple words, all my fears disappear. "Then I don't want to wait another moment." I lead him forward, forcing myself not to touch him as he walks beside me.

The entrance to the deep springs beckons, a wide, tall walkway into the mountainside. Delicate webs light the way inside, leading down a pathway that descends into the mountain. At the end of it, we reach a cavern sparkling with glistening webs made of all colors, not the usual cerulean blue. A set of stone steps leads us down to a deep pool of water set within the floor.

A rhythmic drip echoes around the cavern, and it surprises me

32

to see single droplets of water falling from the same spot on the ceiling far above us, especially because they appear to form out of the stone itself instead of flowing from somewhere else.

I try to remember what Elyria told me about the springs—that it is the only water source flowing directly from Earth's surface. I'm not really sure how that works: it's certainly not dripping from the sky. *Very strange.* But it's a mystery that will have to wait.

Baelen follows me to the pool's edge where we find more steps that will take us deep into the water. I notice for the first time since we entered the cave that his feet don't burn the ground anymore and his steps are slower. His eyes are dark coals; the fire in them almost gone out.

"Baelen?"

He exhales. "I'm okay, but I'm glad we're here. I don't think I can maintain this shell much longer."

A wash of panic spreads through me. I will dive into this pool right now if I have to. I splash down the steps, urging him to come with me. The water is cool and very still. So is the air around us—perfectly still but not stale. I step further in until I'm waist deep. The stones rise as I move deeper into the water, positioning themselves above and beside me where I can see them from the corner of my eye.

Baelen's feet disappear under the surface, followed by his legs and waist. The water rises as he displaces it, lifting to my armpits. I wade further into the pond until it's level with my shoulders, while Baelen follows me. He's so tall he'll need as much water as there is.

I bite my lip as he immerses to his neck. We're both wearing our armor and it feels ironic that we're dressed exactly like the last time we saw each other, when we took the form of gargoyles and fought each other by mistake.

He closes his eyes, shutting off from me. It's not just his eyes, but his whole body. Every part of him shuts down, suddenly empty. It's like watching a lamp go out. He's gone. Completely gone. It's even worse than after he first paused himself. I can't even hear his heartbeat this time. As soon as he immersed himself in the water everything stopped.

His armor reflects light from beneath the surface, a reminder that he's not okay. There's no sudden sign or explosion of power, nothing to indicate any change in the water… or in Baelen.

"Please heal." I wait as he remains still and immersed, watching the cut of his jaw and high cheekbones, the scar running the length of his face, and his eyes that I'm desperate to see, to have him look back at me with his whole self. "Please."

I wait for the longest time.

He doesn't move. There's no indication he's breathing.

I wait for so long that I can't keep watching for a sign. I close my eyes, burning with tears I haven't shed yet: tears for Cassian and the miners who didn't make it, tears for Elyria because she's so broken, tears for Elise and my Storm Command because they're imprisoned, and tears because… if Baelen doesn't come back to me… if I've lost him…

"Marbella."

My eyes shoot open. Hot teardrops leak from them. "Baelen?"

He contemplates me quietly as water swills around his shoulders. His jade-green eyes follow the shape of my face from my braided hair to my pale eyes, my nose, my chin, and back up to my crimson lips. He takes in every detail, every change, his lips parting slightly and a tiny crease appears between his eyebrows.

"You're awake. You're… finally awake." I can't say anything else. My voice catches and sobs rise out of me. I can't hold them in anymore. *Damn, it must be this water.* It's drawing every emotion out of me, so strong that I can't move except to ugly cry every bit of sadness. Tears pour down my cheeks, dripping into the pond.

He's here. Finally, he's here.

Without taking his eyes off me, he undoes the straps keeping his armor on his chest and pulls it over his head, pushing it away across the surface of the pond. The deadly cuts in it make me cry harder. But he isn't bleeding. He isn't hurt anymore. He's healed and he's here, lifting his arms out to me.

"Marbella, come here." He doesn't wait for me to answer, pushing through the water until he's directly in front of me, rising up out of the water a little as he reaches the shallow side where I've stayed, churning the pool around us.

"Come here. I'm not letting you cry alone."

I want nothing more than to launch myself into his arms. "What if…" I sob and hiccup between words. "I hurt you? I can't… take that… risk…"

His lips part. His image blurs through my tears, but the curve of his mouth makes my heart do backflips. "Something tells me you can't hurt me. Not ever."

He slides one arm around my waist and another around my shoulders before I can think twice, drawing me closer. "I've waited long enough to hold you."

All my emotions pour out of me at that single touch. All it takes is the brush of his bare skin across the back of my neck, the briefest graze of his fingers through the loose hair at the nape of my neck for the first time in seven years. I feel everything at once—raging grief, despair, and an opposing sense of overwhelming happiness. I want to scream and weep and sigh all at the same time.

He drops a gentle kiss on my forehead and a bolt of lightning shoots through me—lightning coming from him. The storm hasn't returned to me with his awakening. Maybe it never will. Maybe I'm okay with that and maybe I'm not, but right now I don't care. I just want him close to me. If he felt the lightning, he doesn't flinch, slowly drawing me closer to his chest.

"You're hurting," he says. "I'm here. Let it out."

I do. All of it. I wrap my arms around him and let myself feel every moment of fear and helplessness when Howl pushed me around, every threat Howl made against the women in Harem Hall, the moment when I realized that Baelen and I were connected only to have to sever the connection, nights of freezing in the mines, being subjected to the gloating Elven Command and hearing them talk about imprisoning my friends, and finally, watching Cassian die. I sob all of it out against his chest while the water laps around us, and he strokes my back and my hair and kisses my forehead.

He brushes his thumbs across each of my cheeks, gently wiping the tears streaming down them, kissing the salty trail. "Even your tears are like diamonds," he says, startling me.

He pulls back a little as I stiffen, the corners of his mouth lifting into a smile. "You don't know what you look like now."

The phoenix said I was luminous. I thought it meant I looked happy, or relieved, or just plain alive, since death was in the cards.

Baelen drops a kiss on the end of my nose and brushes his cheek against mine. His breath caresses the side of my mouth. "You are a thousand times more beautiful than the moon—and trust me I know because I met her."

"You met Incorruptible?"

"She came to see me while I waited for you." His lips brush the soft skin beside my ear. The water swills around us with every movement. "You finally called me, and she told me how to leave my heart behind." His forehead crinkles. "Sort of like the ancients did when they gave their lives to become the world around us."

I gasp, finally understanding the risk he took. "You told me you were okay. But if we hadn't healed you in time, are you telling me only your heart would have remained?"

He blinks gently at me. "The Priestess wasn't overreacting. You were hurting. The Queen's heart would have wiped out everyone in that Court by reacting to your emotions. I had to act. No matter the risk. I was the only one who could."

He saved me—all of us actually—from a threat I didn't even know existed until it was over. I place both my hands on his chest, pulling back.

"No, Baelen, the risk is never worth it. If you had died, then I would have completely lost myself. I would have raged like a thousand storms."

"I'll remember that," he says before he drops a kiss on my lips.

The touch is so brief that it's over before I realize it began. My skin tingles where his lips touched mine.

I let the lap of water carry me closer to him, drowning in the sensation of his thumb brushing against the side of my neck. He tilts his head down to mine, waiting for my lips to find his. The water lifts me upward and our mouths fit together so perfectly.

Finally, I can kiss him like I've wanted to for seven long years.

My mouth crashes against his, never wanting the contact to end. He holds me, supporting my back, sinking lower into the water so I can wrap my legs around him while his kiss asks for more and more from me. I gasp for air when the contact breaks, my head tilting back as he trails kisses down my throat and back up to my lips. I try to press closer, my hands running through his hair and across his back, following every line, every muscle of his body.

I can't get close enough.

I hate my armor right now.

He pauses, his breathing not quite under control, taking a moment to study my face, my eyes, and my lips.

"Baelen?" I break the pause by brushing my lips across his.

"Marbella."

I tangle my fingers in the back of his shirt, tugging upward. I hate his shirt. I hate the armor he's still wearing from the waist down. I hate everything between us. "Please?"

His response is a throaty growl. His gaze is so intense I feel like he could burn through the Elyria thread my armor is made out of. He probably could. His eyes aren't filled with flames anymore, but he still controls all of the Storm's power. I sense it in every move he makes, the way he's controlling it, holding it back.

While one of his hands continues to support my spine, the other brushes the neckline of my armor. He doesn't take his eyes from mine as he asks, "How does this come off?"

I shiver, abandoning any attempt to keep my breathing under control, embracing the intensity of everything I'm feeling right now. I release his shirt and slide my legs away from him so I can find my feet at the shallower end of the pool a little further away. I tug at the neckline of my armor, undoing the hidden clasps at the neck and down the side. From there, it's a simple task of peeling it off my arms, torso, and then my legs.

He catches up to me, churning through the water, and stops me before I can start, catching my fingers in his. "Let me."

I want to rip the damn thing off, but he takes his time, sliding it off my shoulders, his hands following the armor's path down the outside of each of my arms as the water swirls around us.

Finally, he slides my armor to my waist, but his eyes remain on mine. I crave his hands against my skin. As if he hears my thoughts, his palms graze my ribcage, his fingers splaying out against the curve above each of my hips. His hands are so big they reach from my hipbone all the way up my ribcage.

It's not enough. I take both of his hands in mine and shift them upward to cover my breasts. Baelen blinks at me in surprise. Then he breaks into a smile, kissing me fiercely as my body burns with every movement of his palms and his thumbs and… *heavens…*

He takes a deep breath and disappears under the surface,

drawing his hands all the way down my body, making me shiver. He pulls my armor off my legs at the same time and I dip in the water to release the garment from beneath my feet. My clothing floats to the surface but Baelen stays under for another few seconds. Sensation floods me everywhere he touches my calves and thighs, before he emerges, his hair slicked back and water rushing off him as he breaks the surface. He shakes his head side-to-side, splattering me with water droplets.

I gasp in surprise. His scar is gone. The scar I gave him the night I became the Storm Princess. It's completely gone. The springs have healed it.

"Baelen, your—"

He doesn't let me finish, pulling me to him. I forget whatever I was going to say as my body responds to the intensity in his eyes and the demand in his kiss.

I tug at his shirt. *Off. It needs to be off.*

He helps me pull it over his head and remove his armored pants, pushing them away across the surface. Our clothing now dots the surface of the springs like multi-colored lily pads. I expected to see a myriad of scars across his chest and back from the battle he fought in the arena in what feels like a lifetime ago, but it looks like the deep springs have healed those too.

He gathers me toward him, and I'm not prepared for the swell of emotion I feel now that I'm finally able to touch all of him. I shiver as my body presses against his, skin to skin. We've been through so much to get here. Almost lost each other so many times. Almost didn't make it…

His expression becomes very serious as he draws back with a question in his eyes: the question he never fails to ask me. "Marbella Mercy, may I have your permiss—"

"Yes."

I take advantage of the water to lift and wrap my legs around him and draw him to me. He doesn't wait and I don't want him to.

Our bodies join and my world spins.

The entire time we've been in the springs, the heartstones have remained quiet above me and Baelen has kept his storm power in check. Now, both ignite.

The air above us glows with diamond light and the water blazes crimson red. Lightning and deep magic clash in the sudden swell, water droplets rise, and lightning curls around us in ribbons. Baelen holds me tight while I wrap my arms around him, neither of us moving, both waiting to catch up with everything we feel.

I can barely form words, but I need to tell him… "We waited such a long time to be together. No matter what happens, I will never let us be torn apart again."

In answer, he whispers, "We will have this again. Not just today."

Finally, he moves. He ignores all the power crashing around us, focusing only on me and our joined bodies, kissing every part of me that he can reach, pulling me closer every time. Sensation floods me and every emotion I've felt for him rushes at me: every cry, every laugh, every battle, every time Baelen protected me, every time I protected him, all of it hits me.

Baelen seems to sense my emotions and in response, power builds in his eyes. Water suspends around us. Droplets hover mid-air. I was already drowning in all the sensations he's sending through my body but now he lets go. Thunder thuds through me. My world shifts.

Our bodies crash against each other and that's all it takes. My world explodes in waves that threaten to tear me apart. Baelen holds me together as he crashes against me, sending lightning rippling out from us. I cling to him in the center of the pond, shaking with the force of what we created.

He holds me tight as we descend, both of us breathing hard, his lips finding mine as he kisses me over and over. "Marbella, you are everything to me. I would wait a thousand years to hear your voice, kiss your lips, walk beside you."

I kiss him back, sighing against his mouth. "I love you, Baelen Rath."

A smile breaks across his face, lighting up his eyes. "I love you, Marbella Mercy."

We stay that way for a long time, floating in the water, tangled up in each other, before he shifts me so I rest in his arms. I stretch against him, already missing the connection between our bodies. Before now, he was always in control. Always careful. But for the first time, here in this place with me, he truly let go. I smile, grin actually. "Promise me you'll lose control like that again."

His answer is to run his fingers across my shoulders, my collarbone, and all the way down to my hips underwater. "Without a doubt."

The water begins to settle around us. The storm we created slowly calms and loses its force. Baelen catches my armor as it floats past us, helping me pull it back on before the water pulls it away again. I catch his clothing but toy with the idea of refusing to give it back.

He grins at me as if he reads my mind. When we were connected by the storm, we could talk to each other without speaking. I have no idea what he'd say to me right now, but he distracts me with a kiss and the faintest brush of his hands across my ribcage. He steals his clothing right out of my fingertips.

Once dressed, he pulls me against him, adjusts my legs around his waist, and strides from the water, taking the steps at the side. Water streams from our bodies as we emerge into the cool air.

"Baelen, you have all the storm power now."

"It's not mine to keep. Part of it belongs to you. I can feel it trying to pull away from me and get back to you. I'm not sure how, but you will get it back."

He doesn't let me go, kissing me again, his big hands supporting my back and head. As he draws back, he runs his fingertip across the crease forming in my forehead. "What is it?"

"Fear has dictated my actions for so long. Fear and rules. Now you're here and I can finally be with you. But I'm terrified that when we go back out there…"

This night is not over. Not by a long shot. There's a whole world of trouble waiting for me as soon as we leave the deep springs. I still have to convince the clan leaders to accept me as their Queen. That's if I even want to be their Queen…

He strokes my back. "Marbella, you have the weight of this world on your shoulders. My shoulders are pretty broad. Let me share the burden."

I break into a smile. Broad shoulders are an understatement. I gesture at the stones with bewilderment. "I have to figure out how *this* happened."

"We'll figure it out together."

I blush. The last time he said that to me we were in a very

similar position to the one we're in now. He lowers me to the ground, helping me find my feet. After he returns to the edge of the water to retrieve the rest of his armor, he holds his hand out to me. I take it willingly. But very soon I remember there's one more thing we need to talk about before we leave the springs.

Baelen was present in the room when Howl forced me to dine with the Elven Command. He must have heard all of their plans, including the truth about his father's death.

I tug him to a stop. "The Elven Command conspired to kill your father."

The muscle at the edge of his jaw ticks as he turns. His hair has grown over the last month and now wet, brown strands frame the sides of his face. "They will pay for what they did."

"They've imprisoned my Storm Command. I can't abandon my ladies. Eli Elder said he was doing everything he could to make sure they were being treated fairly but I'm worried about what will happen when word gets out that I've killed Howl. I have to go back to Erawind. I have to free them…"

He squeezes my hand. "We will go back, Marbella. I know you're worried about them. I am too, but the Priestess is right. You have to secure peace here first."

"To do that, I have to get the clan leaders to support me. Which involves finding out how this happened."

And… I'm back to the stones again.

As we continue to walk up the side of the mountain, I shiver again—this time because I'm cold. "Do you think it would be unwise to use my power to dry off?"

Baelen responds to my violent shiver by swiftly pulling me into his arms, his skin blazing and warm light glowing around both of us. Within moments, water steams off us and I'm toasty warm and completely dry. I gasp as sensation trickles through every nerve in my body before he releases me with a self-satisfied smile. "Let's use mine."

Llion once told me that I smelled like clouds and ice. I discovered how true that was when I lived so close to the Queen's heart and froze everything around me at nighttime. Llion also told me that Baelen smelled like scorched earth and acid rain. It turns out that scorched earth isn't all that bad.

4

─────────

MARBELLA

Baelen whisks me across the air between the deep springs and Crimson Court but this time, he's right beside me. When we reach the other side, I pause at the Court's entrance. It's quiet. A guard is posted at each open side. I don't know any of them, but they stand at attention when I approach. Inside, bodies are lined up in neat rows with their wings folded across their chests. I don't know what sort of funeral rituals gargoyles have. I don't even know if they bury their dead. There are so many to bury.

I sigh, my breath frosting in the air. The nearest guard suddenly shivers. Baelen rubs his hand across my shoulders, catching my hand in his and pressing my palm between his own. It's not until he uses his power to warm the air around me that I realize I was the one making it cold. Grief seems to do that to me. And all of a sudden, it's crashing down on me again.

"They died because of Howl," the guard says, taking me by surprise. "Not because of you, Lady Storm. It's important that you know that."

I'm surprised by the complete lack of malice in his expression. "You were one of Howl's guards."

He quickly averts his eyes, tucking his wings tight against his sides, but holding them slightly forward in a gesture of remorse. "I

42

am from the Grievous Clan, Lady Storm. I was bound to follow my leader."

"In other words: you were bound to follow Howl."

The guard nods. "He was our clan leader as well as our king. Now he is neither." He meets my eyes. "I do not follow him any more."

All of the clan leaders are waiting for me at the Royal Residence. But the Grievous Clan is without a leader. "What is your name?"

"I am Grievous Gallon, Lady Storm. I am Grievous Erit's cousin."

"How will you decide who is your new leader, Grievous Gallon?"

"That is up to you, Lady Storm. You killed Howl, so you get to choose whether you will become our leader."

Well, this night is full of surprises. I study the guard more closely. He looks young, wears ill-fitting armor, and hasn't had a proper haircut in a while. Not that he's alone in that.

I ask, "What if I choose not to take Howl's place?"

"Then you must choose a replacement."

Good. Because I already know exactly who I want to lead their clan. "Thank you, Grievous Gallon. Please return to your post."

But as I turn away, he calls out, "I'm not guarding them, Lady Storm. I'm here to help gargoyles find their loved ones." He lowers his eyes. "We've sent word to the families of the ones who have fallen. When they get here, they won't have to search the faces of the dead to find the one they've lost. I will help them."

"That's…" *More compassionate than I expected.*

"Orders from Denrock Welsian," Gallon explains. "He told us it's what you would want."

"It is."

All three guards bow as I turn away. I walk in silence beside Baelen. Off to our far right, bright lights flicker in the direction of Harem Hall. I fight the urge to go there and make sure my friends are safe, but I have to trust that Roar will take care of them. I need to settle things with the clan leaders now.

The last time I visited the Royal Residence, Howl was practically dragging me along. Now, Baelen and I follow the wide pathway that ascends through the trees toward the palace. In the moonlight, it's even more unnervingly camouflaged against the cliff face that it's built into. The Residence contains a myriad of hallways and rooms with upper and lower levels. I have no idea where I'm supposed to go. Like before, multiple rows of guards stand watch outside of it but I'm relieved to find the old Priestess fluttering around giving them orders.

"Supreme Incorruptible," she says, more like an announcement than a greeting. In response, the guards stand at attention. I try not to eye them warily.

"This way please," the old Priestess continues. "To the meeting hall." She lowers her voice as we pass through the wide front doors. "Which, unfortunately, you are already familiar with."

My heart sinks. There are some rooms that I'd rather not visit ever again. This is the one where I was forced to eat with the Elven Commanders: Elwyn Elder and Pedr Bounty. When we reach the large, wooden door decorated with the silhouette of a golden panther, I press my palms against it, wishing I could destroy this room and everything that happened in it.

Inside, I count twenty-six clan leaders. They sit in what at first looks like a scattered pattern, but as I study them, I realize that they are gathered more on one side of the room than the other.

On the other side, a fire burns in the fireplace. It wasn't lit last time I was here, and it gives off long shadows across the floor. A large, hunched form rises from beside the flames: a male gargoyle I've never seen before. He wears furs across his shoulders that entirely cover his wings, and a chain made out of bird talons and panther claws across his broad chest. He blows out a match as he rises, indicating that he was the one who lit the fire.

The Priestess announces. "I give you the Supreme Incorruptible Marbella Mercy." I watch her carefully as she speaks. She's making a point of looking right past this new man and not directly at him.

He speaks from beside the fireplace, his voice a deep growl. "Well, that's what we're here to determine, isn't it? Whether or not she really is Supreme Incorruptible."

He draws up to his full height, his fur coat sliding away from his wings, held securely across his shoulders by the chain. He shakes out his wings, a casual gesture, but the action reveals a startling difference: where other gargoyles have single wing daggers at their two uppermost wing tips, this gargoyle's wings are topped with multiple waves of sharp, silver tips, razor-sharp edges catching the light.

Baelen jolts beside me, the first sign of surprise he's shown since he appeared at the Court this afternoon. I don't know what it means when he whispers, "Senturi."

At the same time, a tiny face peeks out from behind the man's coat. Gorgeous, brown eyes and rosy cheeks appear as a little girl—maybe only six-years-old—darts out from behind the older man, hands outstretched to Baelen. "Bae-Bae!"

A grin breaks across Baelen's face. He catches the little girl and swings her up, popping her onto his hip as if she's sat there many times before.

"Little Adalie! You've grown!"

I look for my jaw. I'm pretty sure I've dropped it somewhere on the floor.

Adalie is covered in a fur coat too. It conceals her wings, but she pulls out a necklace so Baelen can see it, proudly prodding at the single talon attached to it. "Look, Bae-Bae. I killed my first talon crow." Her little eyebrows draw down. "I'm not scared of them anymore."

"They are not worthy of your fear, little Adalie."

She grins, clawing her fingers and drawing her lips back into a demonstrative hiss. "They are scared of *me* now."

"As they should be."

Adalie turns her gaze to me, her pupils dilating. I was struck silent before, but now her gaze freezes me. I've felt this sensation before. The Elven Commander I killed—Gideon Glory—had tried to invade my mind with his sorcery. I'd sensed it like something sliding around inside my head. This tiny girl is doing the same. I want to push back against the girl like I did with Gideon, but my power is so strong I could kill her.

Her voice becomes older than her years as she whispers, "You are sad, Storm Lady, and worried about your people."

Well, she's right about that.

The older man quickly covers the distance between us. It doesn't escape me that the other clan leaders lean away from him, avoiding eye contact as he passes. Even the old Priestess suddenly finds something fascinating about the floor as the newcomer reaches for the little girl. "Come now, granddaughter, enough showing off."

Showing off? It felt more like emotional invasion. But not an ugly invasion. More like an unwilling one. If this girl has some sort of power, she doesn't know how to control it yet.

Baelen relinquishes the snuggly bundle in his arms to the older man who whispers to the girl, "Remember your manners."

The little girl drops to a knee in front of me, mimicking her grandfather who also bows to me.

Her little-girl voice rings out innocently into the silence. "Greetings, Storm Lady. Greetings, Bae-Bae."

I bite my lip, trying to bury a smile at her earnest expression. Baelen solemnly taps his heart. "Greetings, Outlier Adalie." He also acknowledges the older man with a respectful nod. "Greetings, Outlier Senturi."

Baelen turns to me next, and his expression begs me to go with him on this. I compress my lips. Baelen clearly knows these gargoyles, but to my knowledge, he never set foot in Erador before I brought his sleeping body across the border. He owes me a lot of answers and his expression tells me he knows it.

"Marbella, these gargoyles are from the Outlier Clan," he says. "They are the ones who guard the edges of our world."

The edges of our world are wastelands where the mountains and grass stop, and the ground becomes ash. The wastelands lead only to jagged walls that are thousands of feet high where the Gargoyle King cleaved a space out of the layers of the Earth for us to live.

"I've never heard of the Outlier Clan," I say, digging into my memory for any mention of it.

"That's because we are few and far between, scattered throughout the wastelands," Senturi explains. "We would be even fewer still if it weren't for Baelen Rath. Adalie would not be alive today without him."

More answers I'll need from Baelen, but I won't be distracted from the more pressing question: Why is Senturi here? I highly doubt that any of the other clan leaders invited him judging by the way they won't even look at him. "Well, you're here now. You must have a reason for traveling all the way from your home."

Senturi clears his throat, meeting my eyes. "Members of my clan have Sight. We alone can tell the true nature of things. That is why I have come to you."

He takes a step closer, daring to close the gap between us. "I'm here to answer the question that everyone is asking: What are you?"

5

———

MARBELLA

I sigh. "I know what I am: tired. I lost dear friends today and I want to bury them. I'm not interested in games."

He leans forward to whisper, "Then I'm sorry we will need to play one." He leans back, speaking more loudly this time so everyone can hear. "You will notice that the other gargoyles avoid my attention."

I glance at the Priestess. She's unusually quiet and offers me no guidance about what I should say next. Instead, she glues her gaze to the floor like everyone else in this room except Baelen and me.

I nod. "It hasn't escaped me."

"Yet you yourself hide nothing." His statement isn't a question, but it sounds like one.

"I have nothing to hide."

His response is quick. Accusing. "You know a secret, Marbella Mercy."

I raise an eyebrow. "Probably. In fact, it's likely that I know several."

He is much more skilled than his granddaughter at hiding the invasion into my mind. I sense it like a gentle breeze, so quiet, so soft that I hardly notice it at all. But I *do* notice it.

I decide not to push back.

He gives me a slow nod, indicating his quiet gratitude. "You could destroy my mind in a heartbeat. Yet you choose to allow me inside your thoughts. Why?"

"Because anyone who is brave enough to look into my emotions is stronger than he looks."

A smile breaks across Senturi's features, transforming him so that he looks much younger. I study his face, his eyes, the perceptive way he assesses me. I've seen that look before. Why does it seem so familiar to me?

As if he doesn't want to give me long enough to figure it out, Senturi abruptly adjusts his focus. "Priestess," he says to her. "Would you be so kind as to call Lightsworn Lance and the other clan leaders closer. Please reassure them that I will not cast my Sight upon them. They have my word about that. All I want is what Erador needs: knowledge and peace."

The Priestess unsticks her gaze from the floor. "I know you are true to your word, Outlier Senturi. I will bring them over."

As the Priestess gathers the clan leaders, Senturi's jaw ticks. "She's right about that. I always do what I promise. And I promise you, Marbella Mercy, I already know what you are. But the trick will be convincing the clan leaders. I'm sorry this is a game you can't avoid playing."

Well, if he already knows the answers, then I wish he would just tell me, but it looks like nothing will be simple tonight.

Lightsworn Lance, who is the patriarch of Liliana's clan, hobbles over to me, mumbling, "I should be too old to be frightened of Sighted Ones." He appears to have aged even more since the last time I saw him; his skin is fragile and semi-transparent. He stops at a safe distance from me and looks me over. The other clan leaders soon join him. I recognize only some of them: the leader of the Virtuous Clan is dressed in regal robes while the leaders of the Denrock and Sunflight clans wear earthy clothing. All of them appear worse for wear after the battle today.

I return their gazes. The stones spin around me in the silence.

Senturi addresses them in a casual manner. "When you look at Lady Storm, what do you see?"

With a perplexed air, Lance says, "My eyes show me two things that can't co-exist: An elf controls our ancient Queen's heart."

Senturi's response is sharp and concise. "She is not an elf."

Even I'm surprised, but maybe I shouldn't be. The phoenix once told me that when it looked at me, it didn't see an elf. It said that I was *something else.*

Lance's eyebrows draw down into a stubborn expression. "Well, she is certainly not a gargoyle. She knows nothing of our clans, our history…"

Anger rises up inside me. I will never claim to be a gargoyle but to say that I don't know anything about them is wrong. I cut off whatever response Senturi was about to make. I am not enjoying this game. "I have fought with your people, bled with them, felt their deaths like a blade in my own heart. They are my friends, some of the best and most loyal friends I've ever had—and that includes my Storm Command who are like sisters to me. Do not stand there and tell me I am not a gargoyle. Do not tell me who I am."

All of the leaders blink at my outburst, but I don't care if I've surprised or offended them. My voice lowers to a growl. "Seven years ago, the Storm chose me to carry her power. *Your* storm chose me. She was a gargoyle just like you."

At the corner of my eye, the Priestess raises her hand at me for calm. The heartstones have sped up in response to my emotions and that's probably not a good thing. I'm not sure what she thinks flapping her hands at me will achieve. I try to rein in my emotions as Senturi appraises me.

I have the sense he approves of my reaction.

"The Storm has everything to do with this," he says. "Please, Lady Storm, would you be so kind as to tell everyone what you know about our beloved Storm."

I'm not entirely sure what he wants me to say. But I'm guessing the secret he spoke of earlier is the one Cassian told me. "Her name is Elyria." That alone draws murmurs, but what I say next turns the space around me into uproar. "She was Supreme Incorruptible."

"Liar!"

"Princess Elyria was murdered by your kind!"

"The Storm was a servant girl!"

"How do you know this?" Lance demands.

I could be offended and angry. I could lash out, but I don't. I meant what I said: I'm exhausted. I've experienced everything today from excruciating fear to overwhelming happiness. There's not much more I can feel.

I reach for Baelen's hand. He wraps my fingers up in his, quietly waiting for me to choose my response. The shouting clan leaders fade into the background as I focus on his quiet strength, finding my own within his. I take a deep breath, calming myself. The heartstones settle around me, their agitated movement slowing.

Admiration floods Senturi's features, but his expression changes as he glares the clan leaders down, snarling at them. "You are foolish to contradict her." His voice rises to a shout. "Look at her! Look with your hearts, not your eyes! Look again and tell me what you see!"

"Do not tell us what to believe, Outlier." The Denrock Clan leader is the one who called me a liar, and he is the first to retaliate, striding toward me, his wings tipped forward in an aggressive gesture. I let him come, squeezing Baelen's hand to ask him not to react.

At the last moment, I focus on the Queen's heart and the power I feel inside it. The stone drops into the space between me and the approaching gargoyle. The diamond heart lights up the air, flickering over me, flashing brilliant spears through the room. I sense it reflecting off my skin, even more brilliant than the flames in the fireplace. The gargoyle skids to a stop three paces away, his eyes shooting wide, one big hand flying up to shield his eyes. His eyebrows draw down and his wings suddenly hunch as he peers at me.

I don't know what he sees, but something has stopped him in his tracks. His eyes grow even wider. He shakes his head side-to-side. "How is this possible?"

The other leaders huddle up behind him, drawn forward like moths to firelight. I peer back at them, perplexed by the sudden change. It's probably not a good idea to tell them that my intention in drawing on the stone's power was to knock this insolent gargoyle off his feet.

Senturi withdraws a little to the side, but not before he shoots me a pleased grin. He turns to his granddaughter. "Adalie, would you please tell the Storm Lady the story about our beloved Storm."

"The pretend story or the real one?" she asks, her innocent gaze stuck to me like her brethren's.

"The pretend one, dear heart."

Adalie parrots her words as if she's learned them by rote. "Four hundred years ago, the last Elven King brutally slaughtered our beautiful Queen Bethesda and her two children, including the heir to the throne, Princess Elyria."

The Elven King murdered Elyria's family! No wonder she hated elves. My hand shoots to my heart, to the sudden pain inside it. I'd heard awful stories about our last King and his sorcery. In fact, I suspected he was just as bad as Howl, but to murder Elyria's family… For her to watch them die…

Baelen said that she was caught in the nightmares of her past. Howl had built this palace as an exact replica of the original one. It would be just like the home Elyria grew up in. Being surrounded by the same walls, the place where her family died must have broken her into pieces.

Adalie is still speaking, telling me what supposedly happened next. "Queen Bethesda's brother arrived on the murder scene just in time to see the Elven King escape. He asked an unnamed servant girl to give her life to become the Storm and kill the treacherous Elven King. And so, the royal family was avenged." She tugs on her grandfather's coat, whispering loudly, "Can I tell them the real story now, Papa?"

The clan leaders lean forward. This is clearly a truth they haven't ever heard given their earlier assertions that the Storm was a servant.

Senturi pats Adalie's hand. "Yes, dear heart, go ahead."

Her face lights up. "I saw it in the Storm Lady's eyes just now. It's so much better than the pretend story. Bethesda's brother arrived just in time to see Elyria herself become the Storm. He tried to stop her. She was injured, her wing was broken, but she was determined to kill the evil King. She was her brother's protector, not the other way around. She was going to become his avenger."

Adalie's eyes shine as if the idea of a girl avenging her family means a lot to her. "She became thunder and lightning, a savage tornado. She raged after the elves, killed the King and his advisors, and wiped out half the elven race as retribution for killing her family."

She stops to take a breath, opens her mouth to continue speaking, but Senturi gives her a quick shake of his head. "Well done, dear heart, now go and play by the fire, but mind the flames."

Adalie glances at me. There's more. I can't read her mind like she can read mine, but I know there's more.

"Yes, Papa," she says.

While Adalie settles herself in front of the fire, Senturi addresses me.

"Many years later, you stood at a cliff's edge and risked your life to save Baelen Rath. You were about to plunge to your death when Elyria gave you her storm power instead. But on that night, you did something that had never been done before. You poured part of your power into Baelen Rath. You know that much, but here's what you don't know."

He rolls his shoulders, the sharp edges of his wing tips catching the firelight. The flames reflect against the side of his face as he focuses on me. Pinpoint focus.

"The act of pouring your power into Baelen Rath left a gap inside you that the deep magic demanded be filled. To fill that gap, Elyria passed on her very essence, the very nature of who she was, including her royal blood."

I stumble backward. "She what?"

"She gave you her soul, Marbella."

I shake my head. This is… not okay… There are so many things wrong with what he just said. Elyria and I used to be connected. If she gave me her soul, then the connection with me would have been crucial to her. But I broke that connection. I left her with Baelen. And then I broke it again today… I didn't just break the connection. I broke… *her*.

I can hardly focus on Senturi. He's so calm, and I know I have to be calm as well, but it feels like my world just turned into a hurricane.

"And so began a metamorphosis," he says. "Your body and your instincts changed: your eyesight developed to allow you to see in the dark, the scent of your blood changed, so did your reflexes, and when you came closer to where the Queen's heart was buried, even your skin and hair changed in response to its call. You may not have wings and your ears retain their points, but you are in many ways a female gargoyle."

"Then… I'm not an elf anymore?"

"You are a hybrid. Not an elf, not a gargoyle, but both."

"What about Baelen? Is he a gargoyle too?" My eyes meet Baelen's. My hand is still wrapped in his.

"No. Elyria's essence didn't reach him, but his bond with you gives him the same allegiance to the gargoyles."

Lightsworn Lance is the first to speak into the silence. "Then… she stands in Elyria's place. She *is* Elyria. She is heir to our throne?"

As Lance speaks, something clicks into place: when High Priestess Talia first saw me, she whispered "Elyria." I thought she was distracted by my armor, the inner skin of which is made completely of the unbreakable thread from Elyria spiders. She'd looked at me strangely afterward too. Talia is the only Priestess alive now who can still use deep magic. She must have sensed my true nature the same way that Senturi can see it.

Senturi stands aside to allow Lance to approach me. Senturi says, "Lightsworn Lance, you knew the King. Tell me who she smells like."

I grit my teeth as the old gargoyle leans forward, glad that he keeps at a respectful distance. He closes his eyes. Inhales.

His eyes shoot wide open. "She is our Queen!"

All of the gargoyles shift where they stand. I don't know what they're doing until they sink to a knee, heads bowed.

"As you have Seen, Outlier Senturi," Lightsworn Lance says. "She is Supreme Incorruptible." He bows low to me. "Supreme Incorruptible, I honor you."

The old Priestess leans in discretely and whispers to me. "Now you say: 'I am honored.'"

Somehow I manage to push sound past my lips. "I am… honored."

Each of the clan leaders echoes their allegiance in turn: "Supreme Incorruptible, I honor you."

I repeat my response to each of them until the last when they return to their feet, waiting expectantly. I have no idea what I'm supposed to say now, but as far as I'm concerned, the game is over.

I say, "Howl did a lot of damage. Families are separated from their loved ones, fallen gargoyles need to be buried and mourned. I will help you, but as clan leaders you are responsible for ensuring that every member of your clan is safe and returned to where they belong."

"May we rebuild our nests in the mountains?"

The miners once told me that each mountain used to contain the main nest of each clan. I had spent most of the last month working in Mount Prime where the Prime nest had been ripped out to house the miners instead. "Of course. You must rebuild."

"What about the Grievous Clan?" another asks.

I scan the group. "Is there a member from that clan here tonight?"

They shake their heads. "They alone were allowed to remain on Mount Grievous. None from the mountain have come here for many years. We believe they may be afraid of your retribution now, Supreme Incorruptible."

"Then I will have to speak to them personally." And take Grievous Erit with me, since he is my pick to lead them. I know that Llion would also make an amazing leader, but I will need him here with me after he returns from the border.

I add, "But not tonight. Now…" I turn to the Priestess, wondering what the practicalities of hosting the clan leaders will be. "Is it possible to arrange a meal for the clan leaders? And beds please. I think we're all in need of food and rest."

She nods to me before she hurries away. "I will arrange for food to be brought in."

The clan leaders seem surprised that I want to feed them. I guess basic hospitality has been sparse for the last ten years.

After they acknowledge my gesture with thanks, Senturi draws me aside, away even from Baelen. "You know there's more."

Nobody's listening to us now. The clan leaders have returned to their seats, although they shoot me glances every now and then. Even Baelen is deliberately giving Senturi and me space. I get right to the point. "What did you stop your granddaughter from saying?"

"There's more to Elyria's story. But I'm afraid it would only cloud your rule for it to be public knowledge. Also, it's for Elyria to tell you, not me."

When I read the Queen's journal, I read about Elyria's mother, Bethesda. She had written about a truth that she didn't want Elyria to find out. Whatever it was, I'm guessing Elyria discovered it.

"If Elyria gave me her soul, where does that leave her? I'm really worried about her, Senturi."

He shakes his head. "I can't see her present state, only the parts of her past that have become part of you. But I saw in your memories the moment when you severed your connection with Baelen. You also severed your connection with Elyria. Until that time, she was not separated from her essence. But now, she has no anchor. She will also experience a metamorphosis."

"For good or bad? What will she become?"

He shrugs. "I'm sorry. As I said, I can only see the past. I can't see her now."

I worry at my lip. "How can I help her?"

"You already helped her when you allowed Jasper to take her away. He's the only one who can help her now."

"Well, if you can't see her present, how do you know that for sure?"

He smiles, assessing me. Again, his face loses its years, becoming younger and so familiar. I gasp. I've seen the expression in Senturi's eyes a hundred times on the face of one of my truest, dearest friends.

Jasper.

Jasper was the only one, other than me, who could see the Storm. She used to be invisible to everyone else—she said it was because she chose to be invisible. She was very upset when she found out that Jasper could see her despite her wishes. When we were trying to figure out how Jasper could see her, we guessed that his grandmother had fallen in love with a gargoyle, that Jasper's father was half gargoyle.

If Senturi is Jasper's grandfather that would explain a lot: like how Jasper is so perceptive, how he guessed all that time ago that I'd become the Storm because I was trying to help someone, how he seems to know my thoughts before I do, and how he could see Elyria for what she truly is.

"And now you know another secret," Senturi whispers. "I have long wished to have a place in my grandson's life but having me in his life would have *ruined* his life. Neither elves, nor gargoyles, look kindly on the mixing of our races."

"You can meet him now. He needs to know his family."

Senturi shakes his head. "I want to meet him more than anything. But Elyria needs him more than me. I can't tell you what she is becoming, but I have to leave them alone."

He draws closer, his voice lower still. "Once she is recovered, you must ask her why the Elven King killed her family. The answer is very important to your future."

"I suppose you're not going to tell me." My hand shoots up. "Never mind. I already know the answer to that. But how can you possibly see all of this when I don't even know it myself?"

"Because I see the true nature of all things."

I growl. He said that already. It's hardly an answer. Elves don't have Sight, but some rare elves are Visionaries—they have the ability to see past our world, as far as the surface of the Earth, and to predict multiple future possibilities. But they can't see the inner workings of another person's mind like Senturi can. I'm about to demand a better answer from him when the door bursts open behind me.

Roar stands inside it, his wings spread. "Lady Storm! Come quickly!"

"What is it, Roar?"

His enormous chest rises and falls rapidly. His wings shudder around his body. "It's our wives."

6

———

MARBELLA

Fear shoots through me. I have no idea what might be wrong, but I've never seen Roar look so afraid. Deep fear pulls his features taut, thrumming through every rise and fall of his giant chest. Gilda is everything to him. If something has happened to her… I'm already running, Baelen close behind me.

As I pass by, Roar shoots into the space between Baelen and me. "No!"

Baelen skids to a halt, his silhouette turning acid red as he harnesses his power.

"I'm sorry, Wrathful One." Roar rises up to fully block Baelen before he can step a foot out the door. He doesn't seem to care that Baelen is glowing hot and angry. "This is not a matter for you."

I don't know why Roar's behaving this way, but I ask Baelen to stay put. "Please. I'll be okay."

Baelen glowers at Roar. "I would not yield for any other gargoyle, but I know you protected Marbella in the mines. I trust you with her life." His voice lowers to a threatening growl. "Do not endanger her or you will answer to me."

Roar growls back. "I would not expect any less from you, Wrathful One. The same way I would kill any man who endangers my wife. You have my word."

As I race away through the halls, Roar joins me, running

alongside. "With respect, Lady Storm, may I fly with you so we can move faster."

My answer is to leap into his arms, my feet on his feet and my arms around his waist. He catches me, spreads his wings, and we're airborne in the next breath, soaring through the high ceilings and out of the wide, front doors.

I see it already: some sort of fire, big enough to be visible above the top of the forest.

"Roar! What is that?"

His voice chokes. "They won't look at us. They won't speak to us. They're breaking everything." His voice becomes hoarse. "Including our hearts."

We soar toward Harem Hall over the tops of trees into the eastern clearing. A fire rages outside it, casting light across the verandah and the yellow flags, but it's the screams that hit me straight in the heart. As we touch down, a woman runs from the Hall carrying an armful of clothing—scanty dresses and barely-there underwear flutter in her arms. She throws it all into the fire in one giant heave. Then she screams at the burning items, tears streaming down her cheeks.

"Fuck you, Howl!" She roars again, emptying her lungs into the air, her arms spread wide, her scream turning into a wail as she collapses to the ground. One of the other women catches her, holding her close, both of them sobbing.

A cry rises in my throat. The woman on the ground is Gilda, Roar's wife, her ebony hair flying around her face in the heat of the flames. She seems to remember her hair, reaches into it, and wrenches out the hairpiece Howl made her wear, throwing that into the fire too.

The woman holding her is Carmen. She does the same, hurling her hairband into the flames. Then they claw at their flimsy clothing, ripping that off too, staring as it disappears inside the flames, leaving themselves completely naked. They roar into the fire, screams of agony they were never allowed to utter before.

Other women emerge, throwing cushions, chairs, parts of tables, ornaments, even the giant cherries that Howl made them eat and the scented soap he made them wash with. All of it disappears into the fire. One by one, they rip off their clothes and stand naked in front of the giant flames.

Tears drip down my cheeks. No woman deserves to be treated the way Howl treated them. Not ever.

There's a growl behind me. I don't think Roar looked like this even during the battle at Crimson Court. He wants—*needs*—to kill something. So do the other men pacing at the far edges of the clearing. I recognize Rhain, Carmen's husband, his newly healed wings half-spread as if he's about to take flight and go to her.

"We tried to help them, but they screamed at us." Roar points at a deep scratch on his chest. "Gilda did this. She won't let me near her."

A pale-green light glows at the edges of my vision. It's the Virtuous Heartstone, its empathy filling the air around me. I wrap my fingers around Roar's big forearm, allowing as much of the soothing emotion to warm my fingertips as possible.

"I will help them, Roar. I promise you. But please, tell the other men to wait. Give us space. Your wives need to do this."

He swallows. His throat constricts. "If you could kill that monster a thousand times, it would not be enough, Lady Storm."

"I promise you, Roar, he felt excruciating pain at the end."

I calm the force of the Queen's destructive power as I pick my way along the path toward the women. The power inside me responds to the flames and the women's rage, but it's not anger that I need now. I reach Gilda's side first. She recognizes me but says nothing, her face streaked with ash and tears.

I ask, quietly, "Where is it?"

She points to a growing pile of clothing that the women continue to hurl into the flames. The edge of a jet-black dress peeks from the pile. I recognize the pale-blue filigree and the ribbons that circle the waist. It was the one that Howl made me wear when he paraded me like his trophy in front of the entire Court. It has a large slit up the back that he loved to abuse. I wore it to the mines, but the women came each week unknown to the miners to collect the laundry and deliver fresh clothing. They brought the dress back to Harem Hall with them.

I drag it from the pile, scrunch it in my fist, and pitch the garment into the fire. The heartstones respond to my anger, pushing the flames so high that they curve over the top of us, forming a barrier of flame between us and the rest of the world. I use the stones' power to keep it there, maintaining the height and width of the flames, blocking out the worried men. The women close their eyes, the light flickering across their bodies and their wings.

"They say your new power can destroy things," Gilda says, her eyes still closed. "Can you burn this place too?"

I study Harem Hall. Howl modeled every building exactly on the real palace that he destroyed. Somehow, I don't think the former King kept a harem. "What was this building in the real palace?"

She sighs. "It was Healing Hall. It was where the Priestesses lived."

I say, "Nobody will want to live here now."

"Nobody." She shakes her head, her hair waving around her face, black strands like ropes around her neck.

"Then I will destroy it. Just tell me when."

Gilda opens her eyes. Tears stream out of them. She counts the women around her. "We're all outside. It's safe to destroy it now."

I close my own eyes for a moment. The destructive power in the Queen's heart wants to be released. I let it go and it's scarily easy. Silver light streaks from the heart, forming four giant strands like ropes. Two of the strands stretch around each side of the Hall, extending all the way to the rock face and pulling taut against the external walls. The light spreads outward, sizzling across the surface of the building from verandah to roof, lighting up the entire structure like a skeleton. Wood and material pop and hiss as if the whole thing was dipped in acid. The building creaks, collapses, and dissolves. Just like Howl.

Within minutes, a giant pile of dust remains.

The women clutch each other, sobbing, barely standing. I wait for them, giving them all the time they need, standing with them.

Eventually, I say, "Tell me what you need."

Carmen wipes her streaming eyes. "You must divorce us from our husbands."

I stop myself before I react too quickly. "Divorce you? But your husbands love you. More than life itself."

Carmen says, "We can't go back to them after what Howl did to us."

Gilda nods. "We can't be their wives like this."

Another woman speaks behind Carmen. "We can't share our bodies now."

"Of course not," I whisper. "But if Howl's actions continue to break your lives, then he may as well still be here."

Gilda shakes her head vehemently. "We need to divorce our husbands so we can marry them again."

Carmen adds, "So we can start fresh."

"Oh." Well, thank the ancients because it would have broken Roar apart if Gilda wanted to leave him.

Carmen says, "You know our customs: the woman chooses her mate. We have to choose our husbands again. For some of us, that might take some time. You must tell them… that we will come to them when we're ready. But if they want us… they must show us their worth. They'll know what that means."

The women join hands and turn away from the fire. "We are going to get our children now, Lady Storm," Gilda says. "Make sure the men know their children will be safe."

The wall of flames has blocked the men from seeing behind it for a while now. I wait for the women to disappear into the night before I let the fiery curtain down.

Roar stops pacing, searching the darkness, but the women are gone. "Where are they? Please tell me that Gilda is okay."

"She will be." I turn to them all, waving them forward. "I have to tell you all something and I need you to hear me out before you react. Can you promise me you will do that?"

They are all searching the darkness for the one they love, many of them startled to see Harem Hall reduced to dust.

I begin slowly. "As Supreme Incorruptible I apparently have the power to divorce married couples. Your wives have asked for this." I wait for this news to sink in. Roar is stunned, but I'm proud of the way he and the others recover, indicating they will keep listening.

"Your wives do not exist anymore. They are free women. Free to choose again. If you want them, you must show them your worth."

Roar processes this for a moment before turning to the other men. "Show them… our worth." His face clears and so does theirs. More than a couple sink to the ground and tip their heads back in relief. "Praise the ancients. They still want us."

"They have gone to get your children. They want you to know your children will be safe."

Roar sweeps me up in his arms in a giant hug that turns into flight. As we soar over the forest, he says, "Thank you, Lady Storm. I will return you to the Residence now."

I try to smile against his chest, but the memory of Gilda and Carmen's pain burns my eyes with tears. "What did they mean when they said you have to prove your worth?"

"It means we have to prove to them that we know who they are. In our culture, we do not deserve a woman in our bed until we know their heart and mind first. I will prove to Gilda that I know who she is."

Roar sets me down inside the Residence where the old Priestess waits for me. His wings encircle me for a moment. "You lost much today, Lady Storm. We all did. But there's much to be gained now that we have new lives."

He takes flight before I can say anything else. Exhaustion rocks me. I haven't eaten for a really long time, and I need to see Baelen. I need to feel his arms around me and remember what goodness feels like. I stop the Priestess before she can speak. "Where is Baelen Rath? Take me to him, please."

"As you wish but—"

"Take me to him."

She takes another look at me and spins on her heel, beckoning me to follow her. "I've had rooms made up on the uppermost level for you. That way you are away from everyone else. He wanted to wait for you, but I told him you might be a while."

The whole place is enormous. I'm sure it could house an entire army as well as the clan leaders and then some. She silently leads me through hallways and up three staircases until we reach a final corridor, stopping in front of a solid-oak door.

"This is his room but—"

I reach for the handle, ignoring the warning in her voice. She steps in front of me, pushing my hand away. I stare at her in surprise.

"That is unwise," she says. "You may not go to his bed."

Female gargoyles choose their husbands by going to their chosen mate's bed. I made the mistake of confusing Cassian by climbing into his bed.

I say, "I know your customs. If I go to his bed, it means that I choose him. Well… *I choose him!*"

Her response is equally forceful. "No! You are Supreme Incorruptible, now. You are a gargoyle, now. There are rules you have to follow. You can't… You aren't allowed…"

I wait for her to finish the sentence that seems to be tripping her up so much. "Can't what?"

"Choose an elf."

What? Rage boils under my skin. I grind my teeth. "You will not tell me who I can love."

"The Wrathful One is a formidable ally and we owe him our lives, but our Queen is a gargoyle. Our Queen must not choose an elf."

I back away because if I don't put some space between her and me, I'm going to do something really bad. Like throw her bony ass out the window or burn her to dust like one of Howl's soaps.

I've just come back from consoling beautiful women whose hearts and bodies were abused for years and my own heart is sore and painful in my chest. It will kill me to spend tonight apart from Baelen.

I ask one last time, "Will you let me pass?"

She plants herself in front of the door. "No."

From inside the room, I hear the faint sound of running water: a shower. If Baelen could hear us, he'd be out here in two seconds.

I shake my head. This isn't happening. She isn't actually saying this. Tomorrow I'm going to wake up and this will be some sort of mistake or bad dream, or they will have all changed their minds and I won't be Supreme Incorruptible after all. I will not let anyone stand between Baelen and me again. I close my eyes, using the last of my strength to contain my rage. "Where is my room?"

I open my eyes to see her point to the door at the end of the corridor. "There."

"Right. Good." I turn on my heel and, instead of walking toward the room she says is mine, I walk away from it. I walk away from her bony frame blocking Baelen's door. She knows I could blast her and that damn door into shards. But she also knows that I won't.

Because I'm not Howl.

I won't use force to take what I want. I will find another way.

I start to run. The heartstones fly behind me. I don't want to be the gargoyle's Queen. I don't want any of this. I just wanted to heal Baelen. And I will be with him, no matter what she says.

I find myself outside the Residence, speeding past the guards, dragging air into my lungs, pumping my arms and legs as hard as I can, running down the hill through the trees, past the pile of dust that used to be Harem Hall, rotating right across the cliffs, racing toward Crimson Court. The guards don't try to stop me. One look at my face and they turn back to the cliffs and give me privacy.

Most of the bodies are gone, taken by their families to be buried.

There's only one I need to see.

I drop to the floor beside Cassian. My shoulders slump. I press my hands against the tops of my knees, hauling air into my lungs. My chest burns so badly. I remember the moment he held the Queen's heart and wrapped me up in his wings, telling me to hold on while he took the force of her awakening. I remember his brilliant, blue eyes. I remember when he gave me a mirror and told me not to be afraid of who I am.

The old Priestess told me that I can't choose an elf. Well, the only gargoyle I would have chosen—even if I could pretend for two seconds that my heart isn't completely Baelen's—lies dead before me now. Cassian, the one whose bed I climbed into by accident.

I pull my braid apart, letting my hair down. Then I take hold of his wing and slide under it. I curl up inside the heavy cocoon that saved my life when I would have frozen to death.

He is the cold one now.

"I'm sorry, Cassian." Tears slide down my cheeks, dripping onto his chest. "I'm sorry I couldn't save you."

I've destroyed many things today, but there's only one thing I really want to destroy: *death*.

A long time later, I awake to familiar arms—Baelen's arms— pulling me upward, gathering me against his chest. He strokes my hair, soothing strokes, and I don't care where he's taking me as long as he's there with me. He doesn't use his power, walking every step, carrying me all the way back to the Residence.

Finally, his warmth leaves me, but only long enough for me to see a bedroom, a bed, and a blanket being pulled up over me. The bed sinks with his weight before he wraps himself against me. His strong arms curl around me, drawing my head against his shoulder.

His voice is a low promise in my ear. "Just because you can't come to my bed, doesn't mean I can't come to yours."

I have no words. Part of me wants to laugh because he found a way around their stupid rules. Most of me wants to cry but I don't seem to have any tears left.

7

———

JASPER

Elyria trembles in my arms, a fierce shivering that I can't stop. She clings to me as the phoenix flies northwest, the moon high in the sky above us.

When we took to the air, I leaned over the phoenix's neck and said, "I know you can't talk to me like you talk to Marbella, but I need you to take us somewhere safe. Far away, where nobody will find us. Does such a place exist?"

The phoenix's determined eyes spoke volumes. A nod of its head told me what I wanted to hear. I promised I would contact Marbella as soon as I could, but for now my goal is to help Elyria feel safe again.

We fly for two hours, leaving the palace and Crimson Court far behind. I learned about Erador's geography while I was in the mines, so I'm able to identify Mount Denrock in the distance. It wouldn't be safe for us to land near it, so I'm relieved when the phoenix flies around it toward another, smaller mountain beyond it. We're so far north now that we're close to the wastelands.

The air is crisp and clean but the scent of blood still fills my lungs. I'm covered in it. It can't be helping Elyria. She hasn't raged once since we left the cliff at the entrance to the deep springs. In fact, I don't sense her storm power at all. Her eyes are squeezed shut, her thoughts closed to me. All I know is that she's still afraid and it makes me want to rage on her behalf. A deep exhaustion is

67

settling in my bones, but I would stand up and fight again right now if it would help her stop trembling.

The phoenix glides toward a valley nestled between two hills. A shadow within the valley quickly takes the shape of a cabin as we close the distance. At the far end of the valley, a waterfall sparkles in the moonlight, pouring into a stream that ends in a lake next to the cabin.

I'm wary, but I have to trust that the phoenix wouldn't bring us anywhere dangerous. It lands between the cabin and the lake, angling its strong wing so that I can carry Elyria from its back. She curls up against me. With my arms full, I can't do more than nod a thank you to the phoenix, who settles down on the spot, telling me it isn't going anywhere for now.

The whole valley is quiet, other than the calming whoosh from the waterfall. I carry Elyria up the steps, across the front porch to the cabin's door, nudging it open. It's dark and empty inside other than a bed, table, cupboard, and a fireplace. Tools are scattered across the table. I recognize them all from the mines. This must have been an old mining cabin. I can only guess as to why it's empty, but possibly because Howl ordered the miners to mine the main mountains after he rose to power.

It's dusty and dank inside. It's clear it hasn't been occupied in a long time. I whisper to Elyria, "You're safe now. I'll keep you safe."

She whimpers a response, her head buried against my chest. I can't do much about the dust on the bed, but the blanket looks soft enough.

I bend to place Elyria on it, but she doesn't let me go, her arms clinging hard around my chest. "I need you, Jasper. Don't go."

"Okay." I contemplate the little bed, but if she won't release me, then we'll just have to squeeze into it together. I'm dying to get rid of my bloody clothes, wash off the stain of battle, but there's no chance of that while her arms are wrapped around my chest.

I carefully angle us both onto the bed, surprised when she hooks her leg around my hip, her upper arm sliding farther around my chest, curling into me and trapping me. Her head presses into the crook of my neck, her breath warm against my throat.

She sobs. "Don't go."

I stroke her hair and back, easing through the tangles, my chest hurting to hear her cry. "I won't leave you, Elyria. As long as you want me to stay, I'll be right here."

She inhales a deep breath, a catch in her voice. "Thank you, Jasper. You are a good friend."

We once had a conversation about friendship. She agreed to let me protect her and in return I promised not to die. "I kept my promise," I whisper. "I stayed alive."

I'm supposed to forget the battle—every soldier is trained to move past it—but the cries of the dying never leave me. Watching Cassian fall, hearing Marbella scream for help, and not being able to get to her—

I squeeze my eyes shut and focus on Elyria's warm body. She was trapped along with Baelen in Howl's possession for a month. The miners didn't hold back information about what living in Howl's palace was like. Elyria would have been exposed to violence in the extreme.

Her warmth seeps through my cold thoughts, calming me.

She sounds a little stronger when she says, "You have never hurt me, Jasper Grace."

I grip her body, wishing I could reach into her mind and obliterate her pain. "I'll cut out my own heart before I ever do."

"Don't do that, Jasper," she whispers. "I would miss you."

I continue to stroke her back, easing out the tension in her body for a long time until her trembling finally stops and she falls asleep. When her breathing is quiet, I cast my eye around the cabin. It's basic, but I can fix it, make a stove, maybe fashion a way to get running water into it. Military training taught me how to survive in difficult conditions, but I want to do more than survive here. I want to make Elyria a home.

I stop my thoughts there.

I promised her friendship. She trusts me. There are lines I won't cross with her.

It feels like I closed my eyes for only seconds when her scream breaks through my dreams, jolting me awake.

She gasps beside me, her hands fisting my filthy shirt. "Black bird. Crimson power. Golden vines! Marbella! She isn't safe."

"Shh. It's okay. You were having a nightmare."

Her eyes are wide open for the first time since we arrived. "It felt real, Jasper. Too real."

I stroke her cheek. "Marbella is with Baelen now. She's safe. He won't let anything happen to her."

She drops her head to my chest, breathing out her fear. "I need to bathe."

I nod. "Me too. There's a waterfall farther along the valley. Would you like to go there?"

She nods. "Will you help me?"

"Get there? Of course."

I pull her upright, thinking she'll walk, but she wraps her long legs around my waist. Her dress hitches up around her waist as she drops her head to my shoulder, her wings encircling us. I inhale a quick breath, fighting the urge to close my eyes and find her lips. I remind myself sternly that she's clinging to me because she needs to anchor herself somewhere, not because she wants more from me.

I carry her like that several hundred paces to the waterfall. She relaxes the closer we get to it, the tension draining from her body as the soothing sound of rushing water blocks out all other noises.

I stop at the water's edge. "I should go in first and check the depth—"

"No." Her legs tighten around me. "I'm coming with you."

Since we left the deep springs, she hasn't let go of me once. A reckless part of me doesn't mind. I like the way she feels wrapped around me.

"Okay," I say, a laugh in my voice. "But if you get dunked because I lose my footing, it won't be my fault."

She raises her serious brown eyes to mine. A curious smile plays around her lips. "Are you making a joke, Jasper Grace?"

I shake my head earnestly. "I'm serious."

She bites her lip, a brief hint of her former confidence showing through. "If you dunk me, I'll take you with me."

"Fair enough." I use my feet to remove my boots, awkwardly shifting side to side without placing her on the ground, before I wade into the water, stepping carefully. It's smooth on the bottom and quickly deepens, but it's rough enough to maintain my grip.

The water is surprisingly warm and the minute we're immersed to our elbows, Elyria moans against me, her long lashes settling against her cheeks as she closes her eyes. The tension around her mouth disappears a second before she lets go of my chest, arches back, and drops her torso all the way back into the water, her wings spreading out under the surface while her legs remain wrapped around me.

"Elyria!" I move to grab her, to lift her out, but she stretches out under the water, completely immersed without breaking the contact between our bodies. She wriggles against me and before I can take a breath, her dress rises to the surface and floats away.

I freeze. Completely.

She can't stay under the water forever, but I have no idea where I'll put my hands now, where it will be okay to touch her.

The tips of her wings rise out of the water first, spearing the surface, then flattening out across it. She uses them to lift herself from the water, every gorgeous, sexy curve visible from her waist up. Shaking out her hair, she uses her wings and her stomach muscles to return upright to grip my chest.

She tugs at the bottom of my shirt. Some of the blood is already washing off and swirling in the water, making me cringe. I wrench the fabric over my head, flinging it onto the grass. My pants are filthy too, but at least the movement of the water carries the gore away.

Returning my focus to Elyria again, I resolutely keep my gaze on her face. Not below it.

She waits a beat. Her hands remain on my waist as she rests in the water, her torso separated from mine from the waist up. Her lips part slightly as she meets my eyes.

I don't make a move.

She sighs in a way I can't interpret. She seems content but also possibly a little perplexed. "Marbella was right."

I force myself to speak, my voice thick. "What about?"

"It *is* possible to care for someone without lusting after them."

Damn.

Her arms tighten and her head returns to the crook of my neck. The way she melts into me, her breasts pressed against me, confuses my body and no amount of internal shouting about friendship can stop my intense physical reaction. I thank the ancients she's wrapped her legs around me high enough that she can't feel my physical reaction. She once told Marbella that elves can't be trusted, especially not when it comes to sex and lust.

I don't know what happened in her past, but I make a quiet promise: I will make her future beautiful.

As gently as I can, I slide us through the water to retrieve her dress. She shakes her head as soon as she sees where we're headed. "I don't want that back on."

The corner of my mouth hitches. I scrunch the material in my fist, lift it so she can see what I'm doing, and use it as a cloth to wash her neck, starting at the point beneath her ear where a stubborn drop of blood—someone else's blood—tells me she was exposed to something she never should have seen. I continue washing her across her back and down her arms as she relaxes beneath my hands.

She's chosen to make herself completely vulnerable to me, trusting me, and in return I will keep her safe, give her everything she needs, and I won't ask anything from her in return.

8

———

MARBELLA

I awake to find Baelen sound asleep beside me. When I shift, his arms tighten around me in a protective reflex. I slept in my armor. Without eating. After a lot of crying. And nothing more than Baelen's kisses on my hair and his gentle words in my ears even when I wanted more.

My stomach growls. Loudly. Also, I need to use the bathroom. *Curse the necessities.* I want to stay right where I am.

Nope. Bathroom calls.

I pry myself from his arms, sliding out from under the blankets. I love my armor—it has saved my life countless times—but I need it off my body. I need to be free of all the fighting and battles. I peel it off my arms and legs, inhaling a deep breath as I step out of it. I leave it in a puddle on the floor and head straight to the bathroom, using the facilities before I turn on the shower and stand beneath it, letting the water stream over me.

It runs dark with soot from the fire outside Harem Hall.

I lather and rinse twice before I'm certain I've washed all of the ash out of my hair. Outside the shower, I catch a glimpse of myself in the mirror, the way my hair has taken on a pearly sheen, my skin a moonlit glow. If I cover the tips of my ears and imagine wings, I look like a female gargoyle. So much of the elf in me has disappeared that I don't recognize myself anymore.

Drying myself, I realize I have no clothes or even a dressing

73

gown. *Do I care?* I trust Baelen with my life and I want to be with him. I'm not afraid to be naked in front of him.

I leave the towel behind and prowl from the bathroom to find a very awake Baelen standing right outside. He's dressed in the same clothing he was wearing when he brought me back last night: a long-sleeved shirt and long pants; clean ones he must have changed into while I was out with Roar. It's definitely gargoyle clothing because the shirt has discrete clips at the side to allow for it to be put on around wings.

He misses a beat. He's always had incredible self-control, but I'm certain he wasn't expecting me to emerge naked. He wrenches his gaze from the curve of my hip. Funny, I never thought that would be the sexiest part of my body but the way his gaze lingers on my narrow waist and then rises to my shoulders, following the water droplet sliding from the base of my neck across my collar bone…

My knees threaten to give way in the most ungraceful way. Luckily, I still have one hand on the bathroom door, so I use it to keep myself upright.

He owes me so many answers—how does he know Outlier Senturi?—but right now I have other things on my mind. My chest rises and falls. I tell myself to breathe. "You promised me I'd only have to wait three years, Baelen Rath. Well, it's been seven-and-a-half. We have a lot of catching up to do."

A smile grows on his face, lighting up his eyes. He lifts his chin, appraising me. "You seemed busy all that time. I didn't want to interrupt."

I let go of the door, trading its support for the chance to be nearer to him. After two steps, inches remain between us. I tilt my head back. Damn his height. I can't reach his lips on my own and I have no water to help me this time.

He tilts his head down to mine, drawing a quick breath before his lips descend.

At the last moment… he freezes.

The laughter fades from his eyes, which become very serious. His hands return to his sides. He contemplates me for so long that it scares me. "Baelen?"

He takes a step back. "We can't do this today, Marbella."

Wait... what? I shake my head. Swallow. Repeat what he said inside my head. Did he just say we can't do this? Did he just say no? Please, please don't let it be because he's taking the whole don't-come-to-his-bed thing seriously…

He sidesteps me, walks backward to the closet, and drags it open, all while keeping his eyes on me. He wrenches the nearest garment from its hanger—a silken dress that threatens to slide right out of his hands. He fumbles with it, closes his eyes, takes a deep breath, and hands it to me.

I take it but don't put it on. Stare at it. Stare back at him. "I don't understand."

"We were lucky seven years ago," he says. "But I scent you, Marbella. Give me mercy, the Storm tells me what's going on inside your body. We won't get away with it again."

"What…? Baelen?"

His expression softens. "Wait another week, Marbella. I promise you, I won't turn you away."

Wait another week… Wait a minute… Is he talking about… babies? Shock ripples through me. Howl had scented me too; he'd told me when he first met me that I was way too fertile, and he wouldn't bed me for fear of having children with me.

I say, "But we already did. Last night."

"That was in the deep springs. Nothing operates like normal there. It was protected." He pulls away from me. "This won't be."

"But…"

Baelen heads to the bathroom, stops in the doorway, and clutches the doorknob, his knuckles turning white. "Please don't be naked when I get back out. It's taking every shred of my self-control not to accept what you're offering and embrace the consequences. Because believe me, Marbella, I want children with you. But you have enough going on in your life right now."

I can't speak. I watch the door close behind him. It clicks and then shifts again as if he just leaned his weight against it. I wobble back against the bed and drop to its surface.

If it weren't for the storm's power, he wouldn't have known. We wouldn't have known. I have no idea how I'm supposed to feel about that. Gargoyle women only have two children—always twins. Their whole culture is set up around making sure the woman is free to choose a good mate. Elves, on the other hand, can have multiple children but often choose to cloak themselves in contraceptive spells. If I'm some sort of hybrid, I have no idea what the consequences will be. Will I have twins? Or more? Obviously not *none* or Baelen wouldn't have stopped us.

I examine the dress he handed me, consider the other clothing options, and swap the dress for long pants and a fitted shirt. I find boots in the bottom of the closet and then I sit on the edge of the bed while the shower runs and finally clicks off. I wait for Baelen to emerge, trying to figure out what I'm going to say, trying to push away what I want.

It turns out he was in such a hurry to get away from me, he didn't take any clean clothes either. He emerges with a towel slung low across his hips, water dripping from his slicked-back hair down his broad chest. My heart rate increases. I remember his body moving against mine, his chest beneath my hands, his hands flexing against my back.

I can't share the same space as Baelen and not throw myself across the distance and rip that damn towel off him.

I jump to my feet. "I'm getting breakfast. You can explain all about Outlier Senturi when you're fully clothed. And I do expect answers, Baelen Rath."

Racing to the door, I stop in the doorway, glance back as a smile breaks across his face. Oh no, he doesn't. He can't push me away and then suck me back to him with a single smile and naked muscles and water droplets and…

Oh, I'm clutching the door again. I force my feet to move. *Away* from Baelen.

The Priestess meets me halfway along the corridor. "Supreme Incorruptible, you're awake."

Well and truly.

She seems nervous. I guess she's trying to figure out if I hate her. *Yes, old lady, I do.*

I say, "Good morning, Priestess. I need to know what the situation is with the gargoyles who were imprisoned in Slave Station. I know they were responsible for looking after the whole palace, but I told the miners to free them. I don't want anyone kept here against their will. If that means I have to grow my own food and do my own washing, that's fine with me."

She relaxes, settling into stride with me. "All of the gargoyles—including the slaves and the guards—have been told to return to their families. Many have chosen to remain."

I'm curious. "How many?"

"All of them."

I miss a step. "Why would they choose that?"

"Let me see… You killed Howl, opened the deep springs, allowed everyone to heal before you, ordered the fallen gargoyles to be treated with equal respect whether they were friend or enemy, destroyed Harem Hall, wept over the body of a fallen warrior, led your people to freedom… Shall I go on?"

My people. Freedom.

Suddenly my need to be with Baelen seems so small compared to what the gargoyles have faced: whole families ripped apart, children kept from parents, wives taken from husbands and used as leverage. I study the floor as I walk. "I'm humbled by their trust."

She twists her hands in front of her. "I'm very sorry about what I said last night. I don't want to cause you pain. It's just that… trust is a fragile thing. It was a fight to get the clan leaders to accept you."

"You don't want me to undo it all by choosing Baelen."

"Give it time. He will prove his loyalty to the gargoyles the same way you have, and then they will embrace him too." She tips her head with a cautious smile. "Then we can talk about bending the rules."

"I understand." Wait a week, Baelen had said. Can I get the gargoyles to accept him in a week?

When we reach the food hall, my empty stomach is ready to stage a full-blown rampage, but I rein myself in. The tables are full of male and female gargoyles eating and talking, some are quietly telling their stories, others are crying, many are rebuilding friendships. I stalk straight to the cooking area off to the left, heading for the gargoyles hard at work frying eggs and sausages. They stop what they're doing as soon as they see me.

"Good morning," I say to the man who presents himself to me. He is very thin like so many of them. It makes my hunger seem like a mere twinge.

"He's the head cook," the Priestess whispers at my ear.

I acknowledge him and each of the workers. "Have you already eaten this morning?"

"Uh…" The head cook gives me wide eyes. "We usually eat whatever is left over."

I compress my lips in a disapproving line. "From now on you will eat before everyone else. You can't work on empty stomachs. What's more, you will put down your… uh… utensils right now please and eat something. But go slowly; this food is rich."

"We will eat once we have served you, Supreme Incorruptible."

I open my mouth to object but the Priestess interrupts. "Thank you, Head Cook."

He bows low. "It is our honor to serve the Merciful Supreme Incorruptible Marbella."

He hands me a plate piled high with eggs, fresh bread, sausages, and a bowl of fruit tucked at the side. The Priestess guides me to the only empty table at the head of the hall. I pass the miners on the way, catching their eye. Welsian stands up as I pass, along with Iago, Arlo, and Erit. Two women smile up at me, and I guess they are Iago and Arlo's wives. Roar and Rhain aren't here, but I expect they are doing what they need to reunite their families. Likewise, I can't see Badenoch anywhere, but he once told me that his wife had passed away and he would need to find his children.

I consider joining the men at their table, but the Priestess clearly indicated the empty table is for me and I don't want to stretch my truce with her.

I clear my throat. "I apologize for taking your husbands away this morning," I say to the women. "But I hope they will join me at my table."

Iago's wife responds with a gracious smile. She is older than the other woman and inclines her head with poise and kindness. "It is our honor, Supreme Incorruptible. We understand there is much work to be done. Please let us know if we can help."

The men immediately pick up their plates to follow me to the empty table where Welsian takes a seat opposite me. "We didn't expect to be alive today, Lady Storm."

"You did well after the fight yesterday by ordering the guards to help families find their fallen ones."

He stares down at his plate. "Only General Cassian remains there today. He has no family left."

I knew Cassian had no family, but I'm surprised the Hideaway Clan hasn't claimed him. "Won't his clan come for him?"

Welsian shifts. "They came early this morning, but they weren't sure if they were allowed to move him. You… uh… indicated you might not want him to be taken away when you… uh…"

Wept over the body of a fallen warrior. The Priestess's words return to me. "You're right, Welsian. They're right. I want him to be buried here, not in Mount Hideaway. Can you please help me with that?"

"I'll make the arrangements. It will be an honor for his clan."

I swallow my first mouthful and my eyes water. I tell myself it's because I'm so happy to be eating something. I tell myself it's not tears. I blink them away. "What about the orphanages?"

"I can help you with that," Arlo says, his serious eyes meeting mine as he tucks his wings in tight to his sides. Sitting across from him now, I can't believe we were once forced to fight each other in the mines. "The orphanages are so scattered, it's hard for parents to find their children. I've sent word to the Priestesses who were hiding in each orphanage, asking them to bring all of the children to Crimson Court so families can come here to find them. The first group of children should arrive this afternoon."

"And what of the Priestesses themselves?"

Iago speaks up this time. "With your permission, Lady Storm, I would like to build a new home for them, which will also contain an orphanage for those children whose parents are lost. There is a good site for it further along the ridge to the east of Crimson Court. It is beside a large, rock garden with a small waterfall where the children can play, and the Priestesses can commune with each other."

Iago is a master at building things. I nod my assent, knowing he will create something extraordinary for the Priestesses and children.

Erit is the only one who hasn't spoken up so far. He asks, "How may I help you, Lady Storm?"

"You will have a challenging task, Grievous Erit. I need you to help me build bridges with the Grievous Clan."

He folds his arms across his chest. "Well, you have a few options.

You're their leader now. You can order them to present themselves."

"Or?"

"You could go to them."

"Which would you advise?" I'm testing him. He knows it, but he doesn't know it's because I want him to lead them.

"Lady Storm, I gave up my clan because of their brutal ways. I would like nothing more than for you to order every last one of them to come here and grovel at your feet. But you will show greater strength if you meet them on Mount Grievous. It will show that you are not afraid to step into their stronghold."

"That sounds wise," I reply.

Sudden silence descends over the room but it's not because of what I said. My head shoots up, seeking the source of the change in temperature in the room.

Baelen stands in the opposite doorway. He looks as if he was about to take a step inside when the silence stopped him. The nearest gargoyles hurry out of his way, chairs scrape backward, some even pick up their plates and relocate away from where he stands.

My heart sinks. The gargoyles didn't react this way to me. Not at all. The Priestess was right. When the gargoyles look at Baelen, they see an elf.

Worse, they see a deadly elf: one who took down a whole legion of guards with a single swipe. One who can burst into lethal anger within moments. One they need to avoid at all costs.

9

———

MARBELLA

I begin to stand, my chair scraping in the silence, but the Priestess hisses from her station behind me. "Do not move."

I shoot her an annoyed glance, but Baelen has recovered. Shoulders back, at full Rath height, he strides straight toward me, not once taking his eyes off me even while every single gargoyle stares at him. He takes a knee. "Supreme Incorruptible."

Now I stand. "Rise, Wrathful One. You will bow to no-one."

This draws a gasp. The corner of Baelen's mouth twitches. He hides it well, ducking his head lower. "With respect, I wish only to serve your people."

I contemplate the top of his head. It's a lifetime ago that he took a knee and bound his heart to mine at the Heartstone Ceremony. He is everything to me and I need the gargoyles to see it, but I have to go slow.

"Then allow me to introduce you to my people." I wait for Baelen to tip his head back before I open my palm toward Welsian. "This is Denrock Welsian. He is the new head of my guard."

Welsian is surprised by his new title, but he hides it, giving Baelen a nod.

I indicate Arlo next. "This is Virtuous Arlo. He is my new head of security. This is Sunflight Iago, my head builder." I smile at Erit. "And this is Grievous Erit, who will travel with me to meet the Grievous Clan to secure peace between clans."

81

Baelen draws to his feet, towering over all of them, acknowledging their quiet greetings.

I choose my words carefully. "Meet Baelen of the House of Rath, who is my friend." My best friend, my greatest love, the one who picked me up when I fell, taught me how to defend myself, gave me space to choose, always asks my permission, and makes my knees go weak with a single look. I sigh. The one I'd rather be with somewhere else right now.

I say, "Please join us, Baelen."

One of the nearby cooks stands to hurry back to the kitchen to get a meal for Baelen, but he stops them. "Eat, please. I can get my own."

Chairs scrape again as Baelen passes by. The room remains silent. He's halfway through filling his plate when the far door swings open and Adalie's little voice cuts through the tension. Her bare feet patter across the stone floor as she runs straight to him. "Bae-Bae!"

He drops what he's doing and swings her up onto his hip. She hugs him, her little arms barely reaching around the front of his big chest.

He tickles her feet. "Where are your socks? Your toes are like icicles."

She screws up her nose. "Don't like socks."

He raises his eyebrows, glancing around her as if he expected somebody to be there. "Well, then, where is your grandfather?"

"He didn't want to scare anyone." She speaks in a loud whisper. "He's eating in his room."

Baelen waggles his eyebrows at her. "I think I should have stayed in my room too."

She giggles. "You're not scary, Bae-Bae."

Baelen shovels food onto his plate one-handed, ignoring everyone else now. He hands Adalie a piece of apple. She crunches on it as he returns with her to our table. If the other gargoyles were uncomfortable around him before, they definitely don't know how to react now. They know what Adalie is, and he's clearly not afraid of her. At the same time, she's completely adorable, making more than a few gargoyles grin as he carries her past.

I suddenly know what I need Baelen to do today, and I really hope he'll go along with me on it. I lean forward as he takes a seat with Adalie propped on his knee, allowing her to pick at his meal. "Good morning, Adalie."

"Greetings, Storm Lady."

"A lot of children will be coming to Crimson Court today, Adalie. My friend Arlo is going to find their parents and he'll need all the help he can get. How would you and Baelen like to help with that?"

Her eyes light up. "Children like me?"

"Well, not exactly like you but—"

"Friends?"

Oh, she meant children, as in *not grown-ups*. Senturi said there weren't many Outliers. I wonder how many other children Adalie has ever met. But surely she has a brother?

"Yes, children who could be friends."

She tilts her eyes up to Baelen, dropping her head back against his chest, imploring him. "Can we please, Bae-Bae?"

His gaze hasn't left mine. "I wonder what Lady Storm will be doing while we are busy?"

"I will travel to Mount Grievous."

"Alone?"

"With Erit."

Tension fills the lines of his face. "And who else?"

"Just us."

He's worried. Traveling to Mount Grievous will be dangerous. He would rather come with me but I'm telling him to stay behind. I smile gently. "And these." I tilt my palm up at the stones that float above my head like an extension of my body.

He looks up as if he forgot they were there. I'm actually stupidly pleased that he doesn't see them. He sees only me.

He acquiesces. "We would be honored to help the children."

I relax. So does the rest of the room.

When I finish my meal and push back my chair, I find the entire room follows my lead and stands as well. Then every gargoyle takes a knee, male and female alike. Welsian, Arlo, and Iago join them. So does little Adalie, sliding off Baelen's knee.

Heads bowed, their voices chorus together in a deep resonating pledge. "Supreme Incorruptible, we honor you."

I acknowledge their gesture. "I am honored."

At that, they stand to go about their day, leaving me with a smile on my face and a warm glow in my heart. I wait for everyone to clear the room, but I ask Erit to meet me outside.

"I'll prepare packs for our journey," he says before he strides away.

"Back to your grandfather, Adalie," Baelen says to the little girl.

As the cooks make themselves scarce, Adalie skips after Erit. He holds the door open for her, his giant, warrior arms like tree branches way above her head. The door slides closed behind them.

"Baelen, you have to tell me how you know them: Adalie and her grandfather."

He takes a deep breath and doesn't keep me waiting. "I think you know that I disappeared for three years after military training."

"Nobody knows where you went."

He nods. He studies a point on the wall past my shoulder. He folds his arms, speaking slowly now like he doesn't like the memories. "When I finished military training, I went to my father and told him that I was going to find you. He told me that I couldn't. I told him that he couldn't stop me."

He clears his throat. "I made it as far as the courtyard outside the Storm Vault."

My eyes widen. "You came for me."

"I saw you." He swallows. "You were surrounded by your Storm Command. Your advisor, Elise, was with you. I saw her first and she was clearly upset about something. Then I saw that your storm suit was all cut up. Your hands and knees were bleeding. You were dripping, shivering, shaking. But you grit your teeth and kept your head up. Glaring the world down. Daring anyone to come near you."

He stops. Stops for so long that I don't think he's going to continue.

"Baelen?"

"I felt it, Marbella. I felt the Storm rising off you. I realized then that I couldn't take you away from that. I needed to be *part of it*.

Which meant I had to wait for the Heartstone Ceremony. My father was right.

"But there was no way I could breathe the same air as you and stay sane for three years. So, I walked away. Walked all the way back to Rath land. I followed the mountains south for months. I lived wild, kept away from everyone." His mouth twitches into a half smile. "Grew a pretty savage beard."

I crinkle my forehead, trying to picture Baelen with a beard. *Hmm, no.*

"I reached the wastelands and kept going," he says. "Until one day I heard a scream. It was little Adalie. A talon crow, the biggest I'd ever seen, had just killed her brother, and it was about to rip her apart. I had so much rage… There wasn't anything left of that bird by the time I finished with it."

No wonder Adalie was afraid of the crows if one killed her brother. I've never seen a talon crow in real life. Just like I'd never seen a shadow panther before one attacked me. "So that's how you met them."

"I lived with Senturi for over two years. Went out each day and hunted those birds down until there were hardly any of them left. Killed a bunch of shadow panthers too. For some reason, Senturi never once asked me why I was there. It took me forever to figure out that he had Sight."

He shakes his head with a soft laugh, but the sound fades. "Then one day, he came to me and said I had to go. He told me he had a message from the northern Outliers… that my father had died. He told me I couldn't trust anyone except you."

"I'm sorry, Baelen."

"I cut off my beard, came back for the funeral, and stayed away from the Elven Command. That's when I started planning. I searched the mountains for the best places to hide in case I needed a backup plan. I concealed emergency packs throughout them, but it was when I discovered gargoyle nests where they shouldn't be that I started to ask questions. Carefully of course."

"Then you offered me your heartstone."

"You know the rest."

"I can't imagine you with a beard." I push my chair back, cross to him, and slide my hand across his cheek. For so long, a simple touch like this was forbidden to me.

I bend to press my lips to his. Before our mouths meet, he catches my waist and pulls me to him. Responding to his touch, I slide one leg over his, straddling him. I press against him and plant a kiss on his lips, tasting the warmth of his mouth. My body heats up as his thumbs brush across each of my hips, his fingers spreading out around my waist to shift me closer.

It takes all my willpower to break contact. "I want you to know that I tried to see you at your father's funeral. I wanted to tell you how sad I was for your loss."

Baelen had lost his mother when he was ten-years-old. I was there for him at that time. After that, his father was his only remaining family and it broke my heart knowing Baelen went through his father's death alone, that I wasn't there for him. "They wouldn't let me near you."

He brushes my hair behind my ear, running his fingers across my cheek. "*I* wouldn't let you near me." He swallows. "It was hard enough to stay away from you for seven years. Even in the beginning after the fall, when I couldn't walk, I… uh… would try to get up and leave the house. It was like there was a thread between us and it kept getting shorter, pulling me toward you. I knew that one conversation with you at the funeral, one look in your eyes, and I'd abandon all reason. I'd tear down whatever I had to— destroy whatever I had to—to get to you."

A shiver races down my spine. We had been connected. We just didn't know it was the storm. "I missed you, Baelen."

Such simple words. So much heartache to go with them.

I press my lips to his, drowning in the contact and trying to form coherent thoughts. "I don't want to be apart from you today."

He whispers against my lips. "I understand your intentions. Your people don't know me. They don't trust me like they trust you."

That's the second time he's called them my people. "Our people, Baelen. You've lived with gargoyles longer than I have."

His thumb grazes my lips, trailing across my jaw. "I lived with Outliers. That sets me even further apart. But I promise you, I will do anything to be with you."

How am I going to wait a week? I shiver as his other hand strokes the curve between my waist and hip through my shirt.

He sighs, but it's resigned. "Our time is up. Erit has returned."

He picks me up and slides me to the floor. I smooth my clothing in time for Erit to push through the doors. "Lady Storm, everything's ready."

I steel myself for what's ahead of me. It's time to face the Grievous Clan head on.

10

––––––––––

MARBELLA

I've never flown with Erit before. He was the leader of one of the mining teams, and for a while, he was the last gargoyle I thought would ever be my ally. Over time, I got to know him and heard his story. He'd told me about killing a shadow panther when he was a teenager—that if he didn't come back with one, clan law meant he would be thrown out of his home to starve. Now, he's flying me to the heart of the Grievous stronghold.

After some consideration, I left my armor behind. I don't want to fly into Mount Grievous looking like I'm about to launch a war. Erit has chosen to wear light armor, but that's because it has straps that he has wrapped around me to make sure I don't fall. It's a handy addition to gargoyle armor that is usually intended for carrying bundled weapons but happens to be conveniently Marbella-sized. The safety straps are also helpful when he has to navigate through mountain peaks, tilting on his side or even flying horizontal. We decided early on in our flight that it would be a good idea to stay low and fly through the mountains, rather than making ourselves a target in the clear sky.

He apologizes along the way for the bristles on his chin, which catch my hair as I press my head against his chest. I laugh, thinking it's strange that I'm so comfortable being this up close and personal with a gargoyle, let alone one I used to think wanted to kill me.

When I first arrived in Erador, it was nighttime, and I didn't get to see the landscape. Every time I flew across Erador since then I was bundled into a basket so I couldn't see. Now, it takes my breath away. A spider web of mountains spreads out beneath us, each leading back to Mount Erador where the palace is located. Mount Prime is rust-colored, Mount Virtuous is a deep mossy green, and far, far in the west looms a mountain that is black as ochre: the perfect place for shadow panthers to thrive.

"There it is," Erit says, his voice a rasp as the air rushes past us. "Mount Grievous. The last mountain before we hit the wastelands."

As we near it, multiple villages come into view, located at various points along the mountain range and deep in the valleys, many of them surrounded by thick forests. Erit angles for the far side of the mountain where the shadows are darkest and the sunlight barely reaches.

I ask, "Should we go to the Cavity?" Each mountain contains a place called a Cavity—it's where the main nest is located.

He shakes his head. "Grievous live out in the open. They believe it makes them tougher." He points to a cluster of buildings located at the highest point on the side of the mountain. "Whoever is in charge will be in that village there. It won't take long for them to show themselves once we land."

The village approaches fast as Erit speeds toward the nearest cobbled street. I sense movement below us, swift and stealthy, but when we glide to a stop, there's nobody in sight. The buildings are shuttered and closed. A chill breeze whistles through the gaps between them. Erit unstraps me and I step off his feet, stretching my arms and legs. I love flying but remaining in the same position for hours has left me stiff and sore.

Erit stretches out his muscles while I smooth my hair. He gives me another apologetic glance. He's older than some of the other gargoyles, but no less agile as he unstraps a sword and hands it to me, swiftly reaching for his bow and nocking an arrow. Between us, we have attacks covered both at a distance and up close.

I draw on my power to cast a soft glow across the dark street, the Queen's heart responding to my wish: *Destroy the dark*. I'm still getting a handle on how to use and control this new power. I hope at some point that I might be able to use it to fly on my own, but I'm not sure how yet. Destroy gravity? Probably not a good idea.

Erit raises his weapon, assessing all attack points from the rooftops to the street. "Go ahead, Lady Storm."

I plant my feet in the middle of the street and raise my voice. "I am Supreme Incorruptible Marbella Mercy. You will show yourselves or I will burn your homes to dust."

It's a horrible threat; one I wouldn't normally make, but Erit has schooled me on Grievous culture. They will only respond to brute strength.

A shadow grows from an alleyway on my right and a figure emerges from the darkness, but not so far that I can see who it is. A female voice hisses, "Supreme Incorruptible, you stole something from me that can't be replaced."

I consider shining the heartstone's light into the shadowed recess that hides the newcomer. But I let her have her cloak of darkness for now. "Who are you?"

"I am Grievous Indira."

Erit stiffens beside me. His eyes widen and tension enters his posture. "Careful, Lady Storm. She is Howl's sister."

Sister. Of course. Always a boy and a girl. It's difficult to imagine Howl having any sort of family.

The woman emerges into the light. All female gargoyles are beautiful, but she is savagely gorgeous. Her eyes are such a dark shade of brown that they appear black like her brother's. Her hair matches the color of her eyes and it's glossy, long, and braided down one side. She wears the skin of a shadow panther slung across one shoulder, attached to leather armor that covers her entire body. Female wings don't have wing daggers like the men, but she's made up for it with leather casings that cover the top of her wings attached to which are sharp spikes.

I appraise her as she takes up position ten paces away. She doesn't carry any weapons as far as I can see, but that doesn't mean they aren't hidden around her body.

I say, "I won't apologize for killing your brother."

"But you will apologize for taking his death from me."

My forehead crinkles. That's a strange thing to say. I'm not sure what she means.

Her hands curl into fists as she snarls, "It was my right to kill him. Not yours! You stole that from me."

She wanted him dead? I definitely didn't expect that. "Then I saved you the trouble."

She stalks toward me. Erit keeps his bow trained on her and I ready my sword, although it's the heartstones I'll draw on if I'm really threatened.

She stops three paces away. Up close, I can see there are rips in her wings. It looks like someone took a knife to them, shredding the bottom third into wide ribbons. Llion once told me that to injure another gargoyle's wings was a heinous crime, an act of violence that was meant to subjugate the victim.

"Did he hurt your wings?"

She snarls, "I did this to myself."

Well, she's a ball of contradictions.

"You owe me his death," she says, drawing her right hand slowly up to her left shoulder and toward the first spike on her wing armor. It looks like she's about to scrape her palm across it.

"Stop." Erit lowers his bow, surprising me by separating bow from arrow and raising both in a placating gesture. "Lady Indira, you don't have to do this. Lady Storm was mistreated by your brother the same as you. She had every right to kill him."

"I don't care! He hurt me first. That gave me first right."

"Lady Indira—"

"Nobody calls me 'Lady!' Especially not you."

He tilts his head, taking his time to respond. I'm dying to leap into the conversation with all sorts of retorts. If she claims she had first right to kill Howl, then why the hell didn't she try? Or maybe she did and failed? And why is she so angry at Erit? What did he do?

Erit contemplates her. "So, you do recognize me. I wasn't sure how much I'd changed over the last fifteen years."

Indira scowls back at him, one foot planted slightly in front of the other, right palm resting across her upper chest very close to the spike. I'm still not entirely sure what she was about to do with it, but Erit's efforts to stop her make me worried.

She studies the cut of his stubbly jaw, his gently pointed ears, and slate-gray eyes, taking her time to assess him. Her flinty gaze softens, but only briefly. "They told me you were dead."

"Dead?" It's his turn to appear surprised, but he slowly nods his head. "Of course, that's what my parents would tell everyone to save face, isn't it?"

She whispers, "You got out."

"I did."

"Then you know I have to do this," she says.

He shakes his head. "You really don't."

In a flash she drags her hand across the wing spike, spilling droplets of blood on the street.

"No!" Erit's shout dies in this throat.

Indira's focus returns to me. "Supreme Incorruptible Marbella Mercy, you owe me Grievous Howl's death. I will have yours instead."

Erit sags beside me. The fact that he's concerned makes me concerned. I keep my voice low, trying not to react to this fierce woman. "Erit?"

"She has challenged you to a fight to the death."

The heartstones glow around me. "That seems unwise." But as I speak, the glow dims and all of a sudden, the lights in the heartstones go out.

"Unfortunately, it is a blood challenge. The deep magic is bound by it, which means you will not be able to use the heartstones' power in this fight."

This is news I didn't want to hear. No wonder Erit was trying to stop her. Leaving my armor behind is suddenly the worst decision I made today.

Indira watches my reaction closely, so I keep my response casual, calm. *Just talking about the weather. Nothing to worry about.* "So, it's just me and her?"

"I'm afraid so. You need to know that Lady Indira is a fierce warrior. She will not be easy to defeat but... Lady Storm, I've seen you fight without any power to aid you. Like many others before her—including myself—Lady Indira is underestimating you."

I search his eyes. Indira can hear every word he says. He's deliberately allowing his genuine concern to show through. I consider carefully what he said. First of all, he's trying to psych her out, which tells me I actually need to be worried about her skill as a fighter. But on top of that, he's reminding me of my fight with Arlo, of how I forced Arlo to yield. Whatever history Erit has with

Indira, whatever injustice Indira has faced, to kill her would be a tragedy and it will get me no closer to improving relationships with Grievous Clan.

I place my hand on his arm. "Erit, I can see that you care deeply about the outcome of this fight. I promise you, I will show mercy."

Indira spits from the side. "How very magnanimous of you, Supreme Incorruptible. I assure you, I will not."

It's her turn to try to psych me out. As she speaks, gargoyles emerge from the shadows around us. The street is wide enough for a single gargoyle to spread its wings and land with room to spare, but the alleyways between the buildings are narrow and cramped. Gargoyles cling to the sides of the buildings, hanging off the edges of the roofs, hunched beneath their wings, their faces shadowed, their wing daggers pointed aggressively forward.

Now *this* is the picture of blood-thirsty gargoyles that the elves fear. I'm not sure whether I should laugh or cower. Neither seems like a good idea.

"Well, what are the rules?" I ask Erit. I'm still holding the sword. "Weapons or hand-to-hand combat?"

Indira is quick. "There are no rules."

She takes two steps forward, feinting around my sword, and aims her fist at my face.

I evade Indira's attack just in time. Light on my feet, I sidestep and throw my sword off to Erit in the same movement. I won't use a weapon until she does. He catches it by the handle and hurries out of our way.

Dodging Indira's next attack, I assess her movements, the rips in her wings, and the way she favors her right foot. She won't be able to fly, which makes the fight between us even, but she makes up for it with five wing spikes across each wing, each spike at least an inch long. They remind me of Senturi's wing tips, razor sharp. Of course, she has to make sure she doesn't hurt herself with them so I could turn them into a liability.

She comes at me again, and I discover I was wrong about her wings being completely out of action. She spreads them and catches air that lifts her higher than I expected. At the same time, she shoots forward. My defensive position is too low and her fist crashes down on me like a rock. I'm forced backward, rolling to my feet. She comes in too close, allowing me to land two quick jabs, left-right, on each of her cheeks. As she rolls backward with the punches, she uses her unbalanced position to her advantage to kick her upper leg straight into my stomach.

She knocks me hard up against the wall of the nearest building, where I grab the closest object I can lay my hands on—a ceramic pot with a dusting of soil and dead weeds in it—and crack it against her head. Her arms fly wide, and I use the gap to land several hits to her stomach and face before she grabs my arm, lifting me bodily upward across her shoulders. Her wing spikes scrape across my arms and chest. I'm lucky they don't pierce anything important before she throws me across the street.

Thud. That definitely hurt. *Damn she's strong. Curse my little body.* I'm so light she can fling me anywhere. And she's coming right back at me. I scramble to my feet, but halfway up she attempts to ram my chest with her knee. I lurch backward just in time, pushing down on her leg defensively, but she spins, using her momentum to punch her fist at me. I block and dance backward. She leaps at me, but I crouch, using my shoulder to lift her, and then it's her turn to take a tumble along the street. She lands right next to Erit, jumps to her feet, hits him square in the jaw, and steals my sword from him.

Suddenly the fight is no longer close to equal.

I don't wait for her to unsheathe the weapon. With a roar, I barrel straight into her, grabbing her sword arm as we hit the side of the nearest building. My fingers close around her wrist and my fingernails dig in.

"Lady Storm! Catch!"

My hand shoots out. Somehow, I catch the dagger Erit throws to me. Turning my attention back to Indira, all I see is her fist. Pain explodes in my temple, the hardest hit she's landed. I drop but I don't let go of her sword arm, taking her with me. Once again, we tumble, but not before I nick her cheek with my knife. We roll apart, both shooting back to our feet at the same time.

The sword is out of its case now and my dagger is no match for it. She charges, I defend, and metal scrapes on metal as her sword sings down the blade of my dagger, forcing me to my knees. I'm using both hands on the smaller weapon to resist the sword's force, but I brace, pushing with all my might to set my left hand free to thump her stomach. The impact causes her to flex forward, and I use the small shift in her weight to unbalance her. She tumbles to my left, angling her shoulder to take the fall, ready to roll through it, but I grab her nearest wing, yanking backward on it. She lands on her back with an *oomph*. I land on her stomach, straddling her.

My dagger descends to her heart.

Her sword ascends to my throat.

Both blades draw blood, making us freeze. If we continue, she will slice open my neck as fast as I can slide the blade into her chest.

Neither of us will survive.

11

MARBELLA

This fight started with a blood challenge. The only way it's going to end is with another one. I have no idea whether it will work but I have to try. Without moving any closer to the blade at my throat, I stretch my free hand forward, reaching out to drag my fingertips across the same spike she used when she made her challenge, screaming out the pain in my jaw and all the places she thumped me with those rock-like fists of hers.

"I am Supreme Incorruptible Marbella Mercy. Grievous Indira, you owe me the Grievous Clan's allegiance!"

I take hold of her face with my bleeding hand, curling my fingers into her hair, forcing her to look at me and not the weapon at my neck. "I hold you to your clan's debt, body and soul, for the rest of your life."

Her eyes widen. "For the rest of my…"

I ease my bloody fingers from her hair, too sticky not to catch and pull, making her wince. I don't apologize. "For the rest of your life. Which will have to be very long to pay out the debt that your clan owes."

I pull upward, withdrawing my dagger.

Her arms flop to her sides. The sword clatters onto the street. "What did you do?"

I have no idea, but she stopped fighting me so it can't be a bad thing. The heartstones flicker back to life, telling me the blood

96

challenge has ended. I check my fingers. The cuts have healed, and when I brush my neck, it no longer hurts. Virtuous's heart has done its job and healed me.

Now the Queen's heart casts a soft glow across Indira's stunned features. "I can't fight you now." She scrambles to her feet, sporting a cut across her cheek and another across her arm. "How did you know which blood words to use? You're an elf."

"I'm really not."

Her chest heaves. She roars, long and loud, curling her fingers into fists. "Grievous Clan! Come down from the rooftops!" She picks up my sword and hands it to me, her voice lowering. "We have a new leader."

She takes a wobbly breath. Drops to a knee. Bows her head, her braid falling across her shoulder. "Supreme Incorruptible… I honor you."

The gargoyles swoop down from the rooftops and out of the alleyways, settling down onto the street in neat rows, huddled under their wings, faces hidden, all of them taking a knee. "Supreme Incorruptible, we honor you."

My forehead creases as they speak. Their voices are not quite what I expected… but relief overcomes any uncertainty I feel. "I am honored."

Erit strides forward and retrieves my sword, slipping it neatly into the weapons brace at his back. "Lady Indira, there's something that you and the Grievous Clan need to know. It's important because of clan law."

He waits for Indira to find her feet. I eye the others warily as they retain their hunched positions, remaining concealed under their wings, not revealing their faces.

Erit announces, "Lady Storm killed a shadow panther."

Indira's eyebrows shoot up in surprise.

Erit continues. "It smelled her blood and attacked her. She killed it with her own hands."

Indira is incredulous. "But shadow panthers only crave gargoyle blood."

I press my lips together before I say, "Like I said, I'm not an elf."

But inside, I'm surprised. If shadow panthers only crave gargoyle blood, then that would explain why Erit looked so perplexed when I told him the story about how the shadow panther hunted me. It's just one more piece of evidence to support Senturi's declaration that I'm part gargoyle now.

Erit speaks firmly to Indira. "You know what this means."

Indira contemplates me in the heartstone's light. Her gaze flickers to her people, still concealed under their wings. I notice how they stay out of the light, preferring the shadows.

She says to me, "Very few gargoyles will fight a shadow panther. They leave that job to the Grievous Clan. You are not Grievous, but you have gargoyle blood and by killing a shadow panther you have earned certain clan rights. Since you are also female, there is something you have the right to know."

She takes a step back before she shouts, "Rise, Grievous! Show yourselves."

As one body, the warriors behind her glide to their feet and emerge from beneath their wings.

I gasp. Not wings but shadow panther skins pretending to be male wings to conceal their bodies. From girls as young as ten-years-old to women as old as one hundred, they lift their faces and stand proud before me, each of them holding weapons and dressed in armor, an impressive and determined force.

They're all female: every single one of them.

"When our men were taken away, we learned to defend ourselves," Indira says before she spins to her small army and orders them, "Sentries, back to your posts! Everyone else, back to your duties."

The women disappear into the darkness as silently as they arrived. It's hard to believe that it's actually daylight on the other side of this shadowy mountain. This village is doused in perpetual night.

Indira heaves a sigh and heads off along the street without waiting for us. "Come with me. I need a strong drink."

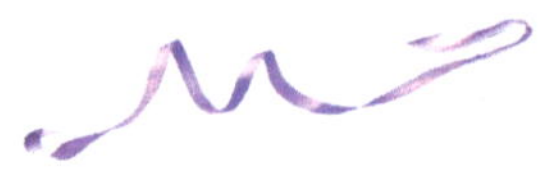

INDIRA'S HOME SITS ABOVE ALL THE OTHERS RIGHT ON THE EDGE OF A cliff, the building itself taking on the attitude of a gargoyle clinging to the precipice by nothing more than the tips of its claws. It suits her.

She pulls off her wing and chest armor and thumps a jug of beer onto the wooden table. Scooping a cup into it, she doesn't drink it, but carries it over to the sink instead. She sucks in a sharp breath as she pours the alcohol over her wounded arm. "Erit, would you pass me the gum, please? Unlike Lady Storm, I don't have the power to heal my own wounds."

He lifts the pot from the shelf she points at but dips his forefinger into it instead of passing it to her.

She scowls as he approaches. "I can do it myself."

"I'm certain you can, Lady Indira." He ignores her exasperated sigh, reaches for her arm, and wraps his whole hand gently around her elbow to keep it steady so he can apply the sticky gum safely. It will keep the wound sealed while it heals. She bites her lip but doesn't pull away.

"You have another cut on your cheekbone," he says, taking a cloth from the sink and soaking it in alcohol from her cup. He lightly dabs the cloth across her cheek. She blinks rapidly, but endures the sharp pain, holding still as he leans in to inspect the wound. Lightly smearing the gum across it, his face ends up close to hers.

Her gaze flickers for the briefest moment to his lips.

I hide a smile. There's definitely history between these two.

When Erit returns to the table to pour three drinks, Indira joins us, choosing the seat closest to him and furthest from me. That's fine with me.

I consider all the questions I have for her. "You hated Howl enough to want to kill him. I wish you had, but something must have stopped you."

She peers into her cup. Despite announcing that she needed a drink, she doesn't touch the liquor yet. "The practicalities got in the way. I couldn't fly myself to him because of my wings and none of the women are strong enough to carry me. I had to wait for him to come to me."

"Which he never did?"

She shakes her head. "Howl took all of the men with him ten years ago. Even the young boys. None of them returned."

"Gone for ten years?"

"There hasn't been a child born here the entire time." She grimaces. "You kind of need men for that sort of thing."

She taps her cup, her fingernails clinking an irregular rhythm against the side. "The consequences weren't all bad. He took all the old brutes away. We were glad to see their backs. After that, it didn't take long for us to figure out that if we stuck to the old ways, our future would be even more precarious."

Erit says, "You mean sending teenagers out to hunt shadow panthers."

"Barbaric practice," she spits. "I outlawed it."

"Good." Erit leans back in his chair. "But I couldn't help but notice that you're all wearing panther skins. You must be killing them somehow."

She meets his eyes, an edge to her voice and a muscle twitching in her jaw. "I kill them, with the help of a group of older women. We don't send kids to do an adult's job. Only cowards use children to keep the shadow panther population down."

She draws a deep breath and swallows a mouthful of alcohol, grimacing as it obviously burns all the way down. She wrinkles her nose and shoves the cup away. "Disgusting stuff."

Watching her, I make a decision. "Erit, I brought you here because I was going to ask you to lead the Grievous Clan."

He gives me a smile and a nod, scratching his bristly jaw. "Your intentions were easy to read, Lady Storm. But I see that you've changed your mind. I think you've made the right decision."

"Wait…" Indira interjects into the conversation. "You aren't leading us yourself?"

I level my gaze with hers. "Grievous Indira, do you acknowledge my power to choose the next clan leader?"

A worried crease appears on her forehead. "I do. But if it's not you, then I want to be involved in the decision. These women have fought to survive with everything they've got, and I don't want some arrogant man coming in and—"

"I want you to lead them."

She blinks at me. "I'm sorry, what?"

"Well, you're already leading them, aren't you?"

She rocks back in her chair, clearly shocked. "Yes, but… I'm… not good at it. Really not good. I'm tough on them and I curse and shout. A lot."

"But you know what they need. You know how they think. I didn't see a single, fearful face out there today. They follow you out of loyalty, not fear."

She splutters. "I don't think you've thought this through, Marbella."

I hide a smile as she takes up calling me by my name. I'm pretty sure it's the shock of my announcement that makes her drop her guard.

"I'm not going to bow and scrape like the other clan leaders," she says. "I won't go easy on you."

I laugh. "They don't exactly bow and scrape either."

"Hah. Grew backbones, did they? Let me guess… right after you killed Howl?"

I'm not sure what to say. The irony doesn't escape me.

Indira blows a long breath through her lips. She reaches across the table for the cup she abandoned and inhales a long drink from it. As the mug thuds back to the table, she says, "Okay. But you need to know right away that I'm not letting those old bastards back on Mount Grievous. If any of them are still alive, you'll have to find somewhere else for them to live."

I ask, "Do you mean men like Gerst?"

"Exactly like Gerst."

"He's dead."

"Good. I'm glad." She stares at her hands. Her eyes water up, but I'm sure this proud woman will never cry in front of me. "Oh, fuck." She hunches over her drink, shaking out her wings as if they're dirty laundry. "How can I lead them when I can't even fly?"

"That's certainly a question I could apply to myself," I murmur gently.

I'm not sure if I'm supposed to ask her, but I'm going to anyway. "How did it happen?"

Instead of answering, she glances toward Erit, blinking hard to try to hide her emotions. "Erit can tell you."

He shakes his head. Apparently, he's not going to go easy on her. "It's not my story to tell."

"Fine." She gnaws at her lip. "It was the night Howl and I were sent out to kill shadow panthers. It was winter. Cold. But I had a plan and it worked. I killed my panther and started carrying it down the mountain before I froze to death. It turned out that my brother had a plan too. He jumped out at me, knocked me over, stabbed a knife through each of my wings to pin me to the ground, and took my panther. I couldn't get the knives out."

I peer at her. She said she'd made the cuts herself. "You ripped up your own wings to chase after him."

"Coming back without a panther means death. So, I tore through my wings to get free. He knocked me down again. Pinned me. *Again*." She hunches even further. "Damn I hated my wings."

"You ripped them again."

"But this time he hit me with a rock. He knocked me out and left me there, bleeding. Right where the panthers would smell me."

She clears her throat, squeezing her cup hard. "I woke up to find Erit standing over me and two dead panthers lying next to me. They would have killed me except for him."

Erit interrupts her and she seems relieved not to have to keep telling the story. He folds his arms across his chest, muscles flexing. "I made you carry them both down the mountain."

She growls. "While you vanished into the trees, you lazy brute." Her eyelashes lower. So does her voice. "I always wondered how you knew I was in danger?"

Erit tips his chin at her. "Because you told me how you were going to kill the panther—trap it while you waited high in the trees, then drop onto its back and stab its eyes out. The panther Howl brought back was killed just like that, right down to the trap marks on its legs. I knew it was your kill, not his."

She leans toward him, her expression softening. "You were gone three years later. What happened to you?"

"Howl was being groomed to take over as clan leader. I had to get out while I could."

"They told me you died, and I thought Howl had killed you. He always found a way to take away everything good in my life."

The blood leaves his face. "No. Not Howl."

Her voice is small. "But you didn't take me with you."

He blinks at her. Swallows visibly. "I didn't think… that you…"

I lean back in my chair. It feels like they've forgotten I'm here, the same way everyone in the room fades away for me when I'm with Baelen.

Indira rustles her wings again, but it's a subdued movement, the torn ribbons fluttering around her. "Was it because of these?"

Erit closes the small gap between them, his arms unfolding and his knees knocking against hers. "No, not because of your wings."

She presses her lips together so hard they turn white. "You were older than me, but I turned eighteen the night you disappeared. I thought you knew my heart. I went to your bed, but you were already gone."

Erit is shell-shocked, frozen, wings half-forward, not quite reaching for her.

I take glances between the two of them and carefully slide off my chair. It's time to go. I'm intruding on a conversation I shouldn't be part of now. I tiptoe away from the table, grateful that neither of them notices my departure.

Outside, I take stock of the mountain and its view of the wastelands. Talon crows wheel across the distant sky. The birds aren't as big as giant eagles, and nowhere near as large as the phoenix, but they're a dangerous predator. Far, far in the distance, our world ends in walls of rock. I never imagined that any clan could survive in the wastelands, let alone on a cold mountain like this one. I feel a deep respect for the Outlier Clan and especially the Grievous women for surviving in these conditions. I shiver, wishing I'd brought a coat. I draw on the heartstones' power, trying to warm myself as I glance at the door behind me.

Nope, not going back in there to get warm. Not until one or both of them comes out.

Five minutes later, Erit emerges, quiet and troubled. He leans against the wall beside the door, his wings tucked tight to his sides, his broad shoulders hunched. I can't see much of Indira through the opening, but she picks up the jug of alcohol and stares right into it.

"I can't be what she wants," he says.

I blink hard. Is he really going to throw this chance away? "What is that, Erit?"

He gestures at our surroundings. "Grievous. I can't return to the clan I gave up."

I funnel as much anger into my response as I can muster while my teeth are on the verge of chattering. "I don't think this is the same clan you left. It's changed dramatically. In fact, it's still changing, and you have the chance to be part of that change."

He shoots away from the wall, obviously taken back by the harshness in my tone. I've never reprimanded him before. "Lady Storm?"

I glower at him. "A proud woman like Indira will only show her feelings once. You're lucky she opened up to you at all. If you want to be part of her life, then go back in there and tell her. Right now."

He glances at the open door.

I point a commanding finger at it. "She's giving you a second chance, Erit. You won't get a third. Now go make a hammock bed or whatever it is you need to do to make it official."

He takes the leaps from shocked to serious to grinning. "I didn't come here for a wife, Lady Storm."

"I know you didn't, Erit, but you're leaving with one. Now get back in there."

"As you wish, Lady Storm."

He pauses in the doorway, his big chest rising and falling. I guess it's a lot to take in. We came here to build bridges. Now he has to build the most important bridge of his life.

He leaves the door open behind him. I turn away from it, giving them privacy as I head up the steps to the right. I'd rather try to find a warm fire somewhere, but the village is not exactly welcoming regardless of the clan's pledge to me.

A crash and a thud behind me draws me right back down the stairs at a run. I seriously hope I wasn't wrong about Indira… or maybe talon crows got in… or one of the clan members doesn't like the way things are going…

I race through the opening and skid to a halt.

Erit lies on his back next to the table, one arm around Indira who has landed on his chest. She clutches the broken handle of the glass jug, brandishing it at his face, shrieking at him. "You don't get to tell me that you love me!"

Golden liquor drips from the edge of the table, trickling from the remains of the jug on the table's surface. I quickly put together the pieces of what I'm seeing: she dropped the jug, he took a step toward her, slipped on the liquid, and they fell together.

I harness the heartstone's power just in case I need it.

He ignores her cry, clearly enjoying her current location. "Lady Indira, you need to know that for the last fifteen years I made my bed wherever I found it." He pats the floor with his free hand. "This patch of rock looks pretty good to me."

She hurls the jug handle at the far wall where it shatters. She shrieks again. "You…!" But she immediately drops her head to his and kisses him fiercely. Drawing breath, she declares, "Now we are married. And you will never break my heart again, Grievous Erit."

"Never," he whispers, drawing her close.

My heart glows—so do the heartstones. I reach for the door handle, prepared to shut it this time, but not before I make my presence known. "When you're finished, you will come back to the deep springs with us, Grievous Indira. You have wings to heal."

She looks up, startled by my presence and my order. She seems speechless for the first time. "Yes, Supreme Incorruptible."

"Good. Now I'm going for a very long walk… around your freezing mountain and I won't be back for some time."

Their happiness follows me out. I close the door behind me. It's time to get a handle on the power in the heartstones. Most importantly, I need to figure out how to fly, because Erit will need to fly Indira back, and I can't ask one of the women to carry me.

I pick my way along the uneven surface of the steep pathway. I don't exactly want to take an ungraceful tumble the wrong way down the street. There are eyes everywhere in this village. I can't see any of the women, but I sense them watching me as I go.

What I really need is to find a place that's safe to test my power. All my attempts to draw on the heartstones to warm myself are failing. The Queen's heart always made me cold, not warm, and Baelen is not here to balance me out. I'm not worried about freezing to death—surely Virtuous will kick in before that happens?—but I'd rather not feel so miserable. I shudder so hard that I have to pause in the middle of the walkway, rubbing my arms.

I hurry to the top of the rise where the trees thicken and follow the pathway through them. The exercise warms me a little and walking uphill forces me to focus on my breathing. It takes over half an hour to reach the highest peak, a jagged patch of rock with a lone tree. There are no caves or openings. As I emerge from the darkness below, the sudden sunlight and view are breathtaking.

On the sunlit side, the mountains of Erador rise up like giants in the distance, but as I turn, the view changes. On the shadowed side —the side of the village—the wastelands are a bleak reminder that our world has deadly edges. So are the talon crows, gliding closer than before but still very far away.

I find a jutting rock, choosing to turn my back on the wastelands and face the sun's warmth instead. I peer up at the heartstones floating around me like a halo, wondering how to trigger them individually. When I first tethered them to me, I thought I heard them speak as if they each had voices. Closing my eyes, I try to block everything out, including the sunlight flaring beyond my eyelids.

Incorruptible's chill is by far the strongest, drowning everything else out. I try to listen beyond her, but she buzzes even louder in my ears. I shake my head, trying to dislodge the noise. So impossible. I can't even sense the other heartstones over her increasing shriek—

Pain explodes in my shoulder. A sharp object rakes across my shoulder blade, lodging in the bone and lifting me upward, tearing through sinew and muscle.

My eyes shoot open, and a scream burns through my lungs as sharp feathers slice across my cheek.

12

———

GRAYSON

The Rath and Mercy Heartstones are laid out side by side on a soft cloth on top of my desk. My palms hover over them, and I take a breath before I touch them, preparing myself for pain.

Gannon Glory waits at the side of my room, a tall, lanky form plastered up against the golden wallpaper. He stands as far away from me as he can get, static causing his hair to spread out across the image of golden vines that decorates my wall.

I've been searching for Marbella Mercy for a month. Now I finally have the means to face her.

Gannon's lips are pinched. "Are you sure this is the best course of action?"

My answer is a narrow-eyed glare. Gannon was Baelen Rath's advisor, but Baelen was smart enough to see through Gannon for the spy he is.

Gannon tries again. "The Elven Commanders—"

"Agree with my plan!" I snap. "Now make yourself useful and bring a talon crow. The largest we have. Place it in a cage outside my room."

"Yes, my lord."

I wait to hear the door close before I lower my hands to grip the edge of the desk. He's not wrong to question this plan. This is possibly the most dangerous step I could take, but I couldn't find

107

Marbella while she was vulnerable. Now that she controls the gargoyle heartstones, it will take all my power to fight her.

Before I can think about it, I take hold of both heartstones.

I jolt at the emotion that flows through me, completely unexpected.

Pure love rockets from the Rath Heartstone to Mercy's—and back again. It races through me as if I were a mere conduit.

I thought I understood what love is, what it looks like. But I've never felt anything like this. It's beyond anything I ever imagined possible.

Gideon was the only elf to show me love, so I only know one kind—that of a guardian to his ward. The power streaming between the crimson and purple heartstones is multi-faceted and rips through me like a hammer cracking all my defenses, chipping away at them. Baelen Rath used this stone to pledge his life to Marbella. He pledged to love, protect, and honor her until death, the purest vow he could make.

I wrench my hands away.

How can two elves who murdered Gideon have the capacity to feel such an untainted love for each other?

I shove the question aside, ignoring my doubts, and focus on the memory of Gideon's dead body. I couldn't protect the one elf who showed me any empathy. Now all I can do is avenge him.

I reach for the stones again, this time to cleave them apart.

When I'm finished, I'm racked with pain, burning the entire length of my spine as if hot pokers have speared through each vertebra. I use the pain, harness it to power my actions, striding across the room and throwing open the door to reveal the talon crow in its cage.

Its black eyes dart to me, its talons stamping the bottom of the cage as it screeches at me. Its instinct is to tear me apart.

It will give me the wings I need to test my new power.

13

MARBELLA

The talon crow drops me, and I fall to my hands and knees, trying not to vomit while my bloody shoulder gapes open at the edge of my vision. The bird soars upward and circles back. Its body is as big as a shadow panther, its wingspan at least eight feet wide and its talons are curved daggers, dripping my blood across the ground as it dives toward me again.

Power surges through me. Incorruptible bursts into life. Light burns through my torso and arms, my palms shoot outward with the force riding my body, and I spear icy death across the distance.

Right before my power would strike the bird, it hits a shield. The crow pulls up sharp only three paces away and settles to the ground, its wings still spread. Incorruptible's light hits a point right in front of it, but the light splits and curves around a protective force. The two forces hiss and spit against each other. I push harder, drawing more power from the stone, but the shield doesn't give way. The bird is completely protected.

It's sorcery. It has to be.

The bird cackles. Its beady eyes stare at me, unblinking. An eerie white substance swirls across its pupils like smoke building on the inside. Its beak opens, emitting a low moan. It's hard to tear my eyes from the tusks rising on each side of its bottom jaw. Talon crows have some of the same attributes as a boar and can use their beaks and giant tusks to maul their victims. I can't let the bird get any closer.

"Marbella Mercy," the crow says as the smoke swirls in its eyes. "I've been waiting to meet you."

I might never have seen one of these beasts up close before, but I know for sure that they can't speak. There is definitely sorcery at play here. "Who are you?"

"I am Grayson of the House of Glory. Gideon was my great-uncle."

An elf! Eli Elder had told me that there were two, new members of the Elven Command who had filled the vacant positions after Teilo Splendor escaped and I killed Gideon Glory.

Grayson must be my age if Gideon was his great-uncle. It's very unusual for someone so young to claim a place in the Elven Command. As the last Rath, Baelen had that right, but the Commanders prevented him from taking up his rightful place. The shield that Grayson is placing around the bird tells me he earned his place because of his mastery of sorcery. If he can withstand Incorruptible's power, then he's more powerful than Gideon ever was.

I shudder so hard that the line of icy power hitting the shield wobbles. Sorcery derives its force from death, which means Grayson is a murderer.

"I assume you have taken his place." Pain rakes through me. I'm still losing blood. All of my energy is being channeled into keeping the bird at bay. My vision is beginning to blur and if I pass out, I won't survive. *Virtuous! Heal me! Please!*

Blood continues to flow down my chest, warming me in the worst way. I'm not healing, and I don't know why. *Virtuous!*

The smoky mist that swirls in the talon crow's eyes spreads into the feathers around its beak and back over its head. Grayson must be drawing on the bird's life to sustain his sorcery so he can speak with me from his true location far away in Erawind. He's slowly killing the animal. This gives me hope. I just have to hold out long enough for it to die. Then I'm getting the hell off this mountain.

"You are not as powerful as they warned me," Grayson says. The bird tilts its head, one eye looking me up and down. "But you are much more beautiful."

The bird takes a step forward, its talons digging right into the rock. The shield moves with it, only two paces away now. I push back but my arms are screaming and fear creeps into me. *What if I can't hold out long enough?*

"It's a shame I'll have to kill you," Grayson says. And in the next breath: "We will give you a month to prepare the gargoyles for surrender. If you do not give yourself up by then, we will begin killing your friends, starting with the head of your Storm Command, Reisha."

The bird takes another step, its wings slowly turning white, its talons scrabbling at the ground. There must be some part of the animal trying to fight back, trying to stay alive.

I scream with the effort of maintaining Incorruptible's power. My arms shake. My breathing is ragged. Why can't I heal?

"Nothing can save you from me—"

An arrow shoots from the edge of the clearing, piercing the bird's side. It explodes into a cloud of white dust. The shield disappears, and Incorruptible's power shrieks to a stop. I collapse to the ground, my arms shaking so hard I can't lift them.

The bird's remains settle gently over the rock, its dust lifting and wafting into the breeze. I cover my nose and mouth, scooting backward, trying not to breathe it in.

A young woman emerges from the pathway at the side of the mountain. "It was about time he shut up."

I can barely focus on her. I need to figure out what was wrong with Virtuous. Searching for the emerald stone above my head, I discover why I can't sense it.

It's not there.

I cry out in fear before I can stop myself, desperately searching the air and ground for it. I find it several paces away, lying on the ground, its glow diminished. Grayson must have knocked it away from me when the talon crow first swooped. But how is that even possible? *How is any of this possible?*

Everyone told me that the Queen's heart was the most powerful heartstone. Were they lying? Were they wrong?

I scramble toward Virtuous's heart, catching it up in my hands and clutching it against my own heart. Dull emerald light returns to the stone, but it's very pale. Luckily, it's enough that the pain in my shoulder stops and so does the bleeding. I don't want to look, but a quick glance tells me that my skin has healed over. It's not perfect though: it's fragile and red beneath my torn clothing.

The girl reaches my side. She doesn't pay homage to me, looking me square in the eyes. "I was told to bring you this," she says, handing me a cloak made of thick, black fur. "But I think you have bigger problems."

I pull the cloak around my shoulders but keep Virtuous close to my heart. I'm starting to shake, but she's right: it's not from the cold. "Thank you. For the coat and for killing the bird."

"The crow was only shielded in front. Whoever he was, he didn't think you'd have friends." She positions herself on my undamaged side to help me stand.

I'm in danger of going into shock. Only the warmth of the coat keeps me in the present as I force my legs to move. "You'd think with all of *this…*" I wave my hand at the stones. "I'd have figured out basic things like how to keep myself warm."

Her response is blunt and forthright. "You're drawing power from the wrong stone."

"I'm sorry?"

She points as we leave the clearing. "You probably can't see because they're above your head, but you only ever draw power from Incorruptible's heart. Since you got here, I've only seen Virtuous shine once after your fight with Indira. The moon is icy, so using Incorruptible's power will only make you colder."

"So… which one will make me warm?"

A secretive smile breaks across her face. She keeps one eye on the steep path and the other on me. "Prime's of course. He was Incorruptible's opposite, fiery and passionate. Some gargoyles think they were lovers."

I ignore that statement. I know for a fact that they weren't, but their hearts belonged together. "What about Lightsworn?"

"Conceited. Totally full of himself. But he was an amazing warrior. If you draw on his power during battle you will fight better."

"Better, huh?"

She ignores my sarcasm. "Then there's Virtuous, who was some sort of healer. Her heart is complicated: sad, lonely. You shouldn't draw on it too often or you'll screw up your emotions."

Well, good thing I've got Virtuous pressed right up against my heart right now then. I sigh, but it's worth the risk that my emotions will go haywire because I need Virtuous close while my shoulder is still healing. And I need to figure out how it got knocked away from me. "How do you know all of this?"

She scoffs. "Because I grew up with it. It's the first thing Grievous children learn: the power of the heartstones. Where do you think Howl got his obsession?"

"Which one of the heartstones will give me the power to fly?"

She shakes her head. "Sorry. That would be Hideaway's heart because of his powerful wings, but nobody found that heartstone and besides… gargoyles don't need the power to fly."

"I guess not." I'm disappointed. I thought I'd at least be able to try. We walk in silence for a long time, finally passing Indira's home, but the girl doesn't stop there.

"Where are we going?"

She points along the street but all of the buildings around us are shuttered and closed. "You're coming with me to see Gretel. She sent me to find you. She can tell you everything you need to know about the heartstones, including how to use them properly."

"I take it she told Howl everything too."

She shrugs. "Not by choice, but that was the way with Howl. I didn't really know him, mind you. Before my time and all."

She's so young, maybe only fourteen-years-old, but she seems like an old soul. "I don't know your name."

"I'm Bethany."

A little while later, we reach a house on the outskirts of the village. Like Indira's home, this one also sits on the precipice of a cliff. A small balcony has been built into the roof and a sentry sits huddled under a fur coat topped with a shadow panther skin: an excellent disguise to make it look like the girl huddled under it is a much larger man.

Bethany waves to her before pushing through the front door. Welcome heat rushes to greet us and I sigh with relief. Like many times before, I only realize I've been drawing on Incorruptible's power when I don't need it anymore. The cold evaporates along with the tension in my body.

The room is sparsely furnished with a table and chairs, a small kitchen off to the right, and a stone fireplace on the left. An old woman sits huddled under a layer of furs on a wooden chair beside the fire. Her silver hair is tied back in a loose bun at the nape of her neck. She immediately shifts and acknowledges me with a hoarse whisper. "Supreme Incorruptible."

One of her eyes is glazed and white. The other is a delicate blue. I miss a step before I realize how rude it is to stare.

She points at her glazed eye. "Howl."

Of course. He may be dead, but the deeper I dig, the further his cruelty extends.

Bethany pulls a chair from the table, positioning it beside Gretel, gesturing for me to sit. Then she sets about putting a kettle on the stove and gathering teacups.

Gretel's gaze slides from my face up to the stones. Her bony finger twitches as she counts them. "Incorruptible, Prime, Lightsworn. But where is Virtuous?"

I open the coat and my fist. "Here. She was knocked out of my control."

"Ah." Her hand lands on my arm, giving me a comforting squeeze. "You can tell me all about that in a minute, but for now, let's focus on what you have, not what you don't."

"What I have?"

"The four most important heartstones: strength, heart, strategy, and immortality."

Is she talking about the same stones? "You missed destruction."

"Destruction? Which heart is that?"

I point to the Queen's.

"What?" She is shocked, her mouth dropping open. "Incorruptible was strong, faithful, and wise. She sheltered her people when they needed courage."

Gretel takes stock of me before she leans forward to peer into my eyes. She tilts so far forward I'm concerned she's going to slide out of her chair. She clicks her tongue, exhaling a disappointed sigh. "I don't need the power of a Sighted One to see that you are deeply fearful of the power you hold."

"Of course I'm afraid. I have the power to destroy anything I want."

"There it is again. That word: destruction. Destroy. Where did you get this from?"

"Well… the Priestess told me that all the good of our ancestors went into creating our world, and all the bad was left in their hearts."

"Pfft! That Priestess! She's all goodness and light. All flowers and meadows; sunlight and twinkling stars. She doesn't see the beauty in a raging thunderstorm or the value of a hot flame to keep us warm. She doesn't understand that the heartstones are neither good nor evil. Their nature is determined purely by the choices of the one who controls them."

Choose. Choose life or death. The memory of Incorruptible's voice returns to me. She'd asked me to choose one or the other, but she hadn't told me which. She left that choice up to me.

I say, "When I first touched Incorruptible's heart, I needed her to kill Howl. Then when I held her heart in my hand… they said I could have killed everyone." Even Baelen had risked his life to stop me.

Gretel nods. "It's true. You could have. But only because you weren't aware of what you were doing. That doesn't mean you have to be afraid now."

"But I am." The admission leaves me relieved.

"Acknowledging fear is the first step to overcoming it." She smiles. "Now, tell me, when you think of the stones, how do you describe them to yourself."

"Well… That is Incorruptible's heart. Her power—"

"No! Wrong!"

I blink at her. "What?"

"It is *your* heart, *your* power. Each power is yours. But each one makes up a different part of you." She points to the stones. "Incorruptible is your strength. Prime is the fire in your heart. Lightsworn is your battle strategy. Virtuous is your immortality. *Yours.*"

Bethany appears with cups of tea, handing one to me and then to Gretel. The scent of rose petals wafts up to me. *Heavenly.* I take a sip and the warmth eases all my tension.

Gretel's hand flutters at Bethany. "Please, dearest, will you bring me my mother's tiara?"

"But that's your most precious possession—"

"And now it will be a gift for our new Queen."

I place my cup on its saucer. "I don't need anything."

Gretel pierces me with a flinty glare. "But you do."

I'm not going to argue with that fact. I sit meekly while Bethany disappears and drink the entire cup of tea.

When Bethany returns and solemnly hands Gretel the tiara, the old woman turns it around in her hands. It is a simple piece of jewelry made up of two thick bands of gold joined at their ends and curved to sit around a woman's forehead, big enough to encircle her head. It is obviously very precious to Gretel.

"Howl wore his heartstones close to his chest," she says. "But you must wear them close to your mind because that is where you fight your battles."

She hands me the tiara, but I say, "The heartstones are too big to fit into this."

"Currently, yes. You must cleave them into smaller pieces the same way you must break down your misconceptions and fears."

I swallow. "How do I do that?"

"Take each one in your hand and seek the power you need. But start with Incorruptible."

I reach out and grasp the diamond heart. It fits neatly into my fist, smooth and oval. She is strength. I read her journal. She wanted to fight back against the humans who forced the elves and gargoyles from Earth's surface. She had the strength of will to do what was right for her people even though her heart told her to run away with Prime. Later, she chose to become the moon that lights the way for gargoyles at night.

I'm reminded of the old, elven song: *spin gold, shelter silver.* Incorruptible was a protective force, not an aggressive one. I felt that force when I reached out to burn Harem Hall, to protect the women from the horrors of their past. I felt it when I was trying to protect myself from Grayson Glory. Is it as simple as banishing fear from my mind? As simple as trusting myself?

I open my fist.

The diamond quietly splits into two pieces. And then two more.

I hold out my palm for the other heartstones and they come to me, each of them splitting neatly into quarters.

I press each one against the tiara, using my Prime power to mold the gold and heartstones like putty beneath my fingertips, smoothing out the corners and tightly encircling each piece of stone and binding them together. I make sure to place the Prime pieces closest to the Incorruptible ones. When I'm finished, the tiara is lined with colorful gems set out in a neat row. Even the pieces of my Virtuous heart have regained their full green glow. I slip the tiara around my forehead.

Gretel beams at me. "Now tell me what happened to Virtuous."

Some of my happiness slips away. "An elf named Grayson Glory attacked me in the form of a talon crow. It happened on top of the mountain. I didn't realize, but on its first swoop, the crow knocked my Virtuous heart away from me."

"It attempted to break the tether between you and your heartstones." She nods, deep in thought. "There is only one way to do that: through an opposing heartstone."

"But elves can't hold gargoyle heartstones."

"True, but they can hold elven heartstones." She sighs. "Do you recall Howl ever asking the elves for any of their heartstones?"

"No… Wait… Yes. He made a deal in exchange for killing Baelen Rath. He wanted the Rath and Mercy Heartstones."

"Mercy is your elven House?"

"Ye-es."

"Then Grayson Glory has taken possession of your heartstone and forcibly tethered it to himself. If he has done the same with the Rath Heartstone, then he is protected against your power."

"So, I can't beat him."

She leans forward. "Of course you can beat him. But you will need your Lightsworn heart to help you come up with a plan."

Lightsworn is strategy. I definitely need to repeat my strengths like a mantra.

Gretel fixes her gaze on Bethany. "My girl, you won't repeat a word of this outside this house. It's up to Supreme Incorruptible how she handles this threat. Panic plays no part in the solution."

When Bethany nods her agreement, Gretel sighs, reclining.

"Now, you'll forgive this old lady, but I need to rest. All this thinking has worn me out. Bethany, please? I need a nap."

"Wait, please." I stop her before she stands. "Come back with me to the deep springs. You can heal your eye."

She shakes her head. "Thank you, Supreme Incorruptible, but some wounds are important reminders of what we're fighting for."

Bethany helps Gretel upstairs, telling me she'll be right back. When she returns, she hands me a large piece of fresh bread and says she will take me back to Indira before Indira comes looking for me.

I still don't know how I'm going to get back to the palace. As I pick my way up the street, I say, "The power of flight would have been useful."

Bethany giggles. "You don't need it."

"Actually, I think I might."

She points. "Nope."

The phoenix is a bright flare in the distant sky, but its voice is even clearer in my mind.

Princess, you need me.

I do, my friend. I will be ready to fly when you reach me.

I hope Erit and Indira will be too, because I need to get back to Baelen and tell him about Grayson Glory's threat.

14

MARBELLA

It's faster to ride the phoenix, so Indira and Erit agree to travel on the firebird with me. The street through the Grievous village isn't wide enough for the phoenix to land but it finds a clearing further up the mountain.

Indira leaves the clan with strict orders to remain on the lookout while she's gone. When Erit moves to help her climb onto the phoenix's back, she gives him a stern look. At the last minute, he picks her up and carries her up the bird's wing. She looks like she wants to pummel him. He arches an eyebrow at her, and she kisses him instead, snuggling into him as they sit together.

Once I find my place at the front, the phoenix soars into the sky. The firebird trills in my mind: *You have a new headpiece.*

I'm learning not to be afraid of it.

And what of the elves? I sensed a dark presence in the sky. It's why I left Elyria to come to you.

I say, *Grayson Glory seeks my surrender. He is a very powerful sorcerer. I fear for my friends.*

He is not as powerful as you.

I sigh. *That's the theory. I will need you, Phoenix, before the month is out.*

The phoenix's answer is comforting: *I will be ready when you call.*

Thank you. And for looking after Elyria. But... how is she? It's such a small question. I want to ask more, but I'm not sure how. Outlier Senturi said that Elyria would go through a transformation now. I saw one part of it: that she is now visible to everyone, but I'm worried about what other changes she might experience.

Jasper is looking after her. He has a way with her, helping her heal, but she has a long road ahead.

When we land at the deep springs, the cliff around Crimson Court is packed with young gargoyles. It's now mid-afternoon and the sound of children travels across the ravine.

Even from this distance, it's easy to pick Baelen out from the crowd. He stands above the others, positively gigantic next to the children. My heart burns. I need to see him, tell him what happened on Mount Grievous.

Indira sidles up to me. I've remained on the phoenix because I need a way to get across the ravine, but she and Erit have already alighted. Erit waits at the entrance to the springs while Indira peers in the opposite direction, her jaw dropping.

"Is that… Baelen Rath?"

I'm surprised. Even the phoenix's appearance didn't draw this much interest from her. "What do you know of Baelen?"

"Only stories of a wild elf in the wastelands." Her voice lowers to a conspiratorial whisper. "They say he isn't afraid to look Sighted Ones in the eye. They say that talon crows fall to their bellies at his feet and all he has to do is growl at a shadow panther and it slinks away. Unless he kills it first."

I try to hide my smile. Maybe she doesn't know that he's with me. But at the same time, that sort of reputation would explain why the Priestess calls him Wrathful One—and why the gargoyles avoid him. Even Howl was worried when he first realized Baelen's sleeping body was in his possession. I thought it was because Howl had killed Baelen's father. But it sounds like Baelen had already made a reputation for himself among the gargoyles—whether he wanted to or not.

Indira's forehead creases before she shrugs. "I thought he had a beard. Oh well."

Erit draws her toward the deep springs but pauses to tell me they won't come straight back to the Royal Residence.

"There's a place I want to show Indira," he says with a smile. "We'll come back tonight."

"That's fine, Erit. Return when you're ready." I wish them luck, knowing that when Indira emerges, she will be able to fly again.

The phoenix ferries me across the ravine, causing a stir among the gargoyle children who point and chatter. I choose to leap off its back because there's no room for it to land. *Thank you, Phoenix.*

I will see you soon, Princess.

Finding my feet, I seek Baelen across the distance. He has already spotted me, his focus immediately zeroing in on… uh-oh… the dried blood all over the front of my shirt. Maybe I should have asked Indira for a clean shirt…

"Marbella?" His intensely unhappy growl cuts across the diminishing distance between us. A little boy clings to his chest while Adalie trots along beside him, running to keep up. A trail of children follow him like little ducklings, and I can't help but smile as he unconsciously pats the head of the nearest child as if he's checking that the little girl is still there when he draws to a halt in front of me.

His glower tells me I definitely should have changed into fresh clothing.

I answer firmly, pulling the ripped material away from my shoulder to show him. "I'm fine. See?" I release the shirt and go straight for a diversion, smiling at Adalie. I'd expected to find her in the crook of Baelen's arm. "I see you gave up your favorite spot."

She becomes solemn. "He needs Bae-Bae more than me."

The little boy looks barely two-years-old, his wings tucked neatly against his side, his head buried as if he finds comfort in the thud of Baelen's heart.

I mouth: *Parents?*

Baelen's concern for me gives way to a deeper sadness. He responds: *Gone.*

The little girl on his right—the one whose blonde head he patted—tugs on his arm, whispering so he has to take a knee to hear her. He nods, after which her gaze darts to me.

She wobbles into a curtsy, her young voice a nervous whisper. "Supreme Incorruptible, I honor you."

I answer, "I am very honored."

"C'mon, children," Baelen addresses them. "Back to the Court."

"One more story!" one of them shouts.

"Yes, please!"

Adalie takes my hand. "Bae-Bae has told us all about battling talon crows and shadow panthers…"

She babbles away as I walk with her, following the children who follow Baelen. Every now and then he glances back to check I'm still there. He might be focusing on the task at hand, but I know it's only a matter of time before he demands to know exactly what happened while I was gone.

Up ahead, I recognize many of the women from Harem Hall. Some of them are obviously waiting for their children to arrive— those are the ones who pace anxiously along the cliff-side of the Court. Then there are those who are helping others, bringing drinks and food and making sure the children are happy. At the nearest corner of the Court, I recognize Gilda, her dark hair flowing freely down her back, watching over a group of children who are occupied with drawing.

I'm several paces away, just about to greet her, when a male gargoyle soars in from the expanse beyond the cliff, lands on the edge, tucks his wings in, and heads straight for her.

It's Roar, his blue-veined wings stained with soot and his boots covered in mud. Gilda freezes when she sees him, drawing up tall, uncompromising and prickly. He keeps his head down, watching where he's going instead of forcing her to make eye contact.

I stop right where I am. Baelen has led the children off to the other side of the Court. He glances back, sees me, sees Roar, and quickly stays where he is, giving the unfolding situation the space it needs.

Roar drops to a knee in front of Gilda as she eyes him warily. He's absolutely filthy, worse than I ever saw him in the mines, covered in sweat and dirt. Her eyes narrow, her back straight, but that's the only reaction she gives to his appearance.

He holds up both hands, one cupped beneath the other, opening his palms to reveal an offering: a delicate white flower, the most beautiful I've ever seen.

Her eyes widen. Her dark hair lifts in the breeze, framing her face as she opens her mouth to speak but stops. His head is still down. Without hesitation, she whisks the flower from his palm, takes one look at it, and crushes it in her fist with a vengeance. She presses so hard that her knuckles turn white.

My heart sinks as she opens her hand and allows the flower to fall. Tears sparkle in her eyes. She stalks away from him while the flower's mangled remains flutter to the ground and land next to his boot.

He scoops it up, finally lifting his eyes to watch her swaying form as she strides away. She doesn't look back.

I race to his side. "Roar! I'm sorry."

He startles me by breaking into a grin, beaming at me, his eyes more alive than they've been in days. "There's nothing to be sorry about, Lady Storm. She accepted my gift."

"Uh… really?"

He hands me the flower. "This is a chrysalis flower. It's only found in the wastelands in muddy bogs. Once you pick it, it wilts after four hours. No time for me to take a shower." He shrugs at his own disheveled appearance. "But look…"

He holds it up for me to see. "Its true beauty is not in its appearance, but in what lies beneath the surface."

The flower has changed color, turning a deep amethyst, and the most amazing fragrance wafts up from it. The scent contains layers of vanilla and roses and immediately makes me feel comforted and warm.

Roar says, "It only releases its perfume when you crush it."

"So… when she crushed it…?"

"She accepted my gift."

Thank the ancients. "I'm happy for you, Roar. So happy." I attempt to hug him, but he quickly sidesteps my gesture.

"Uh, Lady Storm, I'm filthy right now and…" His gaze darts to Baelen who is suddenly a simmering silhouette inside the Court. "I don't think the Wrathful One will appreciate adding mud to what must already be concerning him about the state of your clothing."

Once again, I forgot the blood. "I'm fine, Roar. Totally healed."

"But it was a bad wound. Anyone can see that."

I sigh. "I guess you're not the only one who should get cleaned up right away." I need to shower and change before questions are asked that have complicated answers. I wrinkle my nose at him. "At least I don't stink."

"Thanks, Lady Storm." He pauses, grinning widely at me before turning away. "Nice tiara, by the way."

I've never seen this lighter side of Roar. In the mines, he was always serious, always focused on the task at hand; a hard worker and a dedicated warrior. He still is. Finding the flower would have been difficult to begin with, but he must have flown as fast as the phoenix to get back here from the wastelands in time. To see him grinning now, relaxed and happy to have done something that touched his wife's heart, it makes me wonder how much the oppression of Howl's rule changed his behavior and who the gargoyles would all be if they hadn't been subjected to Howl's cruelty.

I make my way past Baelen, grateful to see that none of the gargoyles are avoiding him now. One of the women passes him a glass of water, telling him to drink something. Two children tug on his arm and beg him to play with them. They aren't afraid of him any longer and that's a vast relief to me.

The sun will go down soon, and the children will need to be brought to the Residence. I want to clean up before that happens. I veer toward him briefly. "I'm going to change. Let's talk once you're back at the Residence."

He growls a response that makes the nearest children giggle. Looks like it's growling-Baelen day. He's not happy, and I hate that he's worried, but I can't give him any assurances that don't lead to more questions right now. I hurry away from him and the chorus of little voices begging for another story.

Inside the Residence, I sneak to my room before I encounter the Priestess or anyone else who will want answers. But especially the Priestess. She'd told me that the stones were destructive, and I guess her beliefs were formed out of fear. I'm still processing what Gretel taught me. I'm still coming to terms with the fact that the stones sit on my head now and that they feel like part of me.

My strength, *my* heart, *my* strategy, *my* immortality.

I remove the tiara in my bedroom, testing how far away from the crown I can move before I feel its pull. Seems like the bathroom is okay. From the doorway, I test whether I can call it to me, reaching out my hand. The crown zips straight into my open palm. Excellent. I could probably move even further, but right now, I need to clean up.

I'm halfway through washing myself—most of the blood is gone—when the bathroom door crashes open in a great gust of wind.

Baelen storms in behind it, a tornado picking me up so I don't slip in surprise. The shower water suddenly transforms into a fine mist, swelling around me in a gentle cloud. He dwarfs the doorway. Every muscle in his body is tense, his chest heaves, and growls rip from his throat. Behind his eyes, the spark of fire threatens to be released.

I don't fight the pull of the storm around me. "Baelen—?"

He strides toward me at the same time the tornado whisks me forward and deposits me, naked and wet, into his arms. Carrying me from the room, his fiery body heat dries me off instantly.

He plants me on the side of the bed but doesn't let me go, dropping to a kneeling position to examine my shoulder. His chest rumbles with thunder as he inspects my skin and muscles, his fingers light at first, then firm as he tests for any lasting damage.

He finally speaks, a threatening vibration. "You were supposed to be invincible. They said you were invincible. How did this happen? Who do I need to kill?"

"Nobody, Baelen. Really. I'm okay now."

"But you weren't!"

My voice is small, trapped in my throat. I try to squash the memory of the talon crow clawing through my shoulder. "No, I wasn't."

"What happened?"

The truth is not going to make him any happier, but there's no way around it. I try to slow it down, keep him calm. "A talon crow attacked me. It was under the control of the Elven Command's newest member: Grayson Glory. He's a powerful sorcerer and… he's forced a tether with our heartstones. It protects him from my power. It's how he got through my defenses."

"Which heartstones?"

"Rath and Mercy."

If he was angry before, now he's pale with fury.

I hurry on. "But I have much better control of my power now. I was afraid to use it before, but I'm not anymore. And the positive side is that he thinks I'm weaker than I am."

Baelen's big hands flex around my waist, his jaw clenching. "I should have been there."

"Baelen—"

"It's my job to protect you, Marbella Mercy. I can't protect you if you won't let me."

"You can't be there every second of every day."

"Watch me." He drops a growly kiss to my shoulder, his determined statement vibrating against the sensitive skin at the base of my neck. His hands drop to my thighs, his thumbs grazing the inside of my legs while his lips travel from my collarbone to my mouth. Warmth spreads through me as I realize where we are, what position we're in, and how much I don't want him to stop, even if he's kissing me in sheer fury about the fact that I was hurt, and he wasn't there to stop it.

I kiss him back, shifting closer to his chest and sighing against his lips. My moan seems to bring him back to himself, but he doesn't push me away like he did this morning. He picks me up and carries me to the closet, hooking one arm around me after he slides me to my feet in front of the racks of clothing.

He asks, "Which ones?"

I point to a pair of long pants and a new shirt, as well as to the underwear drawer. "I take it the Priestess has replenished my clothing."

But he's not interested in where the clothing came from, pulling the underwear onto me, sliding the shirt over my head, and sitting me back on the bed to slip the long pants from my ankles to my thighs. He touches my bare skin every chance he gets. By the time he pulls me into a standing position and drops a kiss on my stomach as he buttons the pants for me, I'm burning all over. Can he rip everything off me now please?

He whispers into my ear. "Soon."

My knees wobble. "Baelen, there's more."

His eyes narrow and tension returns to his body. "How much more?"

"Grayson Glory told me to prepare the gargoyles for surrender. He gave me a month to give myself up. Then he's going to start killing my Storm Command.

Fire leaps into life at the back of Baelen's eyes. "You can't surrender."

"I'm going to fight back. I'm going to free my Storm Command. But Baelen… the gargoyles need time to heal. I can't walk out there tonight and tell them that the Elven Command is planning to take away their freedom after they just got it back. I need time to figure out what I'm going to do."

"You want to keep this threat from them?"

"Not for long. Just for now." I chew my lip, expecting him to argue against it. *I* want to argue against it. I verbalize my thoughts before I can second-guess myself. "Howl has only been gone for a day. Families are still trying to find each other. The gargoyles need time to mourn, reconnect, rebuild. And I…"

I swallow hard, twisting my hands in my lap. "I need to bury Cassian. I need to say goodbye too."

Baelen wraps my hands in his. I thought he would have jumped in already, told me it's the wrong choice, but he hasn't. Instead he says, "Grayson Glory gave you a month. The best thing you can do for your… our people… is to take a few days to get your head straight and start planning. If you need to bring some of the gargoyles into the loop, then do that. But when you break this news to them, you need to go to them with a plan. Otherwise, you'll only bring fear back into their lives."

I blink away the sudden tears swimming in my eyes. "You'll help me?"

"Always. But not only me. You have legions of gargoyles with incredible skills behind you. That gargoyle you healed—Llion?—he was the King's armorer, wasn't he?"

"That's right."

"You'll need his help. And the new High Priestess Talia too. They tell me she has the power to use deep magic to protect gargoyles who are in danger. If you're thinking of heading back into Erawind, then she needs to be here in your place. How long until she and Llion get back?"

"I'm not sure, but with the babies, I'd say another day at least. That's if they don't run into any trouble."

He levels his eyes with mine. "Then we use that time to plan for war."

15

———

MARBELLA

We bury Cassian that night. Welsian found the perfect place—a clearing high behind the Royal Residence. It's surrounded on one side by trees but open on the other, allowing a full view of all of Erador and its vast mountains. Their custom is to conduct funerals at night under the moon. They don't lay ribbons over the coffin like elves do, but they do mourn in silence. Like elves, gargoyles believe there are no words to lessen the pain of losing someone.

A second coffin rests near Cassian's. It contains the former King's wing bones. Howl had kept the bones as an act of aggression after burning the King's body. The bones hum and buzz in my ears like they did in the mines, but now I recognize the sound as a trigger.

While I stand at the head of Cassian's coffin, my tiara glows as my Queen's heart responds to the King's bones, an ancient recognition of royal blood between them and me. It vibrates through me for a final moment before the sensation eases and the bones fall silent.

They conveyed one last message: I must protect the gargoyles.

Baelen stands one step behind me. He has been true to his promise to stay close but not in a way that invades my space. He spent most of the afternoon working with Arlo to reunite the remaining children with their families. I'm both sad and relieved

129

that only a few children remain who have no family left, but the Priestesses are mothering them. A handful of the gray-haired women cluster at the side of the clearing now. They remind me of my Storm Command, dressed in stormy gray dresses. They are older, grandmotherly women, but the air tingles around them: a remnant of the deep magic they once wielded. Talia is the only Priestess who can command it now.

All of the clan leaders are here too, including Senturi. There is no point trying to keep Senturi in the dark about Grayson Glory's threat, so I took him aside at a quiet moment and told him everything.

As I place my hand on Cassian's coffin where it's elevated on top of two rocks, I'm glad I don't have to speak. I can feel whatever I need to feel. Cassian was complicated. The first time I met him he was trying to capture Talia and he really didn't make a good impression on me. Then Cassian was sent to keep an eye on me in the mines. He certainly did that. But over time he changed—so slowly that I didn't notice until his transformation was complete. Then he was my friend and ally, a protective force in my life.

I clutch his bone lash, holding it close. Welsian retrieved it from the battle. He told me that it's my choice whether to keep it or bury it with Cassian: neither choice is wrong.

I clip it to my belt in front of the watching gargoyles. It's the only signal they need. Four, big gargoyles step forward to lower both coffins into the ground.

Then every other gargoyle in the clearing rises off the ground, soaring in a swarm high up above our heads. It's an imposing sight. The men's wings absorb the moon's light, darkening the sky, while the women's wings catch the light like diamonds. They swoop low over the coffins, one last flight for Cassian and the fallen King. Then they soar away into the night.

I wait quietly for the four gargoyles to finish their work. Then they, too, rise up and fly away.

Baelen wraps his arms around me and kisses the back of my head. He whispers, "You haven't told me what happened."

It's true. I haven't told him anything about Cassian. I start to speak and then I can't stop, the words tumbling out of me. I tell Baelen everything while his arms remain a comforting pressure around me. I can't hide from any of it, even though I'm afraid it could hurt him. I don't leave anything out, none of what Cassian said or did.

When all of the words have broken out of me, Baelen adjusts his arms around me, his gaze full of respect as he contemplates the fresh earth.

"He protected you when I couldn't," he says. "For that, I will always be grateful."

A breeze grows beneath my feet. Baelen's storm power springs into life, lifting me away from the graves. The growing wind plucks at my clothing. Other than the fight with the guards, he's barely used his power. A whole lot more of it simmers beneath the surface. He lifts me above the gravesite, carrying me far above Erador, so high that I imagine I can see the border on the distant horizon.

"This is your country," he says. "This is what you're protecting now."

Beneath us, a thousand cerulean-blue lights glitter, each one a gargoyle home.

His body heat increases to counteract the cold air, but I stop him. "Let me try."

I've been practicing using my Prime power, and it's time to test it out. I close my eyes and focus on the golden stone resting against my forehead, the opposite force to my Incorruptible power. Heat washes through me in a rush, from the top of my head to my toes, so fast I gasp. A pocket of warm air builds around me. In response, Baelen's grip relaxes, releasing me to float a little higher.

My eyes shoot open. "Don't drop me."

He laughs. "Never. Remember, I won't let you fall. But… Marbella… you're doing this on your own."

He's not holding me at all. I consider the force around myself, sensing the freezing temperature of the air outside my warm bubble—my Incorruptible power is making it colder out there, which in turn makes me float. "Well. Okay then."

He takes my hand and leads me down through the air. As we approach the ground, a lone figure beside Crimson Court catches my attention. I swerve in that direction, tugging Baelen's hand.

"That's Indira. But I don't see Erit."

"Do you want me to give you a minute?"

"Yes, thank you."

As I touch the ground, he kisses my forehead and disappears into the darkness. He won't go far, but he won't listen in. I cross the distance to the proud woman. "Indira."

The wind whips at her hair and coat as she stares into the distance. "Erit lied to me."

She turns to me, her eyes sparkling with surprising tears. "He told me that he made his bed wherever he found it, but the truth is that he built a home for me. He planned to come back for me, but Howl threw him in prison before he could. It's in a valley not far from here. It's beautiful there, Marbella. Just like a picture. Everything I could have dreamed of. Everything… that I could want to raise a family."

She presses both her hands flat against her stomach, tears dripping down her cheeks. The way she splays her fingers out across her body and what she said about raising a family make my eyes widen. "Are you…?"

"I am."

"But… you only… this morning and… it's only been hours… how can you tell so soon?"

She laughs out loud. "It only takes once." Then she shrugs, giving me a crazy-happy smile. "Gargoyle women know straight away. We only experience pregnancy one time, so we get to enjoy every minute of it. It's the last part that's hard: giving birth to twins with wings."

I shake my head in amazement. Elven women don't realize they're pregnant for weeks. Our cycles are six weeks long and there aren't any physical signs until our next cycle simply never shows up. I break into a grin. "Indira, that's amazing! I'm so happy for you!"

I throw my arms around her, surprising her with one, ginormous hug. But as soon as I let her go, fresh tears spill down her cheeks.

"I wanted to stay with Erit in that beautiful valley and have our babies and pretend that everything is fine." She levels her gaze with mine, her eyes glossy with tears that she wipes away. "But we both know things are only going to get worse."

I exhale a long breath. "Gretel told you about the threat."

"She slipped me a message before we left. I asked Erit to bring me here so I could speak with you about the future of the Grievous Clan. I didn't tell him the real reason. I won't say anything until you decide it's time."

She steps right into my space, her expression hardening. "Gargoyles have long feared retaliation for what the Storm did to the elves. Howl may have abused us, but the Elven Command will wipe us out."

"I won't let that happen, Indira."

She asks, "You have a plan?"

"I do, but it comes with risks. I won't make anyone come with me who doesn't want to."

"Go with you?" Her shoulders draw back. "You're taking the fight to the elves."

Is that admiration on her face? "I plan to."

"When do we leave?"

I laugh. She looks ready to come with me right away. "I'm waiting for Llion to get back because I need a weapon only he can make." Llion created the golden dagger that I used to sever the connection between Baelen and me. The dagger was coated in shimmer beetle husks—the toughest substance in our world, tougher even than a gargoyle's wing daggers. Llion is the only gargoyle skilled enough to make it for me. I need it so I can sever whatever connection Grayson Glory has with the Rath and Mercy Heartstones.

"Grievous Llion? I haven't seen him for many years. Other than Erit, he was the only respectful man in my life."

"You're cousins, right?"

She links her arm with mine. "Llion got away from our clan when we were kids. He made his way to the palace and convinced the King to employ him. We heard about it all the way back on Mount Grievous so my aunt and uncle couldn't claim that he had died."

We make it halfway to the Residence before we reach the spot where Baelen waits. He lifts himself away from a tree at the side of the path, but his forehead quickly creases, his jade-green eyes narrowing at Indira. "I know you."

She suddenly appears sheepish, tugging her coat a little closer around herself. She's taller than me, but still has to tip her head back to meet his eyes. "Greetings, Baelen Rath. Uh… I may have shot an arrow at you once."

"That *was* you."

She glances side-to-side as if looking for an escape route, her shoulders rising and her mouth drawing into a hopeful smile. "So, I guess… I'm sorry?"

"How about 'thank you.'"

She clears her throat. "That too."

I take glances between them. "What's going on?"

Baelen folds his arms, appearing very stern, but the crinkle at the corners of his eyes tells me he's trying not to smile. "Lady Indira was hunting shadow panthers in the wastelands one day. It happened that we were after the same one—a particularly bloodthirsty brute. It was creeping up behind her, but she saw *me*, not it. She shot an arrow at me."

Indira rushes to finish the story for him. "Only to watch this wild elf dive right past me, arrow and all, and rip the jaws off the shadow panther. Right before it would have made a meal of me."

He taps his upper arm. "I used to have the scar to prove it."

Indira gives Baelen another hopeful smile. "A mistake for which I hope I'm forgiven."

"Perhaps. Is that the panther's skin?"

Her fist flies to the skin she wears draped across her wings. Her eyes narrow into a challenge. "You can claim clan rights as loudly as you want, Baelen Rath. I'm not giving you this coat."

He laughs out loud. "I wouldn't dare ask for it."

For a moment, I wonder if the fact that Baelen has killed shadow panthers might be enough for him to claim some sort of status as a gargoyle, but unlike me, he doesn't have gargoyle blood.

Indira stares Baelen down for another moment before she becomes serious. "Speaking of shadow panthers, there's something that's bothering me about your encounter with one, Marbella."

It's my turn to challenge her. "It really did happen if that's what you're questioning."

"Not at all. My concern is more about the location. I'm assuming you weren't in the wastelands at that time."

"It was on Scepter Peak—that's on the border between Rath and Bounty land in Erawind."

Indira considers this information. "The problem is that shadow panthers only inhabit the wastelands. They venture onto Mount Grievous because it's closer to the wastelands than any other mountain. Our mountain allows the panthers to hide in the shadows and feed off animals in the forest."

I see where she's going with this. "So, it would be unusual for a shadow panther to find its way into the heart of Erawind."

She inclines her head. "Very."

Baelen is grim beside me. "There were more panthers there that night on Scepter Peak. I saw a couple in the distance, prowling the mountain range."

"How did they get there?" Indira asks. "Do you think Howl set them loose?"

I chew my lip, my thoughts churning. "The Elven Command promised Howl that they would kill all of the escaping gargoyles. They couldn't send in troops—although they did try that in the end. What if they sent in panthers instead?"

Baelen gives an unhappy nod. "Panthers crave gargoyle blood, so the animals would seek out hidden gargoyles for the kill. And leave pure-blooded elves alone."

Indira is equally concerned. "In which case we need to know: to what extent does the Elven Command control the predators around us?"

I shudder and reach for Baelen's hand.

Indira grimaces, but when she spots Erit waiting for her outside the Royal Residence in the distance, her focus changes. "On that happy note, if you'll excuse me, I need to meet the other clan leaders. *Stuffy old men.*" She strides away from us but throws a final word back at Baelen. "You look better without the beard."

Baelen's humor died with the first mention of the Elven Command. "Grayson Glory possessed a talon crow to attack you, Marbella. It's possible they've been using shadow panthers even longer than that. Maybe for years."

I survey our surroundings. "Why does it feel like the night has eyes?"

He's grim. "Because it might. From now on, we only talk in places we know are safe."

I sigh. "I wish Elise was here." She used to drop us into sound bubbles so nobody could hear our conversations. But something even worse occurs to me. "Llion and Liliana went to the border to get their children. What if there are more shadow panthers there?"

Baelen tries to reassure me. "They are both skilled warriors and they have Talia to protect them."

"I don't know… Llion was worried about the Elven Command's sorcery before he left. He wasn't certain that Talia's power could defeat it. After what I saw today with the talon crow—"

Something tugs at my back. It's quick and sharp, a pull so strong that I stumble backward, losing my footing. Baelen is fast to react, his hand tightening on mine and his other arm swooping around me, keeping me on my feet.

"Marbella? What just happened?"

A quick check behind me tells me there's nothing there. But I definitely felt something attached to my back. My frightened eyes meet Baelen's. "I don't know—"

My heartstones shriek a warning in my ears.

The powerful force tugs again, but this time, the pull is so strong that I fly backward, my feet wrenched out from under me, yanked right out of Baelen's arms. My stomach lurches and my surroundings blur with the speed of movement. I'm flying through the air before I know it.

Lightning shoots through Baelen as he harnesses his power in my defense, leaping after me, arms stretching, but he's already far away.

"Marbella—!" His alarmed shout cuts off.

Darkness closes around me, and everything goes black.

16

———

GRAYSON

I harness my power to travel long distances within moments, arriving at my destination within the Revenant Mountains before I can blink. The gargoyle Marbella protected during her marriage trials is nested here. There was a time I refused to attack him, but my options are limited now. He and his children are the leverage I need against her.

Putting away any guilt I feel about my intentions, I tread carefully between the cliff faces that form a walkway into the nest. It's a clever location, the entrance hidden from the eye due to the angle of the rocks. Pebbles are scattered along the walkway, a simple alarm system, but I harness my power to float above them.

My approach is whisper-quiet.

I stop at the entrance into the nest, reaching out with my senses to determine the location of its inhabitants. A soft blue glow from Elyria web radiates from the deeper part of the cave. I sense three adults located toward the back of the cave, not the single one I thought I'd find, but their number does not concern me. Gargoyles may be bloodthirsty creatures, monsters according to the Elven Command, but they don't concern me. I used talon crows to search Erador for signs of Marbella for a month and the gargoyles I saw during that time showed me that they're vicious creatures with little regard for each other. Granted, I only saw them from afar, but their rock-like bodies and their behavior toward each other confirmed my beliefs.

My intention is to capture the gargoyles in this nest, not kill them, but I won't hesitate to attack if it's a choice between them or me.

The front of the nest is an open area, empty for the moment, allowing me to creep inside.

A soft sound reaches my ears and I spin.

The most beautiful creature I've ever seen glides from inside the cave. She has the appearance of an elf but with rounded ears, and her wings… I catch my breath, mesmerized at the way her silver wings refract the moonlight, her long golden hair falling across her back between them. She has a perfect button nose, a rosebud mouth, and emerald eyes that are suddenly wide with fear and focused directly on me.

She's frozen like I am, her gaze passing from my eyes, to my lips, across the golden runes decorating my chest. I'm naked from the waist up, my shoulders and muscles so broad and bulky that I had to turn sideways to fit through the opening.

What is she?

She turns to face me fully and I finally see the baby she has propped on her hip. It's another creature just like her, a perfectly formed little girl with silver wings. *Surely, she can't be a female gargoyle?*

This can't be so. Female gargoyles are just like males, skin like rocks, bloodthirsty, ugly creatures.

This woman is too perfect for me to believe my eyes.

Fear quickly consumes her expression. "Who are you?"

"I'm here for the gargoyles." I jolt at the way she tore the truth from me.

Her lip curls. "You will not harm us."

The air ripples around her, a power I've never felt before, a power reminiscent of Marbella's but not the same. This is raw and consuming like moonlight streaming right into my bones.

It's a distraction.

I duck and roll, narrowly avoiding the giant fist aimed at me from the side. Now *this* is the kind of gargoyle I know. I pivot and blast my power outward, forcing him to leap away from me to avoid it.

The side of the cave explodes as my power hits it, pieces of the rock wall flying outward.

The male gargoyle doesn't waste time with words. His wing daggers descend one after the other, deadly attacks that I swerve to avoid. I harness my power again, this time casting a containment sphere around him—a large translucent bubble that lifts him above the ground. He shouts, slamming himself against it, but there's no way out. He has no idea the favor I just did him. He would have died if he touched me.

Another woman races forward, a baby boy in her arms, and a dagger in her fist. "You will not harm my children."

So this is the mother.

Unlike the first woman, I don't sense any magical power around this chestnut-haired woman. Her weapon hand shakes and her gaze darts to the child and back to me. The way she holds the weapon tells me she knows how to use it, but she must be afraid of fighting with her child in her arms. She would be equally afraid of putting him on the ground.

I take the burden of choice away from her. My power erupts, encasing her and her child in another containment sphere.

Then I turn to the woman with the golden hair.

"You will die for this, elf!" she says. This time her power is like darkness, sucking all light out of the cavern. It shoots through the air, taking on the form of a black spear. I don't understand the magic she's using. I have no way to know if it can kill me. I react on instinct, flinging my power out, smacking her against the rock face.

She hits her head and collapses.

The spear disintegrates.

Above us, the babies float safely in the air, unharmed. I ignore the gargoyles in the containment spheres to hurry toward the woman on the ground. They both press up against the sides of their spheres, their focus on the unconscious woman, their shouts inaudible from the outside.

With my back to them, I release the hold I have on my emotions, allowing my intense shame to wash through me. My power is too strong and the golden-haired woman is so delicate. I hit her too hard, much harder than I meant to.

Racing to her side, I quickly cast a spell around myself to protect her from my power so I can safely check her over.

Thank the ancients. Her pulse is steady and the cut on her head isn't life-threatening. My power tells me she doesn't have internal bleeding.

I was lucky. Her death would not have sat well with me.

My hand pauses on her cheek, wondering what her skin actually feels like, what it might be like to touch her without the protective barrier between us. If only I could. I gather her up in my arms and carefully form a third containment sphere around her, letting it lift her into the air.

My features harden as I remind myself why I'm here. I have my leverage now. She fought to save this gargoyle and his children once before. She will do it again.

It's time for the Storm Princess to answer for Gideon's murder.

It's time to force her to come to me.

17

MARBELLA

I hit the ground on hands and knees, thrown out of the force that transported me. It feels like my insides have been rearranged, everything moved so fast. I gasp air into my lungs as my surroundings become clear. I'm not outside the Residence anymore.

I'm lying on a cliff—a very familiar cliff. Two soaring cliff faces obscure a walkway that is only visible from an angle. This is where Llion's children were hidden: all the way across the border. Somehow, I've traveled hundreds of miles in seconds.

A smirking voice beside me says, "Every time we meet, you're on your hands and knees."

I scramble to my feet, twisting to face the speaker. A male elf towers over me only two paces away. He has platinum blond hair that is shaved short around the back and sides but is longer on top and jagged at the tips, which end above his pale-olive eyes. His face is almost angelic: perfect cheekbones, perfectly full lips, and a strong jaw to match. He stands naked to the waist, his sculpted chest tattooed with golden runes to enhance his power.

"Well met, Storm Princess. Or should I use the gargoyle salutation and say 'Greetings, Lady Storm?'"

I narrow my eyes at him. Only the gargoyles call me 'Lady Storm' and it worries me that he knows that. How many days, or even weeks, has he been spying on Erador through the eyes of predators?

He rests one hand on the scruff of a shadow panther. The beast is pure white, crumbling into dust as I watch. He must have drained the life out of it to bring me here. Three more shadow panthers sit obediently a step away, their silver eyes vacant of any natural instinct. I shudder as I realize that he has complete control over them.

"You're Grayson Glory." He's a lot more solidly built than Gideon was. Men in the House of Glory tend to be tall, slender, and lethal without the brute force of other houses like Valor and Bounty. Grayson is tall, but he's surprisingly bulky and well-muscled. Baelen and Jasper are the only other elves I've met with broad enough chests to rival a gargoyle's, but Grayson comes close.

I demand to know, "How did you bring me here?"

"The Mercy Heartstone knows you, Marbella, and now it obeys me. I can drag you to me whenever I want."

Oh, great. He thinks I'm his puppet. Well, he may have taken me by surprise this time, but I'm determined that it won't happen again. He must have access to the Mercy Heartstone right now, or he wouldn't be able to use that sort of power on me. But where is it? The bastard is half naked. He's certainly not wearing the heartstone in plain sight like Howl always did.

I retort, "Like hell you will."

"Why are you so unhappy, little—"

"Do not call me 'Doll!'" So far he's called me 'Lady Storm' like my friends and now 'Little Doll' like Howl used to. I take a step closer to Grayson, daring him to touch me. I may not be able to kill him or stop him from toying with my location, but I sure as anything can make his life miserable. Once he uses up the three panthers' lives, he'll be all out of death to sustain his sorcery.

I fill every angle of my body with threat as I say, "I killed the last man who called me that name. Come to think of it… feel free to call me whatever you want. I will kill you regardless."

At the same time as I step forward, I angle slightly to scan my surroundings. The cavity where Talia and the babies lived yawns empty on our left; the side of their home is nothing more than a jagged opening that looks like it was blasted apart. The rest of the cliff is shadowed and difficult to see. The moon definitely doesn't glow as brightly in Erawind as it does in gargoyle country.

At least my friends aren't here. I hope they were long gone before Grayson arrived.

My voice glides into the narrow space between us. "How about you send me back to Erador before I kill you?"

He tilts his head to the side, wipes the dust from the dead panther across his muscled thigh, and pins me in his frosty-calm gaze.

"You don't think you can break." It's his turn to narrow the gap between us, taking a step toward me. "Everyone has a breaking point. I will find yours."

I let his threat wash off me, edging nearer to him. His arrogance has allowed me this close. I just need to be a little closer. I drop my voice to a gentle whisper. "Why don't I find yours first."

He doesn't step away, standing his ground instead, a smile tugging at his mouth. "Feel free to try. You will fail like all the others."

His confidence is unsettling. So is his comment about others trying to break him. But I'm not letting this opportunity pass. He's too far away from the shadow panthers to draw on their lives to give him power to sustain his sorcery. Only his forced tether to the Mercy Heartstone will protect him now and it's time to see how strong that protection is.

My palm shoots out and connects with his chest. My power streams through it and I pour all my destructive thoughts into the contact. If there's a time that I want to destroy something, it's now.

Grayson jolts as the force shoots through him, burning light crackling across his shoulders, racing down his arms and legs. The runes on his chest light up golden, glaring brightly in the darkness. I pray for him to fall, collapse, die, *anything*. I remember Howl: how he'd screamed and burned and shattered. But Grayson remains standing.

His hand closes over mine, pressing it flat against his chest, imprisoning it there. It's almost as if he doesn't want the contact to end. His eyelids lower as he tugs me closer, chest-to-chest, only our arms between us. His other arm slips around my waist, palm resting lightly against my lower back as my power fades. "I think I'll call you Marbella. That suits you best."

I grit my teeth. His touch against my lower back presses and releases, his hand finding a spot to rest where his thumb can graze back and forth against the curve at the top of my hip: Baelen's favorite spot. I try to calm myself, pushing back against the strong desire to unleash everything I have against this man.

Since he seems happy to explain things to me, I ask, "Tell me how you're still standing right now."

Please don't tell me the Mercy Heartstone is this strong...

For the very first time, his expression loses its chill. A hint of anger glints in his eyes and his perfect lips transform as he growls, "Most elves need to kill a living creature to use sorcery. But I was born into death. It's in my bones. I've had this power from the day of my birth. Both my mother and twin sister died that day."

My Virtuous Heartstone flares in empathy but I shut it down. There will be no pity for this elf.

He continues. "It was her own fault. She wasn't built to carry twins. She should have known better than to have an affair with a gargoyle."

My eyes widen. "You're part gargoyle?"

That would definitely explain his larger physique.

"Except that, unlike others, my mother didn't keep it a secret," he replies. "I'm told she was proud of her love." He lowers his eyes to mine, his lips so close to me that his breath tickles my cheek. "You can imagine how I was treated growing up as a known half-caste."

Jasper is part-gargoyle too, but nobody knew about it and his grandmother never shared her secret. Senturi was right when he said that elves and gargoyles don't look kindly on gargoyles and elves falling in love with each other. Not every female elf who falls pregnant to a gargoyle will have twins—Jasper's grandmother didn't. Mixed race children take after their mother so it's easy to hide their heritage. Grayson's mother obviously didn't take advantage of that fact—maybe she didn't know and thought the truth would be revealed as soon as her children were born. Or maybe she didn't want to hide it. Either way, I *can* imagine growing up being mistreated. Every elven child in a minor House knows how it feels.

I say, "I'm surprised the Elven Command appointed you."

"I'm the second natural sorcerer ever born in our history. I convinced them I was their best chance at controlling you."

"Controlling?" I narrow my eyes. "Not killing?"

"Not yet."

My forehead creases, because something's not adding up. "But you killed the talon crow today and the panther just now. If you're a natural-born sorcerer, why did you have to do that?"

"The talon crow was a vessel—a means of speaking with you. It died because of its contact with my sorcery. And it's true: every death gives me more power. But the panther, on the other hand… I touched it to stop it from killing something else."

He steps back, positioning himself at my side, his arm remaining around my waist, a light touch that suddenly feels like a dead weight. The darkness lifts across the cliff. I'm horrified to discover that the shadows weren't natural after all, that it was a trick of the light—Grayson's trick.

Three translucent spheres float above the ground. They resemble giant, pearly globes. Two of them contain female gargoyles: one is Talia, lying on her side, unconscious. The other is Liliana, holding her babies close, her wings tucked around the little boy and girl while tears track down her cheeks. She sees me, gasps and calls out, but I can't hear her. The final sphere contains Llion who is a ball of rage. He slams his wing daggers against the sphere. They cut through and for a moment I think he's going to charge out of there, golden eyes blazing, but the sphere seals up as fast as he can cut it. His shout makes it out for a split second as he slits the sphere with both wing daggers and punches his fists against the side.

"Lady Storm! Run!"

Llion telling me to run is more frightening than Grayson's constant stroking of my hip or the suddenly growling shadow panthers.

"I'm told panthers crave gargoyle blood," Grayson murmurs. "That woman is bleeding."

Talia's forehead oozes. She must have fought back against

Grayson while Llion protected Liliana. Talia's deep magic can only be used in the protection of others; then she is incredibly powerful. But if my heartstone power can't defeat him, not even her deep magic could protect the others. Grayson would have taken her out first, then Llion, and last of all, Liliana.

Fear churns through me. "You told me I had a month."

"I said I'd give you a month before I started killing elves. I never said anything about gargoyles."

I try to wrench out of Grayson's hold. "You will not kill them!"

He smiles a challenge. His arm tightens around my waist, pulling me closer than before. "What will you do to protect them?"

"This, for starters." I spin, step behind him, and blast my power at the panthers.

Grayson jolts, surprising me by leaping away from me. He can't be afraid of my power because it did nothing to him before. Then why the sudden reaction? As my power blazes across the clearing, he turns so that he's facing me again.

Suddenly, it's clear that it's not the dying panthers or my power that worries him. The glimpse I caught of his back when I stepped out behind him tells me where the Mercy Heartstone is: broken into pieces and embedded in his skin all the way down the left side of his spine. What's worse, the Rath Heartstone has met the same fate—broken into pieces and embedded in a line down the other side of his spine.

The panthers' silver eyes and claws light up moments before my power strikes them and they crumble to dust. As the final beast dies, I snarl at Grayson. "If you didn't want me to see the stones, you should have worn a shirt."

His lips compress. He assesses the distance between us and doesn't seem to like it. For a moment, he seems to have forgotten my friends and I'll do anything to keep him distracted. Now that I know where the heartstones are, I need that golden knife to cut the tether Grayson has with them. If I have to slash the stones right out of his back, I will.

But first I need to get my friends away from Grayson as fast as I can. Then we can regroup, make the knife, and after that… we will become the hunters.

His jaw clenches. "I can't wear anything next to the stones. They burn whatever they touch."

I'm surprised. But maybe I shouldn't be. Baelen bound himself to me with the Rath Heartstone. My Mercy Heartstone was connected to me and the Storm. Together, they must burn likc ice, scorched earth, and acid rain combined.

I can't help it. I laugh out loud. "Then how do you sleep?"

He growls in response: an unhappy sound. It's the same sound that gargoyles make deep in their throats when they're upset about something.

I say, "I hear the gargoyle in you, Grayson Glory. You aren't part of the elven world. You are a gargoyle. Which means you answer to me."

He crouches a little, a defensive gesture. If he had wings, I'm sure he would tuck them around himself in a protective gesture right now. My assertion that I control him was a stab in the dark, a desperate call to the gargoyle inside of him, but it looks like I might have hit a nerve.

Again, he assesses the distance between us, taking a step to close it. His gaze darts to my hip and it suddenly dawns on me that I still have Cassian's bone lash. I never asked what the tip was made out of, but Roar once told me that the lash was strong enough to take a gargoyle's head off. I've never uscd one—I don't know how—but I wonder if it could be strong enough to shatter the pieces of the heartstones in Grayson's back and break the tether. I unhook it but I don't unravel it yet, watching for his reaction to determine whether he's worried about it. To my disappointment he ignores the lash, his focus traveling from my hip to my neck in one burning sweep.

His hand flexes.

My body tugs toward him against my will.

My eyes widen. "I will not be your puppet."

His hand flexes again. My power flares. I quickly reattach the lash to my belt, so I don't lose it. I fight the pull of Grayson's power, digging my heels in.

His eyes narrow. A purple glow emits around him, coming from his back. The Mercy Heartstone is working overtime trying to move me, but I refuse to budge. Golden light grows around me in response. It's Prime. It's my heart power. Of course. I've been trying to fight using my strength again, but Prime is my heart, the only power that could fight the pull of the Mercy heart.

Sweat breaks out on Grayson's forehead and chest. He growls, "Come here."

"There's that gargoyle again," I say, hoping I can rattle him even more. "And no, I won't."

He speaks through gritted teeth. "You will come here. If I can't control you, the Elven Command will seek to kill you. Is that what you want?" He actually looks like he cares. What on earth has changed since I tried to shoot my power through him? He's morphed from I-will-break-you-Grayson into I-don't-want-you-to-die-Grayson. What's going on with this man?

My head shoots up as lightning crackles in the distance. Thunder rumbles across the sky, a booming vibration approaching fast. It shakes the air around us: a sonic boom. I wobble backward, but my heart leaps.

It's Baelen. He's coming for me.

"The Storm is coming, Grayson. You won't be able to fight both of us. I suggest you get out of here while you can."

I have no idea if it's true that Baelen and I could defeat him. I'm only now figuring out which power to use against Grayson, and Baelen hasn't fought him before, but at the very least I need Grayson to doubt his ability to fight us both at once.

It looks very much like he does doubt himself. The tug that was pulling against my torso disappears. But his new target is worse. His hand shoots out and the sphere containing Liliana and the babies speeds toward him. Inside the sphere, Liliana jolts backward. I don't have to hear her to know she screamed.

Grayson shouts, "If I'm going, I'm taking her with me."

"No!" My heart-power bursts around me, giving me speed as I race toward him. But this time, I don't try to defeat his power or use mine against him. It wouldn't work anyway. Instead, I collide with him, using the force of my momentum to physically shove him aside, breaking his concentration.

Relief floods me as Liliana's sphere stops gliding toward Grayson. He loses his balance, slides sideways, but at the last moment, his satisfied eyes meet mine, and that's when I know I made a big mistake.

He grabs me. "I knew you'd come to me."

Lightning crackles behind me. A crimson storm wails down on the cliff and Baelen slams down onto the ledge so hard that cracks shatter along the cliff. He is full of rage, more than I've ever seen. His eyes meet mine, his lightning streaks across the distance between us, aimed at Grayson, but it's too late.

Grayson's heartbeat thuds against mine.

One beat.

Two beats.

His power flares. Then we're gone.

18

MARBELLA

Darkness and light speed past me. My stomach flip-flops and I squeeze my eyes closed, until finally the movement stops. I open my eyes to my new surroundings, finding myself inside the most opulent room I've ever seen. Multiple plush seats line the edges, along with an ornate desk and a large dining table, each leg carved in intricate designs and polished to gleaming. Every inch of the wall is covered in wallpaper inlaid with gold—actual gold if I'm not wrong—and the silken curtains are interwoven with gold filigree. The House of Glory controls land that is rich in gold and precious jewels, so I'm guessing that's where I've arrived. Even the gargoyle palace is no comparison to this place. The decadence makes me feel a little ill because elves in the minor Houses have nothing.

I shove Grayson away from me and he doesn't seem concerned about letting me go this time, spreading his arms wide. "Welcome to the House of Glory. Makes you sick, doesn't it?"

I inhale sharply. Is he reading my thoughts? I don't sense him poking around inside my mind. Either he isn't listening to my thoughts or he's very good at masking the mental invasion.

"Baelen will find me! You won't stand a chance against both of us."

Grayson remains calm. "Baelen Rath won't find you here. Nobody will. This entire house and its grounds are cloaked from

150

the outside world. It's impossible to detect by spellcasting, sorcery, deep magic, whatever you try. All anyone sees is a dense forest at the edge of Glory land."

He smiles, but there's no humor in it. An edge of threat bleeds back into the glint of power in his eyes. "This is your golden cage, Marbella."

I stalk around the room, using my study of our surroundings to buy time to consider my situation. Grayson Glory is a natural-born sorcerer, and that alone makes him a match for my power. But on top of that, he has tethered himself to my House's heartstone. Elven heartstones aren't weapons, so he can't use it to hurt me, but so far he has used it in surprising ways—like dragging me around with him. Importantly, he's using it to create a protective force around himself so it cancels out my strength. Worse, he's embedded the pieces of the heartstone into his body, making it nearly impossible to break the tether without cutting the stones out of him.

And if all of that wasn't bad enough, he's also tethered himself to the Rath Heartstone and embedded that too. The only positive is that Baelen's storm power isn't heartstone power, so the Rath Heartstone shouldn't be able to counteract it.

But if the Rath stone can't protect Grayson from the storm, then why has he tethered himself to it? What benefit does the Rath Heartstone give him? Especially since it's probably the main reason he can't sleep on his back at night.

Grayson watches my every movement as I pretend to study the furniture. "I had every intention of capturing you in a containment sphere like your gargoyle friends and bringing you straight to the prison."

My ears perk up at the mention of a prison—the grounds of a cloaked place like this would be ideal for the Elven Command to conceal my Storm Command. I may be desperate to find silver linings about my current situation, but if Elise and Reisha are imprisoned here, then I have to find out where and figure out a plan to get us all out.

I fold my arms across my chest and fake a casual tone. "But you brought me to this room instead. What changed your mind?"

He closes the distance at a prowl but takes his time, calculating each move, keeping it slow as he reaches for my hand, his palm closing around mine. I flinch backward, not because the contact hurt, rather because of the sheer fact that it doesn't. My arm is stiff —I'm deciding whether or not to fight back—but he patiently draws my palm toward his chest at the exact same angle that I shot my power into him earlier.

He explains, "You touched me."

I squeeze my eyes shut. "To kill you," I clarify, since he seems to need clarification right now.

His voice lowers to a soft growl. "But you touched me."

I crack open one eye, then the other, and enunciate each word just in case he didn't hear me the first time. "*To kill you.*"

His perfectly sculpted lips draw up into a smile, one corner hitched higher than the other, not quite in a smirk, but definitely in a silent challenge.

I take a deep breath, trying to remain patient. "Okay, then. Why is touching you so special?"

"Because nobody can."

I eye him with increasing alarm. Fear of the unknown shouldn't be a thing for me anymore but, well, it is. I purse my lips for a moment, trying to decide which question to ask first. Finally, I settle for the simplest one. "Why not?"

"Because I kill what I touch."

My focus flies to my palm, which remains resting against his chest. "I'm not dead."

"You are more powerful than anyone I've ever encountered. The fact that you're alive tells me that."

I have no idea how I'm supposed to respond to that. I'm still processing his revelation that I should be grateful to be alive. "If you kill everything you touch then how…? I've never heard of you. Not that I heard much… but nobody mentioned…"

"What you're trying to ask is why nobody knows about me?" He doesn't release me. His hand continues to rest over mine, pressing my palm against his skin. His touch softens but not enough that I can easily slide my hand away. "Like I said, this place is a cage. I grew up here. Gideon Glory took it upon himself to become my guardian. He created these grounds for me and kept my power a secret. Not hard because everyone who was at my birth died."

Grayson exhales a long breath. "He did try to give me a normal life. He used cloaking spells on me so that my touch wasn't always deadly. That was how I could be fed and cared for as a baby. I can create my own cloaking spells now, so that I can mingle with others, but everything I touch feels…"

"Wooden," I say for him. I'd lived for seven years not being allowed to touch anything. When I needed to train with my Storm Command in preparation for the marriage trials, Elise used a cloaking spell on me so I wouldn't hurt my ladies when I fought them. But touching them while I was cloaked was like touching wood. There was no life in that contact, no warmth or softness. I can't imagine a life of never knowing what another living creature feels like except to watch it die at my touch.

Grayson continues. "When I was older, Gideon sent me to Elven Academy. I pretended to be normal. But word got out about my mother and the fact that I was part gargoyle so… I didn't enjoy the academy very much."

I remember the boys in the major Houses pushing me around. But that was when I had no power to fight back. "You didn't use your gift against them?"

Surprise flickers in his eyes. "It's interesting that you call sorcery a gift."

"Sorcery gained through murder is an abomination—to kill others to make yourself powerful is nothing short of true evil—but to be born with it… You can choose what you do with it."

His hand strokes mine. "To answer your question: No. I didn't hurt them. A sorcerer's greatest power is secrecy." It's his turn to shrug, his broad shoulders lifting and falling, making his muscles tighten and relax beneath my palm. "Of course… if someone suddenly becomes ill and dies, it has nothing to do with me."

I shudder, but sudden anger flares inside me. "Did you create the curse that killed the last Storm Princess?" My beautiful friend, Mai Reverie, who was the Storm Princess before me, was killed by an intricate web of spells that had been made to look like the Storm. It was her death that gave the Elven Command the power they needed to create the curse that would force my husband to kill me. That curse died with Gideon Glory.

Grayson is unfazed by my accusation. "That wasn't me. I had nothing to do with you or Baelen Rath until I took Gideon's place on the Elven Command a month ago. Which is why I was surprised to discover that you are far from the ugly woman Gideon described to me." His gaze travels up to my tiara. He abruptly changes the subject. "The emerald stone flares more often than the others. Why is that?"

I'm wary of answering his question and giving him too much information about my heartstones, but it wouldn't take him much to find out the answer for himself. "That's Virtuous. She was a powerful healer and also very compassionate toward others. Empathetic. Kind. That is my power to heal and perceive other's feelings."

Grayson asks, "So it keeps you alive, but it also senses my emotions?"

If I was wary before, I'm even more so now. "Something like that."

The pressure of his palm over mine eases, becoming even softer than before, but not letting me go. As I consider whether it's time to fight myself free, he reaches for my other hand. Again, he keeps his movements unhurried, measured, watching me while I watch him. At the last moment, he snatches hold of my free wrist, an abrupt change of pace. His hand closes fully around my lower arm, wrapping his fingers and thumb across the delicate bones. His grip is firm, verging on painful.

He snarls, "Does it tell you what I'm feeling now?"

I don't need Senturi's Sight or even Virtuous to perceive Grayson's emotions. "Anger. Vengeance." I swallow. Oddly, I feel curious instead of afraid because there's a deeper emotion forming the foundation of his wrath: pain. "You're angry at me about something. Something that… hurt you."

I'm not sure what it could be. My inner voice quietly asks me a more important question: why haven't I pummeled this guy yet? What's stopping me? Is it Virtuous and all her empathy about Grayson's childhood? My healing power must be working overtime since Grayson hasn't stopped touching me, so it's probably messing with my emotions. Bethany warned me not to draw on Virtuous too much. I can't think why else I'd stand here and let Grayson grab me like this…

I stiffen, but it feels like an afterthought, something I do because

I'm supposed to. Why am I not more afraid right now? Why am I still standing here?

His lips part and his expression changes. So does his grip. He trails his thumb across the end of my sleeve, pushing the material down to expose the sensitive inner skin of my arm. He doesn't stop there, gently dragging his hand all the way back up to my wrist, lightly circling my skin with the pad of his thumb.

He leans in, angling his body toward me. "What about now?"

I shiver, confusion flooding me. For a moment it felt exactly like Baelen was touching me, not Grayson, right down to the soft scrape of Baelen's calloused palms.

I say, "Now you don't hate me at all."

He releases my other hand—the one that was pressed against his chest—running his fingers along that arm, stroking up to my shoulder, grazing his fingertips along my neck, brushing gently against my cheek, tucking my hair behind my ear, gently stroking my neck again…

Baelen's hands… Baelen's fingertips...

Sensation shoots through my spine and all the way to my toes, turning my bones into liquid. Confusion is a storm inside me as Grayson pulls me closer, much closer, guiding my hips to his, one hand caressing my lower back while his other—the one that was playing with my hair—lightly runs across my eyelashes.

"Close your eyes," he says. "Tell me what you feel."

I allow my eyelids to droop as he presses his palm across them, keeping them closed. His breath whispers across my cheek. His lips follow. I inhale and my head fills with Baelen's scent, the touch of his lips against the corner of my mouth, the press of his body against mine. All of this man pressed up against me. All of it is Baelen. My heart rate increases and so does my breathing. I can't control my body's response as need rages through me.

Grayson's exhale teases my bottom lip, not quite connecting but far too close. "Tell me."

I can only form one confused word. "Baelen."

I sense Grayson smile, but the sudden space between our lips is unbearable. Without thinking, I pull him closer to me, reaching for his shoulders. I want to kiss him. I want to press my lips against his, to drown in the taste of Baelen's mouth, losing myself to his touch, to his fingers tangling in my hair and the shivers racing down my spine.

Now my inner voice shouts, *Stop! He isn't Baelen.*

Grayson whispers, "What about now?"

I'm shaking. Shaking so hard. But I suddenly realize that I don't need to tell him. Grayson knows exactly what I'm feeling.

I wrench his hand away from my eyes so I can see him again. For a second—the smallest moment—his true reaction is open to me: he is watching my lips, and he is not in control. He leans toward me for a moment as if the sudden distance between us is painful.

Then a mask drops over his face, over his whole body. He is calculating and measured again. He assesses my reaction, studying my face.

I want nothing more than to hide my response, take back my hands gripping his shoulders, take back the way I pressed into him, stop it instantly, but it's not possible. Baelen's impact on me is a storm I can't control, what I feel for him goes beyond physical. It's emotional and mental and I can't turn that off cold, not like Grayson has. But what really scares me is not the way Grayson hides his emotions so quickly behind an aloof mask.

It's the crimson glow that fills the air around us, a glow that's coming from the Rath Heartstone in his back. What terrifies me is the fact that Grayson was drawing on the Rath Heartstone while he was holding me. Baelen used that stone to bind himself to me for life, promising to love, protect, and honor me until the end of time. Until his death. It contains every emotion of love, need, protectiveness, and worst of all, the soul-searing desire that Baelen feels for me and me alone.

It contains everything Grayson needs to control me.

19

———

MARBELLA

Now I know why Grayson embedded the Rath Heartstone in his body. I wrench backward and he lets me go. My legs are jelly. I stumble like a new foal, reaching for the nearest chair so I can drop into it. I grip the armrest, focus every bit of my rage into it, and stare at my hands as they slowly turn white.

I nearly kissed him, nearly betrayed everything I feel for Baelen. Angry tears burn behind my eyes, but I will not shed them. I will not let him see what his sorcery has done to me.

Grayson says nothing. Does nothing. Observing me with no emotion at all.

My voice is like sandpaper in my throat. "What happens now?"

"Now you stay here. With me."

"For how long?"

He doesn't move. He may as well be made of stone. "As long as it takes for the Elven Command to take control of Erador."

"Why do they want to attack the gargoyles? Is it for revenge because of what the Storm did?"

He replies, "The gargoyles have something we need."

"What is that?"

His only response is a quick shake of his head. He isn't going to tell me.

My accusation is bitter. "So, you're going to attack the gargoyles even though you already have me."

157

"I told you to prepare for war."

I gasp, growl, and laugh all at the same time. "You think it will be easy to conquer them. You have no idea what they are capable of."

He tilts his head with a curious expression, the first movement he's made. "I did not find the gargoyles on the cliff so hard to subdue."

I'm not ready to stand yet, but I will be soon. "Yes, but that was because of your natural sorcery. You won't be there for this fight."

His brow furrows. "What are you talking about? Of course I'll be there. I'm leading the battle."

I can finally stand, lifting myself up off the chair with all the poise I can manage, desperately trying to ignore my despair. Even Cassian was respectful of my body. He never tried to kiss me. *But Marbella*, I tell myself, *that was because he loved you.*

Tears burn behind my eyes again. "You won't be there, Grayson, because you'll be *here*, keeping me under control." I turn to the doorway. Point at it. "Without you, I'll simply walk out that door. There is no other elf powerful enough to stop me."

His eyebrows have risen. "I will place you in a containment sphere."

"Try it," I dare him. "Try it right now. Watch me destroy it."

With barely a gesture on his part, my feet lift off the ground and a transparent shield forms around me, dragging me upward. I press my hands against the front of it, demanding his attention. A blast of Incorruptible light shatters the globe around me in the next moment.

I drop gracefully to my feet and stride toward him, well and truly in control of my legs now. Diamond light shines around me as my Incorruptible power continues to respond to my anger. "Put me behind bars, inside a spelled prison, and wrap it up with as much magic as you can. It won't matter. I'll get out."

I'm close enough to jab his chest, the same chest I pressed up against moments before. "The only thing keeping me here is you. *Your* body. Once you're gone, I'm gone. Good luck to the elves fighting a battle against the gargoyles without you."

He contemplates me with the first sign of real emotion. It's odd to see him fixate on the finger I jabbed him with. I see again the moment of emotion he couldn't hide when I first opened my eyes after he held me just now. I remember the sensory overload I felt when I discovered I was able to touch people after seven years of keeping my distance. I jab his chest again and press my finger there. It's a stupid move, but if he's going to control me, I'll fight back with everything I can, including the knowledge that touch isn't something he's used to.

I say, "I'm tired and hungry and I'm assuming you don't want me to starve. So where is the food?"

What I want more than anything is to see what's outside this room—to get a feel for the layout of the house and where the prison might be.

He snatches a glance at my finger. Then, without warning, he sweeps it up to his mouth and catches the end of it between his teeth, closing his lips around it. The air glows crimson again and delicious warmth shoots through me as he kisses my skin. *Baelen's kisses.* "I'm hungry too," he murmurs.

I drag my finger free with all my might, my heart sinking at just how badly that went.

He lets me go with a laugh that sounds oddly genuine. "If you're going to play that game, be prepared to lose."

"Got it." I clear my throat, burying my finger inside my curled-up fist. I step away from him, knowing that from now on, I need to keep as much distance between us as I can. I wasn't lying though. I'm hungry and tired. I was on my way to dinner right before Grayson snatched me from outside the Royal Residence. It was right after I buried Cassian. Right after Indira admitted to me how much she wanted to stay in her beautiful valley with Erit and never face what was coming. Right after Baelen lost it when he saw me covered in blood.

My shoulders slump. Too much happened today. Time is my enemy. The elven army is about to attack the gargoyles for reasons that Grayson won't tell me. It can't be as simple as revenge, or he would have said so. But the gargoyles aren't ready. Half the army was killed in the battle with the miners and most of the strongest men who were thrown into the mines are still recovering from imprisonment. They aren't prepared for an attack, and that's on me. I chose not to warn them. It's my fault and now I have to make it right. I need to buy time.

I turn back to Grayson. "If I promise to stay here while you go to battle, will you wait the month you promised?"

He is surprised. "Why would you do that?"

"Because it will give the gargoyles time to evacuate their children from the battle zone." I glare at him. "There are villages close to the border, Grayson. Peaceful villages with families and little children. Families who have only just found each other after years of…" I curl my hands into fists, swallowing hard against the emotions rising inside of me. They are families I have just reunited. I won't let them be torn apart again.

"I will not allow children to die," I say. "If you want a battle, then let it be a fair fight between armies. Not a slaughter of peaceful villagers."

The furrow in his brow deepens. Emotions flicker across his face: surprise, distrust, deep thought. "It will be a slaughter if I'm there, Marbella, and that's what you're guaranteeing."

"You're forgetting Baelen."

"Ah." He grants me an acknowledging nod. It looks like he's going to take me at my word that I'll stay put, because he says, "Then a battle between armies it is. I will give your gargoyles a month. By now they will know about your disappearance, so I will send a messenger to the border stating our terms."

"Thank you." It's a small victory but it gives me what I need: time. Time to locate Elise, Reisha, and my Storm Command. Time for the gargoyles to prepare.

Grayson strides to the door located on the opposite wall. Opening it, he gestures me inside. It's a bedroom, equally opulent with a large four-poster bed draped in golden pillows and covered in a silken bed cover. Of course, there's only one bed.

He points to a door at the side and then to various spots within the room. "Bathroom. Bed. Obviously, I can't sleep in it, so you have nothing to worry about. Also, the bathroom has no openings to the outside, so I have no concerns about leaving you alone in there."

I ask, "What's to say I won't blast a hole in the side and walk out?"

"You could. But then our deal would be off. Our army is ready to attack whenever we give the word. I don't think you want that to happen."

I make a straight line for the bathroom, craving space.

"Stop."

I freeze.

He strides to the closet and pulls out a towel and a dressing gown. "You can sleep in this tonight. Tomorrow I will arrange clothing for you."

I gather the items into my arms. I've been sleeping in unfamiliar clothing for a long time now. I've forgotten what it's like to have my own clothes. This is my new normal.

Once inside the bathroom, I close the door behind me, listening as Grayson's footsteps recede on the marbled floor. I'm halfway through showering before everything that happened today hits me. Then I curl down into a ball, letting the water beat down on me.

Baelen.

I want to scream his name. I want to blast this entire building into shreds. But I can't beat Grayson. I have to play within his rules. I thump my fist against the bathroom tiles. All of my heartstones glow at once. They are trying to help me—to give me strength and heart, to help me think and help me heal—but it's all too much. I crawl out of the shower and drag a towel around myself, drying my body before pulling on the dressing gown. I release my hair from its braid, letting it fall to my waist. Then I stagger to my feet, preparing myself to find Grayson waiting for me outside. The lamps have been dimmed but he's nowhere to be seen. Filled with relief, I slip into the bed and pull the covers up to my neck. I ignore my empty stomach—I've gone longer without food before.

Somehow, I manage to fall asleep.

20

———

GRAYSON

Marbella Mercy lies sleeping in my bed while I pace my cage. Even as an Elven Commander, I'm not free to come and go without the other Commanders' permission.

My pacing carries me to her bedside.

Touch. It seems like the simplest thing but carries so much power. Touch can be kind or cruel, but the absence of touch is the cruelest of all. My power to kill everything I come into contact with means I've never experienced simple connection before. Even when I kill, my target's life is gone, that living spark void.

Suddenly, I'm drowning in need for all the touch I've missed.

Nothing prepared me for what it would feel like to connect with another elf, skin on skin, let alone an elf with so much power coursing through her body and mind. A power like my own.

The splintered Rath stones burn against my spine, making me ache with a need, physical and emotional, that threatens to consume me. Marbella tried to rebel against me—she jabbed her finger at me—and all I wanted was more. I would have welcomed her hitting me if it meant she touched me again. When she almost kissed me, it was enough to make me lose control. I could have used the Rath stone to make her sleep with me and she would have come to my bed willingly.

But I couldn't. Because it's a lie.

Touch without honesty. I never realized how important that would be.

The door to my quarters bursts open in the other room and I hurry out there. Elwyn Elder's hunched form barges in, his robes flapping around him.

"Where is she?"

I was supposed to take Marbella to the prison. I'd even intended on killing her on the spot, which is why I allowed her to touch me in the first place. But now, everything has changed.

I step between him and the bedroom door, a physical barrier in case he thinks he's going to barge in there. "She's inside."

Elwyn shouts, "You were supposed to take her to the prison!"

I sense the temporary sorcery inside him. He killed a living creature before he came here, which tells me he's intent on taking Marbella away. Rage flows through me, powered by that damn Rath Heartstone, but this time I agree with it. "Do not question me, Elwyn!"

My power blasts out from me, propelling Elwyn back through the air. He thuds against the wall so hard, he dints it. I advance on him, using my power to push him against the wall and pin him there.

His face reddens with anger. "You let her touch you, didn't you?"

I push harder, hoping his ribs will crack. He can use his sorcery to heal himself and then it will be consumed and he will have to leave.

Elwyn shakes his head at me. "I told you not to touch her."

I growl. "You told me nobody could. You told me that even Marbella Mercy would die at my touch. Well, she didn't!" My voice lowers. "What other lies have you told me?"

I'm satisfied to sense his ribs break, three of them popping under the force of my power. Finally.

"Noth-Nothing," he stammers, gasping for breath. I ease up enough to allow him to heal himself, waiting as his sorcery drains away. Having been forced to use up his power, his tone becomes disappointed, placating, nearly pleading. "Grayson, don't lose sight of our goal. She's a distraction you don't need."

I release him, allowing him to finish healing and stretch out his aching muscles.

"She's more than a distraction," I say.

He scowls. "What are you talking about?"

I hate admitting the truth. "She's the only woman I can ever…"

Elwyn's eyes widen. "Wake up to yourself. She belongs to Baelen Rath. If you want a woman, then cloak yourself and go get one. Get three for all I care. That woman in there will never bed you willingly."

I fold my arms across my chest. As always, he misinterprets my meaning. He assumes I have the same priorities that he does: power and pleasure at the expense of everything else.

He doesn't realize that what I mean is that she's the only woman I could have children with. Cloaking myself during sex is an instant contraceptive.

I want to know what it's like to hold my own child in my arms like the golden-haired woman held the child at the nest. I want to give them the childhood I never had, to make sure they're never ashamed of their heritage, that they know who they are and take pride in what they can achieve. My gargoyle father gave me height and powerful muscles. He gave me physical advantage over other elves. I could rival Baelen Rath in a fight—and yet I am jeered at, hated, and feared. I want that to change.

There's no point in trying to make Elwyn understand. I change the subject. "I've sent a messenger to the border to tell the gargoyles they have a month to surrender. I've told them we have their Queen." I glower at Elwyn, wanting him gone. "Now get out."

Elwyn curses beneath his breath before he whirls to the door. "You'd better know what you're doing, Grayson."

"I do. Don't worry."

The door closes and I stare at it.

I lied. I don't know what I'm doing. This morning, I did. This morning, I had a plan. Now, my intentions are confused. I want things I can't have. I want to change things I can't change. All that does is make me angry.

21

MARBELLA

I awake to loud voices outside the bedroom. The door is open and it's easy to see through to the living area where two men argue. I stay where I am, feigning sleep.

The newcomer is Elwyn Elder. He appears more hunched than the last time I saw him at Howl's banquet. His face is red with anger. "Where is she?"

Grayson steps between Elwyn and the bedroom door, fists clenched. "She's inside."

Elwyn blusters. "You were supposed to take her to the prison!"

"Do not question me!" Grayson's arm shoots out at Elwyn. Suddenly Elwyn is propelled backward, his robes flapping around him as he flies through the air. He thuds up against the opposite wall, pinned there, wincing.

Grayson advances on him, threat hanging between them. If Grayson is the second natural-born sorcerer in our history, then I don't think Elwyn Elder is the first. Elwyn has nothing to kill to fight back against Grayson, but he must have some residual power because he manages to slide to the ground and take a step, pushing into the force around him.

Elwyn snarls, "You let her touch you, didn't you?"

Grayson growls and pushes harder.

Elwyn shakes his head in disapproval, a slow movement against the force of Grayson's power. "I warned you not to let her touch you."

"You told me nobody could. You told me that even the most powerful Gargoyle Queen this world has ever known couldn't touch me and remain alive. Well, she can!" His voice lowers. "What other lies have you told me?"

"Noth-nothing," Elwyn stammers, shaken for the first time. He raises a placating hand, pushing through what must be a suffocating force. "Grayson, don't lose sight of what we want. What we *all* want. She is a distraction you don't need."

Grayson releases Elwyn and the older elf coughs and hunches, shaking out his shoulders and rubbing his neck.

Grayson says, "She's more than that."

"What are you talking about?"

Grayson grinds his teeth. "She's the only woman I can ever…"

Elwyn's eyes shoot so wide it looks like they're going to pop out of his head. "Wake up to yourself. She belongs to Baelen Rath. If you want a woman then cloak yourself and go get one. Get three for all I care. That woman in there…" He points his bony finger in an accusation. "She will never bed you willingly."

Grayson folds his arms across his chest. The golden runes that decorate his muscles gleam in the dim light. He doesn't respond to Elwyn's assertion, changing the subject instead. He's good at doing that when he doesn't like where the conversation is going. "I've sent a messenger to the border to tell the gargoyles they have a month to surrender, or we go to war. I've told them that we have their Queen, and we aren't giving her back." He takes a step toward Elwyn who maintains a healthy distance between them. "Now get out."

Elwyn shakes his fist at Grayson before whirling to the door. "You'd better know what you're doing, Grayson. We need access to the deep springs, and we need it soon. Erador must fall within a month."

"It will. Don't worry."

As soon as Elwyn leaves, Grayson spins on his heel and strides toward the bedroom, heading straight for me. "Don't pretend to be asleep. Nobody could sleep through that." I can't see his expression very well in the dark, but his voice softens. "No matter how tired they are."

I make sure the dressing gown is closed before I sit up. "If you need access to the deep springs, then why don't you ask permission to use it? If somebody's sick—"

He laughs. "We don't want to use it, Marbella. We want to destroy it."

I scoot away from him. "What? Why?"

He doesn't respond. He's a master at not responding. Instead he leans across me, forcing me to press myself flat against the wall to avoid his chest brushing up against mine. He takes the pillow from the other side of the bed along with the spare blanket, pausing to drop a kiss on my cheek, far too close to the corner of my mouth, before he straightens.

I jolt backward, but he has already relocated himself across the floor, choosing a spot between the bed and the bathroom to lay down on his blanket. That way I'll have to step over him in the morning if I want to use the facilities. He'll know if I wake up before him. Every move he makes is calculated. So is the seemingly random kiss on my cheek—a brand of ownership. He pummels his pillow and lies facing me, closing his eyes.

I squeeze my hands into fists. "I need you to stop taking liberties."

His eyes remain closed. "Why?"

"Because my heart is not yours."

A chill enters the room. "I'm well aware of that."

He says nothing more, and I skate back under the covers. Just as I'm about to drop back to sleep, his whisper reaches me. "Be warned, Marbella. I'm determined to get what I want."

22

———

BAELEN

I alight on the pebbled courtyard at the front of the Rath mansion. I don't have time to go inside and see my childhood home or to speak with the elves inside it. I stride forward to the elven messenger being held at sword-point in the courtyard.

Macsen gives me a grim acknowledgement, his sword at the elf's throat. Two other Mercy elves stand at the intruder's back and his other side. They're both ready to kill the intruder if he moves the wrong way.

Last night, I transported Llion, Liliana, and Talia back to the safety of the palace. Then I told them that I was going to tear Erawind apart, find Grayson Glory, and kill him. It was only because Roar, Llion, and Welsian physically restrained me that I didn't. My jaw still hurts from the punch Roar landed on my cheekbone. But it was Senturi who really stopped me. He told me that raging into Erawind would get me nowhere. I had to make a plan and ask every gargoyle to be a part of it. The elves have stolen the Gargoyle Queen. This is bigger than me now.

We spent the night planning until early this morning when a gargoyle flew in, exhausted, to tell me that an elven messenger waited at the border with information about Marbella. It took me minutes to arrive here.

I haven't seen Macsen for a month. I need to speak with him,

168

but neither of us greets the other. There's no time and our friendship doesn't require pleasantries.

Crimson lightning crackles around my torso as I take threatening steps toward the messenger.

Gannon Glory kneels on the pebbles, his head raised in defiance. As soon as he sees me, he shouts, "I have a message for you, Baelen Rath. Once I give it, you will let me go unharmed."

He waits for my agreement.

I would like nothing more than to kill him on the spot, but I restrain myself. "Speak."

"I bring a message from Grayson Glory, the Elven Commander. He says to tell you that the gargoyles must surrender in a month or our countries will go to war. We have your Queen and we will not give her back."

My response is a guttural snarl. "Like hell you won't." I bend to grip his face in my hands. "Where is she being held?"

"In Grayson Glory's personal quarters. You will never find her. His home is concealed from everyone." Gannon smirks. "Grayson seems to have taken a liking to her. Don't expect Marbella to remain untouched. He has the power to take whatever he wants." Gannon grins harder, a crazy grin. "As often as he wants."

My hand tightens around Gannon's jaw. All it will take is a twist to rip his head off, but I need him alive. "You will take a counteroffer back to Grayson Glory: the gargoyle army will attack Erawind whenever the hell we want. We are ready to decimate your corrupt Command and raze your bloated cities to the ground. *Unless* you allow me to see Marbella within the week. If you do that, then we will give *you* a month to prepare."

His jaw drops. He clearly wasn't expecting us to come out swinging. "I will deliver the message."

"You will also give Grayson a personal message from me: If he hurts Marbella in any way, he will answer to me."

Gannon's mouth snaps shut. He presses his lips together, then releases them. For the first time, he sounds afraid. "You have no idea how deadly Grayson Glory is. You don't understand what he can do. We are afraid of him. You should be too."

I shake my head. I met Grayson Glory twice. At the first

meeting, he told me I would walk again. Then, on the night of the first trial for Marbella's hand, he confirmed that he lived in a cage. I had cautiously considered the possibility of making him an ally.

Something has changed since then. Something has made him want to become my enemy when we weren't enemies before, and it feels personal, more than elves hating gargoyles. More than stealing the Gargoyle Queen to anger the gargoyle race.

He wants Marbella, but why?

I don't doubt for a second that Gannon's intense fear of Grayson is real and now my own is rising, but I clamp down on it, suffocating it with anger.

"Howl was feared," I say. "That didn't make him immortal. Neither is Grayson."

I step back, signaling to Macsen to release Gannon. The lanky elf rises, stamping feeling back into his feet. He hurries to the griffin that waits at the edge of the courtyard to fly him away. The phoenix is already circling above us within the cloud cover, ready to follow the griffin wherever it goes. My hope is that Gannon will lead us straight to Marbella. As soon as we know where she is, we'll attack.

After Gannon takes to the air, Macsen approaches me, his steps heavy. He grips my shoulder. "Brother, we will find her."

I sense Roar approach too. I brought him with me—a very unpleasant trip for him because of the speed I traveled. He's still rubbing the feeling back into his cheeks from the force of the wind that churned around him. He grips my other shoulder in his enormous fist.

The two halves of my life are represented in this gathering. Elves and gargoyles. My two loyalties.

I clench my fists, fighting the sense of powerlessness that's invading every part of my mind and body. I try to take strength from the friends standing with me, but I can't pretend, not in front of them. I trust them with my truest thoughts. There was a time when my brief meetings with Grayson—my instincts about the kind of elf he is—led me to believe he was honorable, but now I can't be sure.

My chest rises and falls, the weight inside me threatening to crack me apart. "What if she's hurt? What if he forces her? What if she can't fight back?"

Their hands tighten, supporting me. Macsen's determined eyes meet mine. "She's strong, Baelen."

Pure desperation beats through me. In all this time, I've never felt so afraid for her. Even when Howl sent her to the mines, there were rules governing her captivity. Howl's motivations were clear: he wanted power. It was in his best interest to keep Marbella alive. But Grayson is unpredictable and his true intentions are unknown.

I clench my jaw so hard, I nearly crack my teeth. "I promised to protect her."

Roar circles me, his wings held at a warrior's angle, fierce. "I know what you feel, Baelen Rath. I know powerlessness. Marbella gave me back my power. It's because of her that I'm alive now. Our brother is right. She's strong."

Macsen's eyes widen and then soften. Roar just called him a brother, even though they've never met before. It's a sign of Roar's respect for Marbella that her brother is now his.

Roar continues, his voice stern. "No matter what happens, no matter what she goes through, it doesn't change her worth. You must make sure *you* are worthy of her."

I take a deep breath, fighting my every instinct to take to the sky and rain hellfire on the elves. I'm responsible for the safety of the gargoyle nation now—I am their voice. Marbella has given them her heart and soul. They are her people. When she returns—and I am determined that she will—I will make sure she returns to an army that is ready to fight and a people who have not lost their faith.

I nod. "I will prove my worth to her."

"In the meantime, we'll prepare for war." Without letting me go, Roar gives Macsen a polite nod. "Greetings, brother of Supreme Incorruptible Marbella Mercy. I am Sunflight Roar."

Macsen replies. "Well met, Sunflight Roar. You are not alone in your fight." His eyes meet mine. "It's time for you to meet your elven army, Baelen."

Behind me, elves spill out from inside the mansion. So many elves. At their head are Sebastian Splendor and Eli Elder. They tap their fists to their chests in a gesture of respect.

Still, the elves keep filing from the building, a hundred, maybe more.

Macsen gives me a deadly grin. "We're ready to fight."

23

MARBELLA

For the next three days, Grayson is true to his word: I stay in the room with him. He doesn't leave me alone except when I go to the bathroom. Instead, others come to us. Elves in the minor House of Verity serve the House of Glory and bring us food five times each day. Seamstresses arrive on the first morning to take my measurements. The furthest Grayson moves away is to stand in the doorway, which isn't far enough for me to see what's outside this room. When I push back the curtains at one point, I discover that they're false: there is nothing but a solid wall behind them.

Over the course of the three days, each member of the Elven Command comes to see Grayson. Pedr Bounty and Osian Valor are as frosty toward me as they always were. But the new Commander from the House of Splendor—the one who replaced Teilo—is a surprise.

The servant at the door announces, "Lord Grayson, Elven Commander Priscilla Splendor is here to see you."

There's never been a woman in the Elven Command before. Let alone one as young as me. She glides into the room, tall and lithe, her neck like a swan's, and long legs to match Elyria's. She takes one look at me and plots a path straight for Grayson, asking him outright, "Are you cloaked?"

He puts away the map he was studying and rises from his seat. "For you, always."

She plants both hands possessively on his chest, lifts up on her toes, and kisses him in a way that makes her message very clear: he belongs to her.

I smother a sigh. Does she really think it will bother me?

Still… it's a pity her eyes are closed, and she doesn't see his face. For him, kissing while cloaked would be like kissing a plank of timber. He wouldn't have known any difference before, but unfortunately for me, now he knows what connecting with someone's skin really feels like. She definitely tries her best though, and after a beat where he glances across the room at me, he commits to her gesture, kissing her back.

I rise from my chair and head for the bedroom to give them space. Then I wonder if that's a bad idea because they could be headed there themselves. Then I second-guess myself because Grayson doesn't go near the bed so maybe it's the best escape after all. I stop and start again, but I don't make it two steps before his power tugs me to a halt.

"Stay where you are, Marbella."

I remain facing away from him. If he's broken their kiss to deal with me, then Priscilla will be fuming right about now. "Thank you, but no," I say without turning back. "I'd rather leave you to your business."

My Prime power flares, allowing me to take another two steps before his presence behind me is like a burning wall of flame. I sense him close the gap between us, and then he grabs my arm and spins me around. "You will stay where I can see you."

I whisper in response, "You can't see much with your eyes closed, Grayson."

His glare would make anyone cower, but I really don't need to watch his girlfriend play tongues with him. So, I stand my ground. His fiery scowl suddenly breaks. He actually laughs.

I suddenly realize that despite all the emotions he fakes or masks, his laughter is always real.

"You're right," he says, grinning at me. "I guess I'd better start kissing with my eyes open."

Ugh. Not the outcome I wanted. And definitely not what she wants either. She's murdering me with a glare right now. She adjusts her body language before he turns back to her, giving him a sickly-sweet smile as if anything he wants is fine with her.

Before she can speak, a loud knock sounds at the door and a voice calls. "A message from the gargoyles, Lord Grayson."

My skin is suddenly cold. I have no idea how my people will respond to Grayson's threats.

Grayson stalks to the door and takes the scroll while the messenger bows and waits for his response. A crease forms in Grayson's forehead as he reads. He brings the message to me. "It seems you were right about your people's courage. They've responded with a counteroffer. They will meet the elven army in battle in a month's time, but they won't promise not to attack sooner unless Baelen Rath is allowed to speak with you within the next week."

My heart leaps. The thought of seeing Baelen gives me hope.

Grayson paces the floor, the scroll held loosely in his fist as he considers his decision. Priscilla reaches for the parchment, and he hands it over.

"Let him see her," she says, placing the message firmly on the table. She presses up against him, rubbing his arms in a soothing gesture. "You need to know how to break Baelen Rath in battle, but you won't figure it out unless you meet him and test him." She looks pointedly at me. It's clear they both believe that I will be Baelen's tipping point.

"All right. We will allow Baelen Rath to see Marbella." His lips curve into a slow smile. "But not alone. We will host a celebration in the arena in the heart of Erawind in five days. Marbella will be there. He may bring one gargoyle with him. If he wants to see her, those are the terms."

The arena is where the Heartstone Ceremony was held. It was also where the Elven Command tried to kill Baelen.

I ask, "What exactly are we celebrating?"

He replies, "Your capture."

Priscilla smirks. She kisses Grayson again before exiting the room. "Time for me to get a new dress."

AFTER ANOTHER TWO DAYS OF BEING COOPED UP IN THE BEDROOM, I'm going stir crazy. Even Grayson glances at the fake windows as if he'd rather be outside. On the morning of my sixth day in captivity, still two days before I will see Baelen, I stop Grayson outside the bathroom. Despite his decision not to take his eyes off me, he hasn't given up his own privacy while he showers. He makes up for it by tugging on my body constantly while he's in there, promising me that if I fight it, he will come straight out no matter how undressed he is.

He jolts to find me right outside, but I plow right on with my request. "You have to let me go outside."

"Why?"

"Because I need to see the sun."

"Why?"

Ooh, he's infuriating. I really want to find out where the prison is, but I'm not lying: I need fresh air. Desperately. I try to remain patient. "Because I've been breathing the same air for six days now."

He laughs and tugs my braid over my shoulder. His fingers linger on my shoulder. "You're so pretty when you're all riled up."

I scowl at him, standing my ground. Every morning when he gets up, he puts his pillow and blanket back on the bed, and every night he leans across me to get them—even though he could easily walk around to the other side. Each time he drops a kiss on my cheek and each time, it's closer to my mouth. Last night it was on the corner of my lips.

He smirks. "Fine. After breakfast. There's something I want to show you anyway."

It's still two days until the "celebration of my capture" and Grayson seems remarkably relaxed today. I plow through my meal and wait at the door while he finishes his breakfast. He takes his time, deliberately making me wait for him. Finally, he pushes his chair back.

The door opens without him moving from his seat, but he's not far behind me as I lean into the hallway outside.

"Follow me," he says.

We pass a number of rooms, many of them large, all of them opulent, until we finally leave the building through the back door, heading down a path through immaculate gardens. I veer to the right in the direction of the other buildings. I need to get a look at them to figure out which is the prison.

"Not that way," Grayson says, to my disappointment, pointing to a copse of trees at the end of the path. "This way."

The pathway ends, turning into a rough, leaf-strewn track. The forest is dark and dank compared to the open garden, but he strides right into it. I pause. It's one thing to stay with him in a brightly lit room. It's another to follow him into a dark forest.

I say, "I thought we could walk around the garden." So far I've seen nothing that tells me where the prison might be.

"You thought wrong." He's far enough inside the shadowed woods that his body is a mere silhouette. He tugs on me with his power, making me take a step before I harness my own power to stop him.

He sighs. "I promise I won't hurt you. I just want to show you something."

Said the psycho to his prey.

"Fine, but just because I can't hurt you personally, doesn't mean I can't burn this forest to the ground if I need to," I warn him.

"Noted."

I catch up to him and there's just enough room to walk side by side along the track. I point out: "You know you're walking in the dark."

"So?"

"That's a gargoyle trait. Your eyesight is primed for moonlit nights. Elves need lamps."

It's his turn to be exasperated. "You don't give up, do you?"

I allow myself to smile. "How many gargoyles have you actually met?"

"Uh." He must not realize I can see as well as he can in the dark because he doesn't hide his expression. He looks uncomfortable. "Just the ones on the cliff the other day, and many from a distance, but I've seen plenty of drawings."

I scoff. "Oh, you've seen drawings. The ones the Elven

Command commissioned? Well, then, I guess you've met lots of gargoyles. Were you surprised to discover the women don't look like hideous beasts?"

He shuffles again. "A little."

I say, bluntly, "Female gargoyles are more beautiful than female elves. But not just on the outside. They have truly beautiful souls. It's why the men are so protective of their families. They would die for them."

My emotions are getting away from me. I try to reel them in. "The woman you tried to take with you was Llion's wife, Liliana. She was holding their two babies—the only babies she will ever have. Howl ripped their family apart. She hadn't seen her babies for a year, and then you tried to kill them."

I stop talking because I have to suppress my feelings. I feel like I'm talking to a brick wall. He doesn't want to know about the gargoyles. He has a picture of them in his mind, and they are nothing more than beasts to him. They are the reason he was ridiculed when he was a boy.

Grayson is quiet for a time. Our boots crunch in the leafy carpet, and the air grows colder the deeper we travel into the forest. Then he says, "I didn't meet Howl."

"Howl was just like the drawings, but worse."

"You did us a favor when you killed him." He pulls me to a sudden stop, his grip warm, but firm. "Your mercy is your undoing, Marbella. Howl was ruthless. We were never going to get to the deep springs while he was alive. But you… you won't betray others to further your own interests. You sacrificed your freedom for those gargoyles on the cliff. You *care*. It's your weakness."

I yank myself out of his hold. "I'd rather be weak than your version of strong." I will never get through to him. "Now where is this thing you wanted to show me?"

He points. "Right there."

We've reached an opening to a small, circular clearing. The ground inside it is covered in ash and burned tree trunks, as if a sudden, vicious fire burned in this spot. I sense the remnants of sorcery in the ash, the emotions that burned with the unnatural fire, layered with sadness, pain, and rage.

It's hard to miss the single gravestone in the middle of the clearing.

Grayson loses the mask he keeps over his true emotions. Stepping onto the ashen ground, genuine sadness enters his expression as he says, "I carried him here after you left him where you killed him."

He's obviously not talking about Howl.

I whisper, "Gideon Glory."

Grayson looks at me the same way he did on my first day here, when he grabbed my arm with a vengeance and his expression was filled with wrath.

I say, "That's why you're angry with me. Because I killed him."

He paces out onto the ash, kicking blackened earth up beneath his boots, stopping in front of the grave. "There have been other natural-born sorcerers in our history, but only two of us have survived beyond infancy. Do you want to know why?"

I don't particularly, but I figure he's not really asking my permission to tell me.

He continues, "Because their families figure out what they are and kill them. They leave them to die in forests like this one."

He folds his arms across his chest. "All natural-born sorcerers have a different strength. Some can read thoughts, others can manipulate your actions, forcing you to do things you don't want to do. But me… I killed my mother and sister at the moment of my birth when my power awakened. The healer who delivered me also died. Nobody wanted to touch me after that. They wanted to leave me where I lay and let me starve to death. Only Gideon kept me alive."

I try to reconcile what he's telling me with what I knew about Gideon Glory. The Gideon I knew never did anything for anyone unless it benefitted himself in some way. Even cloaking Grayson would have more likely been for Gideon's own protection than for Grayson's sake. But why would Gideon raise a child he knew could kill him? Why would he take that risk? Grayson must have had something he wanted.

Grayson says, "He was my father when I had none. My protector when I had none. I owed him my life. And then you killed him. You killed the only person who ever cared about me."

The gravestone is like a glaring accusation. Regardless of Gideon's motives, he was the only family Grayson had. I took Gideon away from him. I don't know what to say or do. Grayson is angry, but not threatening, despite what he says next…

"I vowed that I would find you and kill you. I convinced the Elven Command to let me join their ranks. I possessed a hundred talon crows searching for you in Erador, but I never found you. It turned out you were deep underground all that time. But when Howl asked for the Rath and Mercy Heartstones, I knew they were important. So, I broke them up and made them part of me. That was the same day you resurfaced and killed Howl. Now here you are. And you are… nothing like I imagined."

His expression softens as he looks at me, a mixture of confusion and intrigue. Maybe he *was* listening when I was talking about the gargoyles. Maybe I can get through to him. My Virtuous heart is glowing. *Curse its empathy.* I hate that I understand Grayson's point of view. Gideon Glory was the father he never had, and I was responsible for taking that away from him.

He turns to me, open, needing to know. "Why did you kill him?"

My voice is small. "He was going to kill me."

"He wouldn't do that. He wasn't that person."

I search his face for traces of a lie. *Does he truly believe that? Are we talking about the same elf?* His earnest expression tells me that he honestly believes what he said. I'm hesitant, but I have to tell him the truth. "Gideon and the other Elven Commanders killed Baelen. Once they had my storm power, I was next."

"In self-defense."

I blink. "What?"

"Baelen Rath attacked them. They fought back in self-defense."

I can only stare at him, incredulous. "Is that what they told you? They stabbed Baelen *in the back* while he was in the simulation unable to defend himself. If you don't believe me, the cuts in his armor prove it."

A sharp clapping at the edge of the clearing interrupts us. Priscilla steps into the light. "What pretty lies you tell, Marbella."

By the time I spin back to Grayson, he's wearing the mask over his emotions again, expressionless and blank. As I search for any sign that he heard what I said, I'm disappointed. Behind the mask is distrust. He doesn't believe me.

Priscilla smirks as she wraps her manicured fingers around his bicep. I'd give anything to smash that smile right off her face. My power might not have any effect on Grayson, but it would sure sting this woman. *To hell with nice, Marbella.* I grit my teeth, narrow my eyes, and harness my strength, intending to douse her in cold air and freeze that stupid smile on her face. Grayson anticipates me and an invisible shield shoots up between her and me. It's imperceptible—I sense it instead of seeing it—and Priscilla doesn't seem aware of it. My gaze flickers to Grayson's, meeting his silent, warning glare.

Completely oblivious, Priscilla keeps speaking. "Well, I hate to break up this little heart-to-heart but we have a situation we need to deal with. Grayson, if you don't mind, our little princess needs to go back to her cage."

Her fingers play down his forearm as she releases him so he can deal with me. He latches hold of me, gripping my shoulders, his hard gaze clashing with mine. The world spins as he transports me back to the bedroom in an instant. The way he dumps me on the floor when we arrive tells me he's done talking to me.

Even so, before he returns to Priscilla, he asks me one thing: "Will you stay here while I'm gone or will war start tomorrow?" He looms over me. "Remember that no matter where you go, I will bring you back to me."

"I'll stay," I say, not entirely sure if I'm going to keep my word.

"In case you change your mind, you should know that it takes ten minutes to run to the edge of the cloaked area," he says. "You won't make it to the outside world before I get back."

In other words, I should say goodbye to any thoughts of at least getting a message out about my location.

I glare at him. "I said that I'll stay."

He gives me a single nod and then disappears before my eyes. He told me that every natural-born sorcerer has a particular strength. His might be killing at a single touch, but his ability to travel from one place to another in the blink of an eye is dizzying. Even Baelen can't travel that fast. I certainly can't. That doesn't mean I'm not going to try.

24

GRAYSON

The female elf's body is barely recognizable. Her pale hair is matted with blood, her wrists shackled to the dirty prison wall above her head. Her dress is torn and her arms, legs, every patch of skin, including her face, is burned.

She isn't breathing.

Priscilla snickers beside me. "Marbella is going to be so upset."

I spin to Osian Valor. "Who is this?"

He and the other Elven Commanders fill the space inside the cell. I've never been to the prison before, didn't know where to find it. It's buried deep underground beneath the city. The entire place reeks of death. I passed other cells on my way to this one, each of them filled with women dressed in damaged, filthy armor. One of them, a blue-eyed warrior with blood-splattered blonde hair gripped the bars and snarled at the Elven Commanders as we passed. *"I will kill you for what you've done to her."*

Osian is expressionless. "She is Marbella Mercy's advisor, Elise." He gives Priscilla a pointed glare. "Marbella's reaction is exactly what we need to control."

My voice is cold. "They are close?"

"Like sisters," Priscilla purrs. "You will have to control her, Grayson. Marbella can't be so enraged that she escapes. We need this war to go ahead."

"Yes. We do." I agree with her, but I'm starting to wonder if I'm

182

on the right side of it. Marbella tried to convince me that the Elven Commanders, including Gideon, had struck Baelen Rath in the back while he was defenseless. That she had killed Gideon only because he was about to kill her. I need time to process what she said, to decide if I believe her.

I cloaked myself the moment I entered the prison and I maintain the barrier as I reach out to Elise, gently lifting her chin. "What happened?"

Osian shrugs. "We wanted information. We thought she could handle it."

Torture. I swallow down the bile that rises to my throat. I've seen a lot of cruel acts, but the burn marks on her exposed arms and legs make my stomach turn. Every woman in the nearby cells would have heard her screams. I'm not a skilled healer, but if the others are really worried about Marbella's reaction, then all they need to do is—

Osian continues, "We didn't mean to kill her."

Kill her?

I force myself to remain impassive. *But she isn't dead.*

The small patch of perfectly healed skin beside her left ear tells me she is holding on, desperately trying to heal herself. The fact that she isn't breathing has nothing to do with it. She's absorbing oxygen through her skin, just enough to maintain bare conscious thought. She's existing on her magical power alone. Deep inside her mind, I hear her spellcasting, even though she's nearly comatose, her thoughts patchy and intermittent. She's a truly skilled spellcaster to accomplish such a thing.

The Elven Commanders aren't powerful enough to detect her internal life signs.

No matter what Elise did, punishment should be quick and clean. Never this.

I make a decision, hoping it isn't the wrong one.

Pasting a cruel smile on my face, I turn back to the others. "You should give her the burial she deserves. Take her body out into the fields and dump it where the talon crows can pick at it."

Priscilla's eyes widen, her smile growing as she presses against me, stroking my chest. "Mmm, Grayson, that sounds perfect to me."

I return her smile. "Don't worry. I'll take care of Marbella. She won't give us any trouble."

25

MARBELLA

I race for the door. Grayson told me that he would be ten minutes. If what he said is true then I won't make it outside the cloaked area, but I can definitely look around inside it. I speed along the corridor, skidding to a halt to avoid elves from the House of Verity standing around the corner, and impatiently wait for them to move on before I race in the direction of the back door.

Once there, I run as fast as I can to the buildings I didn't get to visit earlier. But as I draw closer, I'm disappointed. One of them is a greenhouse filled with exotic flowers. I recognize some of them from pictures Elise showed me once of flowers that are used in healing potions. As I veer away from the greenhouse, I find that the other building is a stable for winged stallions. Most of the stalls inside it are empty, but three of them contain the beautiful creatures.

Could a prison be hidden under the stable? Or was it never here to begin with? I search my memory for what Elwyn Elder said about it… He'd yelled that Grayson was supposed to take me to the prison. He never said it was here. I just assumed. Which means it could be anywhere.

The nearest stallion nickers. There's no way that ordinary stallions could be kept this close to each other—they're like alpha males and fight each other for control of the herd—but winged stallions are gentle creatures, more like brothers with each other than rivals. Riding one is easy. And they fly much faster than I could run…

My heart lifts but quickly plummets. I won't make it out in time. I've already used up seven of the ten minutes and Grayson said he wouldn't be that long…

A sharp tug on my spine tells me my time is already up. His power is like a wash of electrified air as he strides up behind me, his presence a powerful reminder of my captivity. He rasps, "You said you'd stay put. What are you doing out here?"

I turn on him. It's time for me to ask the questions. "Where is the prison? Where are you keeping my Storm Command?" I face up to him with my demand for answers.

He stands his ground, but he looks… ashen. Troubled. Maybe even a little worried. My eyes narrow in thought. He can't be that concerned about me being out here; as he says, he can pull me back to him at any time. Something else has happened but… what?

He asks, "Is that why you wanted to look around?"

"I need to know where they are. I need to know that they're safe."

He opens his mouth but closes it. Starts again. "They aren't here, Marbella." A tone of urgency enters his voice. "I need you to know that they were never here. That I… had nothing to do with their imprisonment or treatment. I didn't know. I swear…"

He stops. Inhales. Contemplates me. Doesn't go on.

Fear slides into my heart, settling there like a cold chill. "What happened? What was the situation you had to deal with?"

My heartstones gleam. In all the time I've been here, I've only taken the headpiece off so that I can sleep comfortably, and, to my knowledge, Grayson has never tried to touch it. Now he studies it, eyeing it, his shoulders drawing forward like a gargoyle would draw his wings around to protect himself, feet planting, telling me he's bracing for my reaction to whatever he's about to tell me.

I take a step toward him, near panic. Whatever he's going to say, it's bad. My voice rises as I repeat, "What happened, Grayson?"

His gaze drops to mine. "They told me… that your advisor, Elise, was killed."

The floor drops out of my world. My whole body freezes. The temperature of the air around us plummets with my heart. My hands begin to shake, rattling at my sides. My head shakes too, side-to-side. "No. That's not… possible…"

I step away from him, backing up, the cold building in my feet, clawing up my legs into my stomach, filling my chest, and sliding toward my neck. Part of me doesn't believe him. She is my best friend and a spellcaster too. I know what her presence feels like. I know what her power feels like. I would have felt her death. I would have known. I can't… I can't believe…

I demand, "How?"

He is very pale. He doesn't look at my heartstones anymore, focusing on my face, my eyes. "They were trying to get information out of her and went too far."

"Torture?" Now I advance on him. Any sane elf would back away from me, but he stands his ground. He continues to meet my eyes. The runes across his chest are subdued. He doesn't draw on his power even though rage burns through me and crackles loudly in the space between us. The stallions stomp and shift in their stalls, sensing the danger.

I'm two seconds from burning this building to the ground. The only things stopping me are the innocent creatures I'd destroy with it.

"I'm truly sorry, Marbella."

If he had played the evil villain, gone on the defensive and made excuses, even remained aloof or masked his emotions, anything other than what he does next, I could have held it together.

But instead, he offers me his hand. "Take my hand and let it out. I can take your pain."

My chest heaves, my breathing rages, and a scream winds its way into my throat. *Elise. My beautiful Elise.*

It can't be true. He's lying. But if he isn't… I can't hold in my fear anymore. I clasp his hand, gripping hard, knowing that otherwise I'll tear apart the stables, the stallions, the greenhouse, and everything else around us.

I scream out my fear that he's telling the truth. Pain shrieks through our connected hands flowing fast from my body into Grayson's. He flinches as the force hits him. Power shoots though his arm, straight across his torso, and crackling under his skin. It's the same force that tore Howl to shreds. Cracks appear like spider webs all over Grayson's chest, up his neck, and down his arms. His muscles clench, his forearm and biceps bulging. He grits his teeth as I continue to scream, pouring all of my pain into the contact. Despite it all, he refuses to look away. Even when I drop to my knees, dragging him with me, my scream turning into a wail.

It has to be a trick. It can't be real… "I need to see her body."

"No."

My throat is sore, constricted. "Why not?"

"I told them to bury her properly."

I swallow. "They weren't going to, were they?"

"No, they weren't."

I drop my head to my chest, my free hand flopping to my side. "What about my Storm Command."

"They haven't been touched. They're fine."

"Fine is a relative word, Grayson. One version of 'fine' is healthy and safe. Another version of 'fine' is starving and wounded but not dead." At this point, I'm not ashamed to beg. "Please let them go."

"It's not up to me. I don't control that situation."

"Then you don't know that they're fine."

He sighs. Tugs my hand. Pulls me to my feet. I stumble back to my cage, swinging between going into shock and trying to stay alert. I can't allow myself to become vulnerable in this place. And until I see her body or hear it from someone I trust, I won't truly believe she's gone.

Priscilla waits for us when we get back. As we enter the room, she straightens from a lean against the table, flicking her hair behind her ear and smirking at me.

"Oh," she pouts, putting on a sad face. "Is somebody upset?"

Grayson doesn't react, taking me to the nearest chair, finally letting me go. He positions himself in a standing position at my side, his tone neutral. "Priscilla?"

She smiles sweetly. "Yes, Grayson?"

"Get out."

She laughs. "Don't tell me you feel sorry for her."

I may be exhausted and emotionally drained, but I can still access my power. I harness the cold again, wondering if Grayson will stop me this time.

He must sense it, but to my surprise he doesn't put up a shield between us. Instead, he narrows his eyes at Priscilla. "You should be more afraid of her."

Priscilla is taken aback, flicking her fingers at me. "What? Scared of that pitiful, little *doll*—"

My eyes widen. Grayson said he never met Howl, but Priscilla must have. She must have told Grayson what Howl called me. My resolve strengthens. My power crackles, but Priscilla is either too proud, or too stupid, to acknowledge the danger.

Grayson says, "Leave, Priscilla. Before I let Marbella do what she wants."

Her body language changes, becoming instantly threatening. "You'd better not betray me, Grayson."

When he doesn't answer, the furrow in her brow deepens. "Fine, have your little moment. Just remember who will be there when it's all over."

She stalks from the room, glaring daggers at me. I consider turning her perfect ass to dust, but that would rain all sorts of hellfire down on me from the other Elven Commanders, and the consequences would be faced by my people. The gargoyles and my ladies. The Elven Command may not be able to hurt me, but they've made it clear that they can hurt... *kill*... the people I care about.

I shouldn't have waited to come looking for my ladies. I should have stormed into Erawind as soon as Howl was dead. I should have done... something... *anything*...

I jump to my feet and head for the bedroom, closing the door behind me before I crawl into bed and pull the blankets over myself. Grayson lets me go, doesn't try to stop me, doesn't even tug on me.

I close my eyes and let the shock take over.

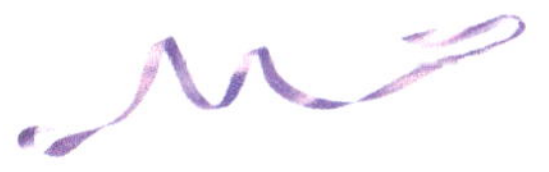

THAT NIGHT, AFTER GRAYSON LEANS OVER ME TO RETRIEVE HIS pillow and blanket, he angles in slowly, as if he's about to drop a kiss right on my lips.

Before he can make contact, I place both my hands on his chest and shove.

He immediately withdraws, dropping to a sitting position on the edge of the bed. To my astonishment, he grins at me, one eyebrow raised. As always, his chuckle is real. "Good. You were so quiet, I was worried I might have lost you."

I scowl at him. "You never had me."

His smile broadens. "There's the Marbella I know." He tugs at the edge of the blanket. "Scoot over."

Alarm replaces my unhappiness. "What are you doing?"

"I have a theory…" He nudges the blanket down and slides one leg inside it. "That your diamond stone makes everything colder. Am I right?"

He's seriously about to get into the bed with me. I hustle to the other side as fast as I can. "You might be."

He pummels the pillow that I just vacated and hands me the one he took, pulling the blanket no higher than his waist while lying down on his side, facing me. The mattress wobbles as he makes himself comfortable. "So, my theory is that even if I roll onto my back and set this bed on fire, your power will stop the flames before they start."

He inhales deeply, holding his breath for a moment as if he expects the bed to burst into flames right then. Nothing changes. He exhales. Relaxes. Closes his eyes. Says nothing else.

I peer at him. He looks far too comfortable where he is. But he hasn't come any closer. In fact, he's very close to the edge of that side of the bed. I assess the gap between us. It's as wide as it can be. But now I can't decide which direction I should face. Toward him might send the wrong signals, but I don't exactly want to take my eyes off him.

Without opening his eyes, he says, "Relax, Marbella. I'm not coming over there. I just don't want to sleep on the floor anymore."

Despite what he says, his upper arm stretches out across the distance, fingertips brushing my shoulder and staying there, the barest connection that I try to ignore as I fall asleep.

I'm not sure if he wants me to hear him when he murmurs, "If only we weren't enemies."

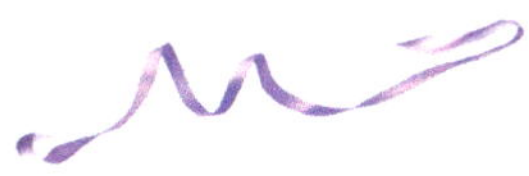

I DREAM OF THE MARRIAGE TRIALS, OF THE COMPATIBILITY TEST, AND the Chair of Truth. The Elven Commander, Pedr Bounty's grandson, a big brute of an elf, sits opposite me, just like he did after the battle in the arena. I hated him for hurting Baelen. I never wanted to lay eyes on this elf again. My voice echoes back at me as I force him to answer my question: *What do you see when you look at me?*

He struggles to get away from me, struggling so hard that sweat drips into his eyes. *I see a storm of power and light. I see burning and chaos. I see a girl on a mountain. The wind's beating at her, lightning's striking, claws are ripping, but she's fighting back. I see life and death. I don't know if you're the one killing me or saving me.*

I awake with a cry in my throat as echoes of my dream repeat on me... *Claws ripping. Burning and chaos. A girl on a mountain.*

War. I can't stop it from coming. Up until this moment, part of me thought I could find a way to stop the battle. I'd planned to take the fight to the elves, infiltrate Erawind, kill the Elven Commanders myself, and keep my people safe. But now... now...

My eyes fly open as the horror of my nightmare fades. Grayson watches me from the other side of the bed. Just as he promised, he hasn't moved from that position.

"I want to ask if you're okay," he says. "You were obviously having a nightmare. But somehow I don't think you'll tell me what it was about."

He's right. Because he is at the center of it. *He* is my greatest fear for my people.

Without answering him, I slide my legs over my side of the bed, preparing to get up.

He gives a resolute sigh at my silence and flops onto his back, staring up at the ceiling. But his eyes shoot wide as he realizes that his back just connected with the bedding. "Oh fu—"

Heat blasts across the room at the same time as the bed blazes, fire lighting up beneath Grayson. I'm only halfway off the other side. I roll back, slap my hand against his chest, and throw my power through him.

As a chill replaces the heat, the fire sizzles and dies. Smoke curls around Grayson's frame. He looks shocked. Grabs my hand. Lifts up off the bed to check the damage to the mattress beneath him. "Uh… thank you."

Not something I ever expected him to say to me. I shove away from him, roll off the bed, and head to the bathroom. He kept his word about staying on his side of the bed. He will keep his word about standing at the head of the Elven Army when it attacks my friends.

As the day wears on, Grayson's mood shifts from quiet to brooding. He seems to remember that he is living in a bubble and that bubble is about to burst. Or at least open up for a while, because today is the celebration, and he has agreed to let Baelen see me. The closer the afternoon gets, the more on edge Grayson becomes. By the afternoon, he is in a dark mood that worries me, his responses to me clipped and sharp to the point where I stop saying anything.

I pace the bedroom floor as he dresses in the bathroom. A box rests on the bed. It contains the dress I'm supposed to wear, but I haven't opened it because I'm trying to delay whatever cleavage-revealing, butt-exposing horror awaits me. My experiences of having my clothing chosen for me haven't gone so well in the past. I heave a sigh as I recall burning dresses with Gilda and Carmen. They needed space in the days before I was captured, so I hardly saw them. I miss them. I also miss my Storm Command. Grayson told me that they aren't being held here. I believe him about that, but not so much about his assertion that they're fine.

He emerges from the bathroom, blond hair slicked back, golden runes glowing across his chest. He's wearing black pants that hug his hips and accentuate his thighs.

I remove the lid from the box and gather the dress into my arms before hurrying to the bathroom and nudging the door closed with my foot. The bone lash hangs from a hook on the wall. I've studied the tip many times, trying to decide if it would be powerful enough to rip the stones out of Grayson's back. I have to break the tether between him and every single piece. The connection between

Baelen and me was a visible thread of deep magic. I don't know what Grayson's tether will look like, and I'm terrified of what will happen if it doesn't break or if I only break some of it.

I drag on the dress, trying not to pay too much attention to it. The corset is made up of an inner skin-colored body suit that pushes up my breasts and makes them look larger, and it's overlaid with fine, white embroidery while the small waistline is decorated with flowers, dropping to a full, white skirt. It's definitely cleavage-enhancing but thankfully not butt-exposing.

I freeze as I catch sight of myself in the mirror. My wavy auburn hair falls free to my waist, contrasting with the dress like a summer sunset. As I position my tiara on my head, I realize that, for the first time, I look like a Queen.

That is… a Queen in a wedding dress.

I close my eyes, fighting sudden fear. Grayson is looking for Baelen's breaking point. Parading me in a wedding dress is Grayson's way of showing Baelen what he can't have. It's the first step in tearing Baelen down. I shudder as I wonder how far Grayson will go today.

26

MARBELLA

It's half a day's travel to the arena from Glory land, so everyone else left this morning, but Grayson transports me there instantly so there's no risk that we'll be intercepted on the way. He steadies me until the dizzying blur stops, and I can focus again.

The arena hasn't changed since the last time I was here: a dais at one end and seating in the upper balconies—empty this time. About forty elves, male and female, are drinking at the tables lining the edges while others dance to the string quartet playing on the dais. The arena is decorated like a fairytale with golden lanterns and flickering candlelight. Everything sparkles.

A dancing couple sways past as I edge out of Grayson's grip. The woman's eyes meet mine for a second, but I recognize her: *Reisha!*

I quickly scan the faces of the other women around me, recognizing each member of my Storm Command. They all wear long-sleeved dresses, but when they move their sleeves ride up and their wrists show, revealing raw skin and bruises from shackles. Their eyes are dark-ringed, their hair lank, and makeup doesn't quite cover the bruises on their necks and faces. They paste smiles on their faces as they dance and pretend to drink. They need food more than alcohol judging by their thin frames. Each of them has a male partner who is clearly military. Just as I feared, my ladies are not so fine after all.

Grayson leans into me. "I hope you can see that there's a lot at stake if Baelen tries anything today."

I spin to him, pushing back against his shoulders. "Let them go, Grayson. They don't deserve this."

He is deadpan. "I can't."

"Please!"

He pauses. "I will let *one* of them go if you kiss me right now."

"Reisha," I say without hesitation. "Promise me you'll send her back with Baelen."

"I promise." He gives me a slow smile. "But you'd better move fast because your window of opportunity is closing."

I don't question his motives. Reisha's life is in my hands. If I can free her and get her out of this hell, it's worth any humiliation. I step into the circle of his arms and draw his face down to mine, determined to make it the briefest kiss in the history of Erawind. I prepare myself for the overwhelming scent and taste of Baelen and the dizzying impact that it will have on my body. What I'm not prepared for is that Grayson stops me in that position before our lips can meet. One of his hands sweeps into my hair to cradle the back of my head and control my movement. His other arm curls around my waist to draw our hips together while halting our mouths a mere breath apart.

He whispers, "One day, you will kiss me because you want to. But for now, you've done enough."

He withdraws, taking a deep breath. Then the mask falls over his feelings again. His emotional shield is perfect and flawless, and I know that the person he was yesterday when he told me he was sorry about Elise—that person is gone.

The emotionless Grayson is the one to be feared.

"You have perfect timing," he says.

A hush has fallen over the room.

I look up, knowing what I'll see, prepared for how it will break my heart.

Baelen is frozen in the doorway, shock radiating out from him in waves. Every muscle in his body is bunched, ready for attack. Lightning curls around his fists, torso, and face, accentuating the cut of his jaw and the bristles growing there. He's growing another beard, and it makes me want to cry.

Don't break, Baelen. Please don't break.

His presence is like an explosion inside of me. I can't dim my feelings no matter how much I try. Everything inside of me wants to run to him. A burning glow at the corner of my eye tells me that Baelen's presence, and my response to him, is having a major impact on the Rath Heartstone; so much so that Grayson winces with pain. He rolls his shoulders, trying to shake it off. He reaches for me without seeming to realize it, pulling me tight into his side. He might use the heartstones to control me, but I'm certain that at this moment in time, the Rath stone is controlling him. He wants me in his arms as badly as Baelen does.

A quick glance around the room tells me that my ladies are in mortal danger, many with daggers held at their backs. Their determined expressions tell me that despite their exhaustion, they want to fight back. But we all know that Grayson controls this situation and things could go bad very quickly.

Baelen is watching me closely enough to follow my gaze. As the situation becomes apparent to him, he relaxes. He knows I can't make any choices for myself right now. It makes my heart break even more knowing how much he trusts me. His lightning dims, but it must be taking every bit of his self-control not to tear Grayson apart.

Whatever happens, I can't let Baelen touch Grayson or Baelen will die.

Baelen steps to the side, revealing the gargoyle with him. Indira glides into the light. I'd expected to see Llion or Roar, maybe even Senturi, but I'm glad it's her. A Grievous gargoyle is exactly what is needed on this mission, especially a ferocious woman like Indira.

Like Baelen, Indira wears light armor and a smattering of weapons. Her gorgeous wings catch the light as she crosses the distance ahead of Baelen, a strikingly confident form who catches the eye of every man in the room. She is even more beautiful than the last time I saw her, the glow in her cheeks reminding me that she's pregnant.

Even Grayson is transfixed. "Who is that?"

I reply, "Her name is Grievous Indira. She is one of the most fearsome women I've ever fought." Then I decide to drop a little bombshell. "She was Howl's sister."

He is visibly taken back. "But she fights with you now?"

My response is a warning to Grayson about trust, but I'm not sure if he will hear it. "That's how much Howl hurt everyone around him during his quest for power."

Indira stops directly in front of Grayson. "I expected a little more hospitality," she says, holding out her hand while Baelen takes his time joining her.

He's assessing every part of the room and its occupants. Priscilla's presence at one of the tables makes him narrow his eyes. He will be able to sense her sorcery. She takes on a casual pose, remaining where she is for now. If the way Grayson is holding me bothers her, she's hiding it. But her response to Baelen is unmistakable despite her casual posture: she's afraid of him.

"I thought there would be dancing." Indira bats her eyelashes at Grayson. Her goal is clear—give Baelen and me space. She shrugs in my direction. "It's not like Marbella is going anywhere."

She reaches for his hand but at the last minute my senses go haywire. He isn't cloaked! I can't let her die. Not her—and not the babies she's carrying.

"Indira, don't touch him!"

She withdraws at my shout. Grayson slides both his arms around me, leveraging me so he's standing behind me. He nuzzles my ear. "Aw, Marbella, no need to get possessive. She just wants to dance with me."

"Grayson, please…"

"I promise I won't bed her." His hands splay across my hips, making me freeze. My stomach sinks with every moment that he continues to touch me. It's obviously all for Baelen's benefit.

Baelen is frozen again. I don't have to read his mind to know his thoughts: if Grayson keeps touching me like that, he's not going to have any fingers left by the time Baelen is done with him. If Grayson were an ordinary man, it would be true.

But Grayson is not ordinary, and we all know it.

I sense Grayson's cloaking spell go up a second before he lets me go. He catches Indira's hand and spins her a few paces away. The music starts up again.

I don't wait.

"Baelen." I run to him as fast as I can, not knowing whether Grayson will jolt me backward and keep us apart. It's likely that he'll give us moments and then deliberately tear me away to demonstrate his control over this situation.

I crash into Baelen's chest, the full force of contact with his body sending my senses into overload. A storm rages behind his eyes kept under tight control, a growing tension in the lines of his jaw, the angle of his shoulders, and the flex of his biceps and forearms as his arms close around me. Up close, I can see dark circles under his eyes and the fury that fills every part of his body.

I tilt my head back, knowing that before Grayson whisks me away, I have to tell Baelen… I have to make sure he knows…

"Whatever you see. Whatever you hear. Please know this: Baelen Rath, I give you my heart. I will love you, protect you, and honor you until the end of time."

His eyes widen before I dip my head to his chest and wrap my arms around him. I just spoke the Heartstone oath. It's the same oath Baelen gave to me in this same arena. It will bind me to him so that nothing Grayson does can force me to hurt Baelen again.

I finish the oath, whispering against his armor. "Until death."

I wait for him to say the words that mean he accepts my oath, which mean he trusts me no matter what he saw, the words that will complete the binding. His heart pounds against my ear. He gently draws back so he can search my eyes, the rage in his expression morphing into an even stronger emotion as he cups my cheek in his big palm. It's the same way he looked at me before he asked permission to kiss me the first time. It's so fierce and so real that my heart shatters.

Finally, he says, "Marbella Mercy, Supreme Incorruptible, Queen of the gargoyles, I accept your promise. We are bound together, live or die, succeed or fail. We will forever love each other."

A shiver races through me from the top of my head to my toes. All four of my heartstones burst into light at once, glowing powerful and bright.

I flinch as a harsh cry breaks across the distance. Grayson

doubles over, curled up on the floor twenty paces away, clutching his stomach. *Did Indira stab him?*

I wouldn't have thought any physical assault would have that effect on him. I also can't believe she got through his defenses.

She backs away from him, arms splayed, bumping into the elves behind her. The shock on her face tells me she didn't do anything. She shouts at the advancing soldiers, "I didn't touch him!"

He clutches his stomach, lifts his head, and roars so loudly that the elves cover their ears and the glass paneling in the ceiling of the arena shatters. Glass shards creak, wobble, and separate from each other like a falling jigsaw puzzle, dropping toward the shocked elves below.

"Grayson!" Priscilla screams as she races toward him, waving away the shards that would strike her or Grayson, sending them in all directions. Whatever anger she felt at him yesterday, she's forgotten it. Her frightened face shoots panic in our direction. But the source of her fear is painfully clear to me: she's not afraid for Grayson. She's afraid for herself. Grayson is her protection. Without him, she's vulnerable.

She screams, pulling at him, trying to make him stand. "Grayson, stop it! Get up!"

Indira also launches into action, speeding toward us just as the deadly glass is about to impale the screaming, clambering elves. "Baelen!"

Baelen's thunder booms and everything freezes, including Grayson and Priscilla—and the deadly glass shards. Just in time.

But not Indira. She plows into both of us. "I didn't do anything! I swear. He just collapsed."

I don't know what has hurt Grayson, but even the thunder hasn't stopped his pain. He's slowly writhing on the floor, clearly in agony. Yesterday, he absorbed my destructive power without making a sound, so the fact that he's shuddering now tells me how much pain he's in. My Virtuous heart glows again, its compassion telling me to help him, that I can't let his pain go on like this.

Stop it! I can't feel sorry for him.

I smother my empathy with fear for my ladies. I have to get them out of here. I spin to Baelen. "Grayson won't be frozen for long. He's too powerful. Can your storm power carry twenty-one women? I need you to get Indira and my ladies out of here."

"Twenty-two," he says, piercing me with his green eyes. "You're coming too."

My voice breaks. "I… can't."

Indira grabs my arm. "We're taking you home, Marbella."

I'm shaking. "Grayson controls me. He controls my location and everything I do. If I run, he'll pull me right back here. You can't touch him, Baelen. He kills everyone he touches. You have to take my Storm Command and go."

Indira's eyes widen. "That's why you didn't want me to touch him."

"Please. Take my ladies and go."

Baelen is powerful and unyielding, a tower of strength as he holds me in his arms. "Grayson controlled you through the heartstones." His eyes meet mine, clear and determined. "I don't think he controls you anymore."

He gently turns me in Grayson's direction.

Grayson is curled up on the floor, shaking, small tremors that would be so much more powerful if he wasn't contained within the force of the thunder. A soft crackle reaches my ears, a popping sound like twigs burning in a fire. Grayson's spine is glowing, and at first, I think it's the Rath Heartstone like before, but this glow is angry, a deeper shade of carmine, like blood. Beneath the heartstones, his skin bubbles and seethes. It's such a shocking sight that I'm running before I know it.

Grayson told me that mercy was my weakness. Maybe it is. Maybe I'm about to make a terrible mistake. But the person he is when he drops the mask over his emotions is the one I want to help.

I ignore Priscilla's frozen form. Her sorcery isn't natural like Grayson's. She can't defeat the storm's power and she will remain frozen until Baelen chooses to release her.

I kneel next to Grayson where he can see me, waiting for his eyes to meet mine. Then I pull him toward me so the side of his stomach rests across my knees and I can reach his back. The stones are loose, boiling his skin. I reach for the first one—part of the Mercy Heartstone—and lift it away from him. It falls into my fingers and the boiling beneath it stops. I repeat that seven times for Mercy and ten times for Rath, gathering the pieces into a pile on the floor while Baelen watches over me. I have no idea what he's thinking now. He must think I'm crazy to be helping this elf. But Grayson is part gargoyle, and it's the gargoyle that I'm helping now.

I glance up at Baelen in the middle of my task. "We broke the tether. When I bound myself to you, we must have broken his connection with our heartstones. The heartstones are punishing him for forcing the link."

Baelen's expression is shuttered, controlled. "We should take these with us so they can't be used against you again."

Indira swoops to place the shards in a pouch at her waist. Unlike gargoyle heartstones, elven heartstones aren't deadly to touch, so they don't harm her.

By the time I'm done, Grayson has stopped shaking, but his eyes leak tears of pain. He squeezes his eyes closed, turning his face away. I guess he doesn't want me to see him like this.

I check the wounds on his back. His skin has stopped bubbling, but it's burning hot. I can't heal him, but I can soothe the pain. I draw on Incorruptible's ice, allowing it to seep from my fingertips into his spine. His skin cools immediately, the redness fading. I run my fingers up his spine again, making sure it's completely cooled before I pause at a spot on his back, considering it. Underneath his golden runes, several strange bumps interrupt his smooth skin, but there's no time to wonder how they got there.

He relaxes, the tension in his body releasing, but his eyes fly open, watching me again. He struggles against the force that binds him, confusion more than fear, filling his eyes as he sees Baelen standing so close by. He probably wonders why Baelen hasn't struck him dead already.

As a warrior, Baelen knows exactly what Grayson is thinking. But Baelen has always fought with honor. His jaw clenches. Lightning crackles around his torso. "This would not be a fair fight. But I will meet you in battle, Grayson Glory. And when that time comes, no measure of mercy will save you."

I lean down to Grayson. Now that the tether is broken, I can leave. Grayson can't pull me back to him anymore, but my feelings toward him are so conflicted. He said last night that he wished we weren't enemies. I wish that too, but not for the same reasons as he does.

I won't love or be with anyone except Baelen, who holds my heart and soul in his strong hands. But I've seen who Grayson is under the mask: he is a gargoyle, and that makes him one of my people.

I take his hand and fold mine inside it for a moment, asking for his trust. "I didn't lie to you, Grayson. I'm sorry I took Gideon away from you. I wish I could change the past. But you need to question everything the Elven Command told you. *Everything.*"

I draw to my feet and use my power to send all the remaining glass shards speeding up and away. I could let them fall on the soldiers but, as Baelen said, with them frozen, this is not a fair fight. The shards quiver where they impale the walls.

Baelen sweeps his power through the room, mini tornados picking up each of my ladies and transporting them toward the door. He wraps me up in his arms and pulls me to his side, lifting Indira with his power at the same time.

"Baelen?" I'm heartbroken, can barely get the words out as I say, "They told me Elise is gone… They said she didn't survive…"

Baelen and Indira exchange glances. "They thought she was dead," he says, "But Elise is alive."

"What?" I stare at him, dreading that I heard wrong, needing him to confirm that she's alive.

"They left her for dead; threw her in a shallow grave out in a field. That's how she escaped. She spellcast a call for help, and I found her. But the location of your ladies was still cloaked, and Elise had been separated from them for days, so it was impossible for me to find them."

Tears of relief stream down my cheeks. I press my hand to my heart, feeling like this pain, at least, is healing. I can't stop the sob wrenching from me. "I thought she was dead. It broke… my heart…"

Baelen plants comforting kisses on the top of my head and forehead, his touch and his arms soothing and warm. "She's okay, Marbella but… after I rescued her she stopped speaking. She says she'll only speak with you."

I wipe my eyes. "Why?"

He shakes his head. "We don't know. She won't say a word."

As we ascend into the late afternoon sky, I ask, "What about my family? Are they safe?"

Baelen smiles for the first time. "All of the elves who were loyal to me have gathered on Rath land—a small army—including the entire House of Mercy. Eli Elder is there too."

"That can't have made his grandfather very happy." Eli Elder is Elwyn Elder's grandson. Eli was one of the first elves to recognize the Elven Command's sorcery, and he went against his grandfather's wishes in the marriage trials.

Baelen says, "They've defended Rath land from every attempt to invade it. That's where we will go now. To your brother."

Rath land is right on the northern border between Erawind and Erador. It sounds like it has virtually seceded into gargoyle territory now.

"Baelen, the entire elven army will attack Erador as soon as they find out I'm gone. I made a deal with Grayson to buy you more time, and now I've broken it by leaving. The gargoyles aren't ready and it's my fault. I should have warned them."

Baelen says, "They're ready, Marbella. Your decision not to tell them only delayed their preparation by a few hours. As soon as you disappeared, a war council was formed."

"With Baelen at its head," Indira interjects, calling across the wind barrier. "He brought Llion, Liliana, and Talia back, and they explained what happened to you. We've spent the week fortifying the border."

"You've bought us enough time already," Baelen says. "We're ready for war."

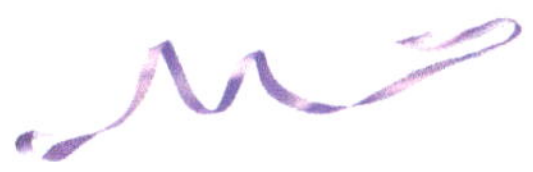

THE FLIGHT TO RATH LAND TAKES A FULL TWO HOURS. BAELEN HAS to fly much more slowly and carefully because he's transporting twenty-one elves at once. Along the way, I try to talk to him about Grayson. "Baelen, about what you saw…"

He gives me a quick shake of his head. His gaze flickers to the talon crows flying in the distance. "Not here."

I try to read his expression. His response was a lot more clipped than I expected it to be, and I'm suddenly worried. Back at the arena, I was sure he'd understood the situation, but now I can't tell if he's upset, betrayed, angry, or something else. He definitely doesn't want to talk about it right now.

We approach Rath land as the sun begins to set. As we fly over it, I can see how prepared they are. A number of gargoyle men patrol the sky while the outposts on the ground are manned with elven soldiers. Baelen signals to them and they lower their weapons, allowing us to pass. We travel onward through the outer village and finally into the center of the Rath mansion. It's not as big as the Royal Residence, but just as imposing. It feels like forever since I spent my childhood in this place.

A group of elves wait for us outside: two male and three female. My heart leaps to see my mother, father, and brother, as well as Jordan and Sahara.

As Baelen sets me down, I don't know who to go to first. They must have figured this out in advance because my mother races to me with open arms. "My daughter!"

"Mom." I haven't spoken to my mother in a year and haven't hugged her in seven. She's crying as she wraps her soft arms around me. I'm a grown woman, fought a lot of battles, but seeing my Mom brings me to tears.

"Marbella, I missed you, sweetheart."

My father wraps his arms around both of us, kissing my forehead. "Darling girl."

"I've missed you both so much." While I was the Storm Princess, I wasn't allowed to see or speak with my brother and father. Only my mother was allowed to visit me once each year.

After a long hug filled with tears, my parents give way for Jordan and Sahara, who are beaming at me. Sahara looks exhausted, but she gives up her position leaning on Jordan to hug me. "Welcome back, Marbella."

Jordan is next, her eyes sparkling with tears. She was the head of my Storm Command before she was married. For many years she was my protector as well as my friend. I hug her for forever before my brother jostles in for his turn. She rolls her eyes at him, squeezing my hand one last time and quickly whispering to me, "We'll catch up at dinner."

Macsen fills my view with his ginormous self, giving me a great big bear hug that lifts me off my feet. I still can't get over how much he's changed. His auburn hair is cut short at the back and sides and is not much longer on top—a soldier's haircut. His enormous chest and biceps dwarf me. He raises his eyebrows at my revealing dress. "Wow, big sister. Who did they make you marry?"

It's a loaded question masquerading as a joke, the kind that only Macsen could pull off, but it's suddenly clear that it's the question they all want to ask me. I instinctively reach for Baelen, but he's further away than I expected, at least ten paces from my location, his expression shuttered and closed. I can tell from the way my family and friends look at me that they're worried. I forgot how much I've changed: my skin, hair, even my physique. I'm leaner and stronger, working in the mine for a month gave me muscles I never had before. Not to mention the new addition of the tiara on my head. But the picture I'm painting right now in this dress… is all wrong.

"Nobody," I whisper. "It was Grayson Glory's way of making me uncomfortable." I lift my chin up. "Besides, I'm a gargoyle now. They have a very particular way of getting married that I will follow when the time comes."

The corner of Macsen's mouth twitches, but he doesn't quite smile. I don't think he's certain whether my answer has alleviated their concerns yet. "And what is that?"

I take a deep breath and say as clearly as I can, "You can ask Baelen after it happens."

Everyone relaxes. After another quick glance at Baelen, Macsen finally breaks into a grin and drops a kiss on my forehead. "Glad to have you back, sister. The army needs you." He raises his voice. "Maybe now Commander Rath will stop raging around like a shadow panther with a sore tooth."

Baelen snorts from across the courtyard. It's a light reply, but it sounds forced. "Don't count on it."

He turns to set my ladies down, finally releasing them from the thunder. They stumble and flinch to the ground, disoriented. Some of them fling their arms over their heads because the last thing they remember was the glass ceiling about to fall on them.

My mother calls for help and more elves race from the house to assist my disoriented ladies. But once they're back on their feet, they gracefully decline the offered hands, striding toward me. Reisha leads them. She hasn't lost any of her elegance or stealth despite the mistreatment she's experienced over the last month. She was always calm and intelligent, thinking before she acted. She pulls to a halt. Each woman holds out her arm horizontal to her chest and rests her forehead on it. It's the elven gesture of remorse.

Reisha speaks without raising her eyes. "Forgive us, Princess. We were unable to protect you."

I'm aghast. "Against Grayson? Nobody could protect me from him." *Except Baelen...* I look for him again, finding him even further away from me. Every time I look up, it seems he's distanced himself even more.

"It's our job to fight for you. To never give in to fear. We failed."

I swallow my tears. I won't let them believe that they failed me for another second. I'm the one who failed them. "Storm Command! Heads up!" I stride between their neat lines. "You have succeeded by surviving. You have protected me by staying alive. My heart would have broken if you hadn't…" I swallow my emotions. "You have made me proud."

I stop in front of Reisha. "Raise your eyes, Storm Commander. You owe me no remorse."

Her voice catches as she swallows back her emotions. "What are your orders, Princess?"

"You will eat and rest, Reisha. All of you must regain your strength for the fight ahead. Go now and allow these elves to help you. You must be ready to fight with me when the time comes."

As my ladies disperse, Mom takes my arm, leading me inside the House. I glance back to Baelen. He's a silhouette against the falling dusk, watching me go. He doesn't make any move to follow me before he turns and heads in the other direction. It seems like the freer we are, the more distant he becomes, and it's scaring the hell out of me.

Mom says, "I know you must be tired and hungry…"

"But I need to see Elise." After the pain I felt when I thought she died, I'm desperate to see her, hug her, and reassure myself that she's okay.

"She needs to speak with you. She's been shaken and distressed ever since she got here, refusing to eat or sleep."

Refusing to speak is one thing, but refusing to eat or sleep is another. I'm alarmed by this news. Elise was always the calm one, balancing out my emotions. It takes a lot to unsettle her this badly.

Jordan and Sahara follow closely behind us. Jordan says, "At first we thought it was because of the torture—"

Rage burns through me. Grayson told me the Elven Commanders were trying to get information out of her—that they went too far and thought they killed her. "Tell me."

Jordan doesn't soften the details, knowing I'd rather have the facts. "She arrived with burns to most of her body."

My stomach turns. I will kill each of the Elven Commanders, slowly, one by one. Grayson can't stop me anymore. I want to turn around right now, find them, and rip them apart.

Mom rubs my arms, a soothing gesture. "She's okay, really sweetheart. Sahara and the other healers have been working on her for two days straight to make sure she is completely healed."

That would explain why Sahara looks so exhausted. Her normally glistening silver-green eyes are dull, her shoulders slumped.

Mom continues, "But nobody can get Elise to eat. She won't until she speaks with you."

"Then take me to her right away."

Jordan leads the way even though I know this house, and all its rooms, far better than any other place. If I wasn't so focused on Elise, I would stop and take it all in. Being back in the Rath mansion is surreal after so long and everything that's happened since I left.

We arrive at a guest room on the lower level. A healer sits beside the bed in the middle of the room, removing a dressing from Elise's arm. "This is the last one, Elise."

Elise catches sight of me and launches off the bed. "Princess!"

I run to her as she slips off the side of the bed before the healer can stop her, her knees buckling immediately. I race to her, lifting her into my arms. She's far too light.

"Princess," she whispers. "Is it safe to hug you?"

The last time I saw her, I'd just found out I could safely touch others again. I answer her by tightening my arms around her. I don't try to stop the tears streaming down my cheeks or the possibility that I might turn into a hot mess.

She's really alive.

"They told me you died."

"Oh, Princess." She drops her head to my shoulder, too weak to hold it upright. "I was very close to death. I had just enough energy to spellcast a death trance. I was injured badly enough that it was convincing. It's how I escaped."

She's very thin and very weak. I help her relocate to the two-seater bench at the side of the room, so she can lean her head into my shoulder. Mom and the others are already retreating from the room.

I wait until they close the door. "It's okay. You're safe now."

She's suddenly agitated, pulling away from me. "Nobody is safe. Nobody!"

"Elise, talk to me. They say you won't eat until you speak with me, and you *need* to eat."

"I know why the Elven Command wants to destroy the deep springs. When they thought I was dead, they spoke freely in front of me. All three of them were there and they didn't guard their words."

I ask carefully, "Which ones were there?" I know I shouldn't care if Grayson lied to me about being involved in Elise's torture, but I need to know.

"The original three: Elwyn Elder, Osian Valor, and Pedr Bounty."

"Not the younger ones? Grayson or Priscilla?"

"Grayson! No, but they talked about him many times. It was his mother who started it."

Started what? I want to ask her so many questions, but I need her to eat something. "Tell me about the deep springs. And then you must eat."

"They said the springs are located in the spot where the Gargoyle King first separated the earth's layers for our new home. Water from the surface of the earth drips into the springs."

Elyria once told me the same thing. She said that the springs are the only water source that flows directly from Earth's surface. I also noticed the strange drip from the ceiling when I healed Baelen—water droplets that seem to form from nothing.

Elise's hand tightens around my arm. "They said there is an unseen entrance in the ceiling of the springs."

"An entrance… to where?"

"The surface," she whispers. "A pathway back to the surface of the Earth."

27

———

MARBELLA

If I had a hundred questions before, now I have a thousand. I try to focus on the most important one. "What are the Elven Command's plans?"

"They want to ascend to the surface."

"But… why? Humans tried to kill us. They almost wiped us out. Why would the Command want to go back there?"

"Grayson's mother was a Visionary. During her pregnancy she had a vision of a world that is vulnerable to sorcery. The Elven Command would be like gods if they made it to surface. There are many human lives to feed their sorcery—many easy deaths to build their power. They're dying here. They don't have much time left. They're feeding off the old and weak. They can't take enough lives to sustain themselves."

Throughout our history, elves with Visionary powers have seen part of the Earth's surface. It's how we know about the cities that humans have built—the skyscrapers and giant monuments. But all of the visions, until now, have told of the destructive power of human weapons—of bombs that would rival the power of Incorruptible's strength. All of the visions have warned against ever trying to ascend again. But now, Grayson's mother has seen a world that the Elven Command could manipulate and control.

Part of me wants those old bastards to leave. But I would not wish their cruelty on the humans.

210

"Once they ascend, they will destroy the springs so nobody can follow them."

I shake my head in shock. Grayson told me they wanted to destroy the springs. Now I understand why. "If the springs are destroyed, it will devastate the gargoyles."

"Worse, Marbella. Our world will collapse. The springs are the center point at which our world was created. Without the springs as an anchor, the sky will fall. The Earthen city above us, the one the humans call Chicago, will also suffer catastrophic damage."

Wide-eyed, I try to come to terms with this information. The Elven Command is basically plotting to destroy our entire world, along with the Earth city above us. I wonder if Grayson knows this will be the outcome of destroying the springs. I exhale my frustration about the sheer magnitude of the Commander's plotting. They've been trying to find a way to access the springs for as long as Grayson has been alive.

"Why wouldn't you tell this to anyone else? Why only me?"

"Because the Elven Commanders have killed everyone who knows about the entrance. Even though I despise their methods, the more people who know, the more chance there is that someone will try to find the entrance, try to ascend, and damage the springs in the process. We can't take that risk. We also can't let the humans find out about us."

I whisper, "Grayson's mother knew."

"That's why they killed her."

I stare at her. "No... the Elven Command didn't... Grayson did..."

She shakes her head adamantly. "They said it plain and clear. Gideon Glory killed her. She was his first kill."

I'm shocked. I told Grayson to question everything he was told but I never imagined how deep the lies went. Elise sags against me. "I don't think the Commanders are completely united in their mission."

"Why do you say that?"

"Before I escaped, Elwyn Elder stormed in very upset and said that Grayson threatened him and accused him of telling lies."

That must have been the night that Grayson first brought me to his home. Elise was still imprisoned then.

Elise continues. "Elwyn said, 'We never should have listened to Gideon. We never should have bound Grayson.'"

"What does that mean? Binding Grayson?"

"I don't know for sure, but binding is something that is done as part of a curse."

I urge her, "What more do you need to tell me before you'll eat something?"

"Only one more thing." She sighs. "It was very strange… When the others thought they killed me, they brought Grayson to see me for the first time. He came with that woman, and she was laughing because you would be so upset, but Grayson… I was sure…" She shakes her head, tiny, trembling movements. "I was sure he saw through my trance. I thought for a moment he was going to tell them I wasn't dead, but instead he told them to take me out to a field and dump me in an uncovered grave where the talon crows could get me."

I shudder. Grayson said he told them to bury Elise properly, but it turns out he really told them to dump her like a piece of unwanted trash. Anger flies through me so fast that I jolt. "That's… Grayson… I'm going to kill him…"

Elise grabs my arm. "No, no. You don't understand… The only way I could call for help was because they took me way out beyond the cloaking spell. They didn't cover me up, so I was easily visible from the sky. That's how Baelen could find me."

My anger turns to utter disbelief. "You're telling me… you think Grayson helped you?"

"He knew I was alive. I'm sure of it. His sorcery is stronger than any I've ever encountered. He could have told them, but he didn't."

Had Grayson really helped her? But why come back and put me through the pain of believing Elise died? Unless… he had to be convincing. Priscilla was waiting when we went back to the room. If I'd looked anything but devastated… she would have known something was off. I sigh. It's very hard for me to understand Grayson's motives for the things he does.

Elise collapses against me. "That's everything I know. Now I can eat."

I immediately call for Jordan and Sahara. I'm relieved to see that they are prepared, appearing with a bowl of warm broth to ease

Elise back into eating food. Before I leave them to their task, Elise snags my arm. "The Storm Command?"

"They're all safe, Elise. They're here in the Rath house. Once you're recovered, you will see them again. But now, you must eat." I stroke her hair as angry tears burn in my eyes. I leave the room with one determined thought: I will meet the Elven Commanders in battle, and I will tear them to shreds.

Mom finds me in the hallway. "She's eating?"

I nod, and Mom gives a sigh of relief.

I say, "It's going to take her days to recover. Thank you for looking after her."

"Of course, sweetheart."

When she links her arm with mine, I ask, "Where's Baelen?"

"He's out with the patrols. They're doubling the guard in preparation for an attack."

"I should be out there with him."

"Not in that dress." She indicates all the cleavage I'm revealing with a barely-suppressed smile. "Come with me, sweetheart. Let's find you something else to wear. And then dinner. No arguing with your mother."

Once I'm dressed in a simple shirt and pants, I follow Mom to the food hall to eat at a long table with my ladies for the first time in a long time. They are tired, exhausted really, but they hold their heads high and go slowly eating their first proper meal in a month. I look for Baelen when I arrive, but he's nowhere to be seen. Mom reads my mind, leaning in before she sits down next to me. "He will eat when he can."

She takes her place on my right while Jordan and Sahara soon join us—Jordan takes a seat on my left and Sahara sits opposite with Reisha. Indira stalks in soon after and sits next to Sahara, tucking her wings in neatly at her sides, so they don't get in the way.

I find myself surrounded by my closest female friends and my heart swells to be here among them. Even though she's thin and frail, Reisha is a steadying presence, Indira is a constantly fierce one, Jordan is unendingly calm, Sahara is kind and loyal, and my mother… well, she's trying not to smother me with all the mothering she hasn't been able to do for seven years. I allow myself to relax for the first time in a really long time, slowly feeling my heart warm as the love of these loyal women surrounds me.

At one point, I reach across the table and take Jordan's hand. "How is Sebastian?"

She glows. "My husband is out at one of the outposts with Eli Elder. They look after the ground patrols while Baelen takes care of the sky with the gargoyles." She laughs all of a sudden. "I never thought I'd say anything like that about gargoyles." Then she throws an apologetic glance at Indira. "Uh…"

The forthright woman grins. "I'm not offended. We have a long history to move past. But I must say I'm enjoying this alliance with the elves." She leans forward and lowers her voice to a whisper. "You have much prettier underwear than we do. I may have to steal some."

I burst out laughing. It's true that elven lingerie is made of silken material, while gargoyle underwear is usually more practical, made of breathable fabrics. The clothing Howl gave me to wear was the exception, but after being stuck in some of the underwear Grayson gave me, I'll take breathable any day.

"Here," Indira says, passing me her pouch across the table. "These belong to you."

I look inside to find the Rath and Mercy stones. I pull two of them out.

Mom exclaims, "Our heartstone! But what happened to it?"

I tell them about Grayson and the stones embedded in his back, the way he used them to keep me tied to him, but I leave out the parts where he manipulated my emotions. I can't have that conversation with them before I have it with Baelen.

Mom runs her hand across the shattered pieces of the Mercy stone. She holds one up next to my face and raises an eyebrow as if she just had a thought.

"What?" I ask her, smiling

"You should add this one to your crown. And one of the Rath stones too. I can have one of the metal workers add it for you if you like?"

"No need." I take the piece she offers and choose one of the Rath stones. Then I remove my tiara. There is enough space on each end of it for one more stone. Closing my eyes and letting my Prime power flow through me, I press the Rath stone into the tiara, manipulating the golden band to embed it, following it with the Mercy stone.

Then I gather the remaining pieces of the Mercy stone into my hand and ask Mom to place all the Rath stones into my other, closing both fists around the pieces. I'd separated the gargoyle heartstones with my power. Surely, I can reconnect the elven heartstones too? I concentrate because this is harder. Why is it easier to break something than to put it back together? These fragments are like Baelen and me right now, breaking further and further apart. I dip my head to hide my tears. Somehow, I don't think this task requires Incorruptible, Prime, or Lightsworn. For the first time, I deliberately seek out Virtuous's compassion, allowing it to flow through me.

Mom gasps.

I open my eyes to find the heartstones whole again. I hand them both to Mom. "They need to be kept somewhere safe."

"I understand."

Halfway through the end of the meal, a group of male gargoyles enters the room. The elves around me all stop eating for a moment. I guess they're still getting used to having gargoyle allies. One of the men is Erit. As soon as he sees us, he heads in our direction. His gaze flickers to Indira for a moment and the smile he gives her warms my heart. Reaching my position, the men all take a knee.

"Supreme Incorruptible, we honor you."

I stand, ignoring the astonished stares from the elves. I'm guessing the gargoyles haven't shown deference to anyone since they got here. My tiara glows in recognition of the gargoyle's fealty. "I am honored."

As the other gargoyles disperse to eat dinner, Erit says, "We've just come off patrol. We rotate on and off so we keep our energy up."

"Was Baelen with you?"

He shifts a little, suddenly uncomfortable, although I'm not sure why. "He was, but he's headed to the furthest outpost to make sure they're prepared if there's an attack in the night."

My heart sinks. The furthest outpost is miles away. It's the smart thing to do, but why does it feel like Baelen is avoiding me? I try to focus on the preparations. "What about the remainder of Erador's border further south?"

"Llion, Roar, Welsian, and Arlo have that covered. There are patrols up and down the border at all times and multiple outposts in the places most vulnerable to an attack. The villages close to the border have been evacuated, and the army is gathered at strategic points further inside the border, ready to defend against any attack. Also, Senturi has gathered Outliers to guard the wastelands on either end of the border."

The gargoyles' resilience and determination constantly amaze me. A little over a week ago, they were devastated by Howl's treatment of them. Now, they are fully prepared for war. "Thank you, Erit. I'm impressed with everything you've done."

He gives me a smile. "It's good to see you safe, Lady Storm."

His gaze falls on Indira. She clears her throat and rises to her feet. "Please excuse me, friends."

Soon after she leaves with Erit, I'm surprised to see the former Elven Commander, Teilo Splendor, bring food around for the newly returned gargoyles. He's wearing a cook's apron and carrying a large plate of boiled potatoes. When he reaches me, he gives me an acknowledging nod, but I can't keep my surprise to myself. "You're working in the kitchens."

He replies, "I'm doing what I should have done when I was an Elven Commander—serving my people."

Sahara, his daughter, gives him a genuine smile. For a while their relationship was strained by the Elven Command's treatment of me, but it looks like they have mended bridges.

Soon after, Sebastian and Eli return from patrol, heading for us first. They bow to me. "Storm Princess."

Like Erit and the gargoyles, they appear tired but focused. "We're pleased to report no incidents at the outposts this evening."

"Thank you, both."

Jordan is already on her feet. I give her a smile as she joins her husband at his table. Instead of heading toward the food, Eli hovers for a moment at my side. "What is it, Eli?"

His crystal-clear, blue eyes remind me of Cassian for a moment, serious and stern. "I understand you encountered my grandfather while you were held against your will."

I recall Elwyn Elder raging at Grayson about not taking me to prison. "Only from a distance."

"Whoever he was before, his soul is gone now. He is nothing more than a predator."

I contemplate Eli. He was always quiet and thoughtful, a lean fighter. He helped me when I was Howl's prisoner by giving me information about my Storm Command. "What are you trying to tell me?"

"I will not hold it against you if you kill him. The grandfather I knew no longer exists. He killed himself a long time ago."

I swallow against the lump in my throat. I can't imagine what he's going through to be fighting against his own people. Against his own family. He spins on his heel, and I return to my seat, feeling subdued.

Neither Baelen, nor my brother, appears during dinner, and afterward, I want to go out and find them, but Mom orders me to go to bed. "A Queen is no good to her people if she's asleep on her feet."

She orders me to my room, waits while I change, and kisses my forehead, extinguishing my lamp as I snuggle into my old bed. "I promise you, we will wake you if you're needed. Sleep well, sweetheart."

My father waits outside the room, and before Mom closes the door behind her, worry passes between them.

"Macsen is at the eastern outpost with Baelen," Dad says as their footsteps recede. His voice is low and moving down the hall, but it's amazing what I can hear when I want to. "They want us to make sure Marbella stays here where she's safe."

Mom's voice cracks. "Our daughter has been through so much." The heartbreak in her words makes my chest ache. I suspected she was putting on a brave face for me, not wanting to show the full extent of her worry about my safety.

Dad replies, "We can't risk that she'll be captured again."

I understand their motives, but I sigh into my pillow. It looks like I've swapped one sort of cage for another. I shouldn't be angry. I've missed my family. I've missed my ladies. If I have the chance to spend time with them, then that is a gift. But it's not my role to be wrapped in cotton wool and put on a pedestal. That's not who I am.

I'll do what they want, tonight—I'll sleep and stay safe—but tomorrow, I'm going straight to Baelen wherever he is. I won't let others fight my battles for me.

For the first time in many years, I sleep in a room alone. For so many years, my Storm Command slept right outside my door, and often one of them would sleep on the floor of my room. That was mostly in the beginning when the nightmares were bad. Then in the mines, I was surrounded by gargoyles. And for the last week, Grayson was always there.

It's only when I'm about to fall asleep that I remember I left Cassian's bone lash in Grayson's room.

28

BAELEN

It kills me to walk away from Marbella outside the house.

I want to tell her how beautiful she is, make sure she feels safe, listen to everything she needs to tell me. I want to tell her how much I missed her. *Damn, I missed her*. Having her back is like finding my heart beating again. But I have to give her the time she needs with her family. She needs them and they need her. Reuniting them is a gift I can give her. I have to prove to her that she comes first. To give her that, I'll make sure Rath land is defended and I'll take care of our war preparations—so she doesn't have to.

My feelings right now aren't important.

Macsen catches up to me before I can take to the sky, forcing me to remain on the ground. "Night patrol?" he asks.

"I'll do it."

He is quiet beside me, keeping pace despite my hurried steps. "Sooner or later, you'll need to sleep, brother."

"I'll sleep tomorrow."

"Hmm."

I glance at him. He doesn't believe me. He's right to distrust my word on this. Exhaustion has become my constant companion. I don't know when I last slept for more than a few hours. Fortifying Erador's borders and evacuating the nearby villages was my first goal; ensuring weapons supply and organizing the army into sections was next. Every other spare moment, I searched Erawind for Marbella's location, every failed attempt widening the painful cavity in my chest. I remind myself that she's safe now. My goal is to protect her until the fight. Even if that means I can't be where she is.

I spend the afternoon and well into the night traveling the width of Rath land with Macsen, checking the outposts to make sure they're secure.

At midnight, I'm called to a scuffle at the southern outpost. One of the gargoyles holds an unknown elf by the collar of his shirt. "I found him creeping through the field during surveillance," the gargoyle says.

I don't recognize this elf. He couldn't be more than fourteen years old. His golden hair indicates he's a member of the House of Glory but he's too young to be a threat. He doesn't even have his tattoos yet.

He squeaks, "I bring a message for Marbella Mercy. If I don't deliver it directly to her, Grayson Glory will kill me."

It's best to make sure he remains afraid, so I narrow my eyes at him, lightning curling around my torso. "Give it to me."

"No, sir. I can't, sir. I must give it only to her."

I peer into his eyes. "How do I know you aren't bringing a weapon onto my land?"

The elf's eyes water as he dangles in the air. Considering the threatening warriors surrounding him, I have to admire that he's still coherent. "Grayson Glory said you wouldn't trust me. He said to remind you that a warrior as intelligent as yourself will know the difference between a threat and a simple message."

I narrow my eyes at the boy. Once again, Grayson is proving unpredictable. I close my eyes briefly, remembering the way we spoke before our enmity began. I thought we could be allies then. Friends, even.

There isn't any hope of that now. I've promised that next time I see him, I'll kill him.

"Very well." I take the boy from the gargoyle and disappear in a whirl of wind.

29

____

MARBELLA

I awake to a commotion outside my door. It rattles hard as wind rushes underneath it. I leap out of bed, snatch up my tiara, and race to the door before it breaks in half. I throw it open to find Baelen about to thud his fist against it. His other fist is busy gripping a disheveled elf by the scruff of his neck. It's the messenger from Grayson's place.

I'm fully awake now. "Baelen?"

Baelen is a tower of stone and rage. The circles under his eyes are even darker tonight. Smudges of dirt cast shadows across his forehead. His arms are bare and his muscles bunch, glistening with sweat. He glares at the messenger. "Speak!"

The elf squawks as electricity crackles around Baelen's shoulders and arms. The elf stutters, "I-I-I have a message for you, Marbella Mercy."

Baelen growls. "The parchment will only open for you."

I take the scroll that the elf holds out to me in his shaking hands. It has my name written on it. Simply:

Marbella.

I've seen Grayson's handwriting on enough documents in his

221

room to recognize it. Taking glances at Baelen, I carefully pry the parchment open.

Marbella,

I warned you about acts of mercy. I may not be able to use the heartstones now, but my injuries healed much faster because of what you did. In fact, I'm completely well, which means I am in a position to annihilate your entire gargoyle army immediately.

However, the other Commanders don't know this. They think I'm still wounded and won't go to war without me.

So, your act of mercy has bought you a week.
Use it wisely.

P.S. This is yours. I sense it means something to you.

The paper disintegrates in my hand as soon as I read the last word. Fine dust falls between my fingertips. He definitely didn't want anyone else to read it.

I'm not sure what the last part of the message means until the elf reaches into the satchel at his waist and pulls out Cassian's bone lash. I take it, dumbstruck. It does mean something to me. Now Grayson has returned it to me and given us a week. *Use it wisely.*

Baelen is all business. "What did it say?"

I take a moment to study him before I respond. He focuses on a spot on the wall right beside my face. I'm suddenly aware that my nightdress is not exactly opaque. Indira wasn't joking about elven lingerie. I fold my arms and pull the translucent material a little closer around myself. Baelen definitely didn't want to be standing outside my bedroom door tonight, that much is clear.

I'm wary of the listening messenger who will no doubt report everything I say back to the other Commanders. Grayson cast a spell on the message so that nobody else could read it—including them. I clear my throat. "Grayson made a lot of threats, but it sounds like he was hurt very badly. We have a week before they can meet us in battle."

"I don't trust him. We'll triple the patrols and prepare for imminent attack." Baelen swings away from me, spinning the elf with him like the man is a sack of vegetables. He drags the elf back along the corridor, striding away from me.

"Baelen! Wait…"

My arm drops back to my side. Baelen is already gone in a rush of wind that whips my hair into my eyes.

There's no way I can go back to sleep now. A glance out of the window tells me it's almost sunrise anyway. I race back into my room, search the closet for something decent to wear, and come up with a sturdy pair of slacks, a black singlet top, and a cropped jacket. I braid my hair, falling into old habits by braiding it down one side of my head and tying a lavender-colored ribbon in it. My fingers linger on the dressing table where Mom has laid out ribbons for me just like she did when I was a girl. We had nothing, but she always helped me feel pretty.

Creeping to the kitchen, I locate an apple and a chunk of cheese to eat on the way.

A voice from the shadows makes me jump.

Indira slides into the light. "They don't want you to go outside."

I grip the edge of the table. "Why not?"

"They're worried about talon crows. Elves can't fly, but the crows are everywhere, spying on us."

"I can burn a crow out of the sky in an instant." I grit my teeth. "I'm going outside, and you'd better not try to stop me, Indira. Or you and I will have a serious problem."

Not that I'd think of beating her up in her pregnant condition, but I'd have some serious words to say.

She throws her hands up, making a gesture at the tiara. "Absolutely not. But I can tell them I tried."

I spin away from her, but she says, "I thought you should know: Baelen never comes back to the house. He doesn't eat or sleep here."

"But… he does sleep, doesn't he?"

"I honestly don't know. That man hasn't stopped since you were taken."

My forehead creases as I recall the dark rings under his eyes. "Where would he usually be at this time of day?"

"Right before sunrise? He'd be at the south-western outpost. I can take you there if you like."

I shake my head at her. My power flares a warning if she tries to insist. "I don't think so."

"Okay, okay. Be careful out there."

I stride away from her. As I exit the house, I dare the elves guarding the door to stop me. I plot a path south, take off the jacket, and jog the half-mile to the southern outpost that is nearest to the border with Erador. The outpost consists of a sprawling, wooden building with a wide verandah and multiple high turrets on its roof where elves stand guard.

When I reach it, I approach the elf standing guard at the door to the building.

He salutes me. "Storm Princess?"

"Where is Baelen Rath?"

"I'm sorry, Storm Princess, you just missed him. He went to the north-western outpost."

I spin. That's miles in the opposite direction. Surely I would have passed Baelen on the way? *Oh, where is Hideaway's Heartstone to give me flight when I need it?* I wonder if I can try that hot-air-cold-air thing I did a while back, but that seemed to be more of a floating thing than a flying-somewhere-fast thing.

Fine. I jog the distance, keeping an eye on the sky and my surroundings. When I finally reach the north-western outpost, I get the same answer, except this time they tell me to go south again, back to the very outpost I came from. I pin the soldier in a glare before he dares to turn away. "Did Commander Rath tell you to say that?"

The guard shifts uncomfortably. "I'm afraid so, Storm Princess."

"Which means he doesn't want me to go east." I shake my head. They want to keep me as far away from the eastern side of Rath land as possible—that's the side most vulnerable to the Elven Commanders. "Well, tell him if he wants to protect me, he'd better come find me at the far eastern outpost."

I spin on my heel, but I haven't made it two steps from the

building before my brother stops me. Macsen steps out of the shadows at the side. "He's not there either."

"Well, then, *where* Macsen? Because I am not going to let him fight without me."

My brother's usually good-humored expression is nowhere to be seen. "I don't think that's what he's trying to do."

"Then what? Annoy the hell out of me? Cut me out of his life? What?"

Macsen is deadly serious. "He said he needs to show you his worth."

Shock shoots through me. I stumble backward, trying to brace myself. The women who were forced into Howl's harem could only return to their husbands by starting fresh. Part of that process involved asking their husbands to prove they knew their wives' hearts. Baelen saw me step into Grayson's arms, and he knows I would never do that willingly. He's trying to follow the gargoyle way by showing me he knows my heart.

Macsen continues. "I don't know what that means, but judging by the look on your face, you do."

I think back to the day before, the way Baelen had flown me straight to my family, stepped back to give me time with them, and then gave me space to reconnect with my Storm Command. And now he's trying to show me that he will work all day and night if it means taking care of me and my people.

But he's got it all wrong. He is part of my world. I need him in my life. And I have to tell him that.

"Please, Macsen. I need to know where he is."

He scrubs at his forehead, easing the furrow that had formed there. He inclines his head toward the Rath mountains. "He said you'd know where to find him."

Where to find him? I spin and consider the distant mountain range. Does he mean the place where it all started?

"Thank you, Macsen."

"Stay safe, Marbella."

I head for the cliffs behind the Rath home, but I stop in at the house on the way. If Baelen isn't taking care of himself then I need to take care of him instead. I pick up a basket of food and flasks of water and top it off with a blanket since he's probably sleeping wherever he lays his head. When Mom catches me and tries to stop me, I kiss her cheek swiftly and look her in the eye. "I love you, Mom. But Baelen needs me. I'm going to him."

Tears form in her eyes. "Okay, sweetheart. I understand."

A solid hour later, I arrive at the top of the cliff that was our secret place. It was the place where the Storm chose me. The place where the wind stole my blue ribbon, and I thought I killed Baelen. So many memories flood back to me. Some of them are breathtaking. Others are heartbreaking. Rath land sweeps across the countryside below me. From here, I can see all the way beyond the Rath boundary, far into elven country. It's the perfect place for Baelen to stand watch.

I find him leaning against the mouth of the cave, head tilted to its rocky edge, one shoulder wedged against it. The bristles on his chin are a growing shadow across his jaw. His chest rises and falls in a deep rhythm.

He's asleep where he stands.

"Oh, Baelen." I creep around him, wrap the blanket over his shoulders, and decide it's time to test my strength. I moved glass shards with a wave of my hand, although admittedly they were a *lot* lighter than Baelen. I concentrate and draw on my Incorruptible strength and my Prime heart, surprising myself when I leverage him gently away from the side of the cave with my power without waking him up, laying him down inside it instead. He murmurs a little before pulling the blanket tighter and remains asleep.

He must be exhausted.

I take his place at the cave's opening, keeping an eye on the horizon. Half an hour later, a talon crow soars across the sky a mile away. I wait for it to fly a little closer and then I stretch out my arm and let loose a little destruction, turning the beast into dust. An hour later, two more crows meet the same fate.

Other than that… it's peaceful. The view stretches in every direction, so any attack will be easily visible. I have no concerns that something might happen on the ground without me. On top of that, I trust Grayson's word. His message was honest. Cynical, that's for sure, but honest. We have a week.

I sense Baelen's breathing change. I turn a little, remaining where I am, even when he jolts upright, disoriented to find himself wrapped in a blanket. "Marbella?"

He squints at me, rubbing his eyes. His gaze shifts to check the position of the sun. His face falls. "What time is it?"

"Don't worry. I kept watch." I shrug, keeping it light. "I killed a few talon crows, but that was easy. You can get more sleep if you want."

"If I want?" His laugh is dry and scratchy. "What I want is…" He shakes his head, squeezing his eyes closed. Takes a deep breath. "Macsen told you where I was."

I turn a little toward the horizon, remaining relaxed against the rock wall. "I forgot how peaceful it is up here."

He rises to his feet, stretching his neck side-to-side, and rolling his shoulders. He bundles up the blanket and drops it at the opening as he draws near to me. He moves at a prowl. I'm not sure what his target is until he swoops to the basket I brought with me and devours all of the wheat biscuits in a few bites, reaching for a water flask to wash them down.

Exhausted *and* starving.

I hide my smile as the remainder of the food—apples, cheese, and bread—disappears within moments. No wonder he was cranky. He holds onto the water flask, carrying it further out across the cliff where he stops to assess the land below us. I remain quiet, unmoving from my station, while he places the flask on the ground, removes his shirt, and takes a knee. Dipping his head, he pours the rest of the water over the back of it, finishing up by scrubbing liquid across his face with his hands.

He rises to his feet again, his broad back to me, water droplets following the curves of his muscles as he scrapes his hair out of his eyes. His chest expands and contracts as he draws in a deep breath, allowing his arms to drop to his sides. He remains in that position for a long time. I don't feel as if he's forgotten me, more that he needs the silence. The air up here is clean and fresh. Quiet. Far away from all the noise. Every inch of my body wants to go to him, but I don't want to break the spell.

Finally, he angles toward me, his chiseled features a silhouette against the sun as he speaks carefully. "Have you… had the chance to spend time with your Mom?"

"Yes."

"And your Storm Command? I know they are like sisters to you."

"Yes."

"Good." He turns back to the horizon for another long moment. "What about your brother and Jordan? Elise too?"

I leave my post, carefully covering the distance to his side. "Yes, yes, and yes."

"What about—"

I interrupt him. "Baelen."

"Yes?"

I bite my bottom lip, reaching up to brush my thumb across his jawbone. A tiny leaf was stuck where he slept on it. "You missed a spot. Right here."

He remains perfectly still.

I brush my fingers across his lips. "And here too."

He doesn't shift, but his breathing increases, washing across my fingertips when his lips part.

I say, "You gave me the time I needed with my family. Now I need time with you." I allow my fingers to drop to the curve where his neck meets his shoulders, running my hand down his arm and pulling it around my waist.

He responds by drawing me closer, his gaze falling to the lavender ribbon in my hair. Cautiously, he slides it loose, careful not to tug as he loosens my braid, allowing my hair to float around me in the breeze.

He folds the ribbon into his fist, but a smile breaks across my face as I decide it's time to set that ribbon free. The last time we stood on this cliff, the wind stole my ribbon out of his hand. That was the moment I raced after him to tell him I loved him, only to be struck by lightning that turned me into the Storm Princess.

I capture his hand, easing the ribbon out of it. Then I let it go, watching it twist and turn in the wind, disappearing into the blue sky.

"There," I say. "Not stolen this time. Given."

He matches my smile with one of his own, his full lips taking on curves that make my heart miss a beat.

I reach up on my tiptoes, very slowly, and whisper, "Baelen Rath, may I have your permission?"

With a fierce growl, he tightens both arms around me, pulling me flush against him. His kiss is more intensely demanding than it's ever been before. I respond with a ferocity of my own, arching up against him and sliding my hands into his wet hair, every part of my body responding to his. My skin tingles from the top of my head to my toes, and my breathing becomes erratic. I can't get enough of his mouth on mine.

He growls at me when I separate from our kiss. "Come back."

But his breath hitches when I slide off my jacket and pull my top over my head, abandoning both on the ground. I'm wearing underwear, but it's an elven bra that reveals more than it conceals. I crash back into him, all of me burning.

I smile against his mouth as I kiss him again. "It's been a week."

His muscles flex around me as he hesitates, pausing, taking a deep breath, and creating a small gap between us. "We don't have to rush this. You've been through a lot."

"So have you…" I kiss his jawline because unless he dips his head, that's as far as I can reach. My heart rate is slowing, because Baelen and I still need to have a conversation about Grayson. "Baelen… I… About what you saw…"

He stops me with a kiss, a gentle one that demands nothing in return. Then he draws back to give me a serious smile. "You bound yourself to me."

I bite my lip, a half-smile forming and fading, not sure what he's thinking. "I did."

An answering smile breaks across his face. A grin, actually. The first today. "Then nothing else matters."

My heart expands. I rise up as far as I can, drawing his face down to me so I can kiss each corner of his smiling mouth, tasting his skin with my tongue, sensing his body respond to mine.

I inhale his sigh. "Baelen Rath, thank you for being so protective of me, but I don't want to wait."

His response is a slow ignition of lightning around his torso as his burning gaze zeroes in on mine. Above us, storm clouds gather in the sky, forming out of nowhere, darkening the cliff face. My eyes widen as the clouds descend, stopping fifty feet above us where they curve and seal to the rock face, creating a cloak over the space at the top of the cliff. Within moments, Baelen drops us into darkness, our own safe cocoon, lit by a gentle spider web of lightning flickering inside the clouds.

His grin turns into a lazy smile at my amazement. "Come here, Marbella Mercy."

My lips meet his and each of my heartstones bursts into life, making me feel like time is slowing down around us. Baelen lifts me up against him, but he doesn't carry me inside the cave—only to its entrance where the blanket rests. I should take a breath but I can't stop kissing him. Or dragging my clothes off. Or tugging off his clothing. He slows us down, beats of time to kiss me everywhere: on my lips, my neck, my stomach, my thighs. Spreading the blanket across the ground, he draws me down to lie beside him.

By the time he's done touching me, I'm glowing. Everywhere.

He leans over me, his lips caressing mine before he pulls me upward again so I'm straddling him. When our bodies join, time stretches. I have no idea whether it's been moments or hours. I'm not afraid of the lightning that sparks between us, or the glow from my heartstones that reaches out to meet it, the two powers winding into each other like a lattice that settles over our bodies as we move together.

Even though we're as close as we can get, I want more of him. I inhale the scent of his skin, the storm, and the condensation in the air, and drown in the intensity in his eyes as he reads my reactions. I tip my head back as he winds his hands in my hair and strokes its waves all the way to my lower back. Raindrops fall from the clouds and glide across his broad shoulders, down his hard chest. Moisture drips down my cheeks and arms, making my skin glisten.

The lattice of power around us glows brighter as the intensity builds, my breathing goes wild, but still I want more. More of him. More of the storm. More of… *my* storm.

I gasp as the lattice of storm and heartstone power contracts around us, sealing hard against our bodies, and binding us together.

"Baelen!"

To my astonishment, he smiles. "Let go. Don't be scared."

He kisses my mouth and I grip his shoulders as powerful

sensations build inside me, shivers racing up and down my spine. I hold on tight, knowing I have to let go of my control, that I have to trust him. I crash against him, meeting his movements, abandoning my fear as a bright spark builds between us, a ray of light expanding and growing.

At the last moment, right before I lose control, Baelen closes his eyes. When he opens them again, they're full of lightning, full of storm. He flattens one palm across my heart, the other against my temple.

He whispers, *"Yours."*

He lets go and my world explodes.

Lightning pours from his body into mine. I scream and cry, soaking it up, drinking it in, absorbing the storm while every other part of me splinters into a thousand rocketing sensations. I fall into his arms as we shudder and tremble. We may as well have survived an earthquake, we're both shaking so hard. All we can do is wait for it to ease. I slide my arms around him, dropping my head into the crook of his neck, wanting to find my voice, wanting to speak, but I don't know how right now.

He strokes my back, his big arms gentle and calm. "Marbella. Tell me you're okay."

"I'm okay," I whisper into his neck. "Are you okay?"

"Very."

"Did I… just get my storm power back?"

His vocal chords rumble against my forehead. "Why don't you try it and see?"

Without shifting my position, still snuggled against him, I lift my hand to examine my fingers, the back of my hand, my forearm. Lightning prickles under my skin and tiny sapphire pulses flicker along my fingers. Its familiar crackling reaches my ears before I shut it off. I exhale my amazement. "Did you know that was going to happen?"

"I suspected it might. Everything was different in the deep springs, but this is where you got your power. It's right that you should get it back here."

I sigh into his neck, nuzzling his ear only to find that my hair tangles in his bristles. "It's time to shave this beard off, Baelen Rath. You don't need it anymore."

I sense his jaw shift as he smiles. "Okay, Marbella, but first..."

He lifts me up, muscles bunching, keeping my legs wrapped around him. A fat raindrop lands on my cheek a moment before he says, "Look up."

I tip my head back. A gentle rain shower patters down around us, rinsing the sweat off our bodies. I squeak as the river of water runs toward our clothing, but Baelen laughs. "Don't worry, they'll dry." He lowers me to my feet, letting the warm water wash over both of us, following it with his hands, making me sigh all over again.

I ask, "How did you get so good at this?"

He raises an eyebrow at me. "Good at what?"

I blush. "I mean controlling the storm."

"Practice." He grins, water droplets running down his face as the rain shower eases. He shakes his head, splattering rain drops across the space between us, making me laugh. "Lightning is your strength, rain is mine."

Acid rain.

I lean into him. "I want to try something... Do you remember when you were asleep? We combined our power without realizing."

"I remember." The depths in his eyes pull me in. "I waited a long time for you to call me."

I entwine my fingers in his, closing my eyes, listening for his heartbeat like I used to. I sense the connection almost straight away. Sooner than I expect, his whisper reaches me as if from a distance, a rumbling laugh drawing me back to myself. "I don't think we're doing our clothing any favors."

I open my eyes. Crimson raindrops rise upward from our bodies, lifting into the cloud cover: raindrops in reverse. One of them loses altitude, drops to the rocky cliff, and sizzles right next to my jacket. I break the contact with an "Oops." Baelen might be able to dry our clothes off, but it would take a miracle to sew them back together.

He pulls me close, brushing the hair out of my face. He exhales a long sigh. "Do you really think we have a week before the elves attack?"

"I do. Grayson is unpredictable, volatile sometimes, but when he gives his word, he keeps it." *Sometimes for the worse.*

"Okay, then. I'll reduce the patrols. Keep everyone rested."

It's my turn to take a deep breath. "There's something I need to do now that I have my storm power back. Senturi told me that my future depends on it."

"Yes?"

"I need to see Elyria."

30

MARBELLA

Before we leave Rath land, we head back to the house to let everyone know where we're going and to pack supplies in case we're gone longer than expected. I consider testing out my new storm skills to fly to Elyria's location, but only the phoenix knows where she and Jasper are. After I call the firebird to me, we detour down the border where Baelen points out our defenses from his position sitting behind me, arms wrapped around my waist.

I'm impressed to find that most of the outposts aren't visible from the sky—which means they will be even less detectable from the ground. I remember the day we came across Llion after we rescued Talia: he'd camouflaged himself against the rock, so we didn't know he was there until he chose to reveal himself. Male gargoyles are particularly good at blending into their surroundings. When Baelen points at the fifth invisible outpost, I squint back at him. "How do you know it's really there?"

His answer is to drop a tantalizing kiss on the side of my neck. He seems to be enjoying the fact that I'm snuggling up against him right now. He's definitely a lot more relaxed now that he believes we have a week before we go to war. "Ask the phoenix to take us down. I'll show you."

The phoenix circles a few times, finally locating a place to set down on a precipice at the top of a ravine. The firebird hops

234

impatiently from side-to-side as if it's standing on hot potatoes until Baelen and I slide from its back. Then it rapidly returns to the air. I'm not sure what all that was about until the ground shifts beneath my feet.

"Whoa!" What I thought was solid rock isn't rock. Instinctively, I harness the breeze around me, lifting myself and Baelen up and away from the surface.

He seems pleased that I moved him instead of the other way around. "Look at you," he says. "Taking a crash course in flying."

"It's about time," I growl, circling the structure and trying to find an opening, because one step on it told me that I was standing on a building, not a rock face. Baelen circles around with me, clearly amused at my bewilderment. He glides in close, slipping an arm around my waist. "You won't see them until they want to be seen."

I clear my throat, peering at the structure that blends seamlessly into the cliff. There is a small platform on one side of it that I choose to descend to, finding my feet on what is actual rock. "They're watching us right now, aren't they?"

Baelen makes a smooth landing right behind me. "Yep."

I straighten, attempting to appear as regal as I can. I am their Queen after all. Even if the way Baelen creeps up behind me and nuzzles my ear before stepping back again makes it look like he's the one in charge. *Hmm. If he keeps dropping kisses on my neck like that...*

The rock-like structure shifts. A man strides from an opening that quickly closes after two other gargoyles appear close behind him. He's beaming at me.

"Badenoch!" I hug him before he can take a knee. "Don't worry about all the Supreme Incorruptible stuff. I'm honored to see you safe and sound."

He grins at me. He's an older man who holds his wings in such a way that they always move fluidly with him.

"I'd like to introduce my son and daughter," he says. "They will fight with us."

Badenoch's wife died soon after she was forced into Howl's Harem. Badenoch told me his children were living in an orphanage. He'd gone to find them after the fight with Howl in Crimson Court.

Two teenagers step up on either side of him. His son is a younger version of him but without the pale scars crossing his chest. His daughter is gorgeous and no doubt takes after her mother with mahogany hair and brown eyes shot through with silver flecks.

I'm surprised. "Somehow, I pictured your children younger."

They smile back at me good-naturedly and bow their heads. "Supreme Incorruptible, we honor you."

"I am honored to meet both of you."

They show me inside what they call a "cavern" and introduce me to the thirty other gargoyles inside.

"It's sort of like a mini Cavity," Badenoch explains, showing me how the building is painted to look like the rocks around it and covered in strong, protective material that Talia has used her deep magic to conform and meld into the surroundings. I'm really happy this means that Talia is testing out her powers. I haven't seen her since Grayson caught her on the cliff top.

Badenoch shows me the openings in the base and top of the structure and the gazillion arrows stockpiled at one end. "If the enemy travels by foot through the ravine below us, we will use these openings to fire on them from above. If they fly over us, we will use the upper openings to shoot them out of the sky." He reveals one basket of five arrows that are all gold-tipped with shimmer beetle husks. "These are only for a dire emergency."

These arrows can slice through any armor, even cut through a gargoyle's wings. They will bring down the most heavily protected foe, but the danger is that the weapon will fall into the enemy's hands and be used against the gargoyles.

"Only if absolutely necessary," I say, thanking Badenoch again.

Taking to the air with the phoenix once more, two hours pass before we soar toward the north-western corner of Erador, the firebird's steady wings propelling us around Mount Denrock and toward a lush, green mountain beyond it. Baelen rides behind me, arms wrapped around me, his head resting against my shoulder. He's very quiet and relaxed. Somewhere along the way, I discover that he has fallen asleep, and I don't want to wake him.

The phoenix has been mostly quiet until now, but sings into my mind: *It's lucky that you came back when you did. Baelen Rath was a burning candle with no wax left.*

You were checking up on him?

He called me to help find you. I flew over Erawind many times looking for you, but you were hidden from everyone. So were Elise and your Storm Command. Baelen did not sleep. Not even a Storm Prince can survive without sleep for a week.

I pull Baelen's arms closer around me, enjoying his trusting weight against my back. I'm determined that he will sleep in a proper bed tonight.

I ask the phoenix, *What else did you see when you flew over Erawind?*

An army, Princess. Not only of elves, but of winged stallions, griffins, and giant eagles.

During the trials for my hand, the Elven Command had called on magical creatures to fly the champions to Scepter Peak for the first trial. Now they will use those creatures against us.

I say, *The gargoyles won't dominate the air like I hoped.*

I also saw cages filled with talon crows and pens of shadow panthers, the firebird replies. *It will be a fierce battle in the air as well as on the ground.*

I say, *We need to protect the deep springs at all costs. I won't let our world collapse.*

The phoenix's voice is a gentle admonishment as it asks, *Have you told Baelen what the Elven Commanders intend to do?*

Guilt rushes through me. I haven't told him about the Commander's plans to ascend and destroy the springs. I consider waking him up since our current location is probably one of the most private places we could be, but his deep breathing stops me. He needs to sleep.

I will tell him as soon as I can.

Very well. We are nearly there. The phoenix circles over a valley nestled between two hills. From up here, I can just make out a cabin at the base of the valley next to a lake, but it's the waterfall at the far end that catches my eye. From the air, the rushing water sparkles like diamonds. I imagine this is like the place Erit built for Indira—the beautiful valley she didn't want to leave.

The phoenix lands beside the lake, several hundred paces from the cabin. I'm very reluctant to wake Baelen, but the firebird rustles its wings and it's enough to cause him to raise his head. I swing to face him, careful not to kick him in the process. "We're here."

He scrubs at his forehead. "I passed out."

I take his face in both my hands. "You need rest. When we get home, you're sleeping in my bed."

His green eyes light up. "Your little bed? My feet will stick out the bottom of it."

I kiss his laughing mouth. "Then you'll just have to curl up."

His chest rumbles. "Yes, Ma'am."

We slide off the phoenix and it settles down onto the grass to wait for us. I make my way carefully toward the cabin, listening for its inhabitants. The rushing sound from the distant waterfall grows louder as we approach. Twenty paces from the door, Jasper emerges, striding down the steps. His straight, brown hair is longer than it was last time I saw him, hanging loose to his shoulders. He's wearing simple clothing, no armor or weaponry. His broad shoulders are relaxed and his gold-flecked chocolate eyes gleam.

I stop dead in my tracks.

He's… smiling.

He greets me first, pulling me into a hug. "Marbella, it's good to see you."

"Jasper… you…"

He pulls back, a full half-smile gracing his lips. I always suspected that when this man smiled he'd blow the socks off any woman around him, but *whoa*, where did *this* guy come from?

His forehead crinkles. "What?"

"You're… uh…" I swallow. "You look happy."

"I am." He turns to Baelen. "Brother. It's good to see you."

"You too, Jasper."

They bear hug, and once again, I'm struck at how loyal Jasper is to Baelen and me. He meets my eyes. "You're here to see Elyria."

For a moment, I forgot that he is Senturi's grandson, but the way he looks at me, seeing more than he should, reminds me that there's a conversation I need to have with him about his heritage. "Can you please take me to her?"

"She's waiting for you by the waterfall. She knew you'd come." His smile dims, becoming serious. "Ever since you broke her chains, she's had visions of the future."

I give a start. "She's become a Visionary?"

"It's best if you talk to her yourself."

"Thank you, Jasper."

I leave him and Baelen outside the cabin and follow the river upstream several hundred paces to the place where the waterfall crashes. Elyria sits on a wooden bench at the side, far enough away from the spray, but close enough that the roar is deafening. Her long lashes blink gently across her deep-brown eyes, her hair washes down one side to her hips, and one of her long legs is tucked neatly beneath her bottom. She looks completely relaxed. Even her broken wing flutters in the breeze without tension.

"This is the only place I can hear myself think."

Despite the roar, I can hear her clearly. I suspect there is some sort of spell cast over this spot, but I can't be sure whether Elyria herself cast it.

She turns to me as I sit on the chair beside her.

"Everywhere else—even the cabin—is full of noisy possibilities," she says. "But here, I can make sense of things."

"Jasper said you're having visions."

She gives a short nod. "I know it must seem impossible. Visionaries are elves, not gargoyles. But Jasper helped me see that I am a bit of both now." She smiles, a gentle lifting of her lips. "Like you."

"Jasper is taking good care of you?"

Her eyes light up as she talks about him. "He helps me understand what is real and what is not. At first, I was sure I was having waking nightmares—that the things I saw were really happening. Now I can tell when I'm having a vision." She reaches for my hand. "I'm glad you came to see me, Marbella. You have a difficult path ahead of you."

I gasp at the warmth in her hand. Whenever she touched me before, she felt transparent—there but *not* there. Now, her touch is as normal, as solid and real as any other gargoyle's.

I nod. "There's a war coming."

Her hand squeezes mine, but her brown eyes demand my attention, suddenly so deeply sad that I nearly drown in them. "You don't want to kill him, but you must."

I blink at her, keeping my question careful. "Who?"

"Grayson Glory."

The day suddenly seems very cold, the waterfall much too loud. She's talking about killing Grayson, but I won't do that unless I'm forced to. I speak very carefully. "I will defeat Grayson Glory. I will make him surrender."

"You have to kill him."

My question is sharper than I intended. "Why?"

She doesn't blink. "Because I see only two futures: one in which he succeeds, and we all die. The other in which he falls, and we all live."

"But killing him? He is not my real enemy. The Elven Command is my enemy. They are the ones who have plotted and killed for their own ends."

She inclines her head. "Yes, but Grayson is the *true* threat."

I can't deny that what she says is correct. The Elven Command will draw as much power as they can from sorcery for the fight, but it is Grayson who could turn the battle in their favor.

She persists, "You are conflicted because he has been misled. The forces in his life have taken him down a bad path—a path he might not have walked if not for them. You see the possibility of redemption for him. That he will learn the truth and change his mind."

I remove my hand from hers. "Grayson has been lied to his whole life. If I was him and I believed that the elf who raised me was a good person and someone murdered them, I'd want revenge too…"

She glances upward at my forehead, and I can only guess she's assessing my glowing Virtuous heartstone. "You feel pity for him."

"I *relate* to him. I lived a life caged from everyone too, not being able to touch anyone for fear of killing them. But I was lucky enough to have my Storm Command, my friends, to keep me grounded. He has nothing but those twisted, old bastards telling him lies all his life."

She studies her hands, remaining calm. "You aren't wrong to feel the way you feel. In fact… you wouldn't be who you are if you didn't." She bites her lip, studies the stunning blue sky and the sparkling waterfall. "Did you ever wonder why I chose you?"

I laugh but it's wry. "All the time."

"When you stood on that cliff top… No… Let me go back… When I raged through Erawind after first becoming the storm, I completely lost myself in grief. My brother and mother were murdered before my eyes, and I wanted to kill every elf… But when that first Storm Princess, that tiny, fragile little girl ran into the Storm Vault and stood in front of her mother—stood between me and the one she loved—she reminded me of *me*. She was willing to give up everything to protect her mother just like I gave up everything to avenge mine. I let her take my power into her body, absorb it, and calm me."

I hesitate to ask, "And me?"

"You stood between a lightning bolt and Baelen Rath. You gave your life willingly for his. You were worthy of my power. Which is why I know how hard this is to hear right now. I know you don't want to kill Grayson."

I clench my hands into fists. Grayson isn't Howl. Death isn't the only answer. He hasn't gone so far down his path that there's no chance left for him. I'm determined to find a way to turn him around. "You keep saying *I* have to kill him. I know I have to face him in battle but Baelen—"

"*Can't* kill him," she says firmly. "Baelen can't. Talia can't. Elise can't. I can't. Not even your heartstones can. There is only one way to defeat a natural-born sorcerer, and that power rests solely in your hands." Her eyes meet mine. "I gave it you."

"You mean the storm power." It's my turn to persist. "But Baelen shares the storm with me."

"He has a derivative of it. And, yes, he was a custodian of the original power for a time, but it was never his. Only you have my original power. I gave you my heart and soul. Only you can stop Grayson…"

I demand, "How do you know Grayson can't be stopped another way?"

"I know because I did it."

My forehead creases because I don't understand her.

She explains, "The Elven King who murdered my family… He was the first natural-born sorcerer in our history. I stopped him when nobody else could."

I sink back against the chair, my eyes wide. "The Elven King was a sorcerer from birth? I knew he practiced sorcery but…"

She sighs. "A natural born sorcerer is not like a spellcaster. Sorcery by its nature is dark and malicious. Deep magic, on the other hand, is inherently good. But me… I became the first *destructive* source of deep magic. It was the only power strong enough to destroy the Elven King's sorcery."

I clench and unclench my hands, hating the choices that are left to me. "So now it's up to me whether Grayson lives or dies."

"It is your choice. But before you make any more choices, you need to know the truth about everything. Starting with the Elven King."

"There's more?" *I don't think I can take any more.* I wait for her to continue as fear and uncertainty rise up inside me.

She says simply, "He was my father."

I gape at her, trying to digest this new information. Underneath the simplicity of her statement is sadness. The Elven King tried to kill her. Which means that her *father* tried to kill her… killed her mother and brother… and then Elyria gave her life to destroy him…

"Elyria… I'm so sorry. I can't even begin…"

She uncoils her foot from beneath her, sliding to her feet. "You read my mother's diary, so you know that everyone warned her about him, but she didn't listen. He visited for her wedding, brought expensive gifts, but he took more than he gave. After that, he didn't come back for eighteen years."

She reaches down to the water, running her hand through the wash. "My mother kept it a secret, but he realized the truth as soon as he saw me. He said I had his eyes."

"Is that why he tried to kill you?"

"He had no children. There was no elven heir. He could not allow me or my brother—*filthy gargoyles*—to make a claim for the elven throne. He grabbed my wing… broke it… I screamed and that's when my mother ran in…"

She covers her face with her hands. Stands very still for a long time. Tears seep from beneath her fingers, but she wipes them away.

"Elyria," I whisper. "You didn't deserve that to happen to you."

She takes a deep breath, swallowing, focusing on the waterfall for a moment before she finds her equilibrium again. "What's important now are the consequences."

She surprises me by dropping to her knees in front of me, taking my hands. Her palms are still wet with her tears. She asks me, "Whose soul made you the Gargoyle Queen?"

I whisper, "Yours."

"I was the heir to both kingdoms."

I gasp. "You're not seriously telling me…"

"You are the heir to the elven throne. You are Queen of both worlds."

31

MARBELLA

I am frozen. I'm sure my heart has stopped beating. I barely hear her next words.

"It's why the Elven Command has been so desperate to kill you."

"But how... did they even know? You killed everyone who knew: the King, his wife, his advisors, thousands of elves..."

She presses her lips together, suddenly trembling. "After Grayson's mother had her vision, the Elven Commanders sought every means possible to take over the deep springs. After a time, they turned their sights on me. They thought the storm power would get them through the gargoyle's defenses. So, one night, fifteen years ago, before you became the Storm Princess, Gideon Glory stole into my mind to find out what I really was and how to control me. He saw all the secrets of my past."

A tear trickles down her cheek. "But it was not what he saw that truly devastated me. My secrets are awful, but they are nothing compared to who he killed to give himself power to see my thoughts."

Her hands shake around mine. Her emotions are making me afraid. Like the other Commanders, Gideon's sorcery was always fed by death. He killed Mai to create the marriage curse. Now Elyria is trying to tell me about someone who died fifteen years ago... when I was... ten-years-old...

I force the single word to spill from my tongue. "Who?"

"Baelen Rath's mother and unborn sister."

My wail cuts across the clearing, sharp and painful. I double over, trying to breathe. Baelen's mother… his sister… their deaths had such a profound impact on him and left his House without a future. Baelen's father was a fierce but wise elf who would have recognized the Elven Command's sorcery much sooner than I did. Gideon Glory struck right at his heart, trying to break him, the same way Grayson tried to break Baelen: by taking away what he loves the most.

"After I made you Storm Princess and you showed signs of controlling the storm, the Elven Command took what they already knew about me and put the pieces together. They know you are the rightful heir."

Elyria runs her hand through my hair, trying to comfort me. "I sank all of my rage into the storm to avenge my family. You avenged Baelen's family when you killed Gideon Glory. But now your greatest battle is ahead of you. I'm sorry, Marbella. I'm sorry to tell you these things. But now you know everything."

Tears drip down my cheeks. A drastic change of air pressure alerts me moments before Baelen drops to the earth beside the lake, his feet pounding in my direction. He felt my pain. "What happened?"

Elyria intercepts him, placing her hand over his heart. "She weeps for you, Baelen Rath."

Elyria heads toward Jasper who is striding up the slope toward us, concern written all over his face. She takes his hand and speaks with him for a moment. He casts a worried glance in our direction before following her back to the cabin.

Baelen takes a knee in front of me. He reaches for my hand, quietly checking me over. "Marbella?"

This great, giant of an elf, who can literally rip a shadow panther apart with his bare hands, is so concerned about me, so careful with my hand, that I just want to cry harder. I swallow my tears and tell him everything.

I start with Elyria's story, the Elven King's treachery, and the consequences of me taking her soul. Then I tell him about Grayson's mother, her vision of Earth's surface, the Elven

Command's plans, the threat to the deep springs, the consequences if the springs are destroyed—and the fact that I'm the only one who can kill Grayson. Last of all, I tell him about his mother and sister.

Baelen cycles through every emotion—emotions he isn't afraid to show in front of me: anger, shock, disbelief, rage, and finally… grief. He bends his head over my hand, dropping his forehead to it, and stays like that for a long time. Quiet.

Finally, he says, "We will end this."

I nod. "One way or another."

When we return to the cabin, Jasper is collecting his weapons and Elyria is packing a satchel of clothing.

I try to stop them. "You don't have to come back with us."

"If the Elven Command wins the war, this valley will be rubble within a week," Jasper says, sliding his sword into its scabbard. He turns to Baelen. "I'm going to need new armor."

Jasper's last armor was beaten up before we even arrived in Erador. It was so damaged that Llion gave him the nickname Twisted Metal.

"I have the perfect armor for you," Baelen replies as they descend down the steps together.

I reach for Elyria. "Are you sure you're ready for this?"

She covers my hand with her own. "I'm ready to heal my wing. I'm ready to face the world again." Her smile turns wonky as she rolls her eyes. "As a new gargoyle-slash-elf-slash-whatever-I-am."

She hasn't once judged me for taking away her power, but as I observe the way she seeks Jasper's help climbing onto the phoenix's strong back, taking his hand without hesitation, I realize that she doesn't want the storm power anymore. She's happier without it. I pause a moment, wondering if she knows the way Jasper looks at her, wondering if they've told each other how they feel. Because it's plain as day to me: Jasper loves Elyria, and she loves him back. I hope they don't leave it too late to tell each other.

JASPER'S SMILE BECOMES FAINTER THE FURTHER WE FLY AWAY FROM the valley. By the time we reach Mount Erador, he has become deadly serious and increasingly protective of Elyria. I've chosen to sit behind Baelen this time so I can look back at both of them more easily.

After we finish off the food we brought with us while we fly, she whispers to him, "I'm okay," but he doesn't seem convinced.

He calls to me from where he sits behind her with his arms wrapped carefully around her. "Can you take us directly to the deep springs?"

"Of course." I speak to the phoenix and we eventually set down right outside them. The ledge outside the opening to the springs is cast golden in the late afternoon sunlight, the cliff face above it is a soaring expanse of mottled brown and gray rock.

Elyria takes a deep breath before she slides off the phoenix. "I'm ready."

I give them space as they head inside, but as soon as they're gone, I spin to Baelen. I don't even have to say it.

He gives me a knowing look, his eyes twinkling. "I don't think they've admitted it, let alone acted on it."

I can't help but smile. "Can you give Jasper a nudge?"

"Hmm. No." He grins. "She's a gargoyle who will follow the gargoyle way. It's up to her, remember?"

I blush. *All that "going to his bed" business.* "Okay, so her relationship with Jasper aside, what is the best way to protect her now? She used to be untouchable, and I'm worried she'll forget she's vulnerable now."

"I think we have two choices: one is to take her to Rath land. The Elven Command is less likely to focus their attack there because it's too far north to provide a good pathway to the springs. Also, the elven army will be more reluctant to attack other elves. On the other hand, it's closer to the front of the battle."

"Our other option?"

"Keep her here in the Royal Residence."

"But this is their target."

"It is… but Indira had an idea that I supported… And given that I now know the deep springs must be protected at all costs…"

He glances up.

I follow his gaze.

The cliff face shifts above me. Pieces of mottled brown and gray rock slide away from each other, pulling out and up, rising and taking on new forms: muscled legs, broad wings, determined faces. Almost the entire cliff face peels off as seventy gargoyles materialize. From beneath their massive wings, smaller gargoyles emerge, all female, all armored and armed to the teeth.

There is only one clan whose wingspan is broad enough to hide other gargoyles within it: Hideaway. And there is only one clan whose women are as ferocious as these: Grievous.

Baelen leans in to me. "Indira made an agreement with the Hideaway Clan. She said that both Grievous and Hideaway made up the greatest numbers in Howl's army, and that they owed the royal line a debt."

I chuckle. "She guilted them into this?"

"Actually, I think they would have done it regardless. The respect you showed Cassian didn't go unnoticed. He was apparently very protective of his clan. He kept many of them alive when Howl would have killed them."

Bethany and the other women fly down to the ledge, followed by the men. There are so many of them that they fill the space, and some have to hover above us. They either take a knee or bow their heads. "Supreme Incorruptible, we honor you."

"I am honored," I reply. "And grateful that you will protect the deep springs from the elves."

Bethany saunters toward me, stopping with her hands on her hips, beaming at me. "Supreme Incorruptible, I hope we meet your expectations."

"This is… truly amazing, Bethany. Thank you. Is Gretel safe?"

"She stayed on Mount Grievous along with a quarter of our women. I hope you understand, we still need to protect our homes from the panthers."

"Definitely. The more of those beasts you kill, the better."

As the gargoyle warriors disperse, the phoenix breaks into my thoughts. It says, *I will also be here to protect the springs.*

Phoenix?

It shakes its feathers, shivering hot sparks into the air around me like fireflies. Opening its mouth, I catch sight of fire rumbling in its throat. *I was born in the age of dragons*, it says. *I will pour molten wrath over anyone who dares approach this place.*

I consider the firebird with awe. *Thank you, Phoenix.*

Running footsteps draw my attention back to the entrance to the springs. Jasper shoots through the opening, skidding to a halt beside me before he slides right off the cliff.

"Jasper!"

"Marbella, come quickly."

"What's wrong?"

"She… Elyria…" Trusting me to follow him, he runs back in the direction he came from. Baelen is close on my heels as we descend through the wide entrance into the tunnel, racing along the pathway lit by spider web. The cavern at the end glistens a rainbow of colors around us while the rhythmic, single water drop echoes in the silence.

Elyria stands near the middle of the pond but at the shallower side closest to us. She is wet and shaking, immersed to her waist, eyes wide, chest heaving.

I consider her carefully as we pull to a halt at the water's edge.

Elyria doesn't look quite right…

"I came here to heal my wing." She presents her back, speaking over her shoulder through chattering teeth. "But now my wings are gone."

32

MARBELLA

My first instinct is to rush into the water and drag her out of there, but my next instinct is to stay as far away from the pond as possible.

Water drips from the ends of her hair as she shivers. "I thought I was prepared for anything, but it turns out I'm not. I don't know what I am now."

It only takes me a heartbeat to know. "Elyria! You're… human!" When I first saw Llion's baby girl all that time ago, I thought she was a human baby because of her rounded ears and delicate skin. Only her wings told me she was a gargoyle. Without our pointed ears and the luster of our skin, elves could appear human too. Male gargoyles are the furthest from human in appearance. Now, without wings, Elyria looks just like I imagine a human looks.

"Human!" Elyria takes a step back, splashing involuntarily as her legs buckle.

Jasper jolts beside me. He's ready to race into the springs to help her, but he pauses before his foot hits the water. His hesitation tells me that, like me, he doesn't want to go in. I study the waves, the sparkle within them, casting my gaze upward to the single drip falling from the ceiling. I'm not afraid of the springs themselves, but some instinct tells me not to go in there at the same time as Elyria. The deepest magic is at play here to cause this final stage of

250

her transformation. That sort of magic should be treated with the greatest respect.

Remembering Senturi's advice that Jasper is the only one who can help Elyria, I withdraw to Baelen's position off to the side, reaching for his hand.

A tear tracks down Elyria's cheek. She's frozen, panicking, unable to move.

Jasper's soft inhalation is both worried and determined. He hovers at the water's edge before he seems to make a decision. "Elyria, come out. You'll be okay."

She shakes her head, wet hair slapping against her small waist. "I don't think I can."

Instead of softening his approach, Jasper becomes stern, an insistent crease settling on his forehead. "Come out of there, darling."

Her eyes widen, surprised at what he called her, before she gives way to panic again. With a small shake of her head, tears spill down her cheeks. "I can't, Jasper."

"Then you're never going to know what I want to say to you."

Her body language shifts, a flicker of curiosity overcoming her fear. She takes a step, but the water laps at her hips and she sucks in a breath. "What if I can't come out? What if I disappear? I died four hundred years ago. What if my wings are just the beginning?"

Jasper's jaw tenses, his eyebrows drawn down. "You know I won't let that happen."

His response seems to jolt her out of her panic. She pushes through the water, inhaling sharply as it washes around her, jumping at every splash. She reaches the stone steps at the side, ascends, but stops on the top one, her feet mere inches beneath the surface, water spilling from her clothing, fear washing over her so fast that she turns deathly pale.

He's three paces away, but he doesn't close the gap, waiting for her to take the last step on her own. When it's clear she's not going to budge, Jasper plants his feet, but he visibly relaxes.

"Elyria," he says softly, making her crane forward to hear him. "I want you to come here because I want to tell you…"

She tips forward. "What?" she whispers. "Tell me what?"

"You'll never know if you don't take a chance."

She worries at her lip as she stares at the final step between them. "I can't."

"Why not?"

"Because I'm scared."

His posture doesn't change. He's still relaxed, but his voice takes on an edge. "I won't hurt you. Ever."

I'm surprised, but I shouldn't be. Jasper has Sight, and he must have seen that it's not only the water and its effect on her body that she's afraid of now, but of what her relationship with Jasper will become. It's plain to me that he loves her, but sometimes you can't see what's right in front of you. The uncertainty must be killing her.

She sucks in a breath. "That's not true. You'll break my heart."

He considers her words in true Jasper style, without fuss, taking them in like a wave sweeping up over him before responding. "Love can't break your heart, Elyria. Only mend it."

Elyria is the polar opposite in her reaction. She's suddenly a hot mess, tears streaking down her cheeks. "You can't mend my heart, Jasper Grace. Nothing can do that."

"If that's what you choose." He's still incredibly calm, much calmer than I would be. Just when I think that's all he's going to say, the corners of his mouth move in an upward direction. A slow smile breaks across his face.

Yeah. I'm never going to get used to seeing that.

Elyria suddenly sobs, gasping, pressing her hand against her heart. "Are you… smiling at me right now?"

He shrugs, slowly, deliberately. "I guess I am. Because I just realized something."

"Wh-what's that?"

"You wouldn't be so upset if you didn't love me back."

She hiccups and cries at the same time. "I… what?"

That same slow, compelling smile rests on his lips. "Come here, darling."

"Okay," she whispers. She climbs the last step and sloshes to him, her wet feet slapping on the stone. She's drenched, wingless, barefoot, and completely vulnerable as she turns her face up to his.

He gently brushes her hair back from her forehead, searching her eyes before he brushes soft kisses against her cheeks and finally kisses her lips. She melts into him, their bodies drawing closer to each other.

Baelen and I take glances at each other and quietly leave them alone, heading up the pathway and out into the open where the phoenix patiently waits for us.

Baelen grins. "No nudging necessary."

I lean into his side, urging his arm around me as I contemplate the setting sun. "It's too late to head back to Rath land now. Let's stay the night here at the Residence."

"Good," he growls, pulling me flush against him, dropping a lingering kiss on my lips. "They have bigger beds here."

My heart flutters and my pulse speeds up. I blush as one of the gargoyles higher up on the cliff clears his throat—a gentle reminder that we're not alone. Baelen doesn't seem to care, kissing me again before we approach the phoenix.

I ask it: *Can you come back for Jasper and Elyria? And bring them to the Residence?*

The firebird answers: *With pleasure.* Then it pauses before asking, *Have they finally admitted what they feel?*

They have.

The firebird chuckles. *It's about time.*

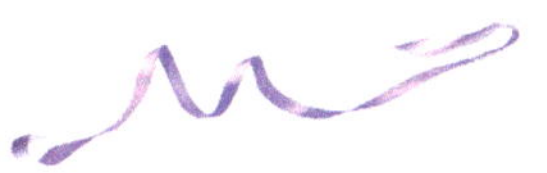

Llion, Liliana, and Talia are waiting for us when we reach the Residence, along with the old Priestess. I embrace each of them and marvel at how the babies have started walking in the last month. Liliana is glowing, and Llion seems happier than I've ever seen him. To my surprise, Talia hugs me the hardest. My skin tingles with the same strange sensation I always feel when she's close by. Her deep magic is like a force around me.

"Thank you," she says. "For saving our lives on the cliff."

I'm surprised when all of my gargoyle friends arrive over the course of the evening: Welsian, Arlo, Iago, Roar, and Gilda, even Rhain and Carmen. Then Indira and Erit fly in with a group of strong, male gargoyles who carry Reisha, Jordan, and all of my Storm Command with them. All of my ladies are here.

They tell me that Sebastian and Eli have remained behind in Rath land to help my brother continue to protect it—and that Elise is still too weak to travel, but my ladies have seen the healers and are fully recovered. They look so much better than the day before: bright-eyed, determined, all of them smiling again. Several of them give me wide-eyed blushes as they talk about the men who flew them here. Each of my ladies gave up a normal life to join my Storm Command; most of them have never had boyfriends, let alone got up close and personal with a man like they would have when they were flown here. I try to hide my smile but don't quite succeed, ending up laughing and joking with them.

Later, Senturi makes an appearance with little Adalie who runs to the babies to hold their hands as they totter around the room.

To their credit, none of my friends seems to care that Senturi and Adalie are Sighted, speaking with them openly and welcoming them to the dinner table.

When Elyria and Jasper arrive, the gargoyles and elves welcome them too, making room for them and filling their plates with food. Nobody asks about Elyria's wings, and my heart swells to realize that race and appearance no longer matter in my kingdom.

After dinner, we sit around the glowing fire in the meeting hall and my friends take turns giving me updates about our preparedness for battle. Only Iago has a different kind of news, proudly telling me that the new home for the orphans and priestesses is half complete already.

"At first I thought I should be on the battlefront," he says. "But Baelen Rath helped me see that building a new home for the children is just as important as the fight ahead. We have to look to our future with hope, not fear. He gave me a team of builders— gargoyles he could have easily sent to the border instead. I never would have gotten so far without them."

"I'm grateful for your work, Iago. I can't wait to see your progress."

As the firelight flickers and begins to die, Senturi approaches me, dropping to a knee, his wing spikes gleaming in the light the same way they did the first time I saw him. He is very solemn.

"Supreme Incorruptible," he asks in front of everyone. "May I have permission to speak with my grandson?"

I cast a quick glance at Jasper. He is sitting with Elyria snuggled close to his side, but Senturi's question causes a hush that grabs his attention. He raises his head from the kiss he dropped on her forehead, peering intently at the older gargoyle.

Senturi stands and turns. Recognition flashes instantly across Jasper's face. He's quicker to see the resemblance between himself and his grandfather than I was.

I say, "I believe you have much to talk about."

Beside Jasper, Elyria is in a state of awe, her mouth dropped open and her eyes wide. "Jasper, you are descended from Sighted Ones!" Happy tears leak down her cheeks before she can stop them, and my ladies crowd toward her, asking if she's okay. She accepts their hugs and their concern, smiling and crying at the same time. "This has been a very emotional day."

Jasper rises to his feet, eyeing the older gargoyle's spiked wings and the chain of talons he wears around his neck. The two men stand head-to-head, their facial structure and the color of their eyes so similar despite the very different color of their skin and the fact that Jasper doesn't have wings.

Senturi begins, "Greetings Jasper, son of Grace. I am Senturi of the Outlier Clan."

At that moment, Adalie runs over and tugs on Senturi's hand. "Is this my uncle, Papa?"

Jasper startles, studying her and the way she uses her power unwittingly when she looks up at him. She breaks into a sweet smile.

Senturi grins from her to Jasper. "And this little one is—"

"Adalie," Jasper says for him. "I somehow know… that her name is Adalie."

Adalie beams at him.

Senturi says, "She has wanted to meet you for a very long time. As I have."

Jasper gives his grandfather a sincere nod and gestures to the seat nearest to Elyria. "Please, we should talk."

Everyone gives them space to get to know each other, and I

spend the rest of the evening mingling with my friends and ladies until eventually, they all start heading to bed.

Before I leave, the old Priestess draws Baelen aside, beckoning him to lean down so she can whisper something into his ear. He gives her a curious glance and then a formal nod. He promptly spins on his heel and leaves the room.

He is already gone before I can ask what's going on. "Baelen—?"

The Priestess hurries over to me. "Please don't worry, Supreme Incorruptible. The Wrathful One has something he needs to take care of, but you do not need to be concerned."

The last time Baelen tried to take care of everything, he almost pushed me away. I'm reluctant to agree, but it doesn't look like I have much choice. "Oh. Okay."

She waves to someone at the side of the room and the Head Cook approaches me with a bowl full of berries that makes my mouth water despite the big meal I just ate. "We have prepared a special dessert for you, Supreme Incorruptible, in honor of... uh... your return to us."

As I take the bowl, he quickly adds, "And before you ask: yes, the kitchen staff all enjoyed a hearty meal earlier this evening."

I smile. He knew exactly what I was going to say. It's been a long time since I enjoyed dessert. Even Grayson didn't eat sweets. As I take the first mouthful, I'm suddenly aware of Elyria's gaze, her mouth pursed into a wondering "oh" before she quickly returns her attention to Jasper and Senturi. They are the last to leave before I finish eating and stretch my legs, handing the bowl back to the Head Cook with my thanks.

"It is our honor, Supreme Incorruptible, to serve you on this night."

The old Priestess walks with me to my room. Before we reach it, I admit to her, "I don't know your name."

She seems surprised. "I am Dorothea of the Prime Clan."

"The same clan as Badenoch," I exclaim and then point to my headpiece. "The Prime Heartstone."

"The most passionate heartstone." She shows her dimples as she smiles and her rainbow-colored wings glisten.

We enter the corridor to my room, and I head toward the end, but she stops me before I reach it, her bony, old arms snaking around me in a sudden hug.

I return it, surprised. "Hmm?"

She grips both my arms and turns me to the right—toward a closed door that is closer than mine. She gestures, palm out toward it as if she wants me to go in.

I raise my eyebrows at her. "That's Baelen's room."

"Yes," she says simply. "It is."

"But he's in *my* room."

"No. He isn't."

My eyes widen, remembering her whisper to him earlier.

I'm standing in front of Baelen's bedroom, and she isn't blocking my way. "May I… go in?"

"I will not stop you. But the choice is yours—and yours alone." She withdraws with a cheeky grin. "Although… you did already eat the royal wedding berries so you may not be able to back out now…"

She skips her bony ass along the corridor and disappears around the corner before I can say anything else. I press my palms against the wooden door.

This is Baelen's room.

With Baelen's bed.

And Baelen.

I don't wait another moment, pushing on the handle, swinging it wide. He stands in the middle of the room, in front of the bed, naked to the waist, water droplets dripping from his hair onto his broad shoulders and down his massive chest. His head is down, his strong hands loose at his sides. I remember the first moment I saw him inside the Storm Vault's waiting room. His head was down then too; he'd dropped to a knee and held his heartstone out to me, offering it to me even though it might mean his death.

I close the door behind me and the sound of the lock clicking makes him look up. The intensity of his gaze sets my body on fire, but he doesn't move. He won't move. Everything from this moment is my choice.

I cross the distance, craving his hands and mouth, his strong arms, but instead of touching him, I whisper, "Wait for me, Baelen. I won't be long."

As fast as my wobbly legs can carry me, I race to the bathroom, turn on the shower, and let the water run over me, my body already tingling with the electricity in the air around Baelen. If he wanted to, he could blast this door down and whisk me into his arms, but he won't. He waited an eternity for me while he slept. He waited seven years for me while I was the Storm Princess. He will wait again because I asked him to.

Drying myself off, I remove my headpiece before I return to the bedroom, wanting nothing on my body when I go to him. He hasn't moved from the spot where I left him on the other side of the room, except to half-turn, one corner of his mouth lifting into a sexy smile as his gaze runs from my dripping hair all the way past my naked parts to my toes.

I clear my throat, my voice a low rasp. "If I'm going to come to your bed, Baelen Rath, I think you need to be in it."

Without speaking, he removes his clothes and lies himself down, his big body filling most of one side. He doesn't take his eyes off me.

My heart thunders in my chest, but I have no doubts.

As I lie down beside him, I inhale the wild air around us, his power igniting mine, and I welcome the storm we're about to create in his room. In his bed.

When my lips find his, I finally understand why the gargoyles and my Storm Command came to see me tonight. Not because they knew I was going to make my choice, but because we only have a few nights left.

In five days we will go to war. We will fight for our lives and our future. We will fight for our world and our freedom. We have to love while we can, live while we can, share our stories while we can, and fight for each other while we can.

Because there might not be a tomorrow. We might not have any more days.

I open my heart and share every part of it with Baelen, giving him all of myself, accepting every part of him in return, a whole world of love while we have it.

33

MARBELLA

A blood moon rises the night before war begins. Incorruptible's light shines crimson across the mountains of my kingdom and all the way across Erawind. I find Baelen outside, alone on one of the balconies, studying the sky, his sword at his side. His armor and mine wait in our room. Everyone else has left for the border except the gargoyles and the phoenix who will guard the springs. All of the children and the elderly have been evacuated to Mount Denrock, the safest mountain and furthest from the battle.

Baelen and I will travel when the moon is at its highest to join the army on the border. We will arrive before daybreak when the battle will begin. We slept most of the day, curled up against each other, knowing that in the final hours before war, we would not be able to sleep at all.

I take his hand, "Promise me, Baelen."

He meets my eyes, his own a blazing green.

"Promise me you will be alive at the end of this battle."

He crushes me up against him, kissing me hard, but he makes no promises, leading me silently back to our room where we help each other into our armor.

Baelen dresses in armor that belongs to the House of Rath: armor that has no weaknesses, that nothing less than sorcery can pierce. That is what I am afraid of today: the five sorcerers we will

259

face, including Grayson. Baelen's storm power will be equal to their power, but he is not invincible like I am. When we are done dressing, every inch of our bodies is protected. Baelen is in finely-molded metal plates decorated in red and black markings; I wear my suit of shimmering Elyria web overlaid with golden segments.

After Baelen hands me my sword, my daggers, my bow and arrows, I click Cassian's bone lash onto my belt. I spent the last two days practicing how to use it under Llion's watchful eye to make sure I didn't take my own head off.

Baelen and I stride to the nearest balcony, where he hooks an arm around my waist and takes control of the breeze. I could fly myself—I know how—but I can't fly as fast as Baelen, and I want him close to me right now. The air pressure increases before I step into his side. He supports my head with his big hand and places a lingering kiss on my lips before he lifts off.

I press my face against his chest as the sky rushes past us, lightning shrieking through me as he speeds up and across Erador. It's not the same as Grayson's instant transportation. Flying with Baelen brings all of my senses alive, calling to the storm inside me. Lightning and thunder crackling and crashing through me. My storm power and heartstones existing in harmony.

When the border appears, we fly over the gargoyle army amassed across every access point. Up and down the mountains half of the gargoyle force is on the ground, the other half in the sky. Thousands of gargoyles are ready to defend our home. Baelen doesn't slow as much as I expected, heading upward in an arc before we drop, slamming down with a massive *crack* onto the top of the highest peak. Dark storm clouds curl across the face of the blood moon, and lightning streaks behind us, flooding the ground for miles in brilliant, crackling light.

I turn to face the elven army camped at the base of the cliff. We've landed right on the border. Right in front of their main force.

Thousands of elves are suddenly alert, heads upturned. They are massed on the gentle slope up to the base of the mountain. The mountains here are not as high as further inside Erador, only a thousand feet, so it's easy to see the large banners flying above the elven army. They stand in neat squares, each one representing an elven House. There would be thirty of them if the House of Mercy and Rath were present. It makes me angry to see that the minor houses form the front line, including Jasper's House of Grace, while the major houses take up the back rows and will only have to fight if the minors fall against the gargoyles.

I lean into Baelen as my gaze sweeps the elven army. "I could use my heartstone power and wipe them all out right now. I could stop this war."

He answers me with a smile. "I could burn the earth they stand on and turn them to molten ash. But we won't do either of those things. Because the elves are our people too."

I can't contain my anger. "Look how the Elven Command has put the minor Houses in greatest danger at the front."

"They don't care about our people, Marbella. They never did."

My heart lifts when ten thousand gargoyles raise their voices, roaring a challenge into the night that booms across the distance. There are ten thousand more hidden in caverns all along the border, ready in case any elves get through the initial defenses.

A single answering form flies upward from the elven force.

Grayson lands on the cliff's edge, keeping his distance from us, his olive-green eyes shuttered, his emotions closed off. The storm light flickering around us highlights his pale hair and the golden runes across his chest. He still isn't wearing a shirt, and he is unarmed—not that he needs weapons.

In the distance, the sun threatens to rise. The daylight will bring death.

I say, "Turn back, Grayson. Take your army and go. Stop this war."

"It's too late for that, Marbella."

I dare to close the gap, knowing that I'm the only one he can't hurt. Even Baelen will have to keep his distance. "It's never too late. We don't have to be enemies."

His response is a growl—a gargoyle growl—but he doesn't hide its origins this time. "Today I will fight the gargoyles I am descended from. I will fight the elves who have betrayed their own people. I will fight the storm." He acknowledges Baelen before he pinpoints me. "And I will fight the woman I want."

Baelen thrums beside me, but he's far too smart to slug Grayson in the face.

"But at the end of this day, I will get what I want." Grayson spins toward the cliff, ready to descend to his army again.

Right before he is about to leap from the edge, I call out, "You didn't kill your mother."

His mask falters. He half-turns. "What?"

"She knew too much. She was Gideon Glory's first kill."

Rage floods his face. He seems to forget everything as he advances on me, a force growing around his fists, deadly malice building in his eyes. "You will not tell me lies!"

I remain steady, knowing that I alone can kill him. "I'm not afraid to tell you the truth, Grayson."

Inches away from me, he searches my eyes, breathing hard and fast. The air between us crackles as my lightning builds, ready to defend myself if I have to. At the last moment, his eyes widen as he realizes… I have my storm power back. I got it back after I escaped from him.

He inhales sharply, whispering, "You're the one with the power to kill me."

"Yes."

A painful laugh escapes his mouth. "Why did it have to be you?"

He backs away from me, one careful step at a time.

I call to him, "Ask Elwyn Elder why they bound you. Ask him, Grayson. Only the truth will save us today."

"Us?"

I sweep my arm in the direction of the gargoyles and then the elves. "All of us."

He arches an eyebrow at me then shakes his head, exhaling. "We will see."

He takes a step off the edge and drops from view.

We are minutes away from war.

On the next cliff top to my far right, my friends are dressed in Rath armor, awaiting the elven horde. Indira and Erit are stationed there along with Roar and Gilda. Baelen unlocked the main vault under the Rath mansion and distributed all of the Rath armor to as many gargoyles as possible. To an onlooker, they appear to be defending the mountain, but actually, they're protecting Elise.

On the cliff top to our far left, Llion, Liliana, Welsian, and Arlo have taken up position, protecting Talia. Each cliff top is a hundred paces deep and wide, and Talia and Elise are standing as far to the back as they can. They spent the last few days comparing spellcasting and deep magic, sharing their knowledge with each other, and they have a plan today.

Gargoyles from the Outlier clan form our first line of defense in the sky. I nod across the distance to Senturi, giving him silent thanks, as he and the other Outliers coast the air in a row beside us that stretches far in either direction from my left to my right.

Jordan, Sebastian, and my Storm Command soon join me on our wide cliff top, along with Jasper and Elyria. They are also dressed in Rath armor, their bodies gleaming, and Talia has painted my ladies' cheeks with runes. Elyria refused to go to the safety of Mount Denrock with the others, but I know that Jasper will protect her. Everyone on this central cliff top has been with Baelen and me since the beginning. It feels right that they will fight beside us today.

"We're ready," Jordan says. She was my friend and guide the whole time I was the Storm Princess, looked out for me, protected my body and my heart.

"Thank you, Jordan." My throat suddenly constricts. "Please stay alive today."

In the final dying dark of night, a hundred flying creatures approach from Erawind. Winged stallions soar toward us, along with giant eagles, each of them bearing an elven rider.

At the front of the swarm, three golden griffins carry the Elven Commanders: Elwyn Elder, Pedr Bounty, and Osian Valor, each of them hunched and twisted, their bodies misshapen and their skin gnarled. Priscilla rides an eagle with white-tipped wings, its wingspan stretching far wider than the others.

They stop and coast the air only ten feet away. Their eyes have turned blood red. Full of death. My stomach turns. *How many lives did they take in the night to give themselves enough power to fight us?*

It will take a lot to kill them today.

Below us, Grayson stands at the head of the elven army right where he promised he would be. He tilts his head back and his gaze seeks me out, focused on me. Far behind him, behind the bulk of the elven army, a cage full of shadow panthers waits to be opened, but they'll do that once enough gargoyles are wounded so that the scent of gargoyle blood will drive the panthers into a frenzy.

To get past our defenses, the elves will have to either fly over the cliffs on their winged creatures or fight their way through one of two ravines below us. The ravines are wide and will allow many elves through at a time if we can't stop them. The sky is clear and the mountains here are not as tall or jagged as others.

The Elven Command chose this place of attack well.

Our plan of defense is simple: the airborne elves are the greatest threat because they can travel the farthest distance, so we need to take them down fast. While we're doing that, we also need to block the ground forces from getting through. It's Baelen's and my job to protect our army from the Elven Commanders.

The elves are singing, and it makes me shudder. The gorgeous voices of the House of Splendor rise above the others while Priscilla smirks at me. Her gaze shifts to Jordan. They are both from the House of Splendor where the song originated. Sebastian sang this same song to Jordan to tell her that he loved her. But in battle it means something very different.

They sing, "Spin gold, shelter silver."

They intend to spill blood and bury us.

My gargoyles respond by beating their wings—once, twice—rising into the air, many of them staying aloft, while others take up positions on the ground, forming a thick barrier with their bodies and invincible wings. A synchronized roar blasts across the sky, twenty-thousand male and female voices shouting in unison, sending shivers up and down my spine.

"SUPREME INCORRUPTIBLE, WE HONOR YOU!"

The elves fall silent, which makes me grin. The gargoyles' loyalty to me has silenced them.

I raise my voice, louder than ever before, filling my whole body with thunder and roaring into the sky, "I AM HONORED!"

I lower my arms. Then the gargoyle army shocks me by shouting again. "HUSBAND OF SUPREME INCORRUPTIBLE, WE HONOR YOU!"

Baelen looks as surprised as me. He tips his head back and roars, shaking the sky around us, "I. AM. HONORED!"

My skin prickles, but it's not entirely because of the gargoyle's display of allegiance. I sense a force near the ground, a far off disturbance. It feels like pain… It feels like Grayson… He didn't know I was married…

The sensation shuts off fast, gone as quickly as it started.

My gargoyle army waits for my command.

The sun rises.

I inhale the cold air and meet Baelen's strong gaze. We both remove our swords and hold them aloft, powerful electricity lighting up around our bodies at the touch of metal. I hear his voice inside my mind for the first time in a long time. *I will love you, Marbella Mercy. Until death.*

It's time to fight.

34

MARBELLA

The Elven Commanders raise their hands in unison, deadly, green light extending between them to form a death spell. They focus on the Outlier gargoyles, rather than on me. They must intend to blast through the gargoyles, make an opening, and create a quick path through our defenses. Their only target is the deep springs, and they want to get there as fast as possible.

We won't let that happen.

We're ready.

My left arm shoots up and out—the signal that Talia and Elise are waiting for. They immediately let loose their magic, their arms splayed out, deep magic and spellcasting pouring from their bodies, mingling and combining the strongest elements of both. A glistening shield shoots up all along the border in line with their position at the back of the cliff. The shield extends all the way to the ground, all the way up into the clouds, and thousands of feet left and right.

Because of where they're positioned, those of us on this side of the shield can fight the airborne elves, while the remainder of the gargoyle army is protected behind the shield—including the ground forces.

Now the elves won't be able to proceed through the ravines. Not until Grayson figures out how to bring the shield down. He's the only one powerful enough to do it, and it's going to take him a while because Talia and Elise have deliberately created layers of spells on top of deep magic, weaving a complicated magical web for him to untangle.

The Elven Commanders shout to each other as soon as the shield springs up. They lower their hands and allow their death spell to fizzle out, right before they urge their griffins to turn around and retreat. Priscilla hesitates, glaring across the distance at me. She wants to fight. I can sense it. But a heartbeat later she turns around, taking up position with the others much further in the distance.

"Cowards!" They know their power isn't strong enough to get through the shield and they'll have to fight Baelen and me if they stick around. They're going to let others fight their battle for them while they wait in safety for their next opportunity to get past us.

The elves who sail up to take their place are all too familiar to me. These elves are not from a minor House.

Rhydian Valor smirks at me from twenty feet away, drawing the reins on his winged stallion so tight that the poor creature's neck is strained. Rhydian Valor was at the heart of the attack on me in the arena during the marriage trials. He tried to take my storm power by force. I've never had good experiences with the House of Valor, but Rhydian's behavior took the cake. While Rhydian molested me, the other men had fought dirty to keep Baelen from intervening. One glance at Baelen tells me he has a score to settle with Rhydian.

Baelen's growl could be straight from a gargoyle's throat. "With all due respect, Marbella, Rhydian Valor is mine."

"I won't get in your way." I focus on the rider beside Rhydian. Another Valor man. In fact, there are many of them. They must not have any idea what they're facing if they volunteered for this part of the battle.

That's okay. I'm used to men underestimating me.

Baelen's muscles bunch.

My heart rate increases.

Together, we run to the edge of the cliff and leap from it, our swords raised, lightning licking the air, flying straight at the elves.

A thousand Outlier gargoyles follow us, razor-sharp wings spread for maximum impact. They will try to spare the stallions and eagles if they can, aiming for the riders instead.

Baelen crashes into Rhydian, lifting him bodily off his stallion, one big hand around his throat, holding him mid-air as the stallion bucks in terror and tries to escape. As soon as Rhydian's legs leave the saddle, the stallion flees while Rhydian kicks the air.

Baelen says, "You were a fool to come here, Rhydian."

Rhydian snarls. A glint of steel is the only warning before he thrusts a dagger toward Baelen's ribs. I quell a split second of fear. Baelen has the storm power, but he isn't invincible…

Before the dagger even nears him, Baelen punches Rhydian straight in the heart with a blast of lightning. It's fast and brutal. Then he drops Rhydian's lifeless body into the masses of watching elves below.

An Outlier zooms past me, cutting a nearby elf from his seat as I hit my target. His sword is raised, and he kicks his stallion to make it turn and dodge me while slicing across the air at my neck. But it's hard to dodge my power. I duck and a single brush of my hand on his skin is all it takes for my destruction to shriek through him. I grab the back of his armor as I fly upward, wrenching him away from his ride so the death stroke doesn't kill the innocent horse too. The elf crumbles into dust in my hands.

My body fills with lightning as I snatch up a dagger and fling it, electrified, straight into the next elf's chest. Another elf screams as Senturi rips him from his ride and there's a crash as Baelen knocks two elves into each other, breaking both their necks. Their deaths are savage, but quick.

My concern now is Priscilla. I knew she couldn't stay out of the fight. She soars past me, close enough to get my attention, but far enough that I can't get to her quickly—not with the other elves and gargoyles in my path. Her target is my Storm Command. As usual, she wants to strike where it will hurt me most. On the rocky precipice, my ladies brace, swords and shields ready while Jasper and Sebastian take up battle stances beside them, shields raised. They can't fly up to meet her. All they can do is brace for the impact. An emerald death bolt grows in her hands as her eagle soars toward them. She wants to take them out in one blow. I'm seconds behind her. Close. But too far to get in between them. I can't throw my destructive power across the distance, or I could hit my friends…

I scream, using my storm power instead to churn the air around her, upsetting the eagle so it wobbles and tips, but she stays on.

Damn! No!

She's only a breath away from releasing her power when Senturi soars out of nowhere, razor-sharp wings glinting in the early sun. Priscilla jolts and aims the death blow at him instead. My heart leaps into my throat but he darts to the right, spreads his wings to full capacity, avoids the death blow, and flies right at the eagle.

I feel a moment of pity for the bird…

Priscilla screams as Senturi's wings cut right through the animal, barely missing her legs. She launches herself off the dying creature and lands on the cliff top in the middle of my waiting Storm Command. My ladies are ready, ducking and spinning, fighting with grace and heart as Priscilla tries to kill them with her power.

She really should have learned how to use a sword.

My Storm Commanders are everywhere and nowhere all at once and within moments Priscilla rocks beneath the blow of a dagger to her heart, screaming out her frustration as she wrenches the weapon out and flings it back at Jordan, missing her by a mile. Priscilla is full of sorcery and will be hard to kill but Jordan attacks her with a savagery I've never seen before, whirling and stabbing Priscilla three more times in quick succession, before slitting her throat and screaming, "That's for Elise!"

I zoom over the top of them, shouting, "Jordan! Get clear!"

I wait another moment for my friends to leap out of the way…

Then I release my power straight at Priscilla. At the last moment, she drops and rolls and the deathblow strikes the rock instead. She rolls straight over the edge of the cliff, stretching her hand out as she falls, compelling the nearest creature to fly to her. A stallion with an empty saddle soars beneath her and she drops onto its back, landing on her stomach in an ungraceful heap before righting herself. She darts away.

She wants to hurt me. She'll be back.

On the other cliff top, Indira, Erit, and Roar fly upward to meet airborne elves who make it as far as the cliffs. Their swords flash as they drop five elves from their rides while Gilda finishes the enemy off after they fall onto the rocky surface. Indira's flung dagger finds the heart of another rider as he attempts to cut Erit from the sky. On the third cliff, Llion, Liliana, Welsian, and Arlo are a blur of movement, protecting the position in front of Talia, taking out any elves who try to get past, flinging the bodies down onto the waiting forces below.

I return to the fight, and after that, it's fast and bloody.

The gargoyles fight with everything they've got, and the elves are at a disadvantage because they can't leave their rides. What's more, the gargoyles use their wings as shields, avoiding every attempt to stab or maim them. They have every advantage in the air.

What feels like moments later, a cry of triumph goes up from the gargoyles as the last airborne elf falls. Winged creatures flee as fast as they can from the battle now that they're free from their riders. The only airborne elves now are the Elven Commanders, coasting in the distance, glaring and red-faced, while their griffins gnash the air like angry beasts.

Something tells me that the danger isn't over.

A horn blows from a distant location and Priscilla is the first to tip her stallion, urging it down toward the ground in a rush of wind. The other Elven Commanders are quick to join her as they drive their griffins toward the earth.

As I float in the air in front of the cliffs, Baelen returns to my side, his brow furrowed like mine. His voice is a low growl, a rumbling tone I'm hearing a lot today. "Where are they going?"

Also responding to the horn, the elves on the ground drop, crouch, and ball up their bodies, slipping their shields across their backs. The Elven Commanders dismount and join them, hunkering down, disappearing in the mass of bodies.

"Something's coming. But… what? Shadow panthers?" I search the ground, but the cage is still closed.

Below and to our right, Grayson finally makes a move.

So far he has stayed out of the aerial fight, remaining beside Talia and Elise's shield at ground level, studying it. Now it seems he's ready to fight back.

He flies up into the air, hovering halfway between the ground and the cliff top, one palm pressed flat against the protective barrier, his other arm outspread toward the crouching elven army. His power washes over them, a glistening barrier just like ours growing and spreading a few feet above them, sealing over the back of the last elf, covering the entire army.

I soon see why.

A black cloud tears toward us.

It's talon crows. Hundreds of them.

They will kill indiscriminately. Even the elves are in danger, which is why Grayson has protected his army. At the same time, he is putting enormous pressure on our shield. He wants to break it to allow the talon crows through. On the other side of our barrier, Talia and Elise scream with the effort to maintain their power, their voices muffled through the shield. Their arms shake. Their heads are thrown back. Grayson is hurting them, sending torturous pain through the shield right into their bodies.

My heart wrenches because there's nothing I can do to help them. Tears burn at the back of my eyes. *Don't give up, Talia. Hold on, Elise.* Our shield *must* hold. The talon crows can't get through. It's bad enough that the gargoyles on this side of the shield will face the vicious, black birds. We can't expose our entire army to them.

On the cliff tops, my gargoyle friends rally and prepare. My elven friends, including Elyria, are most vulnerable because they can't fly away. Gratitude floods my heart when Jordan orders the Storm Command to form a defensive shape, urging Elyria into the middle and asking Jasper and Sebastian to join her. Sebastian gives his wife an admiring grin before he knuckles down—he's secure enough in himself to listen to her. In fact, I'm pretty sure he thinks she's damn sexy taking charge of this situation. He lifts and links his shield with the others to create a box around themselves, swords resting against the arc cut out of the top of each shield, ready to spear any crows that fly into them.

Senturi joins Baelen and me in the air, along with the other Outliers, lining up in defensive formation as we wait for the horde to arrive. He is covered in blood, a gruesome sight that sends shivers down my spine.

He asks Baelen, "Do you still remember how to kill a crow, Wrathful One?"

A scary grin breaks across Baelen's face. "We will make new chains today."

Senturi jiggles the chain around his neck, and for the first time, I realize it's actually two, not one. "I wasn't sure if I should give yours back."

One of them is Baelen's?

Baelen continues to smile. Just like a wolf before it bites. "No need, brother."

The black birds soar toward us, only three hundred feet away and closing. They are a large, black mass of razor-sharp feathers, brutal tusks, and giant claws. Fighting them one by one will take a lot of time. Time that Elise and Talia don't have. They won't hold out that long.

My nightmare returns to me. Pedr Bounty's grandson's voice echoes in my mind. *I see a girl on a mountain... lightning's striking, claws are ripping, but she's fighting back.*

I suddenly speak up. "I have an idea, but it involves spoiling your fun."

Baelen raises an eyebrow at me. "Just as long as I'm part of the plan."

Senturi opens his arms wide. "Of course, Marbella, please tell us."

"Senturi, would you please ask the Outliers to get behind us. Far back, please." My heart swells when he immediately obeys me without question. He trusts me. Completely.

When Senturi and the Outliers are safely located near the shield, I whisper to Baelen, "You are always part of my plan, Baelen Rath."

In the back of my mind, I pray: *Hold on Elise and Talia. Not much longer.*

I reach for Baelen's hand, connecting our power. He grins as he understands what I want to do, and our power combines in a flash.

Acid rain.

I listen for his heartbeat as he closes his eyes for a moment. Connecting with him is like coming home. Everything he feels for me rises to the surface. Even in the middle of battle, his thoughts are for me. And mine are for him.

The birds are only fifty feet away. I open my eyes, turning to face Baelen, meeting his burning gaze and drowning in the smile he gives me. Drops of acid rise up from our skin, filling the air around us for ten feet in all directions, forming a thick, crimson barrier. Lightning ignites between us at the same time, crackling from his body to mine and back again.

The birds are almost upon us.

We turn to face them. Wait a moment longer…

Then we release our power.

Giant ropes of electricity shriek out from our bodies, striking into the middle of the flock of birds and out to the sides, circling them completely. Acid rain rushes along each charged rope, splattering everything in its path. The birds screech and scream, pulling up, beating their wings, trying to get away. The ones closest to the lightning light up for a split second before they disintegrate instantly. The birds further away are unluckiest, cawing as their wings light up, burning, holes growing where the acid rain touches them. Hundreds fall within seconds, most of them turning to ash before they reach the ground.

Our acid rain won't harm the elves below us because of the shield across them, although a big part of me hopes it will upset Grayson's concentration. I follow the falling crows, checking Grayson's response. He hasn't taken his eyes off me. I jolt with surprise as he continues to watch me, his eyes half-open slits— even when each drop of our acid rain onto his protective shield makes him flinch with pain. His hands are shaking. Talia and Elise have stopped screaming but their arms drop to their sides, the shield wobbling. Worry races through me because the reason they've stopped screaming is because they are almost unconscious.

It looks like Grayson isn't faring much better.

"Marbella!"

Baelen's shout has me spinning back as a final crow spears down toward me from above. It must have been right in the sun for me to miss it. Baelen's open hand flashes out between us, ready to pluck it out of the air in front of me, but before he touches it, its body explodes.

I gasp in surprise. Baelen jolts. White dust floats over us.

White dust… That's sorcery…

I spin to Grayson in the distance. His eyes are wide open now. For a second, his gaze burns me across the distance.

Did he just kill the bird so it couldn't hurt me?

He looks away, and I force myself to focus on Talia and Elise. Baelen's worried glance tells me the shield is about to break. He flies back toward the cliff top. We need to prepare for when the shield comes down; we need to get Talia and Elise out of here because they'll be vulnerable and unable to defend themselves.

As soon as he speaks to them, Llion and Liliana immediately rise up and fly toward Talia, stopping in front of the shield, ready to carry her away as soon as it breaks. Erit and Indira head toward Elise. They will take them as far behind the battle lines as they can to give them time to recover.

It's time for the Outliers to do the same.

"Senturi!" I call to the older gargoyle. "You have fought bravely. You've protected us all. Now I want you to take the Outliers and go to the back of our army. I need you to regain your energy and form our final defensive line if the elves get through."

He places his hand on my shoulder, his wings beating the air across my body. "We will be ready."

Baelen calls our gargoyle friends together onto the central peak. As I land on the cliff top beside him, Jordan and my Storm Command are shaking their heads. Baelen has just told them to leave as well. Jasper and Sebastian are also determined to stay and Roar, Welsian, and Arlo plant their feet next to my ladies, but Roar kisses Gilda fiercely and tells her to go with Indira.

As Gilda reluctantly flies away, casting glances back at her husband, a *crack* tells me that our shield is finally gone. The glistening barrier disperses into nothing, and Talia and Elise drop to the ground, hunched over their knees, heads low, barely conscious. They've done so much for us. I wish I could fly to each of them, hug them, and tell them to be safe, but the battle on the ground is about to begin.

I race to the edge of the cliff with Baelen close beside me, assessing where we are needed most.

The protective shield that Grayson placed over the elven army dissolves and a shout goes up as Grayson mobilizes them. Inside the ravine, the elves surge forward, screaming a battle cry. The sound of clashing swords echoes up to the cliff top, sending a shudder down my spine. I want to fly down to fight them but the gargoyles who had been safe behind the shield spring into action, ready to meet the elven army in combat.

The elves are skilled fighters, but the gargoyles have everything to lose. They fight with their clawed feet and wing daggers that can slice through rock and make easy work of elven armor. Twenty gargoyles rise into the air with elves in their claws, ripping them apart. The hidden caverns also open up, sending a volley of arrows into the attacking elves.

Golden-tipped arrows fly toward Grayson, piercing his chest and arms, sending him spinning before he can use his power against the gargoyles. My eyes widen in amazement at the resilience and power of my people. The way they don't cower in the face of his sorcery. The way they fight back with everything they've got.

But what truly surprises me is the restraint Grayson shows. Plucking the arrows out, he doesn't retaliate with magic, floating above the elves and shouting orders while he dodges the next volley of arrows. Like me, he could decimate the enemy army, but so far he has chosen not to. Maybe it's the gargoyle inside of him, but despite what he said earlier about killing my people, so far he has chosen to allow the elves and gargoyles to fight each other without his interference.

Baelen seeks my attention with a gentle touch to my arm. "The shield is down but the Elven Command hasn't tried to fly past us yet."

"We need to find them before they do."

"And end them," Baelen says. "One way or another."

The Elven Commanders, along with Priscilla, have disappeared into the groups of elves located at the back of their army—among soldiers in the major Houses who have not engaged in battle yet and furthest from the battlefront: an unexpected move.

"There," Baelen says, pointing. "Elwyn Elder is with his House. I'll go after him."

I look for Pedr Bounty and locate him among other elves in the House of Bounty. "I'll take Pedr Bounty. I don't see the other two yet."

"We'll find them. Be on the lookout."

"Be safe, Baelen."

He kisses me before we separate.

I zoom toward Pedr, covering the distance in several seconds, a tornado shrieking around me. The Bounty elves see me coming and scatter, shouting to each other, forming a large ring around the space where I land. I hit the ground only paces away from Pedr, my knees bending to take the impact so I can land firmly on my feet.

The tension in the air is palpable. A glance tells me that the soldiers are angry. Their faces are stony, full of rage, but it's odd… because they're glaring at Pedr, not at me. I'd expected them to swarm at me, but their swords are sheathed, daggers nowhere to be seen.

What have I just landed in the middle of?

Pedr squares his shoulders, turning from the soldiers and facing me instead, power glowing around his clenched fists. "Marbella Mercy, you won't live to see the end of this day."

I don't validate his statement with a response. I strike with lightning first, testing his ability to withstand my power. It's safe enough to hit his bulky body without endangering the nearby elves. His eyes widen as he throws his hands up to defend himself, using his sorcery to deflect the impact, fighting back with a shot of his own: a streak of green death. I nearly dodge it and then decide not to because… if it doesn't hit me, it will hit his people and—to my disgust—he doesn't seem to care.

I have no love for these elves, but the surrounding soldiers haven't challenged me or tried to get in my way. The death blow hits me square in the stomach and the watching soldiers inhale an audible gasp as I drop to my knees.

Pedr gloats and I let him have his moment. Sure, it hurt like an iron fist, but I'll be okay. A single glance at the soldiers tells me they are downcast, crestfallen, one of them even reaches for me as if he's going to help me up.

That is *not* the reaction I expected.

With that single attempt to hurt me, I sense Pedr's power wane. He used up a lot of his energy creating that death bolt, and I haven't even used my strongest power yet. Pedr may have taken a hundred lives in the night, but only Grayson can withstand my destructive strength. I roll with the next flash of death that Pedr throws at me, sensing his energy fade even more. The bolt grazes my shoulder, but I heal instantly.

He scowls as I leap to my feet, completely unharmed.

Lightning crackles in the air all around me, licking toward every living thing nearby as I focus all of my power into my hands. I leap toward him, dodging the next blow he aims at me—a paralyzing shot. It sizzles past my ribs as I ram him, both hands planted on his flabby chest. My storm power shrieks through him: lightning and wind together. His head snaps back and he flies backward. The watching elves open up like a splitting river, steering clear of him as he falls. His body bounces and flops, landing half on his side.

I approach carefully, quickly scanning him for signs of life. I'm not convinced he's beaten…

I'm bent halfway to him when his hand shoots out, fist punching into my throat. The impact of the bone-splitting blow thrusts me halfway across the clearing. I cry out as my head hits a rock and pain explodes through my spine, my legs going limp.

This time, I'm hurt.

My throat burns and my head throbs. I sense Virtuous healing me, but I took the blow full in my neck and it's going to take a few seconds.

Seconds I don't have.

Pedr Bounty clambers to his feet and pounds toward me, his big body shaking the earth as he runs across it. He's leaking sorcery everywhere like slimy oil, which tells me I've hurt him badly—he can't control his own power.

He holds his hand, palm out toward me. I'm vulnerable and he's going to finish me off the same way I tried to kill him.

35

MARBELLA

I scream at myself: *Get up, Marbella! Now!*

All I manage is a groan. With horror, I realize that my back is broken. His sorcery shattered my spine. Virtuous is healing me, but I need another few seconds.

You don't have seconds. Get up!

I push with my hands, screaming. My legs won't work no matter how hard I try. As I attempt to roll onto my side, my vision fills with boots…

Soldiers… lots of soldiers… moving to stand in front of me…

Astonished, I follow the nearest pair upward from thick thighs to a bullish chest and a face I never wanted to see again. Pedr Bounty's grandson, Gwynn, the man who pinned Jasper during the fight in the arena all that time ago, who was complicit in hurting me and almost killing Baelen, the man who told me he saw me fighting on a mountaintop, plants his feet, lifts his sword, and tells his grandfather, "Stop right there."

Pedr's eyes are filled with blood as he skids to a halt, his robes swooshing around him. He is unfocused, deranged. "All of you! Get out of my way. I will finish her!"

Gwynn's voice rises to a roar. "You killed our mothers in the night. You killed daughters of the House of Bounty. Do you want my blood on your hands too?"

"I am not your enemy. That woman is—"

Gwynn doesn't let him finish. "We're done listening to you. We won't kill for you today."

A glance tells me that the soldiers on the other side of Pedr are closing in, but not on me. They're targeting the Elven Commander.

Pedr snarls, "You would rather follow this bitch than your own grandfather?"

Gwynn casts a glance at me. "I will follow my Queen."

Pedr startles, blustering, "What are you… talking about?"

"We know the truth. We're not stupid. There's no way you'd spend this much time trying to capture her if she couldn't challenge your rule."

Pedr roars in anger, blood-filled spit flying from his mouth. His hand shoots out. A death bolt flies straight for Gwynn.

But Gwynn has given me precious seconds. Virtuous has finished healing me.

Gwynn's boots are right next to my feet. I flick one leg out, hook it around Gwynn's ankle and pull, sweeping his feet out from under him so he falls onto his back. The death bolt flies over the top of him, narrowly missing the other elves. Luckily, Pedr was aiming for Gwynn's face, and he's almost as tall as Baelen.

Gwynn's reflexes shoot into action. It was a hard fall that will leave him bruised, but he rolls and punches off the ground, returning to his feet. The other men roar at Pedr, their anger palpable.

I spin into the space Gwynn left behind, leap to my feet, and close the gap between me and Pedr. The men have left enough space around him for me to do what I need to do.

It's time to fight the old-fashioned way. My knee connects with his stomach. An uppercut breaks his jaw. My left fist follows through, knocking him flat on his back where I drop a knee onto his chest. I press my open hands against his temples and fill my whole body with destruction.

As Pedr's eyes meet mine, there's nothing living in them. They are wide pools of bleeding darkness.

"Goodbye, Pedr Bounty."

Brilliant, white light streams from me into him. He opens his mouth, a soundless scream, before cracks appear beneath his skin, burning from the inside, turning to dust. Within seconds, he is gone. My knees hit the ground and I roll through the cloud of grit that remains.

I find my feet to silence.

Gwynn Bounty takes a knee. The remaining Bounty soldiers follow him, all hundred of them in a cascading wave. I can't decide if I'm shocked or in awe of this strange turn of events. They're drawing attention from the other Houses, and I have no way of knowing if the others feel the same as these soldiers or if they'll attack me. If each of the Elven Commanders took lives from their own Houses, then the elves of Splendor, Valor, and Elder might carry the same anger as the Bounty soldiers, but there's no way to know.

Gwynn's voice is a rumble. "What are your orders, my Queen?"

I once told Gwynn that I never wanted to see his face again. It's strange to be glad that he has forgotten that order. I consider my options now. I won't order them to attack other elves. I could test my power and fly them all across the gargoyle border to join the gargoyle army to provide support. Or…

"How many lives?"

He knows exactly what I want to know. "Fifty women, including my mother." He points to particular soldiers as he speaks, and they return my questioning look with expressions of rage and betrayal. "His mother. His aunt. His grandmother. His sister…"

I inhale a sharp breath, shaking my head at the extent of Pedr Bounty's cruelty. "Then I order you to go home."

Gwynn is taken aback, his chin jolting upward. "My Queen?"

My eyes swim with the pain of so many senseless deaths. "Go home and bury your loved ones."

"But… don't you need us…?" He gestures to the battle a thousand paces away.

"It's true that I do need your swords. But what I need more is that your swords are not raised against me. Please, take your soldiers and do what is right for your families."

He rises and advances on me. He is a giant. I once thought of him as a bull, and that is still an accurate description. He presses his lips together, turning them white, his emotions spilling over. "You could make us stay and fight for you, but you have chosen not to. You are already a better ruler than we have ever had."

He spins and signals to his House, roaring. "House of Bounty! Fall out!"

They march away, their boots thudding resolutely on the ground. The other Houses watch them with alternating expressions of surprise and alarm as the empty space where the House of Bounty used to stand grows wider and wider. Confusion grows on the faces of the other elves. Some of them grab their weapons and aim them at me. Others are having trouble picking up their jaws. There's nobody here to give them orders and they don't know what to do.

As Gwynn and his soldiers march away, they walk right past the cage of shadow panthers. I approach it as the beasts growl at me, baring their teeth, their hackles raised. Their silver eyes flash in the sunlight, steel claws extended, gripping the earth. They smell my gargoyle blood.

Erit once told me that the ancient gargoyle Grievous only gave his life to become part of our new world because it was an opportunity to give birth to such dreadful creatures as shadow panthers and talon crows to forever remind the gargoyles that life is cruel. I take hold of the bars, gritting my teeth as the nearest panther leaps for me, its jaws open, ready to rip my hands apart. I release Incorruptible power into the entire cage, lighting it up like a bonfire. Every beast glows for a moment, skeletons burning bright beneath their skin before they shatter.

Seconds later, the smoke clears. Piles of dust waft away in the breeze. The panthers won't hurt my friends now.

Nearby elves back away from me as I stride away from the spot where the cage used to be. I scan their faces and raise my voice. "I could kill you all. Just like that. But I won't. Because you are my people too."

Their confusion grows, but I don't have time to say anything else because an explosion nearby has me running. A banner bearing the crest of the House of Elder floats past me, half-shredded.

Baelen!

As I take to the air, searching for him, I quickly assess the progress of the elven army at the border. Despite the gargoyles' ferocity, the elves have made ground. My heart sinks to see Grayson fighting a gargoyle as he advances further along the ravine than I anticipated.

But I'm confused as I realize… he's fighting with his hands, not his power. *What is going on with him?*

And where is Priscilla?

I find her soaring to my right. She smirks at me before she sails away on her stallion, headed for my ladies again. I spin between Grayson and Priscilla, assessing both threats.

I shudder hard because I know I should go after Grayson, but my ladies are more vulnerable right now. Speeding after Priscilla, I finally locate Baelen to my right, on a cliff top further along the border. Elwyn Elder is throwing everything he's got at him, his sorcery colliding with Baelen's storm. The air around their battle explodes and shards of rock blast in all directions as Elwyn aims a death blow at Baelen, narrowly missing him. Baelen retaliates by creating a tornado that tosses Elwyn into the air. It looks like Baelen has deliberately drawn Elwyn away from the main battleground to avoid collateral damage, but it places him much too far away from me.

My head spins as I reassess my priorities.

The gargoyles in the ravine need me. My Storm Command needs me. Baelen needs me. And they're all in different places.

Priscilla doubles back, zipping past, stinging me with a painful blow to my side. She's definitely trying to get my attention. She hits me again, her next shot more insistent, striking the side of my neck. Grayson told her to be afraid of me, but she obviously didn't listen. She ducks the lightning I send in her direction and soars straight for my ladies, drawing me away from both Grayson and Baelen.

Curses. She knows I won't leave my ladies unprotected. I speed after her, mere seconds behind.

On the cliff top, my Storm Command forms another protective box, prepared for Priscilla's attack. As she flies over the top of them, cackling her heart out, their shields open and I'm surprised when Elyria leaps up from the middle, boosted high into the air.

Elyria slides neatly up beside Priscilla and slices open her leg with a dagger. The stallion Priscilla is riding bucks at Elyria's sudden appearance. Priscilla screams, scrambles to get away from the knife, and ends up falling off her ride. As soon as she hits the platform, Welsian and Roar leap out from behind the protective shields and leap toward her, tearing at her with their clawed feet. She screams and flails as she heals and breaks, over and over.

Her power is fading. Her screams tell me that. But I also sense that she is building for another explosion. My friends, my Storm Command, even Elyria, won't survive if Priscilla releases her full force right now.

Light builds around her edges, casting her silhouette green like an emerald stone. I soar toward her, stretching out to grab her before she can release it. Roar and Welsian see me coming and jump out of the way. My electrified fist closes around Priscilla's arm, and I wrench her upward, using all my strength to fling her into the sky, creating a tornado to compel her higher.

Just in time. Her power explodes harmlessly inside the storm. She screams with rage as she fights to escape the tornado that I've imprisoned her in.

Once I get my friends out of the line of fire, I'm going to end her.

Jordan is covered in blood, her hair dripping. "Marbella!"

"Go!" I shout. "All of you!"

Reisha's determined face fills my field of view. Like Jordan, she is bloody, her blonde hair streaked dark red. "We won't leave you."

"Priscilla wants to hurt me by killing you. She will target you until you are all dead, and then my heart will break." I draw breath, trying to contain my emotions. "She is mine to fight."

Reisha begins to argue, glancing at the rest of the Storm Command. That's when I see the bodies lying at the side of the platform. Five of my ladies have already fallen. Pain shoots through my heart. *My ladies... my friends...*

"She attacked us while you were gone," Jordan says, quietly standing beside Reisha.

"Jordan. No more. Please."

She nods, taking Reisha's arm when it looks like the other woman is going to persist. "We will go to safety now. But we will join the Outliers. If the elves break through, we will defend Erador to our dying breath."

I breathe out my relief. Knowing they are safe for now is all I need.

"You too," I say to the gargoyles and I'm relieved when they don't argue with me. Sebastian joins them as they race after my Storm Command, forming an extra barrier of protection around my ladies. Elyria and Jasper are the last to leave.

Elyria hugs me suddenly, whispering. "Don't forget what I told you."

She told me I would have to kill Grayson. I can't forget it.

Jasper and Elyria follow after the Storm Command, deftly navigating the rocks and disappearing down the safe side of the mountain.

I check Baelen in the distance. Now that my Storm Command is gone, he's moving in my direction, drawing the fight with Elwyn toward me. *Good.* The only Elven Commander I don't have a location for right now is Osian Valor, but I'll have to focus on one at a time.

My tornado breaks and Priscilla drops to the cliff top. Her hands fly out and a rope of light whips around my waist, yanking me closer to her. *Does she really think that's a good idea?*

The rope tightens, winding around and around me as she circles like a panther. I let her think she has imprisoned me for now. It's better if she underestimates me.

"It's time you and I had a chat," she says.

I take advantage of her arrogance to assess how much power she has left. All I need to know is how much it will take to end her.

"I noticed that your spellcaster friend is alive after all," she says.

I freeze a little but force myself to relax. She means Elise. They dumped Elise's body in a shallow ditch after they thought she was dead. And then Grayson came to tell me about it.

Priscilla smiles, tilting her head, pausing. "I thought it would be too cruel, but Grayson was determined to figure out what would make you cry. It turned out that killing your friend—or at least telling you about it—was enough to turn you into a blubbering mess..."

She's trying to make me believe that it was all Grayson's fault. I narrow my eyes, but don't respond.

She sidles up to me. "You're very quiet Marbella."

"Because every word you speak tells me how insecure you are. I know Grayson had nothing to do with Elise's treatment."

An angry edge enters her voice. "Okay, fine. Grayson didn't know about it." She shrugs. "You can't blame me for trying to mess with you. I hate the way he looks at you. And you… the way you look at him." Her voice turns into a sneaky whisper as she runs her finger across my shoulder. "I wonder if Baelen Rath knows what happened in Grayson's bedroom night after night…"

Okay, that's it.

I break the rope and grab her arms. She screams, shock shooting across her face as she tries to leap away from me, struggling against my strength, releasing a shot of power into me. Her eyes widen when I don't flinch, let alone release her.

"You thought that would hurt me." My power builds, glowing and sizzling from my headpiece all the way down my arms…

Sudden terror fills her eyes. She opens her mouth to scream again.

Before I can release the killing strike, a voice shouts, "You'd better not do that."

I spin to find Osian Valor riding a griffin that touches down on the other side of the cliff. The beast paws the stone, its beak and claws dripping with blood. Osian is splattered with gore that chills me to the core. He reaches behind him and drags someone off the griffin's back… a woman whose wings flop at her sides, her hair spilling around her face, her body limp. I shove Priscilla away from me, fear spiking every nerve in my body.

I know those wings…

Priscilla teeters, almost losing her balance, before she flicks her hair back and saunters toward Osian. "You took long enough."

She pulls back the female gargoyle's head to examine her face.

Indira's eyes are closed. Blood drips from a head wound above her right eye. Cold fear takes over my body.

"That's her," Priscilla says, dropping Indira's head. "She means something to Marbella. Doesn't she… *Supreme Incorruptible?*" She sing-songs my title before breaking into a satisfied smile, planting her hands on her hips.

I am both hot and cold at the same time. "What did you do?"

Indira was with Erit at the back of our forces. She left a while ago with Talia, Elise, Llion, and Liliana… The only way to capture Indira would be to fight and defeat all of them. Their faces flash before me as rage and fear build inside me. I want to grab Osian and use my power against him, but he's holding Indira…

He drags her toward me, stopping only a few paces away. "She isn't dead."

"Yet," Priscilla clarifies. "But she will be soon." She bends to flip open a flap of armor hanging loosely at Indira's side, showing me the wound in her side from which she's slowly losing blood.

They've stabbed her in the stomach.

I whisper, "She's pregnant."

Priscilla tips her head to the side, her eyes empty of any emotion. "Oh. Pity."

My anger spirals out of control, rushing out from my chest, out from my broken heart through my arms and up into my head, turning me blind with anger. Grayson isn't here to absorb my rage this time. I inhale a breath, knowing that I have to let it out, that I can't contain it, but I have only one coherent thought left: *Don't hurt Indira.*

I tip my head back and hurl my power into the sky, screaming it out as hard as I can. My scream builds and builds. A storm grows above me, the darkest storm I've ever created, lightning crackling and scorching the sky, a wind tunnel forming, picking up dust and debris. Elwyn Elder rushes through it and Baelen storms after him, but Baelen's focus is not Elwyn anymore. It's me.

Elwyn suddenly spins and casts a spell back at Baelen, a barrier that stops him in his tracks. Baelen crashes against the invisible surface. He recoils, throws himself against it again, and tries to burst through. He flies higher only to hit a surface above him, and then another behind and on either side. Somehow, Elwyn has boxed him in.

Someone drops onto the platform beside me and grabs me. My power seeps out from the place where he touches me and my gaze lowers, following the lines of Grayson's silhouette all the way to the hand he wraps around my bicep, the hand that absorbs my rage, soaking it up and leeching it out of me so the storm dissolves and then… there's nothing left.

He observes Priscilla and Osian, and finally Indira, assessing the slow drip from her body. "What's going on?"

Priscilla straightens. "We're speeding things up. Your way was taking too long."

"Where's Pedr?"

"He was distracting Marbella," Osian replies.

Priscilla adds, "Until he wasn't."

Grayson studies Indira for another second. He recognizes her. He danced with her at the arena when Baelen came to rescue me. "She's dying. She doesn't have long."

Priscilla crosses her arms. "Exactly, and I think Marbella knows there's only one way to save her."

My world no longer has any foundation. An empty pit has opened up inside me. *The deep springs. Only the springs can save Indira now.*

Grayson doesn't miss a beat, speaking to me now. "I'm the only one who can get you to the springs fast enough. But it means you have to let us in. You're going to have to decide how badly you want your friend to live."

My voice chokes in my throat. "You want me to take you to the springs willingly."

"I…" For a minute I think he's going to say something else, but he ends up repeating: "If you want your friend to live."

In the distance, Baelen plants his hands on the surface that cages him, the muscles in his arms bulging. Red-hot lightning spears across it, slowly burning through. He's roaring but I can't hear him. It will only take him a minute to get out, but Indira doesn't have long, and Grayson is right—he's the only one who can get her to the springs fast enough. Her face is already deathly pale; her body is so limp. Even Baelen can't fly that fast.

I sense Grayson cloak himself a second before Priscilla sidles up behind him and wraps her arms around his waist. Osian drags Indira across the rocks, making me wince every time her knees bump into the ground. He places his hand on Grayson's shoulder as Elwyn lands right next to us, taking hold of Grayson's other arm.

Elwyn's dark eyes gleam at me. They are empty pools. He wants to kill me as soon as he gets the chance.

Grayson is already holding onto me, ready to move.

It's my choice.

Baelen is almost through the trap. He will come for me.

He will find me.

I grit my teeth. "Take us to the springs."

36

MARBELLA

The deep springs are quiet when we land. Peaceful. The rock face above me is perfectly still. But it's not empty. It's covered in motley brown and gray bodies that look exactly like rocks: the Grievous and Hideaway gargoyles are exactly where they promised they'd be.

Indecision grips me. If the gargoyles attack from above, Osian will retaliate. He hasn't let go of Indira, and it would only take the weakest death bolt to kill her. I turn and kneel in front of her. He holds her high enough that I would be eye-to-eye with her if she were conscious. I gently lift the hair away from her face, making sure it's obvious who she is. She is the Grievous Clan's leader. That alone should be enough to make the gargoyles positioned on the rock pause before they attack.

I speak as loudly as I dare without raising suspicion. "I brought you here. Now I'm taking her inside to heal her."

I hope my message to the gargoyles is clear: Don't attack until she's healed. I close my eyes for a second, trying to sense the phoenix's location, it promised it would be here too. I can speak to it without the Elven Commanders knowing.

I swallow my relief when I hear the firebird's voice. *Princess! What has happened?*

They hurt Indira. I had no choice. Please make sure the gargoyles don't strike until she's healed.

289

I am on the other side of this mountain, the phoenix says. *How can I help you?*

You need to find out what happened to the others: Erit, Llion, Roar, Jasper, Elyria… So many of my friends… I'm afraid…

I gulp, trying to steady my thoughts. *Please fly to the border as fast as you can. If they are hurt, I need you to bring them here. If they are still fighting, I need you to find a way to stop them. The elven army is without leaders now.*

What about the springs?

Inside my mind, my voice is cold. *I will defend them.*

Consider it done.

Osian snorts beside me, dragging Indira along the platform toward the entrance to the deep springs. I said that I would take her, but he won't let her go until he's sure I won't retaliate. She is his only protection from me.

I don't dare look up as we pass the gargoyles hidden at the entrance. The Hideaway clan is perfectly still, totally camouflaged. I also avoid looking at Grayson. I'm worried that the gargoyle inside of him will sense their presence, and he'll alert the other Commanders. I don't want to give him any indication that we aren't alone.

He strides beside me, not afraid to take my arm, but his grip is loose, almost gentle, guiding me inside. Very soon, we enter the sparkling cavity, our boots drumming in time to the drip, drip, drip from the ceiling.

Elwyn Elder is triumphant, spreading his wiry arms as he walks right up to the water's edge. He is the smallest of the Commanders, but tough like weathered rope. His eyes are a very pale azure blue, tapered at the edges like the other members of his House. "At last!"

Priscilla is giddy as she strides to the end of the path and tilts her head back to study the ceiling. This is the only place where the Elyria spiders spin webs of all colors: rose-gold, silver-green, sapphire, sunset-orange, and lilac. Even Grayson seems awed by the beauty of the springs.

"Careful," Elwyn warns Priscilla as her toes almost enter the water. "This water will not tolerate our sorcery."

Only Osian is unmoved by the cavern's beauty. He is a large elf, built for war, but not quite like a Rath. Elves in the House of Valor always had an inferiority complex about the fact that the House of Rath defended Erawind. Unlike Pedr, Osian hasn't let himself go. He shoves past Grayson, grabs my arm, and gestures at the water.

"If you want to heal her, get in. I will pass her to you."

I'm not sure if I can trust him. He could easily kill her as soon as I enter the water. His gaze flickers to Indira as if he hears my thoughts. The whole time he's held her, he's barely acknowledged her. She is a *thing* to him.

A dark smile breaks across his face. "You think I will kill her." He leans down to me, shoves his big face in mine, and pokes my chest with one thick finger. "It's in my interests to keep her alive. As long as she lives, we control you. Now get in."

I barely avoid the spittle that flies at me as he snarls. *Disgusting old elf.* I slide out of his grip and step down into the pond, reaching the bottom step before I hold out my arms for Indira.

Osian laughs at me, juggles Indira so he's gripping her shoulder, and slings her out into the middle of the pond. A stomach-turning *pop* tells me he just dislocated her shoulder. I clench my fists, directing my anger into them as Indira hits the water on her back, her broken wings spreading out across the surface before the water sucks her down, toes first, then legs, torso, neck, mouth…

I splash out to the middle as fast as I can, my armor dragging. *Can someone drown in the springs?* I can't take that chance. I have to keep her face above the surface. Osian knew exactly what he was doing, throwing her this far out to keep me busy.

Right when her nose would slide under the water, I hook my arms under her from behind, grab her shoulders, and lock her arms between mine so she's resting on my chest where I can keep her head above water. It's so deep here that I have to tread water and the waves I create lap dangerously at Indira's face. I kick my legs and use my free arm to glide us back to the steps, keeping her head tilted and clear of liquid. Then I lower myself onto the middle step, grip both my arms across her chest, staying beneath her, my cheek pressed against hers.

My back is to the Commanders. Before I reached the edge, they were clustered at the side of the springs, studying the wall. I'm vaguely aware of Grayson's presence nearby—he hasn't joined them. I guess he's my guard as usual.

Now that I'm facing the other way, none of them can see my face or the tears burning in my eyes. My tears burn so hot, like acid rain leaking from my eyes. I squeeze my eyelids closed and beg quietly for Indira's life. She started out as my enemy, a fierce one, but she became my friend. A true friend who fought beside me.

"Please live. Please, Indira." My whisper cracks into little pieces. I slide my hand to her stomach, gently floating there. "Please be alive, babies. Please… please…"

"Babies!"

I jump. Freeze. The upset water sloshes around me.

Grayson's face appears beside mine, his hands planted at the edge of the water, not touching it, leaning out over the edge, his mouth a compressed line, his eyes narrowed. "Why did you say 'babies?'"

He wasn't there when I told the others that Indira was pregnant. "Osian stabbed her in the stomach."

"But gargoyle women only experience pregnancy once. She won't have any more children."

I'm briefly surprised. So, he *was* listening.

His face disappears from beside mine. I crane to see as Grayson strides over to Osian, grabs him, and punches a fist into his face, knocking him hard against the cavern wall.

Crack. Blood streams from Osian's nose as he drops to his knees, eyes wide, his hand darting to his face to check the damage.

Priscilla shrieks, "What the hell, Grayson?"

Grayson picks Osian up by his shirt-front as if the heavy elf weighs nothing. "There are some lines you don't cross. When we reach the surface, you'd better watch your back. If you pull anything like that again, I will kill you."

He drops Osian with a disgusted growl. The older elf glares murder back at him, but Grayson doesn't seem concerned. His trump card is always his ability to kill at will.

Osian jumps to his feet, bearing down on Grayson. "You little—"

Elwyn throws an arm in front of Osian, stopping him in his tracks, giving him a strong warning glance; a strong shake of his head. "Let it go."

In my arms, Indira gasps. Flails. Gasps again. "Erit!"

I lock my arms around her before she can jump out of the

water. Then I press my cheek to hers, whispering, "Shh, Indira. It's okay. You're with me."

"Marbella?" She cranes to see who is holding her but in doing so, she can now see the Commanders too. Uncontrollable wildness enters her face. "I will kill them. I will tear them apart…"

I keep my voice low. "And I will join you, but first… Can you…" I take a deep breath, barely able to ask the question. "Can you sense your babies?"

She freezes. Shudders. "I… don't know…"

"Forget everything else. Focus, Indira. Before we fight back, I need to know. *You* need to know."

She exhales. The tension in her body is so high, I'm worried she might not be able to relax enough to sense them. She's scared too, trembling in my arms, afraid of what she'll find out.

She gasps, inhales. "They're alive."

"Oh…" I drop my face to her shoulder and let the tears flow freely as she quietly sobs in my arms. Grayson returns to guard us again. His expression darkens as he sees our tears, fists clenching.

I don't know why, but I whisper up to him, "They're alive."

His darkness clears. His smile is always real. He gives me a single nod and that is all before the mask drops back over his features.

My own smile fades. *Remember who he is. Remember what you have to do.*

Indira's hair floats freely around us as she shifts in my arms. I murmur into her ear, "You have to keep yourself and the babies out of harm's way now. They will use you to control me. I know you want to fight them, but I need you out of danger. Can you do that?"

She exhales, chomps down on her lip, and squeezes closed her angry eyes. She doesn't like it. I wouldn't either. But she needs to protect her children now. "As you wish, Supreme Incorruptible."

"Stay inside the water where nothing can hurt you. Even if they strike you, you will heal. They won't dare set foot inside the pond. Sorcery and deep magic can't combine."

She answers me by swimming further out, far enough that they can't grab her. I climb the slippery steps carefully, water sloshing away from my armor, dripping down my arms and legs. Last time, Baelen carried me out safely and made me warm. This time, I harness my Prime heartstone, intending to use its power to warm my skin and dry my clothing.

I step right into Grayson. One of his arms closes around my waist, the other runs freely from the top of my head down my shoulders and back, leaving my hair and torso dry.

He doesn't look happy. "I'm sorry."

There's a lot for him to be sorry about. "For which part?"

He presses his lips together; his jaw clenches. "Come with me willingly and it won't hurt as much."

Like *that's* going to make me go with him. "I don't think so."

On the other side of the cavern, the Elven Commanders point at the wall, running their fingers over it, finding particular grooves, pointing at others.

Grayson says, "You don't have a choice. You saw what they did to Indira. The gargoyles guarding these springs won't survive a fight and you know it."

So, he *did* see the gargoyles outside the springs.

When I dig my heels in, he shakes his head at me. "Why are you so hell bent on stopping us from ascending? I thought you'd want us to go."

"And let you destroy the springs?"

He shrugs. "The gargoyles will be like everyone else—reliant on healers."

"Grayson… destroying the springs will collapse our world. These springs are the pivot point on which our world was built. The Earth city above us will also be destroyed when this enormous pocket of air beneath it caves in. If it was a matter of just letting you go, trust me, I want you gone."

He flinches. "You want me gone."

Of all the things I just said, he's going to focus on that. I glare at the Commanders who continue to run their hands over the wall as though they are painting on it. "I want *them* gone. You… oh… I can't figure you out. But I won't let you kill my people."

Grayson's eyes become narrow slits. I suspected that the Elven Commanders hadn't told him about our world collapsing, but if this news means anything to him, he doesn't show it. A rope made of light springs up around me, twining around my waist and chest.

Unlike Priscilla's, this one is surprisingly strong. I guess I keep telling him things he doesn't want to hear.

He orders, "Come with me. Or they will kill your friend first and then the gargoyles outside."

I struggle against the binding. "They can't touch Indira in the springs."

"No, but they can curse her to drown."

I don't know if that's true or not. After a glance at Indira, I follow Grayson, but reluctantly. When we reach them, Elwyn takes my chin in his claw-like fingers. His hands are wet and slippery from poking at the wall, and it makes me shudder.

"When the ancients descended, they built a fail safe to protect the pathway back to Earth's surface. Only royal blood can open it." His fingernail trails down the side of my neck and rests against the sensitive hollow at the top of my left collarbone. "In fact, we need the living blood of *both* royal lines. Lucky for us, you carry both."

Off to the side, Priscilla gives me a mock curtsey. "Don't worry, my Queen, we aren't going to kill you. Unfortunately."

Elwyn's fingernail grows longer, sharper, about to pierce my skin. "We just need you to bleed a little." He yanks me forward and thuds a fist into my stomach, forcing me to bend around Grayson's ropes. "Right here on this spot."

There are markings carved into the rock—both on the wall and the ground. The spot over which I bend is right above a large carved circle. As soon as his fingernail pierces me, I will drip blood onto the cavern floor. I close my eyes as his fingernail turns iron-hard and sharp as a dagger, its tip cutting a hole in my skin.

I will not do it.

Virtuous flares and my skin closes over, healing as fast he can cut. Elwyn scowls. Presses harder. Makes his fingernail sharper.

I continue to heal. At the same time, my Incorruptible power grows. Quietly. Slowly. I need them all close by so I can end them at the same time. Then Indira will be safe.

I close my heart to any regret I feel about killing Grayson too.

I grit my teeth. "I refuse."

He gives up on his fingernail and grips my throat, his fingers tightening around my neck as he lifts me, choking me. "I will drown your friend. I will burn your gargoyles. I will kill the traitor elves—"

I snarl, choking, "I will still fight you!"

Power grows around me now. Not so quietly. Not so slowly. My eyes fill with lightning, my heart fills with strength…

A whisper of wind touches the back of my neck. A prickle of lightning gives me goose bumps.

"Baelen." I choke-whisper his name a split second before he wails through the opening to the springs, a burning torpedo as he spins upward into the high ceiling. His eyes burn, full of flame, just like before he healed. Full of wrath. There is nothing gentle about him now.

"You." He points at Grayson who releases the ropes from around me. "You will die first."

Grayson scoffs. He splays his arms at his sides. "By all means, you can try."

Baelen shocks me by flying straight at Grayson and plucking him from the ground beside me, shooting back into the air with him. He dangles him above the water while his fist connects with Grayson's surprised face. Grayson jolts backward, ducking Baelen's follow-up fist, freeing himself at the same time.

How is this possible? Baelen can't touch Grayson without being killed.

And then I realize… and it seems so simple… Baelen is cloaked. Elise has cloaked him. I close my eyes with relief because not only is Baelen safe to fight Grayson now, but it means that Elise is alive and safe too. The cloaking spell is difficult to create and wears off, but it will last long enough to protect Baelen for this battle.

Elwyn keeps hold of me, spinning me so I'm facing the fight, wrapping one arm painfully around my throat and the other across my stomach. I draw on my power. I'm ready to fight, but Elwyn hisses in my ear, "Don't try it. I've already cursed your friend to drown. I only have to release the spell."

I grit my teeth, quiet my power, but keep it waiting. Ready.

Grayson and Baelen remain in the air. They don't bring their fight to the ground. They don't use their power. Neither of them can afford to damage the springs or the walls around us, either by crashing into it or blasting it with their power. This is a fight the old-fashioned way. Grayson spins past Baelen, his fist shooting out, but Baelen grabs it, twists, and Grayson flips over in the air, flying right back with another blow.

The two men are evenly matched. Scarily so. There aren't many men who can fight Baelen and remain conscious for long. Llion once did it, and I was glad I never saw that fight. This one has my heart in my throat.

Baelen finally lands a dizzying *crack* against the side of Grayson's head, almost knocking him unconscious. Grayson hunches, tries to steady himself, but drops toward the water before catching himself above its surface. Somewhere in the middle of the fight, his mask has disappeared and now he is… darkness… rage…

He flies back at Baelen, fakes a hit to Baelen's stomach, while his other hand wraps around Baelen's throat.

Something changes.

The air charges with a force I haven't sensed from Grayson before.

Baelen's skin crackles and the fire dies in his eyes. It's so sudden and so terrifying that I lose my footing, slipping under the weight of dread. Their fight has brought them closer to us. I could run three paces and leap to reach them, which means I can see and hear everything.

Grayson snarls, "You thought you could cloak yourself against me. People have been coming after me my whole life. I figured out long ago how to defend myself. I figured out long ago how to break a cloaking spell."

No…

Another *crack*. Another *pop*. Flames light up along Baelen's shoulders, down his arms, making his armor glow. He grabs Grayson's arm, grips his hand, pushes with all his might, roaring against the power Grayson is pouring into him. His grip on Grayson's arm would have crushed an ordinary man's bones but not Grayson's.

Grayson roars, "Everyone lives at my mercy. Everyone!"

Baelen's eyes are half-closed, but he isn't looking at Grayson. He's looking at me. "What do you want, Grayson?"

"I want what you have."

Baelen gives the smallest shake of his head, the barest

movement he can make within Grayson's grip. "What I have is earned, not taken."

Baelen jolts as he tries one last thing, thunder. It washes over us and the pond, freezing the waves, freezing Indira, silencing the wind whistling through the cavern.

But not the Elven Commanders. Not Grayson.

Priscilla chuckles softly, her breath tickling my neck as she leans in to me, pressing up against Elwyn. "The beauty of sorcery is that it learns. We figured out how to beat your little trick after the arena. There's no saving your precious love now."

I wrench out of Elwyn's hands but she's right. If I release my power into Grayson, I will kill Baelen too. I can't see a way through this. I can't see a path that keeps Baelen alive.

Grayson says, "You have three seconds before I destroy the cloaking spell and you die, Baelen Rath."

Baelen's hands slide away from Grayson's arms. His skin is on fire now, burning, crackling, acid rain running in rivers from beneath his armor, dripping into the water. Wide, crimson rivers.

Baelen's eyelids droop but he forces them to remain open, his eyes meeting mine. His chest rises and falls. A final smile lifts the corner of his mouth and everything he ever said to me, every time he loved me and protected me shatters my heart.

Until death.

Grayson drags his hand down Baelen's face and closes Baelen's eyes.

37

MARBELLA

My heart tears into pieces in one devastating moment as I make a choice. I thought I'd lost Baelen once when the Commanders stabbed him. I can't lose him now. I won't let him die. Not when I can do something about it.

My scream echoes around the springs. *"Grayson! Stop!"*

A sudden tension in Grayson's shoulders is the only indication that he heard me. I listen for Baelen's heartbeat. It's weak and fading, but he's still alive. I run to the spot on the cavern floor beneath the place where they float, tipping my head back, desperate for Grayson to hear me despite his battle rage.

I'm glad Baelen's eyes are closed so he can't see me when I say, "Grayson? You can have what you want."

His focus snaps to me. He is full of fury from fighting with Baelen, blind with it. "What?"

I bite down hard on my lip. My hands are shaking. I'm slowly folding up my heart inside myself, making it smaller and smaller, shutting it down, stopping it from feeling.

"I'll be what you want." My throat constricts but I force myself to speak. "I will be with you."

Grayson's eyes widen as he finally hears what I said. Very slowly, he pulls Baelen to the rocks beside the water, still holding him upright, and turned to me.

299

Baelen groans, acid rain leaking from his eyes as he tries to open them. "No… Marbella…"

I finally raise my gaze to Baelen's. "Baelen Rath, I promised to love, honor, and protect you. Now I'm going to do all of those things, but most of all I'm going to protect you. Baelen… my Baelen… I won't let you die."

I turn to Grayson, asking, "Please. Will you let Baelen live?"

A crease grows across his forehead. "You would make this choice to save his life?"

"Yes." As my final act of love for Baelen, I will wrap up my feelings for him and put them far away from my heart, even if it kills me inside and I am only a shell afterward.

Grayson releases Baelen, but doesn't drop him, guiding him to the ground instead. Baelen slumps over his knees, trying to lift his head. I don't touch him. One touch and I will change my mind; my heart won't let me do this. As soon as Baelen's strength returns, he will come after me and try to stop me. So, I cast a gentle whirlwind around him, allowing it to pick him up and contain him while he heals, just like he contained me when he strode into Crimson Court after I killed Howl. He can't fight my storm power because it's stronger than his. He won't escape from behind the shield until I'm gone.

I consider unfreezing Indira, but Baelen can do that once I'm gone. In the meantime, I don't want her to see any of this. I turn, wooden, and say to Elwyn, "You want to ascend but you can't open the pathway without me. I won't open it unless you promise you won't destroy the springs when you leave."

Osian Valor scoffs and Priscilla rolls her eyes.

Elwyn folds his arms. "You expect us to believe they won't come after us?"

"Nobody will come after you. You said that it will only open with royal blood, and I am the last of both lines. Nobody can ever open it again if I come with you."

Grayson draws level with me. He is quiet now, far from the raging man he was before. "You're really going through with this. You're going to ascend with me."

"You always keep your word, Grayson. I will keep mine."

Elwyn considers my offer before turning to the others. Priscilla glares for a full minute before shrugging. "We can't open it unless she chooses."

Osian gives a nod. "It is agreed."

Grayson hardly seems to hear any of it, contemplating a spot on the wall, his gaze far away.

I shut my eyes, closing off the world, taking one last moment, one last free breath, to say goodbye. Then I hold out my hand for a dagger. Osian Valor hands me the one he used on Indira.

For a moment, I consider trying to kill them all. They are standing close enough to me to do it, but at the back of my mind is fear—an awful, overriding fear. *What if it all goes wrong and Baelen dies?* The only thing keeping me standing right now is the knowledge that he will live. My only sure path is to go with them. And once I'm there, I'll find a way to stop them.

The knife wobbles. *Damn.* Why is my heart still beating? Why can't I stop feeling already? I slide the blade over my wrist and open a vein, allowing my blood to flow freely onto the stone circle before I heal the wound again.

The change in the cavern is very quiet, almost peaceful. The entire ceiling of the deep springs fades and dissolves, opening up to reveal a crystal-clear blue sky: the real sky. With real clouds. The view of the surface is from the ground, looking up. To our left is the gentle slosh of water as if there is a water source flowing—a river maybe? To our right, a massive curved building soars into the sky, glittering in the light of the real sun, bright, blinding reflections glinting off soaring panels of green-blue glass. Other sounds filter through the opening: human voices, shoes tapping the pavement, a constant low mechanical thrum that grows and fades like many machines moving past.

Chicago.

Earth's surface.

"There." The Elven Commanders' excitement makes the hairs on the back of my neck stand on end.

Elwyn spins to Grayson. "Time to fly, Grayson."

I shiver as Grayson slides one arm around my waist from behind me, his other reaching for the knife, his big hand gently gliding down my arm before he pries the blade out of my cold fingers and drops it to the ground. He makes no move toward the older Commander, causing Elwyn's brow to furrow.

Grayson kisses the side of my neck and whispers, "Not like this, Marbella."

He must be talking about the knife. Or the sky. Or the way we're about to ascend. Or what… I don't know. I've given up trying to figure him out.

He sighs against my neck, holding me fast, unmoving, and says, "Tell me again how my mother died."

A confused crease grows on my forehead. "You didn't kill her."

"Shh. Not you. *Them.*" He lifts his head, still cradling me, relaxed, as if he's asking nothing important. "Elwyn?"

A deep furrow joins the wrinkles on Elwyn's forehead. His mouth turns down. "You killed her when you were born."

"Hmm. Gideon told you that, didn't he?"

"It happened, Grayson. We were all there to see it. Now, let's get on with it. The pathway won't remain open forever."

"All of you were there, right?" Grayson chews his lip, tilts his head, not budging. "Why were you all at my birth?"

Elwyn falters. "Your mother had a vision of the Earth. You know that."

"Yes, but what did that have to do with me? You're all very important people. Yet you took time out of your day to be there when I was born. Why?"

"We…" Elwyn looks to Osian, clearly floundering.

The big Commander clears his throat. "Her vision involved you."

"In what way?"

Osian licks his lips. "The pathway… It isn't easy to get through. It looks like the surface is right there in front of us, but we are two miles under the surface."

Grayson nods, still holding me. "You need me to transport you. I guess my mother saw that too?"

Osian pauses. "She did."

"Did she tell you her vision willingly? Or under force?"

Above us on the ceiling, the image of the city fades at the edges, the rock face reappearing as a ring around it. It's a slow transition, barely a few inches, but it's visible.

It's closing.

Elwyn turns an angry red, appearing increasingly agitated. "Grayson, keep your eye on the prize. The city is right there! You'll have a new life. You can start fresh. You'll even have Marbella. Now, why don't we—"

"No! We aren't leaving until you tell me the truth."

Elwyn glances at the ceiling. The opening is still wide, but smaller than it was before. Whatever placating response he was going to give disappears as another three inches of rock appear around the edges. He strides right up to Grayson. "Take us there. Now."

"Or what?"

"Or I will compel you."

Grayson carefully untangles himself from me, nudging me out of Elwyn's way. "You can't."

Osian advances on Grayson too, both Commanders standing much closer than I expected. Grayson returns their threatening glares with one of his own. "Be warned, I'm not cloaked."

Osian retorts, "We know."

Without hesitation, his hand shoots out to take hold of Grayson's arm. Elwyn grips the other, his fingers like claws around Grayson's bicep.

I brace, expecting them to burst into flames like Baelen did, hoping they will.

They don't. Their mouths split into wide, malevolent grins.

They haven't… died.

Grayson's shock is palpable. It fills every angle of his body, his expression now confused and alarmed. I jolt backward, plastering myself up against the wall as he retaliates against them, pushing, using his power to fling them both against the opposite wall. Priscilla shrieks as they crack against it, scrambling away from the fight. She already used up most of her sorcery fighting me. It will only take one blow to finish her.

The older Commanders fight back, flinging light in the shape of crimson arrowheads into Grayson's chest. His cry of pain tells me that they are fighting with a different kind of sorcery now—not death, because they don't want to kill him—but torture. He roars and shakes, his arms still outstretched, trying but failing, to keep them away from him.

Elwyn finds his feet, pushing through Grayson's opposing force. "The pain will stop when you take us up. Not before."

Grayson gasps a breath. "How are you… still alive?"

Elwyn's face lights up with cruelty. "Your mother didn't tell anyone that your father was a gargoyle. In fact, she tried very hard not to tell us anything. We found out when you were born."

Osian snarls, "You were a freak!"

"An elf… with wings!" Elwyn twists his hands mid-air and the arrowheads in Grayson's chest turn to and fro, making him roar with pain. His knees buckle but he refuses to kneel.

Elwyn says, "Dirty… filthy… gargoyle wings."

Osian sneers, "We cut off your wings."

Elwyn forces his way back to Grayson, his gnarled features cast in crimson light from the arrowheads. "Then we cursed you to kill whatever you touch."

"And told everyone you were half gargoyle," Osian says, looming over Grayson now too. "So, you would never know any kindness."

I stare, wide-eyed, at the Elven Commanders, shocked by what they're saying. Even I never imagined the depth of their betrayal. How far they'd gone to get here. To control Grayson.

Elwyn laughs. "You can't kill us. We're the ones who cursed you."

Grayson roars out his pain. "Who did you kill for the power to curse me?"

Elwyn gloats. "Gideon killed your mother. I killed your father. Pedr killed the healer. And Osian killed your baby sister."

Pain, not physical, floods Grayson's face. He drops to his knees, broken. His head tilted back to the ceiling. He exhales a moan of the deepest pain I've ever heard, tears leaking from his eyes.

"Give in, Grayson. Take us up. Then all your pain can be over."

Grayson's chest rises and falls. His chin drops to the runes lining his collarbone. He is beaten, empty, but he whispers, "Run while you can, Marbella. Take Baelen and get out of here. They can't ascend without me, and I won't live much longer." His eyes meet mine while he ignores Elwyn's and Osian's snarls. "You can beat them. You always could. Don't show them mercy."

"Grayson…" My hands drop to my sides. I didn't realize I'd flung them out in front of me, prepared to use my power. I brush Cassian's bone lash: my only non-magical weapon.

My resolve hardens. "You should know by now… I don't run from anything."

Anger rushes hot and strong through me. My Lightsworn power flashes bright sapphire—it is my skill in battle. I snatch Cassian's bone lash off the hook on my belt and take a step into position as it unravels with a *snap*. The lash snakes out, straight and true, singing past Grayson, wrapping around Elwyn Elder's neck. I spin and rip and the deadly tip does its work.

Elwyn's head tumbles across the ground.

Priscilla screams.

Osian freezes, panic spreading quickly across his features.

The arrowheads fall from Grayson's chest, and he inhales a free breath, dropping forward, shivers racking his body.

My focus now is Osian, who roars at me, eyes wild, as I advance on him. As if he can stop me by shouting at me. He flings a death bolt at me, but I absorb it and keep walking.

Four paces is all it takes.

Osian's lips draw back. His teeth are bared. "You will not kill me."

"This is for Indira. And Grayson's sister. And everyone else you hurt or killed." I force my palm against his chest and release Incorruptible.

Osian screams as his bones light up and blinding, pure light courses through him, burning him from the inside out. I hurry through the dust that remains. Priscilla is the only one left now. She's already running, but not away. She races toward Indira, sliding to a stop at the edge of the water.

Her hair flies around her as she shouts wildly at us. "Stay back! Or I will drown her."

I pause, drawing on Lightsworn to help me strategize. Indira is still frozen, vulnerable. Priscilla has probably already cursed her. If Priscilla forces Indira below the surface, then I need to end her before Indira runs out of air. I will have precious seconds…

Grayson rises to his feet, rolling his shoulders, easing out the residual pain he must be feeling. He shakes his head at Priscilla. He sounds tired, resigned. "Enough, Priscilla."

"Don't tell me what to do. You're a traitor! You're a… filthy gargoyle!"

I sense Grayson harness his power a moment before he disappears. The sound chokes in Priscilla's throat as he reappears right beside her. In a flash, he catches hold of her wrist. She screams and tries to lurch away from him, but he holds on tight. Her scream dies as she realizes that she's still alive. "But… you're not cloaked."

"Curses die with their makers. You know that. Now…" He releases her wrist to run both his hands across her face, drawing her forehead against his, breathing slowly, trying to calm her. He's as close to begging her as he can get. "Please, let it be enough."

She's breathing hard, shivering, gripping his shoulders. "I chose to be a killer, Grayson. I'm not like you. I never hated it. I had a choice and I made it years ago. I need the power. I *like* it. I won't stop killing. You can't make me—"

A blast of light flashes between them.

Priscilla goes limp in Grayson's arms, and he catches her… pulls her close, slides to his knees holding her, gently supporting her lifeless head and neck as he gathers her up against his chest. Her hair falls across his lap as he strokes it, staring at nothing. He doesn't say anything as he sits with her.

He is quiet and still for a long, long time.

I wait for him to feel whatever he needs to feel. To think whatever he needs to think. Elyria told me that Grayson had to fall if we were going to survive. I'm not sure how literal her vision was, but I decide this is close enough.

Above me, the entrance to Earth's surface finally closes. The clear blue sky, the shining glass and metal building, and the droning, mechanical hum fade and disappear.

I wonder what it's like up there: if humans have to fight for their families and loved ones. Fight to protect them like we have to. Somehow, I think they probably do. Maybe not with swords and magic, but I'm sure it's a battle all the same.

Across the distance, cocooned in my whirlwind, Baelen waits for me to release him. I press my lips together to try to quell all the emotions I feel as he contemplates me, the look on his face telling me that he loves me, the lifting of one corner of his mouth pulling me toward him because… he seriously can't give me that look when I'm not in his arms.

I breathe out all of the fear I felt for him, exhaling it from my body, and then I breathe out all the emptiness I *made* myself feel, promising myself I will never do that again. I release the whirlwind at the same time, allowing him to touch ground. But as I walk toward him, he lifts his hand cautiously. *Wait.*

Grayson rises to his feet, carefully holding Priscilla, his fingers tangled in her hair and her face pressed against his chest. His voice is hollow. "I'm going to disappear for a moment, but I will be back very soon, and I would appreciate if you don't view my return with suspicion. I will not harm you."

I'm not sure what that's supposed to mean or what he intends to do, but I nod. "You have always been true to your word."

"Thank you." He's gone as quickly as he speaks.

That's when I run to Baelen. He pulls me into a fierce hug, his lips finding mine. "Marbella, don't do that to me ever again."

"Never," I promise him.

As soon as I crash into him, everything unfreezes around us. It takes Indira two seconds to assess the danger and find us alone and safe. She rushes to the edge of the water and sloshes out of the springs, dripping beside us. Even though the Elven Commanders are gone, she is pale and afraid. "Osian Valor hurt Erit. Badly." She winds her hands together in front of her chest, her voice breaking. "I don't know if my husband is alive."

A blast of air whips around us as Grayson reappears. He is crouched, holding the wrists of two gargoyle men who appear beside him, both lying on their sides, bloodied and barely breathing.

Indira screams into action. "Erit! Llion!"

Grayson barely glances up. "There are more," he says, before he disappears again.

I take one look at Baelen.

"I'll get them into the springs," he says.

"Keep their heads above the surface. If there are more, we'll need help." I wait only long enough for Baelen to carry Erit into the water, handing him to Indira. Then I race to the entrance of the springs, calling for the Grievous and Hideaway gargoyles.

Bethany is the first to respond. "Supreme Incorruptible!"

"Quickly, I need at least ten of you. Injured gargoyles are being transported here and we need to help them into the springs."

In a flash the rock wall comes alive, and ten women glide to the ground, following me inside with several of the Hideaway men.

Bethany speaks firmly to Baelen as she slips into the water and takes over helping Llion. "I will take him. He is Grievous after all."

Baelen doesn't argue, returning to the edge of the water to wait for more wounded gargoyles. When Grayson returns with Welsian and two members of my Storm Command, Baelen immediately carries them into the water with help from the Hideaway men while the Grievous women hold them safely until they heal.

Before Grayson disappears again, I touch his arm. "Have they stopped fighting?"

He focuses on a point past my shoulder. "The war is ended. The elves are returning home to wait for their new Queen's orders."

He slips out of my hold. "There are more, Marbella."

I step back. "Of course."

Grayson comes and goes, and I lose count of the number of times he appears and disappears. Erit and Llion are healed. So are my Storm Command and Welsian. After the most badly wounded have been saved, Grayson brings those who are beaten and bloodied, but not at death's door. After that, he brings the ones with cuts and bruises. As soon as each is healed, one of the Hideaway gargoyles flies them away, taking them to their loved ones, then returns to help transport the next one.

Indira and Erit are the first to leave. She pulls me into a hug, telling me, "I'm going to bawl my eyes out now, and you'd better not tell anyone about it."

The hours churn on. Baelen and I and the Grievous women keep working to make sure nobody is left unhealed. By the time Grayson staggers to the far corner of the springs and drops to the ground exhausted, nearly two hundred gargoyles and a hundred elves have been saved.

Bethany helps the last gargoyle from the water, gives me a tired nod, and tells me she will see me at the Royal Residence. Baelen brushes the hair from my face, kisses my tired lips, and says he'll wait outside with the phoenix until I'm ready. He knows I have one last thing to do.

I approach Grayson with caution, not because I'm afraid of him, but because I don't want to force him to speak if he doesn't want to. He found out so much about his past today; the truth about the death of his whole family, that the people he trusted were the ones who killed them, and the fact that he had wings and lost them.

He rises to his feet as I approach, steadying himself by planting one hand against the wall. "Marbella Mercy," he says, stopping me in my tracks. He contemplates me, his gaze traveling from my headpiece to my disheveled hair to my tired eyes. The golden runes across his chest glow in the soft Elyria light.

"Yes, Grayson?"

He looks me in the eye. "Now we are no longer enemies."

I respond, softly, "Agreed."

He falters. "I don't… know how to be around people."

I choose my words carefully. "Neither did I. But I think you'll find that *your* people—the gargoyles—are incredibly tolerant of new and unique friends."

I gesture to the front entrance, inviting him to come with me. "Please?"

He shakes his head. "I think it's better if I disappear for a while. I have to figure things out."

"If that's what you need to do."

He gives me a solemn nod and then he's gone.

38

———

MARBELLA

We bury our dead the next day. I declare a week of mourning so that all of the fallen gargoyles and elves can be properly buried and mourned. I lay my five fallen ladies to rest on the crest of the mountain beside Cassian. On that same spot, I also bury Badenoch. My wise and kind friend had flown from the safety of the cavern he was hidden inside and taken the death bolt that Osian Valor had intended for Elise. His children stand beside me, heads bowed, as we lower his body into the earth. Now they have lost both their parents.

I don't have enough tears.

The day after we bury Badenoch, I make my way with the old Priestess Dorothea to the highest room in the Royal Residence where the Queen's journal waits. It is mine to write in now. Dorothea hands me a quill and ink and leaves me to choose my words. The pages will turn the color of my life as soon as I write my name on them.

My hand moves across the page.

Marbella Mercy.

A gentle lilac spreads across the page like ink through water— the color of my heartstone. Then a crimson red grows in the

310

middle of the page, unfolding like a rose, spreading outward—the color of the Rath Heartstone. But they're both quickly followed by pristine white that bleaches the page clean again, the same color as Incorruptible's life. I guess I am a little of all of them.

I start at the beginning, from the day I became the Storm Princess, and I write about everything that happened since, writing long into the night about taming the Storm, about my Storm Command, the marriage trials, Baelen's near death, my heartbreak, mining with the gargoyles and fighting with them, finding the heartstones, fighting Howl and losing Cassian, everything Grayson said and did, the war… until Baelen appears in the doorway, filling it with his massive body as I stifle a powerful yawn. He doesn't tell me to come to bed, simply gathers me up in his arms and carries me there.

At the end of the first week, Baelen and I travel to Erawind to meet with all of the elven houses. We take a handful of gargoyles with us. Talia's rosebud mouth opens in awe at the elaborate elven architecture—the sandstone buildings and sculpted gardens. At some stage within the last few days, she has quietly taken over for the old Priestess in the role of my gargoyle advisor—apparently that is the job of the High Priestess—while Elise remains as my elven advisor. I am honored to have these two, strong women at my side.

Eli Elder meets us on the city's outskirts to escort us to the arena where representatives from the elven houses wait to speak with me. As we enter the stadium, I'm glad to find there is no spellcasting at work here today. It's simply a meeting place.

If the changes in my appearance stun them, Talia's beauty makes them gasp. She has regained her strength in the last few days and now she glows. Her emerald eyes are radiant, her hair is a river of gold, and her gossamer wings are sparkling silver. As soon as I can, I plan to order the destruction of all the monstrous gargoyle images that the Elven Command used as propaganda to spread fear.

There's a lot to be done to restore trust with the elves. I start the meeting by opening the Heartstone Chest and returning the heartstones to their Houses. The Elven Command had hoarded them, but they belong in the hands of their people. The representatives gladly accept the stones, grateful to have them returned. Then I address the need for new leaders in the Houses of the dead Elven Commanders, giving the representatives of those Houses the choice between holding an election or allowing me to choose for them.

A representative from the House of Glory takes a knee, saying, "Our minds have been clouded by sorcery for many years. We do not trust our own judgment. We request that you choose for us. We will hold elections in the future once we trust our own minds again."

Impressed by their insight, I name Eli Elder, Gwynn Bounty, and Sahara Splendor as leaders of their Houses, knowing they will be fair, wise, and most importantly I can trust them. It's harder to choose for the Houses of Valor and Glory. Grayson has not reappeared so I can't ask him what he wants to do. And as for Valor, I've never trusted any of them.

Luckily, Senturi agreed to come with me to this meeting. I hide a smile when the representatives from the Houses of Glory and Valor take a step back as he descends from the dais to study them. I don't blame them. Senturi is in full, ferocious form. Along with a fur coat cast across his shoulders, he's sporting his double chain of talons, making him appear wild and fierce.

He stops in front of one of the Valor representatives. The older elf is the only one who doesn't look away. This elf bears a scar above his eye, and his features are hardened. He isn't the one I would have chosen but Senturi gives me a nod, returning to my side to murmur to me, "He is a loyalist who believes in the Crown. He is ferocious and will bring his House into line."

I ask, "And Glory?"

Senturi points at the man who asked me to choose for them. "That one's daughter. She was instrumental in the protest after you were mistreated in this arena. Since your disappearance, she has worked tirelessly behind the scenes to free imprisoned dissenters."

"Dissenters?"

"Elves who protested against the Elven Command. They have all been released now."

"Thank you, Senturi." I turn back to the representatives. "Now, let's talk about the future."

I'm exhausted by the time we're done, but I've begun building bridges, and that is the most critical thing right now.

That night, we stay in my old quarters. It is surreal being here now. So many memories are caught between these walls. So much heartache. As night falls and the moon shines full, I head to my old bedroom, taking Baelen with me. I lead him to my old bathing room and close the door. This time, he won't leave this room without holding my hand and more.

The days blur over the next month with all the work that needs to be done in both countries. While I go about restoring peace, strange and random things begin to happen in Erador. First, the talon crows disappear. Then the shadow panther population decreases rapidly—almost as if someone is hunting them mercilessly. The Outlier Clan reports that sightings of crows and panthers have become very rare. They bow deeply to Baelen when they tell us that the predator population hasn't been this low since his time in the wastelands. Then, the day after Iago and his builders finish the new home for the Priestesses and orphaned children, elegant wooden furniture and plush seats miraculously appear in the living and dining areas. It looks suspiciously like the furniture from Grayson's cage. The children love it.

At the end of the first month, I awake in my bed in the Royal Residence with a start, sensing… a force I haven't felt for a while. Baelen tugs on me when I slide out of bed, half-asleep, but I whisper for him to go back to sleep—I'm okay. I dress quickly and head out into the dark before dawn.

My living arrangements for now are quite nomadic. I plan to spend two months at a time rotating between the Royal Residence in Erador and my quarters in Erawind, visiting my family on the way through. Iago is already making noises with a gleam in his eye about building me a new palace right on the border between the two countries. I tell him, "All in good time."

I follow the tingle in the air all the way past the new home for the children, past Crimson Court, and to the springs. I tread carefully inside, pausing at the spot where the walkway opens up into the cavern.

Grayson stands at the edge of the water with his back to me. He doesn't move, but he knows I'm here. Without turning, he says, "I wonder what would happen if I went in."

I cross the distance to stand by his side, considering the glistening pond. Sorcery and deep magic don't combine, but I'm not sure to what extent those rules apply to Grayson—a natural sorcerer whose power doesn't derive from death. I've already asked Elise to undertake as much research as she can about natural sorcery, but since Grayson is only the second ever born, we're in unknown territory.

He finally turns to me as he asks, "Would the water kill me? Or would it give me back my wings?"

My lips part a little. He's grown a beard. He wears a chain of talons and claws around his neck. It seems to be a thing.

He steps back from the water's edge, appearing to decide against stepping in. "Sorcery and deep magic are like fire and kindling. A bad combination."

"I think you're forgetting..." I tap my headpiece, my finger landing on Incorruptible's iciness. "I can put out flames before they start."

Elyria lost her wings in this place. Maybe Grayson can get his back. I plant my feet and access my power, lowering the temperature in the air to a point where my breath frosts.

He's startled. "You're serious?"

"I am. You deserve to have your wings back."

"Deserve? Hardly." His jaw clenches. The tension in his shoulders makes him hunch a little.

I shake my head at him. If he had wings, they would curl around him right now, forming a protective shield. He doesn't even know he's accessing those muscles in his back. I become very stern. "Grayson Glory, I am Supreme Incorruptible, and I order you to go in."

He searches my face for a long moment as if he's trying to see the future—does it contain new wings or death?

Then he removes his boots. He doesn't take it one step at a time, diving straight into the water. I brace for impact. Despite what I said, I'm not sure what's going to happen. Maybe he'll never come up again. Maybe the water will explode. Maybe I've been really, seriously, stupidly reckless...

His head emerges. He reaches up to slick back his hair, wiping the water off his face. I let out the breath I was holding.

He looks at me. I look at him.

We're both waiting.

He slowly tips backward, a strange expression flooding his face. Then, in an increasingly loud shout, right before he topples backward, arms flailing, he yells, "Holy fuck! They're heavy!"

Gold glitters beneath the water's surface, a growing mass attached to his back. The Elven Commanders had described Grayson's wings as dirty and filthy, but they aren't. Not at all.

He scrambles to right himself, managing to roll to his side, paddling through the water, and finally crawling up the steps. Giant wings fall across his back and spill across the rocks as he claws his way on hands and knees to dry land. He collapses against the stones, staring side-to-side from one wing to the other. His wings are golden, shot through with silver swirls, glistening and strong.

"Well," he pants, raising a hopeful eyebrow. "I guess I'll be camouflaged against… I don't know… the sun?"

I burst out laughing. I'm finding it very hard not to make a derogatory comment about the fact that it's his turn to land on his hands and knees in front of me. I hold out my hand to help him stand up.

"Wait," he says. "I can do this."

With an expression of great concentration on his face, he slowly rises to a knee, testing his balance, testing his strength, appearing to acclimate to the massive new weight across his back. Hunching forward to maintain his balance, thigh muscles bunching, he very slowly rises to a standing position, but closes his eyes. Probably to help himself focus.

He takes a step toward me, his eyes still closed. His wings slowly rise, extending then retracting as he tests them out, his balance gradually returning, muscles working less and less hard to keep himself upright.

Finally, he opens his eyes and takes another step. And another. His wings extend and curl around me. Very carefully, he draws me into a warm hug. "Thank you."

He releases me, but I return the hug, murmuring against his

chest. "Come back to the Residence now, Grayson. There are gargoyles you need to meet."

He gives me a cautious smile. "Okay."

"And get rid of that beard."

"Yes, Supreme Incorruptible."

By the time we reach the Royal Residence, the sun has broken across the horizon. I lead Grayson to the food hall since there's no point taking things slowly. Silence descends as soon as he appears; the gargoyles stop talking and put down their knives and forks.

At the back of the room, my warrior husband scrapes back his chair, rises to full Rath height, and strides toward us with purposeful steps, a challenge written across his face. He stops two paces away from us and considers Grayson's wings and the row of talons around his neck.

Grayson tucks his wings tight into his sides, holding them low and non-threatening, his chin tucked slightly down. It's such a gargoyle thing to do, a gesture of respect, that the challenge fades from Baelen's posture. Something unspoken passes between the two men.

Finally, Baelen breaks the silence. "I got the same reaction when I first arrived. It will change." It's not exactly a welcome, but it's the closest that Grayson will get.

The tension leaves Grayson's shoulders, and I shoot Baelen a grateful smile, but we haven't made it more than a few steps when my name is called from the door.

Talia glides into the room. "Marbella—"

She freezes as soon as she sees Grayson, her eyes widening. She gasps at his wings, her own drawing back as if she's about to take flight and escape. It caused Talia a lot of pain when Grayson broke her shield during the battle—and that was on top of knocking her unconscious on the cliff top when she was defending Llion and Liliana's children. She opens her mouth. Shuts it again, her jaw clenching.

Head high, she promptly spins on her heel and stalks away.

Grayson hunches beneath his wings, his chest deflating. He's only had his wings for two seconds but he's already exhibiting all his emotions with them. There's no point hiding behind a mask anymore. He walks quietly, as if he's afraid he'll startle everyone more than he already has.

After he takes two steps toward our table, Adalie jumps down from the breakfast table and runs right up to him, staring wide-eyed at the chain around his neck.

Without a word, she holds up her own chain, proudly pointing at the single talon on it.

A faint smile lights up Grayson's face. Adalie is a very little girl, small for her age, and the acknowledging nod he gives her says that the fact she has killed a talon crow—even a small one—is impressive.

She holds out her arms to be picked up and his eyes turn into saucers. He glances left and right.

I shake my head with a laugh. "She doesn't mean me."

Adalie says, "Golden Gargoyle, you need a hug."

She calls him a gargoyle. His eyes widen even further.

Baelen grins at them both. Any hint of distrust on his part disappears. Adalie can see right into Grayson's soul, and if she trusts him, then none of us have anything to fear from him. Baelen swings Adalie up and deposits her into Grayson's arms. Grayson catches her and she giggles, throwing her little arms around his big chest, snuggling her head against his heart.

"Careful, Grayson," I whisper as I glide past. "She will steal your heart and discover all your secrets in a single beat."

Grayson is frozen. He holds Adalie as if she'll break, apparently shocked when she doesn't. Thawing with each second, he drops his head to briefly press his cheek to the top of her forehead. He seems full of amazement. "Her hair is so soft."

He has never held a child before. I widen my eyes at him with emphasis. "You should hold the babies. They have the softest skin you've ever felt. But first… breakfast."

After that, Grayson works very hard to assimilate into the gargoyle way of life, taking up work with Iago and traveling all over Erador repairing damaged homes and rebuilding ones that Howl destroyed long ago.

One morning, I enter the food hall to find him sitting with Roar and Gilda and their two children. He and Roar have similar wing structures and I find them comparing the patterns on their wings.

Afterward, Grayson tells me, "I'm trying to find out who my father was. I think he might have been from the same clan as Roar —the Sunflight Clan."

"That's also Talia's clan."

He falls quiet. "I have one more apology to make, but I don't know how to make it."

"Not to me, surely."

A self-satisfied smile touches his lips. He almost laughs, but not quite. "The only thing I'll apologize to you for is that I'm not sorry."

I try not to smile.

"No, this apology is to someone who did nothing but try to protect her friends…"

I purse my lips. I've seen the way he looks at Talia. He wants to bridge the gap but doesn't know how, and she is definitely not making it easy for him. If anything, she has become even more fierce and distant. "Talk to Roar. He may have some ideas."

Grayson nods and goes on his way.

I hardly see him for months. Winter comes and goes. My peoples' battles become smaller. A crop that fails, a storm that destroys several homes (not my doing), and finally, the hilarious debate about how to fit the elven crown on my head at the same time as my headpiece.

Ten months after the battle, I awake to the day of my official coronation. Today I will receive both the elven crown and the mark of the Supreme Incorruptible.

As my eyes open to the new day and sunlight drifts through my window, Baelen strokes my hair, kissing my forehead and then my lips. "Good morning Supreme Incorruptible."

"Good morning, Wrathful One."

He gathers me up against him so I'm lying on top of him. I push up so I can see his face, my auburn hair falling like a curtain around his face. He strokes my back, a slow smile growing as he finds the base of my shirt and my bare skin. His feather-light touch scatters shivers all the way to my toes.

I will never get tired of the look in his eyes that tells me our bodies are too far apart. "I love you, Baelen Rath."

He rears up beneath me, gathering my legs around his waist and raising us into a sitting position. "I love you, Marbella Mercy."

My answer is a kiss. There are no adequate words to tell him how much I feel for him. Only actions. A long time later, a discrete knock at my door tells me we're late. I throw the door open, fully clothed and dressed now, surprising Talia and Elise who both wait for me and probably expected me to be scrambling to dress right now. They're both wearing simple, elegant gowns, and their smiles make them glow. Behind them, my family beams at me, rushing forward to hug me until I'm breathless. My brother knocks the air out of my lungs with his enormous bear hug.

We are in the Rath House because this is where I have chosen to be crowned.

Elise flaps her hands at Macsen. "Don't crush her dress."

The way he grins back at her and drawls, "Yes, Ma'am," makes me narrow my eyes between them. Before I can think too much about whether there's something going on between them that I don't know about, Mom squeezes my hand and says, "We're so proud of you, sweetheart. You have brought peace to our land."

Baelen prowls up behind me, dressed in full Rath armor. He whisks me down the hallway while my family follows. I wanted to have my coronation in the courtyard at the front of the house, but Talia insisted I needed to be somewhere up high where everyone can see me. The Rath mansion is built with a wide, flat roof from which soldiers can be stationed with a view in all directions. It's a good compromise. We climb the wide staircase that opens out onto the back of the roof. My family wasn't allowed near me when I was officially named the Storm Princess. Now, they will stand beside me for my coronation.

The phoenix waits for us, guarding the elven crown that sits on a tall pedestal at the front of the roof. It was Llion who came up with the solution for wearing both crowns at the same time, simply lifting the elven crown and placing it on top of my headpiece. Since my headpiece has a flat band at the top, the more elaborate crown only needed a size adjustment to sit neatly on top of it. He did a perfect job.

The phoenix's body provides a screen against the crowds. I can already sense the mass of gargoyles and elves who wait for my appearance. I take a deep breath, too far back to be visible to them yet.

I've barely taken a step with Elise and Talia at my side when a form streaks down from the sky, speeding in from the mountains. Grayson drops from the sky, his golden wings curved to slow his incredible speed. He slams down onto the roof, Baelen-style, wrapping his wings into his sides in a fluid movement. He is filthy with mud streaked across his cheeks and chest, splattered across his wings, and coating his boots. His destination is Talia, who has frozen beside me.

He takes a knee, head down, holding his hands up to her, palms cupped one beneath the other. Inside his upper hand is a beautiful, white chrysalis flower.

Talia glares at it. She swipes it out of his hand, waiting for him to say something. He stays perfectly still, head down, hands raised as if the flower is still inside them, bowed, waiting, allowing her to choose her reaction. His only movement is his rapid breathing. He could have transported himself instantly from the wastelands, but he chose to deliver it the right way—by flying his heart out to get it here before it wilts.

The tension releases from her body. She bends carefully in her dress, crouching and using her wings to maintain balance so she can rest at eye level with him. "Grayson?"

He fixates on a spot on the ground but for the barest second, his gaze flicks to hers and away again.

"Look," she says, waiting for him to do as she asks. When he meets her eyes, she closes her fist around the flower. "Watch what happens."

When she opens her fist, the flower is crushed, bruised, but the petals slowly blush pink in the middle, swirling to gold at the edges. Its calming scent washes over all of us.

Talia says, "It was crushed and hurt, but now it is even stronger."

His lips part. She is leaning so close to him that their faces are only inches from each other.

His chest rises, inhaling, and it's obvious that it's not only the flower's scent that mesmerizes him. "I'm sorry I knocked you out on the cliff that night."

"Well, I was about to kill you." She sighs. "We are both changed now, Grayson. You are kinder. And I… am fiercer."

She rises up, head high, throwing her speech back to me before she strides toward the phoenix, "Marbella, if you will?"

Grayson can't take his eyes off her as she glides away. He shakes himself, adjusting his wings as he rises to a standing position. "Forgive my appearance, Supreme Incorruptible."

"Forgiven."

He takes a position at the back of the rooftop as Baelen and I proceed to the front. The phoenix greets me with a nod before moving to the side, revealing thousands of gargoyles and elves gathered in every available space in the courtyard, across the gardens, down the slope, and even on the rooftops of nearby buildings.

A roar goes up as I appear, and it takes a full five minutes for it to die down. Elise spellcasts her voice to project clearly to the farthest onlookers. "Our people, today we crown and mark our Queen!"

This time it takes forever for the cheering crowd to calm down. The crown resting on the pedestal sparkles in the sunlight. It matches the golden flecks in my ivory gown. The dress I wear has two circular cut-outs on either side of my waist that Baelen found irresistible while we were getting dressed, but they serve an important purpose today.

Elise lifts my united crown from the pedestal. At the same time, Talia places her open palm against the bare skin on my left hip. As Elise lowers the crown onto my head, she and Talia speak in turns, their voices projected as loud as thunder across the landscape.

Elise smiles, "We crown you…"

"And mark you…"

"Queen of Erawind…"

"Supreme Incorruptible of Erador."

And together, they say my name, "Marbella Mercy."

The crown is light as it nestles onto my head and Talia's touch is gentle. As she removes her hand, I'm amazed to see the simple mark she has placed on me: a golden circle, representing life.

I can't help it. I'm glowing.

Two steps behind me, Mom is crying and smiling with Dad and Macsen at her side. Below us in the courtyard, all of my friends and loved ones have gathered, all of the miners and elves who fought beside me and for me: Reisha and my Storm Command beaming with pride, Jordan and Sebastian, whose love for each other inspired me, Llion and Liliana who fought so hard to be together, Roar and Gilda who proved that love can conquer anything, and Indira and Erit holding their two tiny babies—new life, the future of our country.

And Baelen… my heart, my love, my forever.

Their voices rise up in unison, a swelling roar. "Supreme Incorruptible, Queen Marbella Mercy, we honor you."

My heart is full as I lift my voice and arms to my people. "I am honored."

EPILOGUE

ALESSIA RATH - 21 YEARS LATER

I close my eyes as air rushes past me and the earth beneath my feet changes in an instant. Liam's strong arms are a steady force around me, his power to jump distances tingling through my back and neck.

He sets me safely upright in the ash that covers the wastelands on the western border of Erador, a teasing twinkle in his emerald eyes. "You okay, Alessia?"

I scowl at him as he releases me.

"Absolutely fine." I could fly myself here using my storm power but it would take me an hour, and today I don't have time to waste. I'm already breaking the rules by disappearing on the morning of my wedding trials.

The sun rises over the horizon, the new dawn breaking across the barren ground, as Liam folds away the golden wings he inherited from his father, Grayson Glory. Liam's eyes are bright emerald like his mother's, the High Priestess, Sunflight Talia. She will soon pass her title onto her daughter, Liam's twin sister, Della. Like Liam, the blood of both a sorcerer and a priestess runs through Della's veins. She and Liam are as powerful as I am. For that reason, there are many elves and gargoyles who believe that only Liam can be my equal as a mate.

I do love him, but not like that. Not in a way that makes my heart skip a beat or steals the breath from my throat. I don't love him the way that my parents love each other—or the way that *his* parents love each other for that matter. Theirs is a love forged out of fire, unshakable despite every challenge that could have torn them apart.

I want that kind of love, but… I haven't found it.

So instead, I've thrown myself into making our world better—a revegetation project to turn the wastelands into fields.

Liam gives me a grin that would make any woman's knees turn weak. "Are you going to break my heart at the first trial today?"

I jab him in the ribs with my elbow. "Oh, Liam. We both know where your heart truly lies."

He gives me a genuinely blank look. I smother an inward sigh. I've been trying to open his eyes for weeks now, but my subtle prods have gone unnoticed. He has no freaking idea that he's totally and completely in love with my dearest friend—

"Adalie!" He hurries away to intercept the brown-haired woman. Her face and body are obscured behind the largest boulder I've ever seen, which she's attempting to carry on her own.

She sways so she can see around the rock, her brown eyes as lustrous as tempered chocolate, but her cheeks are rosy with annoyance. She's wearing gloves, so she doesn't skin her hands, along with leather pants and a thick, plain shirt that doesn't reveal anything of the curvy figure she hides beneath it.

"Sunflight Liam Glory, I don't need… your help!" She's scolding but there's a puff in her voice. "I am… perfectly capable… of carrying this…" She gasps for breath. "By myself!"

Adalie has always been fiercely independent. Seven years older than me, she's been at my side all my life. In that time, I've never seen her take off the chain she wears around her neck, which now sports multiple talon crows and panther claws. She has proven herself to be a ferocious warrior and a true friend. While my older brother acts as my protector, she's the one who listens to my worries.

"With respect, Outlier Adalie," Liam says, keeping his hands at his sides while he shuffles through the ash so he can keep time with her labored steps. "I am certain you can carry that boulder on your own. However, you will get the job done much faster if I assist you."

Liam could easily use his sorcery to lift the boulder from her arms without even touching it, but he would never show her such disrespect.

"Very well," she says, bending her knees and tipping one end of the tall stone. He braces his arms against it, his enormous biceps bunching as he guides it down so that they can each carry one end of it. He's larger even than his father, as tall as my brother and just as physically strong.

Clearing the dead earth has been our biggest hurdle. New boulders fall from the top and sides of the cliff daily. Some gargoyles and elves whisper that one day the edges of our world will crack apart completely and we'll have no choice but to return to the surface.

I see the problem a different way. The cracking cliff face is only due to the splintering of the earth at its feet. The earth breaks because there's no vegetation to bind it together. By ensuring that trees and grass can knit the soil, we can stop the instability and preserve our land. Uncle Iago agrees with me and it was he who originally supported my idea and got me started.

So far, we've succeeded in rejuvenating half of the southern wastelands and we're now working our way along the western end toward the north.

I tell myself that coming here today has nothing to do with escaping the responsibilities waiting for me at home.

Adalie side-eyes me as she and Liam pass. "You should be at home, Princess. Today is an important day."

"Not without you, Adalie."

She hides a smile. She is as relentless as I am in our pursuit of mending the wastelands. She grew up here, lost her brother to its savagery. There's nothing more important to her. Except perhaps Liam. She's always there for him.

"Did you come to fetch me, then?" she asks.

"Yes," I call, even though we both know it's an excuse, not the truth.

They carry the boulder away from the cliff face farther inland where it won't obstruct the new earth. Liam maintains a respectful tone when he speaks in a puffed voice. "Will you permit me to lower the boulder into position, Outlier Adalie?"

She looks relieved but hides it when he glances in her direction. "That would be fine, Liam. Thank you."

She thinks she's too old for him. Well, she's never actually told me that, but she's implied it whenever I've tried to encourage her to act on her feelings. To my mind, seven years is nothing. If anything, Liam needs someone who doesn't swoon at his wings or fawn over his power like some of the girls at the palace. He needs someone who isn't afraid to tell him when he's wrong or to ask him to consider life from other points of view. She challenges him in good ways.

I admire that he's been raised by his parents to respect power and never take advantage of it. I don't know all the history between his parents and mine, but I know that things nearly went very wrong between Grayson Glory and my father. Once the real evil was destroyed, it was only through acts of faith and forgiveness that our land healed after the war.

Liam lifts the boulder with his power and Adalie rests her gloved hands on her hips, catching her breath. Despite his task, Liam barely takes his eyes off her. She has no idea how beautiful she looks with her hair rumpled, her cheeks glowing, and her breath coming fast from her efforts.

Deciding to give them some space, I incline my head at a distant patch of mud. "I'm just heading over there for a minute. I won't be long."

"Don't go far," Adalie calls, giving me her attention for a scant moment. "Sol bears have been seen around this area in the past week."

Creatures we call sol bears started appearing after the war, around the time that the talon crow and shadow panther populations were finally brought to extinction. Unlike shadow panthers, they come out in the day, so we named them after the sun. Some gargoyles believe the bears rose from the malevolent force of Grievous, whose deep magic can never be extinguished—in the same way that our moon endures. Others believe that the bears are born from the slain bodies of the murderers who followed Howl and the elves who followed the Elven Command. All I know is that even my parents are worried about them. Dad fought one and was injured despite his strength and power. In the last few years, sightings have been rare, causing new theories that they're fighting and killing each other.

I banish the beasts from my mind as I give Adalie and Liam space. Maybe today, they'll finally recognize what's right in front of them.

I hurry away from the present with the speed with which I want to escape the future. Using my storm power to move is too easy. I need to feel the impact of the earth thudding through my legs, kick up the ash, and convince myself that all I need is a husband who is kind and intelligent, who understands that my people's welfare will always be my priority.

I don't need love.

I reach a group of boulders at the far end of the clearing before I realize how far I've traveled. Before I turn back, a patch of white in the mud ahead right next to the soaring cliff face catches my eye.

Chrysalis flowers! They're incredibly rare. I haven't seen one in years. I turn to call back to Adalie, discovering that she's a mere speck in the distance and won't hear me, let alone see me.

Hurrying to the flowers, I bend over them. Not one, but ten! My heart lightens at the sight. It's like a ray of light in my day. I brush my fingertips across their brilliant surface, dying to pick and crush one to inhale its glorious scent for the first time in years—

Crack! Thud, thud, thud—

The cliff face shudders beside me and the earth splits apart beneath my feet. I jump back onto solid ground, ripping the chrysalis flower out of its bed before the earth opens up beneath it, swallowing the entire flower bed in a fissure three inches wide.

No! It's my fault.

My weight must have been all it took to shift the brittle earth. To my relief, the ground stops splitting several paces along, but the cracking sound wasn't all I heard.

My head snaps up.

Boulders thud down the cliff face from thousands of feet above me, smashing against each other as they fall, crashing into smaller boulders, cracking off new ones. An avalanche of rocks is seconds away from falling on me.

Mom taught me that fear is not failure. Fear can help me act faster and think more clearly. But right now, I'm frozen to the spot, unable to move as a mountain of rock falls toward me, rocks that will smash my body to pieces. My inner power won't let that happen despite my frozen thoughts. It rushes to the surface. Virtuous, Prime, Lightsworn, and Incorruptible, the powers that Mom carries in stones on her crown, I was born with them in my blood. I sense them sizzle through my body, my storm power melding with them, causing the air to move around me.

Oomph!

A massive warm body slams into me and I fly backward under the force of the movement. An enormous hand and two strong arms cushion my back and head as we hit the ground. Shocked to my core, I stare up into the deep brown eyes of a gargoyle I've never met before, a gargoyle whose determined gaze meets my own. He releases his wings with a *thump*, the largest, blackest wings I've ever seen spreading across the air above me and completely obscuring my view of the falling rocks, forming a shield between me and the danger.

"Stay beneath my wings!" he cries.

"But I..." *Don't need your help.*

My whisper is lost in his roar of pain as the first rock hits his back, striking so hard that he jolts down onto me, his bare chest pressing into mine for a moment. For a crazy second, my gargoyle instincts kick in and I inhale his scent. He smells like earth and wood, like a slowly burning campfire. Warm. Capable of igniting into a furious flame. I've never inhaled such a scent and it fills my head, overwhelming me, forcing me to lie still beneath him.

The muscles of his stomach and chest tighten against mine as he quickly slides his arms out from beneath me and punches his fists into the earth on either side of my head, pushing up so he doesn't crush me, bracing for the second wave of rocks.

Rational thought returns and I struggle to move. I should be protecting him, not the other way around. It's my duty, my job, to protect my people from harm. *Doesn't he know that? Doesn't he know who I am?*

The vibrations through his body, the way he dips toward me as the rocks hit, tell me that they're tearing his skin to shreds. He clenches his fists hard enough that they flush pale with blood loss.

The rocks are breaking his back. A sob of fear rises inside me. He'll be killed trying to protect me.

If he dies…

I can't heal the dead.

My power roars to the surface, ready to push him out of the path of the falling stones, but the thunderous downfall stops as suddenly as it started. The final pebbles clatter along his wings and join the others forming piles on either side of us.

He retracts his wings with a groan, his head tipping forward. He's barely conscious and his body slowly lowers toward mine. I arch up against him and for another crazy second, my senses go wild, my body flushing hot in a way that shocks me. I fight a sudden need to shift my legs and hook them around his hips, wrapping my arms around his massive chest instead and using my inner strength to lift him carefully upright into a standing position.

His head drops to my shoulder. He inhales, his breath tickling the skin beneath my ear and making me tingle to my toes. "You smell like dewdrops on lilies." He sighs against my neck. "This is a good way to die."

I cast him a fierce look, sliding my way beneath one of his arms, supporting him as I maneuver my way under his wings around to his back. I guide him to the ground so that I can kneel behind him, leaning him back against me. Fear is sharp inside me as his wings droop on either side of me, indicating he's close to death.

His back is broken, bones jutting from skin, ribs crushed, skin flayed. He won't make it to the deep springs in time. It's up to me.

With a cry of dismay, I gently run my hand over the worst wounds, drawing on Virtuous to heal him. Mom was never able to use Virtuous to help anyone other than herself, but it's an innate skill for me, the first I used as a child. Healing this man is harder because his body is heavy and the damage a thousand times worse than skinned knees.

For the next ten minutes, I work to repair his bones, broken flesh, and finally his skin. The gorgeous perfume from the crushed chrysalis flower fades as I work, a forgotten beauty.

Finally, I rest him against me, taking a selfish moment to wrap my arms around his chest from behind, telling myself I have to do that to move him again. He is easily as tall as Dad and just as muscled, a warrior's build, which makes it even more confusing that I've never met him. Dad keeps a close eye on every soldier in the united army, which means I should know this man.

I place my head against his back, listening carefully. His heart beats are so strong that I can hear them through his back, a resolute *thud-thud.*

"Are you a spellcaster?"

I startle, shocked that he's lucid again. My cheeks flame, wondering when he woke up.

He scoops up the crushed flower as he twists at the waist so he can see me. All healers are spellcasters, so it's logical for him to think I'm one. He doesn't shake me off, catching and steadying me as I hurry to release him, making me pause.

His eyes are the deepest brown, but they have golden flecks in them that remind me of Uncle Llion.

"I have the power to heal others," I answer, trying not to lie.

He clearly doesn't know who I am. Even though that's impossible. Every gargoyle and elf knows my face. My parents made sure of it. They vowed that there would not be secrets and rumors among our people like there used to be—false reports of what gargoyles and elves were truly like.

I ask him a question that I don't want him to ask me. "What's your name?"

He considers me with a crease in his forehead. "I don't have a name."

I splutter. "But… what did your parents call you?"

"My mother left me at an orphanage when I was a baby. She didn't give me a name. The matrons call me…" He takes a deep breath, the crease in his forehead deepening. Despite the intensity of his gaze, his hands are soft around my shoulders, his thigh angled against my knees. I sense him brace for my response. "They call me 'Dread.'"

My lips part in shock. I can't help my explosion of outrage. "That's not a name for a child. Why would they call you such a thing?"

His expression softens, a hint of relief passing across it. "You're not afraid."

"Of you? Why would I be? A name means nothing."

I check myself. A name means everything to gargoyles and elves alike. My father was called Wrathful One. At one time, he was feared but now he is loved. My mother was, and still is, Lady Storm. Grayson Glory is the Golden Gargoyle, a name Adalie bestowed on him. Names reflect how someone is viewed. Names have power.

I search for Dread's clan mark on his lower stomach. He isn't lying. He doesn't have one, which means no clan claimed him. I struggle to understand why. To begin with, it's unheard of for a female gargoyle to give away her baby, let alone for that child to be raised alone.

"Do you know if you had a sister?" I ask gently.

"I was told she died during birth and that my mother wished I had too."

He speaks so matter-of-factly that it makes my heart ache.

I make a decision. "I will call you whatever you want to be called. Pick a name and it will be so."

"That requires some thought." His eyes crinkle at the corners, a hint of a smile that brightens the golden flecks in his eyes. His features are not perfect, far from it. His jaw is strong, his eyebrows dark, his skin paler than some, but his wings darker than all. His lips… They *are* perfect.

They curve into a smile. "I owe you my life. Will you tell me yours?"

I shake myself. "My what?"

The corner of his mouth hitches up. "Your name."

I avoid his question. "You don't owe me anything. You put yourself in danger because of me."

"I'm glad you're unharmed." His voice is low, quiet, his gaze passing across my own lips like a caress. He releases my shoulder to hold out the flower for me. "I'm sorry this was ruined. I'd pick you another, but they've been consumed by the earth."

The chrysalis flower is the farthest thing from my mind right now. He's sitting far closer to me than most gargoyles would dare and the scent of kindling fire is messing with my senses. Only Liam is free with his affection around me. Even Uncle Macsen and Aunty Elise's three sons—my own cousins—treat me with polite respect.

Dread has identified me as an elf because of my lack of wings and he thinks I'm a healer. He isn't treating me like a princess because he doesn't know I am one. *The* one. As soon as I tell him my name, his attitude will change.

But I hate deception. I won't base any relationship on lies or misconceptions. I sigh, my shoulders sinking as I take the flower, staring at it. "My name is Alessia."

He's silent.

I look up, expecting to see him hustle away from me, but he doesn't budge. He considers me intently. His expression doesn't change. "Supreme Incorruptible, you have honored me with your presence."

There it is. The silent wall rising between us.

I stare down at the flower again. "I didn't want to tell you who I am."

His thumb strokes my arm, a soothing gesture. "Why not?"

"Because you'll treat me differently now." I dare him to contradict me.

"Because I owe a debt to a Supreme Incorruptible."

"Dread, you really don't."

I didn't mean to call him such an awful name, but he doesn't flinch. "Tell me how I can repay it?"

I meet his intense gaze. He means servitude, but I would never cage him. A gargoyle like him needs the wild; in fact, he seems to belong in this place of burned ash in the way that an ember does. It's a heat I want more of.

A reckless, wicked notion passes through my head. I don't know anything about him other than he was raised nameless. I only know that he appeared out of nowhere and nearly killed himself saving me. I also know that his scent is driving me crazy and so is the space between us.

A smile breaks across my face. I tip my chin with a challenging look. "I will take a kiss."

He jolts away from me, rising to his feet. He towers over me but quickly steps backward. It's as if dark clouds have descended over his expression, shuttered, and distant. "Forgive me, Princess. You don't know what you're asking."

"I think I do—"

"No, you don't!" His roar echoes around us. His chest rises and falls with a deep indrawn breath, his voice dragging out of him, his speech forced. "There's a reason they called me 'Dread.'" His fists clench. "They call me that because—"

His focus shifts to something behind me and his forehead suddenly creases again. His lips purse and his eyes narrow. "That's a—"

I swivel to follow his gaze just as his expression clears and alarm shoots across his features.

"Mama bear."

I explode to my feet. The approaching animal lopes toward us at full speed, a ferocious creature with mottled amber fur and claws that can cut halfway through a fully-grown man's torso.

Lightning crackles around me, the air shifting and I push with my hands, sending a whirlwind at the beast to slow it down.

The bear races right through the force.

What the...?

Dread spins to me. "Your power is from deep magic. It doesn't work on them."

He leaps forward, running toward it.

"No! Dread!"

My own father, the unbeatable Baelen Rath, was hurt fighting a sol bear. Dread will be torn apart. I race after him, fueled by fear, running into the danger instead of away from it.

Dread moves faster than I expected, lifting and using his wings to spear toward the creature, dropping back to the earth to run again when he's only a few paces from it.

At the last moment, he drops his shoulder, his wing daggers held back. He slams into the bear's underbelly, pushing up at the same time, flipping it onto its back. I skid to a halt, shock raging through me as the creature flies backward, lifted several feet above the ground before it crashes into the earth with an audible *thud*. Dread's boot thumps into its belly before he wrestles it back to the ground, every muscle in his back straining, the muscles in his thighs bulging. His wing daggers dart forward, piercing the bear's chest, once, twice.

With a keening wail, the creature falls silent.

I blink hard, shock still spiraling through me. I wait for the bear to rise up again, but it doesn't.

Dread killed it.

Just like that.

He straightens, turns to me, then pauses for a moment before walking slowly back to me, stopping a few paces away.

I stare at him. Can't stop staring.

He clears his throat. "I apologize for my appearance, Alessia."

Blood drips down his wings. Gore is splattered across his cheek and chest, but he doesn't wipe it away. He has nothing to wipe it with.

Even Dad nearly died killing one of those creatures.

Yet none of the blood is Dread's.

My voice is hoarse. "How many bears have you killed?"

"Many."

Then he's the reason their numbers are diminishing. I purse my lips. I don't know which question to ask first. How? Why? *Who is he?*

He backs away from me, his gaze distant again, focused on a point past my right shoulder. "I hope to see you again, Alessia."

He spins, spreads his wings, and takes to the air.

"No, wait!"

He doesn't stop, rising against the cliff face. Within seconds, his body and wings blend into it and I can't distinguish him from the rock. He could still be there, or he could be far away by now. I can't tell.

A rush of air beside me tells me Liam has arrived. He holds Adalie at his side. She cries, "Alessia! Are you hurt?"

Liam races toward the dead bear while Adalie checks me over. Satisfied that I'm okay, she spins in the direction of the bear, her eyes wide. "Did you kill it?"

I shake my head. "No."

"Then how is it dead? What happened?" She peers into my eyes. "You look flushed… and…"

She stops herself. She has never used her Sight on me as far as I know, but she's so skilled at it, I wouldn't actually know if she did. She leaves me to wonder how I look. Shocked maybe. Bereft possibly. The scent of woodfire remains in my lungs and I want it back. I want to slide my arms around that chest again. *Dear ancients*, I only met him moments ago. How is such a feeling possible? If Adalie can discern even a hint of what I'm feeling right now…

I close off my expression, shutting down my feelings.

"Liam!" Adalie calls. "Please take Alessia home. She's in shock and needs a warm bath. Tell the Queen what you saw here. I'll follow after you." Her eyes meet mine, unusually firm. "Your marriage trials start in two hours. The outcome will determine your entire future. You need to choose a good husband today. You need to focus."

Liam reappears at my side, wrapping his arms around me. "I'm taking you home."

It's only as the world shifts around me that I realize I'm still clutching the chrysalis flower.

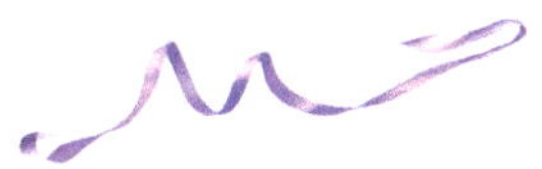

We reappear in the hallway outside my bedroom. Liam is circumspect enough not to transport me directly inside my room given how that would look.

A commotion down the hall tells me Mom has sensed my presence.

"Alessia! Sweetheart!" She races toward me with Aunty Elise on her heals.

I hurry into her open arms. "Mom! I'm sorry I disappeared."

She kisses my forehead before arching an eyebrow at Liam, giving him a pointed look that only a mother can give. "Your parents are looking for you, Liam."

He grimaces. "That's my cue to leave." He gives me a formal parting nod. "I'll see you at the trials, Princess."

Damn. He's still going through with it.

Mom's hand captures mine, her astute gaze missing nothing. She turns my palm up, the crushed petals peeking through my fingertips. Her expression softens. "Did Liam give you this?"

I shake my head. There have never been any lies between us. "A gargoyle. I don't know his real name."

She glances at Elise before returning her blue eyes to mine. I didn't inherit her red hair. Mine is light brown like Dad's, but I do have the same blue eyes she has.

She's deliberately controlled as she asks, "You didn't identify him?"

I've learned to recognize her reactions. When she's worried, she becomes quiet and still, poised, ready to take instant action.

"He had the blackest wings," I say. "The darkest eyes. The strongest arms. He fought a sol bear and killed it—but he wasn't hurt."

"How is that possible?" Mom spins to Elise, but she doesn't have to ask for Elise to know what she wants.

Elise is already hurrying away. "I'll find out everything you need to know."

Mom turns back to me with a quick smile. "Your father and brother will hear of it and come raging in here any second, but before they do, tell me everything you can."

I nod, but for the first time, there are some things I can't tell her.

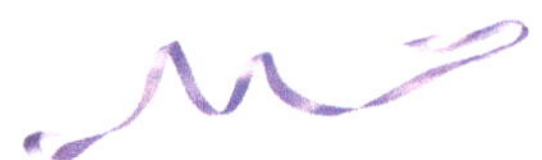

TWO HOURS LATER, I HAVE NO NEW INFORMATION ABOUT DREAD'S identity. Elise asked Grayson to bring one of the matrons to the palace, but the old woman remained tight-lipped and refused to answer any questions, so Mom sent her away.

Mom is hiding her worry well, but my brother, Raiden remains at my side every step I take. Not that he wouldn't have done that today anyway. He towers over me in his protective way, his light brown hair and green eyes catching the light as we ascend to the dais.

Uncle Iago—my honorary uncle rather than my biological one—built Mom a new palace on top of the highest mountain in the center of the border between Erador and Erawind, a place for both races. He didn't attempt to replicate Crimson Court, instead creating a large gathering spot at the side of the palace, a hundred paces long and wide, surrounded by pebbled footpaths leading to a dais at one end that is hewn out of the mountain itself. It's been divided in half, with the front half for the contenders, and the back for the spectators. It's not nearly big enough for the crowd that has gathered, their numbers extending all the way back along the mountain, many of them observing from flying griffins and winged stallions.

Two spaces have been cleared on either side of the dais—one for family and close friends, the other for the leaders of the gargoyle clans and elven houses.

My dress is lavender to honor my mother's house, a silken material cinched in at the waist that falls softly to my ankles while I wear a crimson jewel at my neck to honor my father's.

Raiden is dressed in Rath armor, his stern expression daring anyone to approach me, but his attention is momentarily diverted to the elves and gargoyles gathering in the family section, where Sebastian Splendor and his wife, Jordan, wait with their two daughters. Raiden's smile is for Skylar, their oldest. Like Liam, I wish he would hurry up and propose already. It's clear that Raiden and Skylar adore each other, a match I know my parents approve.

I arch an eyebrow at him. He gives me a blank expression in return. But he lowers his head to me with a growly smile as I ascend to the sound of the cheering crowd. "I will marry after you do, little sister."

He means it playfully, but it fills me with sadness. Everyone's fates are tied up with mine.

Mom waits for me on the dais with the High Priestess Talia behind her on one side and Elise on the other. They're a breathtaking sight in their bejeweled gowns while Talia's wings reflect light across the stage.

I take my place beside Mom, and Raiden chooses a protective location close behind me. Dad joins him there, giving my shoulder a quick squeeze as he does so, lowering his head to mine like my brother did. "I'm proud of you, Alessia. I know you'll make the right choice today."

Mom gives him a smile, pausing for a moment. The look that passes between them makes my heart swell.

Grayson Glory also stands on the stage off to the side with Della, a few paces behind Talia. They're a golden-haired family that exudes so much power. It could be threatening, but I find it comforting. Grayson gives me a friendly nod and Della casts me a shy smile. Despite her growing power, she's one of the gentlest women I've ever met. Unlike my parents, Grayson and Talia don't catch each other's eyes, but the connection of power between them is so strong, it takes my breath away.

Mom clears her throat and raises her hands to encourage silence. When she speaks, her voice is amplified by the thunder in her soul. "As you know, these trials have been brought about by accord. Participation is voluntary and the outcome is determined by my daughter, Princess Alessia. There are only a few rules that you must abide by."

She sounds relaxed, but oh, the politics that led to this occasion. Today is not only about my marriage. It will also settle the line of succession. According to gargoyle culture, the daughter must always take the throne and must do so at the age of eighteen. She's also required to marry at that age. But that's all based on the birthing cycle of gargoyles. Mom gave birth to Raiden first and then a year later, I came along.

In contrast, according to elven culture, the firstborn takes the throne, but only on the death of the reigning monarch.

My older brother is a Rath through and through—he announced that it was his job to protect the throne, not sit on it. Mom announced that she refused to sit on the throne forever. And I announced that there was no way in hell they were going to force me to get married at eighteen years of age.

So a compromise was reached that was supported by all the clan and house leaders. Based on the original Storm Princess protocols, a set of trials will be held today, on my twentieth birthday. Any man can compete, not just the chosen few. Failing a trial does not result in elimination or shame. The purpose is to give me a chance to choose my husband based on his strengths and the personality I deem to be compatible with my own.

Ideally, I would already know where my heart belongs and the trials would be a show, a jovial event for the men (and women if they're so inclined) to show off their skills and have some fun.

But I don't know my heart.

Because of that, there's an edge of tension in the air right now.

Elves and gargoyles are not immune to the allure of power. There are some who see a chance for their clan or house to gain elevation.

Mom continues. "First rule: Any man who wishes to marry my daughter must present himself on this day. She will not choose a husband except from those who offer themselves.

"Second rule: No powers! You must come to these trials willing to put your body and your heart on the line without any magical advantage." Mom glances in the direction of the family section, where Liam stands a head taller than other elves around him. He grins back at her, a disarming smile that she can't help returning.

"Third rule: You may bow out of any of the two trials at any time and it won't affect the outcome." She eyes the crowd, speaking pointedly. "Sometimes, in fact, it is smart to avoid danger."

She takes a breath. "Now that the rules have been announced—"

"Wait!" I step up, catching her startled gaze. "There will be a third trial."

She blinks at me, but I charge on before she can ask me questions. "Both trials have been set by me. I have the right to add another. I will not consider any man unless, at the end of the day, he is willing to challenge me in a fight."

Mom's eyebrows rise. She lowers her voice. "Alessia, what are you doing?"

I wish I'd had time to talk with Mom about this, but I wasn't sure I'd need a third trial. Now that Liam has decided to take part after all, I'm left with desperate measures. I need to implement my backup plan and I've come prepared to see it through. I'm confident I can beat him in a fight—I used to whip his ass all the time when we were kids. I don't want to cause him shame, but I need a solid backup to make it clear that I won't choose him. Also, the idea of knocking some sense into him—literally—is appealing to me right now.

But to my mother, I say, "I can't marry someone who isn't willing to question me, Mom. You and Dad challenge each other all the time and we have far better outcomes for our people because you aren't afraid to voice your thoughts. I want someone who isn't afraid to face me. *Despite* my power and position."

"Very well." She turns to the clan and house leaders, always preserving diplomacy by seeking their views. "Does anyone have any contrary thoughts about this additional trial?"

They unanimously shake their heads. Many of the elven leaders smile. I'm guessing they're the ones who remember Mom's own challenge at the start of her marriage trials when she declared she would fight for herself.

She turns to the crowd. "All those who intend to offer their hand, please step forward now."

She steps back now, her role in conducting the proceedings at an end. It's my turn to run things.

The crowd buzzes. Liam steps into the area in front of the dais and I'm sure I hear someone groan. Nobody knows what the trials will be except me and Elise, whose spellcasting I needed to devise them. But the onlookers will expect one of the trials to be physical combat and nobody wants to face Liam—even without his magical powers.

I acknowledge him with a formal nod. "Welcome, Sunflight Liam Glory."

Nobody else moves.

Damn. No. I won't marry the man my best friend's heart belongs to.

A commotion at the side makes Mom start. I glance at her, reassured by the smile growing on her face. A regal woman strides up to the family area next to the dais, speaking into the silence. "Sorry we're late. We had a small problem with this one." She gestures to the baby on her hip before she smiles at Mom.

"Elyria!" Tears sparkle in Mom's eyes. She doesn't hesitate to race across the stage, head down the steps, and throw her arms around the other woman.

"Marbella!"

They hug each other tightly before Mom relieves Elyria of the bundle on her hip, squealing with delight as two toddlers appear beside her. "Babies!"

Their father also steps forward, leaning across to hug Mom and kiss her cheek. He quickly races after his toddler son before the little boy wobbles into the contender's area, causing the entire arena to burst into laughter.

I bite my lip, unable to hide my happiness. Jasper Grace is one of Dad's oldest friends. He and Elyria lost twins—heartbreakingly stillborn—before their eldest son came along the same year I did. They didn't stop there. At last count they have seven children. They live a simple, farming life away from the palace. I don't know the whole story, but Elyria never visits the original palace in Erador. All Mom told me was, *"Too many memories."*

I haven't seen them for years. I certainly don't recognize the fully-grown man who steps out from behind Jasper and makes his way quietly to the area at the front of the dais. He stands as tall as Liam, his hair straight brown like his father's, but his chest is broader and his biceps have… clearly… been honed from hard work on the farm. He's the kind of man my father would normally insist join the armed forces, but Dad would never force Jasper's hand.

Mom returns to the stage with a toddler on her hip and inclines her head to me. "Sorry, sweetheart. Please continue."

I consider the new man with a smile. "Welcome, Zachary Grace."

At that, another man moves out from the side near the family section while the onlookers clear a way for him. He is savagely gorgeous, his wings dark brown, his hair the same glossy brown cut short at the sides and tightly braided across the top and back. He wears a shadow panther skin slung across one shoulder and bears scars across his naked chest. He's only two years older than me, but Grievous Edric has lived the life of his clan.

I search for his parents in the crowd, finding his father and sister standing in the spot he left behind, and his proud mama over with the other clan leaders. They're only separated because of her duties.

Grievous Indira gives Mom a broad smile, while Erit beams on the other side of the arena. Mom looks like she'll swoop between them and hug them both, too.

"Welcome, Grievous Edric," I say, accepting his smile. He may look fierce, but he has a warm heart.

So far there are three contenders, only two of whom I would consider, but within moments, another three men step out from the crowd—two elves and one gargoyle, all of them respectful, although I don't know them well.

I wait another moment, my heart suddenly empty and my lungs yearning for the scent of woodfire. "Are there any final contenders?"

The sunlight glints at the edge of my vision and a spot flies toward me from the distance. My heart hammers as a gargoyle lands within the crowd, too far away to identify, but the darkness of his wings...

It has to be Dread. *Please let it be him.* But how did he know?

The crowd parts for him, whispers growing as he takes careful steps through the throng, keeping his wings close to his sides so he doesn't bump anyone.

Adalie runs up to the family section on my right at the exact moment that Dread enters the contender's area. She gives me a nod. Did she bring him? But how did she know about him?

I stare at her—I have so many questions—but she doesn't approach the dais, and I can't demand answers from her across the distance. She cranes her head, looking around the family area. She must be looking for Liam...

Her face falls when she sees him in front of the dais, but she quickly pastes a smile on her face when Elyria hugs her. She won't fool Elyria for a second and I'm glad that the older woman is there for Adalie right now.

You fool, Liam! He just broke Adalie's heart.

Liam, on the other hand, is oblivious to her reaction because he's watching Dread.

In fact, everyone except Adalie and Elyria is eyeing him. Now that he stands beside the others, it's difficult to miss how massive and brutal he looks. A shiver runs down my spine, but it isn't fear.

I wish I had another name to welcome him by. "Welcome, Dread."

His name causes a stir. Mom shifts at the corner of my vision, but she doesn't say anything.

I swallow hard. "We will proceed. The first trial is a trial of strength. Contenders, please separate into a single line. Elise, if you will?"

She steps up, lifting her hands. High partitions appear between the contenders, blocking them off from each other. They each stand at the head of a lane that ends fifty paces away—the length of the cleared area.

Within each lane, a large boulder, as big as the one Adalie tried to carry this morning, appears on the ground at their feet. At the other end of each lane, a gilded statue appears, even larger than the boulder and with a thick base of gold. A warrior stands on the base, both hands outstretched.

I call to the contenders. "You each stand in a lane containing a boulder and a statue. They are both real. Their weight is real. Your goal is to make the boulder touch the statue. There is no time limit to this trial. It is not about how quickly you finish. However, you may not use flight to accomplish your task. You may start now."

Five of the men, including Grievous Edric and Liam, immediately attempt to lift their boulders, their muscles bulging. They walk them several paces before putting them down so they can rest.

Zachary Grace leans on his, testing its balance. After a few nudges, he tips it over and begins to roll it, carefully and slowly pushing it along the lane, guiding it between the walls.

Mom glides up to me, a curious look in her eyes. "What is this test, Alessia?"

I create a sound barrier around us so nobody can overhear us. "I want to see how they solve it."

Her eyebrows rise. "Then it's not only a test of strength."

I neither confirm nor deny. "Not everything is what someone tells you it is. I want to see if they consider every possibility."

Liam continues to carry his boulder, making it much farther much faster than the other men, but Grievous Edric puts his down, glaring at it. With a growl, he slams his wing daggers into it, cracking it apart into much more manageable chunks. He then proceeds to carry each smaller piece to the end of the lane, piling them in front of the statue so its hands touch them.

Liam's show of physical strength, carrying the boulder whole, makes the crowd go, "Ooh," especially when he reaches the halfway mark.

But I turn my attention to Dread, who hasn't moved, his forehead creased in a thoughtful expression as he taps the top of the boulder, studying the distance between it and the statute.

He finally bends to the boulder and picks it up without effort, hoisting it all the way onto his shoulder. Mom jolts with surprise and the crowd stirs. He bounces his knees a little, as if he's testing the boulder's weight before he puts it down again.

I lean forward, a thrum of anticipation striking through me when he leaves the boulder behind, the first man to do so, and walks down the lane to the statute. He studies it in the same way that he studied the boulder, placing his hands on it, leaning around it to consider all its angles. It has the appearance of solid gold, certainly heavier than the boulder.

A smile breaks across my face when he bends his knees and wraps his arms around it, tips it across his shoulder, and picks it up as if it weighs nothing. Strolling back to the boulder, he positions the statue in front of it so that the warrior's hands touch the boulder perfectly.

He leaves his lane, returns to the space in front of the dais and takes a knee, his head down.

Zachary Grace finishes next, followed by Edric, then Liam and the others. They each return to the foot of the dais and take a knee.

Mom's eyes are alight with curiosity now. "Was the statue hollow?"

"Yes," I say. "And made of the lightest wood in our land. Dread is the only one who didn't judge it by its appearance."

I release the sound barrier and give nothing away to the contenders as I approach the front of the stage again. "You all succeeded in your task."

I pause before I announce the second trial. I decided on it months ago, but now it seems dangerous—even if the crowd and the contenders expect it.

I swallow hard. "The second trial will be hand-to-hand combat. There are seven of you, so one of you will fight my brother, Raiden."

That causes a stir. Raiden steps forward. He and I spoke about this possibility many times if there were an uneven number of contenders and he assured me it wouldn't be a problem.

I continue. "Fights will be drawn by chance. But I warn you: How you fight is more important than whether or not you win."

Most of the men give me wary looks at that statement, but both Zachary and Dread wear thoughtful expressions.

Elise produces an opaque golden sphere, which she carries from one man to the next. Liam, Edric, and Zachary pair off with one of the other men. My heart leaps into my throat when Dread is left to fight Raiden. They stand to the side as each fight occurs in turn.

Liam wins his fight by subduing his opponent in a neck hold and forcing him to yield. Edric wins by sheer brute strength, his opponent walking away with a very bloody nose. To my surprise, Zachary wins his fight with a single punch, knocking his opponent clean out. He immediately leans down and helps him stand, calling for a healer and waiting beside him until the healer gives the other man the all clear.

Dread waits quietly at the side, observing each of the fights. I watch him watching them, studying the way his expression changes with every move the fighters make as if he's playing the fights within his own mind.

A crease appears in his forehead that tells me he thinks they've made the wrong move—right before they're defeated. His forehead clears when Zachary knocks out his opponent, and a look of wary respect crosses Dread's face when Zachary calls for a healer. Finally, his focus falls on Raiden, watching the way my brother descends from the dais, studying his movements, the powerful steps and controlled head movements.

Raiden is as well-feared as my father. He will soon take over commanding the military forces.

Raiden takes to the field, rolling his shoulders. I sense the crowd hold its breath as Dread steps up to him and the two men face off. My stomach twists. I grab Mom's arm, pulling her up into the air and away from listening ears, surrounding us in a wind tunnel. "I think I should stop this."

"You can't. The others have already fought." She rubs my arms in a comforting gesture. "You've seen your brother in combat. Nobody beats him."

"Mom, I watched Dread annihilate a sol bear. You don't understand. He *crushed* it."

Mom shakes her head in thought. "It's your call, Alessia, but if you don't let this play out, it will look like you want Liam to come out on top."

"But I don't!"

Her eyes widen farther. "What?"

"I don't want to marry Liam."

She's taken aback. "Alessia… We thought…"

"That I love him?" I keep my voice low, trying not to let my emotions show. We can't be heard, but we can be seen. On the field, Dread and my brother have stepped back from each other to wait for us.

"I love Liam like a brother," I say. "But he's in love with Adalie. The foolish man just won't listen to his heart."

"Adalie!" Mom gives a soft exhale. "So that's why she was so upset before." Mom appears perplexed, her blue eyes radiating concern. "So… who will you choose?"

I gesture to the field. "They all have worth. Zachary is quiet and intelligent. He thinks before he acts and finds unique solutions to problems. Edric is passionate, sometimes reckless, but he will always follow his heart and defend me to the death. They are both incredibly strong. But Mom…"

I catch Dread's eye, my heart suddenly burning inside my chest.

Mom's mouth drops open. "You only met him this morning—"

"Love has to start somewhere," I say.

She bites her lip. "I don't know, Alessia. Something's bothering me. I just can't put my finger on it."

I hug her. "I trust you, Mom. When you know what it is, let me know. Until then, I guess I have no choice but to let this fight go ahead."

We return to the stage, but Dread suddenly spins from Raiden and approaches the dais, raising his eyes to mine. "Supreme Incorruptible Alessia Rath, will you please ask your spellcaster to bind my wings for this fight?"

"Wh-Why?" I ask, surprised.

"So I don't inadvertently use them to my advantage against your brother." He lowers his voice. "You're worried about his safety. You have reason to be. But I promise, I will not use unnecessary force."

Mom murmurs beside me with a glimmer of respect in her eyes. "It's an honorable request."

I agree. "Elise, please?"

Elise whispers beneath her breath and Dread's wings instantly pull tightly to his sides. Without fuss, he returns to face Raiden.

Raiden is well-versed in all sorts of warfare, including psychological. With a calm expression, he says, "You shouldn't have given up your advantage."

Dread replies with a bow to Raiden. "We'll see."

Raiden bounces on his heels. Give him a sword and he's an expert, but ask him to use his fists and he's in his element. He's done talking. He steps in and takes a quick swipe at Dread's face. I'm shocked when Dread lets it land, not even putting his fists up, the blow cracking across his cheek. He barely moves, absorbing the blow, shifting only slightly. He takes the next blow to his stomach and then one to his shoulder, shifting minutely to accommodate the knocks. Raiden narrows his eyes at Dread and steps back, taking quick stock of knuckles. They're already bleeding.

A smile crosses Dread's face that would make anyone's blood run cold before he mobilizes, moving so fast that the crowd gasps. Raiden evades the rock-of-a-fist Dread smashes at his head, but he doesn't avoid the lightning fast punches to his chest and stomach, followed by an upper-cut to his jaw.

My brother flies backward in a spray of blood, landing to the screams of a crowd who are suddenly on their feet. Skylar cries out from the side as Sebastian and Jordan grab her just in time. She was ready to fly across the field. I'd pity Dread if she got to him.

Dad steps up beside me, his power glowing crimson and swirling around him. I hear the tension in his voice when he says to Elise, "Be ready to heal my son if he isn't able to heal himself."

Mom grabs my hand, her face pale. "Crushed a sol bear?"

"You didn't believe me."

"I do now."

Dread towers over Raiden as my brother groans and spits blood. Nobody has ever put him on his backside with such efficiency.

Dread says, "With respect, Supreme Incorruptible, please stay down. If you get up, I will continue fighting you."

Raiden twists to grin up at him, his mouth covered in blood. He punches off the ground and bounces back to his feet. "Like hell I will."

He takes another swipe at Dread, who ducks it this time and returns a punch that Raiden avoids, deftly dancing out of the way. For the next minute, they evade each other's hits, ducking and sidestepping until Raiden clips Dread's temple and follows up with a roundhouse kick that cracks into Dread's chest so hard, it would have put a bull out of action.

Dread stumbles backward, digs in his heels, and charges forward, grabbing Raiden around the waist, but Raiden was prepared, pummeling both his fists down onto Dread's shoulders before ramming his elbow into Dread's face. They crash to the ground and roll to their feet in opposite directions, charging back at each other without pause, this time colliding midair, both of them landing head knocks that send the other spinning and thudding into the ground.

I sense Raiden fighting his instinct to draw on his power to heal himself, but Dread has already had his wings pinned. It would be dishonorable for Raiden to use his power now. He leaps at Dread, who lands a kick on Raiden's chest that breaks his ribs. The arena is so quiet that I hear the pops.

Raiden grabs his chest, wheezing as Dread strides over to him. Blood slides down Dread's face and neck where Raiden's fists and boots have cut him.

He roars, "Supreme Incorruptible, you will yield!"

Raiden struggles to his feet, one arm wrapped around his chest. "A Rath never yields."

Dread exhales, his head lowering, but his eyes piercing Raiden's. "Then this fight is unwinnable."

Raiden wipes his streaming nose. "Why do you say that?"

"Because I could beat you to a pulp and you wouldn't surrender." He takes a deep breath. "You could beat me, and I wouldn't surrender, either. Not all fights can be won."

Pure surprise passes across Raiden's face. "Very true."

He rises to his feet but raises his hand, palm up to show Dread that he isn't about to attack again. He harnesses the thunder in his voice to direct a statement to me. "Sister, I can keep fighting this gargoyle for as long as you like, but if you say you have seen enough, then I will follow your wishes."

My fist is pressed to my heart. "Well and truly enough. Please heal yourself, brother."

Raiden exhales and closes his eyes. Within seconds, the strain in his face eases, his wheezing stops, and he straightens fully again.

Without thinking, I head straight for Dread, crossing the distance at a run, my dress swishing around my legs. He watches me coming with wide eyes, casting a questioning glance at Raiden, who gives him a shrug before jogging away to the family area. Skylar will need to see him.

I stop in front of Dread, fighting my need to move closer as I reach for his face. "Come here, please."

He bends his knees and then kneels, a little too unsteadily, indicating that he's hurting. I place my hands across his cheeks, close my eyes, and draw on Virtuous, my thumbs stroking across his jaw. Healing warmth spreads from me to him and back again, knitting his broken skin. This close to him, I inhale the scent of wild air, ashen ground, and burning embers, unable to fight the pull, swaying closer to him.

I open my eyes to find him looking up at me, his lips slightly parted. "Thank you, Alessia."

I'm suddenly aware that everyone is staring. I didn't heal any of the other contenders, but I hold my head high. These are my trials, not anyone else's.

"Elise," I call, trying to sound matter-of-fact, my fingertips still lingering on Dread's jaw. "Please release Dread's wings."

I sense the magic lift a moment before he breathes out his relief, returning to his feet as he rolls his shoulders and eases out his wings. With a *thump*, he releases them fully, stretching them out with a groan. They're even darker in the sunlight, pure black, ochre like the wastelands.

A scream from the dais makes me jump. The field suddenly drops into darkness, the sun disappearing behind boiling, black clouds. Mom rises from the dais, lightning shrieking around her. Dad flies close behind her, their powers melding and filling the space between them with lethal light.

Confusion shoots through me. They're coming toward us…

They're coming for Dread, but I don't understand why.

Instinctively, I step between him and them, but he places his hands around my waist, shifting me out of the way before he closes his wings and kneels again, this time to my parents.

Mom's eyes fill with lightning. Her voice is thunder as she demands to know, "Who is your father?"

Dread's response is so quiet, I hardly hear it over the wind wailing around us. It plucks at my dress, tugging at my body, trying to drag me away from Dread, but I fight it with my own power, determined to stay where I am.

"Supreme Incorruptible," he says. "Please forgive me. I don't want to speak his name."

Her voice rises, cracking like a lash. "You will answer your queen."

His shoulders slump forward, his wingtips sinking low, his arms dropping at his sides.

"I am the son of Grievous Howl."

Howl. The gargoyle who enslaved Erador and committed unspeakable acts of cruelty. The gargoyle who killed Cassian and nearly killed Mom.

Mom recoils, inhaling so fast that the air sucks around us. Her power explodes, lightning ripping toward Dread, swirling around him. "Were you born before or after he controlled a heartstone?"

"Before," he answers. "I wasn't born with heartstone power."

"Then why are you here, son of Howl? State your intentions."

He remains on the ground, his wings tugging in the ferocious wind. He raises his head, but I am his focus. "I came for Alessia." His jaw clenches and he drops his gaze. He exhales as his wings curve around his body, angled forward in a gesture of deep remorse. "I let my heart rule my mind."

"Your heart!" Mom cries. "Do you have one?"

My hand flies to my own heart. Mom suffered cruelly at Howl's hands. I know that her words are born from pain—that Howl's actions were monstrous—but a gargoyle without a heart would never have risked his life for me this morning.

Dread's gaze shoots up. "I am not my father." He meets Mom's angry eyes, tilting his head and baring his neck. "If you think I am, then you have my permission to kill me. I will not stop you."

"No!" I push through Mom's power, calling on all my strength to fight her, stepping directly into the path of her lightning. "He will not be harmed."

I push back against her, drawing on my own storm power to combat hers. Mom has never been unreasonable. Her reactions now can only be born of bone-deep fear. Howl imprisoned her, killed gargoyles she cared deeply about, and kept her and Dad separated.

"The only way to settle this is through Adalie," I say, firmly.

Mom blinks at me, the lightning clearing from her eyes. She glances at Dad as they slowly lower to the ground. Adalie was the one who, at the mere age of six years old, declared Mom to be the Gargoyle Queen.

"We will accept her word," Dad says.

I grit my teeth. "Even though I believe you should trust my judgement."

I spin before they can argue. "Adalie, please!"

She's already hurrying forward with Liam close behind her. In the background, Grievous Indira edges forward with Erit and Edric close by her side. Howl was her brother, which makes Dread her nephew. Judging by the shock on her face, she didn't know about him.

Dread remains kneeling on the ground. I sense his thoughts like a whirlwind. He has several choices right now. He could stay and listen, stay and fight, or fly away and never come back. I will him to stay where he is. "Please stay."

If he heard me, he gives no indication. He's become like stone, withdrawn in a way that hurts my heart. I whirl to Adalie as she arrives. "Did you bring Dread here?"

She nods, making Mom gasp. "I found him after you left this morning. I already knew who he was."

"Then you've seen into his heart?"

"I have."

Mom holds her breath while Adalie addresses her. "You have nothing to fear from Dread. His name was wrongfully given. Yes, he has his father's strength, but he has never used it against another living creature." She gives him a ferocious smile. "Except sol bears."

She turns back to Mom. "Grayson Glory once stood in Dread's place. Do you remember?"

Mom and Dad give a single nod before Adalie continues. "I looked into Grayson's heart and, because I trusted him, you embraced him."

I gasp as Grayson's voice sounds behind me. He approaches with Della and Talia. Liam waits a few paces away, his focus firmly on Adalie.

"You were the first child I held in my arms, little Adalie," Grayson says, his gaze changing, as if he's remembering.

He's an imposing force beside Mom and Dad. I've heard whispers about the fight between him and Dad and shudder every time I imagine it.

Adalie smiles back at him. Nobody else could get away with calling her 'little.' "Golden Gargoyle, you had much to redeem yourself for, but you found your way. Do you trust me when I say that Dread can too?"

"Without question," he answers.

"Supreme Incorruptible?" she asks, addressing Mom and Dad. "Do you?"

Mom reaches for Dad's hand, the last of her lightning fading as they both nod.

Adalie raises her voice, roaring to the crowd. "People of Erawind and Erador! I am Outlier Adalie. The faint of heart do not dare suffer my Sight."

Her voice is fierce. It's true that many gargoyles will avoid her, never look her in the eye for fear of what she will see in their hearts. My mother's word is law, but Adalie's is sacred.

"Dread has suffered my Sight. He has lived a life in darkness, not by choice, but because others told him that was where he belonged. He has stepped into the light now. We who live in the sunlight must never forget that it is only through the darkest night that we find our true strength. Dread is not a threat to us. His heart is true."

There is a pause before the crowd erupts into cheering.

Dread jolts at the uproar. Despite their acceptance, his expression closes off more and more with every passing second.

I draw nearer to him, sensing the tension in his shoulders, the thrum in his wings. He's on the verge of flying away.

Please stay.

Indira races past Mom, slowing before she reaches Dread, dropping in front of him. "Do you know who I am?"

He shakes his head.

Tears fill her eyes. "I'm your father's sister. You're my nephew. I don't know how you can forgive me, but I didn't know about you."

"Forgive you?" He jolts. "What is there to forgive? I lived where I belonged."

Her face falls as Dread rises and backs away from her, his black wings stretching. She reaches for him. "No, you can't believe that…"

He turns his focus to me, his dark eyes drinking me in for a moment. "Alessia, you can only be a dream."

He turns away from me, his paces quickening as he strides away, powerful steps.

He can't be walking away from me.

"Stop!" I cry.

He doesn't look back. "No."

What?

I stride after him, having to walk twice as fast to keep up. "You came to these trials, which means you agreed to the rules. You have to finish."

His forehead creases but he doesn't slow down. He wasn't present when I announced the third trial.

"You must fight me," I say.

He finally pauses. "Fight you?"

"That's the rule."

"I don't follow the rules." He resumes walking.

My storm power rages through me. A whirlwind rises up around him, forcing him to halt.

His dark eyes pierce mine as I draw level with him, using my power to rise up to his height.

"You wish to fight me?" he asks.

"I want you to complete the trials."

His expression is shuttered, controlled. "Do you realize how strong I am?"

I glare at him. "I do."

"Do you know that if I fight you, I could hurt you?"

I swallow. "I do."

His gaze softens as he runs it across my face. "Then know that I never will."

He releases his wings, pushing through my power, shocking me when he breaks through it.

I slump to the ground, whispering, "If you walk away, you're giving me up."

He only half-turns. "To keep you safe, I would sacrifice anything."

It doesn't matter what Adalie said. It doesn't matter that everyone has accepted him. It doesn't even matter that Mom was swayed in his favor. Dread has lived his entire life believing himself to be evil, not worthy of anything more than a life of isolation. He knows what his father did. I see the fear in his eyes that he, too, will turn to darkness. He would rather stay away from me than risk that.

My throat fills with thunder. I have to convince him that he will never be like his father, but before I can harness my voice, he begins to run. With three strong steps and a savage downward sweep of his wings, he lifts into the air, soaring away from me. Within seconds, he's gone.

I turn to the silence behind me.

Grayson, Talia, and Della watch Dread fly away. On the other side of Mom and Dad, Indira, Erit, and Edric are poised to take off after him.

I don't know what to do. I can't cage him. I won't.

Mom approaches and takes my hands, lowering her voice. "Your father once walked away from me. He told me later that it killed him."

"Then why did he do it?"

She considers the sky, where Dread is a fading speck. "When you met Dread this morning, you were in danger. He knew his place in that situation. Here in this place of safety, *he* is the danger. My guess is that he thinks he's protecting you by staying out of your life." She takes a deep breath, her hands tightening on mine. "I let fear rule my reaction to him before. I'm sorry, Alessia."

I shake my head. "Mom, you're wise. A leader doesn't have the luxury of making costly mistakes. I can follow my convictions because I know you're here to pick me up when I fall."

A tear slides down Mom's cheek. "Today, you learned how to land on your own two feet. Go after him, Alessia."

I cast my gaze across my family and all the love between them. Jasper and Elyria hold their gorgeous babies, standing beside Aunty Elise, Uncle Macsen, Sebastian, and Jordan. Raiden and Skylar hug each other at the side.

Zachary approaches Della with a blanket that he places gently around her shoulders. She looks at him in surprise and then appreciation. Every moment of tension would have been triggering her protective instincts, draining her. I'm grateful that Zachary is taking care of her.

Liam draws Adalie aside and I hear him murmur to her. "I have no excuses. Please forgive me."

She tips her head back, fiercely defiant. "Perhaps tomorrow."

He carefully slides an arm around her waist. "Today," he insists. "Forgive me today."

She searches his eyes and a slow smile grows on her face. "Tonight." She pulls his arms closer and wraps her own around his waist. "I will forgive you tonight."

Mom tips her head at the sky, but I don't need any encouragement. My storm power bursts through me and I rise up into the air, knowing that it will take everything I've got to convince this stubborn gargoyle that he has a place in my life.

Lightning crackles around me as I burn through the sky, closing the distance to Dread within seconds, veering around him and landing on the nearest cliff top with a thud that sends hairline cracks through its surface. My dress floats around me, silken lavender wafting in the breeze.

Dread pulls up sharp since I dropped myself into his flight path. The air is crisp, the sun bright, accentuating all the shadows across his face as he lands on the edge of the cliff. He grips its edge dangerously as if he'll take off again at any moment.

My voice fills with thunder. "Don't treat me as if I'm fragile."

His eyebrows rise, his lips parting as he studies me, running his gaze from my narrowed eyes to my stern lips. With steady hands, I remove the jewel at my throat, pulling the necklace over my head. At the same time, I release my hair into the wind and deftly shimmy out of my dress. I was prepared for the possibility that I would need to use the third trial today, so I'd come prepared for combat. I thought I'd have to fight Liam to get him to see what's really in his heart.

Now, I will fight Dread.

Fine leather armor covers my torso, strapless so it wasn't visible beneath my dress, sculpted to the shape of my breasts, waist, and hips, extending to the tops of my thighs. I step out of my slippers. I fight better barefoot anyway.

He freezes, definitely thrown.

I say, "Did you really think I was going to let you fly away?"

"Yes." It's a simple enough declaration.

"Well, if I'm going to kick your backside, you'd better choose a new name because I will not call you by your old one when I declare my victory."

A smile ghosts around his mouth. He shakes his head. "Alessia—"

"Pick a name or I'll pick one for you."

Still he hesitates.

"Trueheart," I say.

He screws up his face in disgust.

I arch an eyebrow at him as I edge forward, approaching on his right side. "What then? Appleblossom? Sugarspice?"

He laughs, a great gusty sound.

I inch up closer, inhaling his tantalizing scent as I check his reaction to each suggestion. "Ash… Coal… Blaze…" He's allowed me to get close enough that my breath whispers across his shoulder, then his collarbone. His body heat is intoxicating and I'm not afraid to lose myself to it. "*Inferno.*"

His right arm whips around me, pulling me so close so fast that the air whooshes out of my lungs. I arch back across his arm, my left leg rising to hook around his hip. He growls at me, an intense sound only a male gargoyle can make, his head tilting to mine as I slide my leg back down his. My mouth is a scant breath away from his. With the lightest brush of my lips across his—a touch that nearly turns me senseless—I hook my ankle around his leg… and pull.

He yelps, flails, loses his balance, and tips back off the cliff. His wings thump out, but not in time before I dive after him, sailing through the air, harnessing the wind around me to crash into his chest. His eyes widen, his wings beat, but it's futile. I drive him toward the jagged cliffs below. "Fight or yield!"

He grins at me as he snaps his wings closed at his sides, freefalling. "Neither."

He wraps his arms around me, his muscles flexing as he slides his hand across the back of my head, drawing me down to him. Gravity pushes me in the other direction, but he fights it, whispering against my lips, "This is also a good way to die."

His kiss is like catching fire, his mouth molding to mine, his lips coaxing mine apart. My heart thuds, erratic in my chest. The air rushes past us as his hands run the length of my spine and across the backs of my thighs, drawing my legs around his hips. We tip upright and I don't know how we changed direction until I hear his wings thump.

"Hold on," he says before he claims my lips again. His wings sweep and he propels us up into the air, infuriating me with his ability to break through my power. My indignation evaporates as he carries us high above the peaks. The border between Erador and Erawind stretches out beneath us, once a line between two races, now united.

I fold my hands across the back of his neck and hold on tightly with my legs. I can harness my power so I don't fall, but I've never trusted anyone to carry me in the air. I settle against the strong arm he holds against my hips, leaning back into the one that supports my shoulders.

I catch my breath, satisfied that his chest is rising and falling, his heart is thudding, and his fingertips seek the bare patches of skin my armor reveals.

"What are you going to do with me, Alessia?" he asks, giving me a perplexed smile before he nuzzles my cheek with his. "I don't belong in a palace."

I draw back in surprise. He must think it's all plush lounges and royal bedrooms. He doesn't know that half of the palace is a training compound, where my warrior father and brother spend their days teaching new soldiers so that we're ready if our world is ever threatened again. Anyone who dares harm our land or our people will meet an army more ferocious than any before it.

A worried crease appears in his forehead, and my heart aches that he trusts me to be so vulnerable with me. "I don't belong in a time of peace," he says. "I'm built for war."

"So am I," I say.

He considers me with surprise, his dark eyes questioning.

I shrug, lightning burning inside me, lightning that is part of my soul. "I am a Rath."

His gaze intensifies before he whispers. "I am… Grievous Inferno."

He kisses me as we spiral slowly in the air, his hand a burning brand against my thigh, a promise of more.

I gasp against his mouth. "Please tell me you make your bed in the sky."

"I will make my bed wherever you are."

I sigh. My soul is light, my arms are full, and my heart is certain. "The sky is perfect."

THE END

ALSO BY EVERLY FROST

KINGDOM OF BETRAYAL

(Fantasy Romance)

1. A Sky Like Blood

2. A Sin Like Fire

3. A Soul Like Glass

DARK MAGIC SHIFTERS

(Dark Urban Fantasy Romance)

1. Wolf of Ashes

2. Bond of Flames

3. Crown of Fate

SUPERNATURAL LEGACY - COMPLETE

(Angels and Dragon Shifters)

1. Hunt the Night

2. Chase the Shadows

3. Slay the Dawn

4. Claim the Light

BRIGHT WICKED - COMPLETE

(Fantasy Romance)

1. Bright Wicked

2. Radiant Fierce

3. Infernal Dark

DEMON PACK - COMPLETE

(Dark Paranormal Romance)

1. Demon Pack

2. Demon Pack: Elimination

3. Demon Pack: Eternal

SOUL BITTEN SHIFTER - COMPLETE

(Dark Urban Fantasy Romance)

1. This Dark Wolf

2. This Broken Wolf

3. This Caged Wolf

4. This Cruel Blood

ASSASSIN'S MAGIC - COMPLETE

(Urban Fantasy Romance)

1. Assassin's Magic

2. Assassin's Mask

3. Assassin's Menace

4. Assassin's Maze

5. Assassin's Match

ASSASSIN'S ACADEMY - COMPLETE

(Dark Academy Romance)

1. Rebels

2. Revenge

3. Rogue

MORTALITY - COMPLETE

(Science-Fantasy Romance)

Mortality Complete Set: Books 1 to 4

1. Beyond the Ever Reach

2. Beneath the Guarding Stars

3. By the Icy Wild

4. Before the Raging Lion

STORM PRINCESS - COMPLETE

(Fantasy Romance)

1. Storm Princess: Book One

2. Storm Princess: Book Two

3. Storm Princess: Book Three

<u>Stand-alone fiction - dark romance</u>

Corrupt Me: Immortal Vices and Virtues

ALSO BY JAYMIN EVE

Shadow Beast Shifters

Book One: Rejected

Book Two: Reclaimed

Book Three: Reborn

Book Four: Deserted

Book Five: Compelled

Fallen Fae Gods

(Romantasy Duet)

1. Gilded Wings

2. Crimson Skies

Demon Pack

(Dark Paranormal Romance)

1. Demon Pack

2. Demon Pack: Elimination

3. Demon Pack: Eternal

Supernatural Academy

Year One

Year Two

Year Three

Supernatural Prison Trilogy (Urban Fantasy)

Book One: Dragon Marked

Book Two: Dragon Mystics

Book Three: Dragon Mated

Supernatural Prison Stories

Broken Compass

Magical Compass

Louis

Royals of Arbon Academy Series (Dark College Romance)

Book One: Princess Ballot

Book Two: Playboy Princes

Book Three: Poison Throne

Dark Legacy Series (Dark High School Romance)

Book One: Broken Wings

Book Two: Broken Trust

Book Three: Broken Legacy

Secret Keepers Series (Paranormal Romance)

Book One: House of Darken

Book Two: House of Imperial

Book Three: House of Leights

Book Four: House of Royale

Titans Saga

Book One: Releasing the Gods

Book Two: Wrath of the Gods

Book Three: Revenge of the Gods

Curse of the Gods Series (RH Fantasy Romance)

Book One: Trickery

Book Two: Persuasion

Book Three: Seduction

Book Four: Strength

Book 4.5: Neutral (Novella)

Book Five: Pain

NYC Mecca Series (YA Urban Fantasy)

Book One: Queen Heir

Book Two: Queen Alpha

Book Three: Queen Fae

Book Four: Queen Mecca

A Walker Saga (YA Fantasy Series)

Book One: First World

Book Two: Spurn

Book Three: Crais

Book Four: Regali

Book Five: Nephilius

Book Six: Dronish

Book Seven: Earth

Hive Trilogy (YA/NA Urban Fantasy)

Book One: Ash

Book Two: Anarchy

Book Three: Annihilate

Storm Princess

(Fantasy Romance)

1. Storm Princess: Book One

2. Storm Princess: Book Two

3. Storm Princess: Book Three

Sinclair Stories (Contemporary Sports Romance)

Songbird

ABOUT THE AUTHORS

Jaymin Eve is the Wall Street Journal and USA Today Bestselling author of paranormal romance, urban fantasy, and sci-fi novels filled with epic love stories, great adventure, and plenty of laughs. She lives in Australia with her husband, two beautiful daughters, and a couple of crazy pets. To date, she has sold close to two million ebooks, and still can't believe that she gets to create fantasy worlds as a job.

Everly Frost is the USA Today Bestselling author of fantasy romance, urban fantasy and paranormal romance novels. She spent her childhood dreaming of other worlds and scribbling stories on the leftover blank pages at the back of school notebooks. She lives in Brisbane, Australia with her husband and two children.